The Winter Rose

Rita Bradshaw was born in Northamptonshire, where she still lives today. At the age of sixteen she met her husband – whom she considers her soulmate – and they have two daughters, a son and six grandchildren. Much to her delight, Rita's first novel was accepted for publication and she has gone on to write many more successful novels since then, including the number one bestseller *Dancing in the Moonlight*.

As a committed Christian and passionate animal-lover her life is busy, and she loves walking her dog, reading, eating out and visiting the cinema and theatre, as well as being involved in her church and animal welfare.

BY RITA BRADSHAW

RITA BRADSHAW

The Winter Rose

PAN BOOKS

First published 2021 by Macmillan

This paperback edition first published 2021 by Pan Books
an imprint of Pan Macmillan
The Smithson, 6 Briset Street, London ECIM 5NR
EU representative: Macmillan Publishers Ireland Ltd, 1st Floor,
The Liffey Trust Centre, 117–126 Sheriff Street Upper,
Dublin 1, D01 YC43
Associated companies throughout the world
www.panmacmillan.com

ISBN 978-1-5290-4982-4

1 3 5 7 9 8 6 4 2

A CIP catalogue record for this book is available from the British Library.

Typeset by Palimpsest Book Production Ltd, Falkirk, Stirlingshire
Printed and bound by CPI Group (UK) Ltd, Croydon, CRO 4YY

Visit **www.panmacmillan.com** to read more about all our books
and to buy them. You will also find features, author interviews and
news of any author events, and you can sign up for e-newsletters
so that you're always first to hear about our new releases.

To my lovely readers who in this horrible year
of COVID-19 have still written such heartwarming
letters, cheering me up and spurring me on.
Couldn't do it without you!

Acknowledgements

The following books helped with my research for this story:

Consett, A Town in the Making, Tommy Moore
Consett, Derwentdale Local History Society
A Nostalgic Look at Consett, Derwentdale Local History Society
Consett, The Past Relived, Derwentdale Local History Society

Contents

Prologue

Rose was dreaming. Even in her sleep she knew it wasn't real, but that didn't matter. She wanted to stay in the dream where she was safe in Davey's arms and he was smiling down at her, his brown eyes alight with love. But then his arms weren't gentle any more. They were rough, pulling at her nightdress, and whisky-soaked breath hit her full in the face.

She reared up in terror, fully awake now as a hard weight descended on her. Her legs were being forced apart, and as she struggled and then screamed, the flat of a man's hand slapped her violently across the face, jerking her neck so that she felt as though her head had been torn off.

Muttered obscenities and the rank smell of male sweat added to the horror of what was happening, and on the periphery of her mind she realized her screams had woken Betsy, who was crying and calling for her. In spite of the crippling pain in her neck and the sheer weight of him that was squeezing the breath out of her chest she continued to resist, kicking and biting and pummelling at his thickset body for all she was worth. Even when she felt him enter her she didn't give in, and when he tried to adjust his position to grab her hands, she managed to twist and wriggle out from beneath him – but before she could escape he'd caught her again, pinning her on the edge of the bed now as he attempted to enter her once more.

Betsy's cries were frantic, and it was this, her child's distress, that gave her a burst of superhuman strength. From somewhere she found the power to push at him so ferociously that – perched as he was on the edge of the bed straddling her – he lost his balance and went catapulting backwards with a crash that shook the house.

Her only thought was to get to Betsy before he came at her again . . .

PART ONE

Judas

1902

Chapter One

As soon as David O'Leary opened the back door of the house and stepped into the kitchen he knew something was wrong. There was no dinner cooking in the range oven, no pans simmering on the hob and no Rose turning to greet his arrival with the smile that always lit up her lovely face.

He stood stock-still for a moment and then, as he heard a low moan coming from upstairs, he hurried into the hall, calling her name as he did so.

Before he'd put a foot on the stairs, Kathy Bates, the local midwife, appeared on the small square landing, her plump face red and perspiring. 'Oh, it's you, lad. That time already, is it? By, the afternoon's flown by.'

Ignoring that, he said, 'What's happening?'

'The babby's coming, that's what's happening.'

'But it's not due for another two weeks.'

'Well, it clearly didn't get the message 'cause it's on its way, lad. I dropped by mid-morning and Rose was having pains then so I stayed. It shouldn't be much longer from the look of things. Now you're here put some water on to boil and while you're about it, make a pot of tea. I'm fair parched.'

'In a minute, I want to see Rose.' He took the stairs two at a time and when he entered the bedroom he saw his wife lying amidst the tangled sheets, her face flushed and her big eyes expressing the pain of a wounded doe. The bedroom was uncomfortably stuffy, the June day was a hot one, and as he reached the bed and kneeled beside it, he said softly, 'I'm here, lass, I'm here. Why didn't you send word to the shipyard?'

'Send you word?' It was the midwife who answered, having followed him into the room. 'Don't be daft, lad. What would have been the point of that?'

'I could have come home to be with her.'

'Oh aye, and likely lose your job in the process? Where would we be if a man came home before the end of his shift just because his wife's having a bairn? No foreman would stand for that and rightly so. Now get out of my way so I can see to her.'

David had always liked Kathy but right at this moment he could have cheerfully throttled her. Rose was clutching his hand and trying to stifle another moan, and as he stroked the damp tendrils of hair from her brow, he murmured, 'You're doing fine, lass, just fine. I love you so much.'

Kathy shifted her feet behind him, clearly uncomfortable at the show of affection, and her voice reflected this when she said, 'All right, she knows you're home now.

Go and put that water on and make yourself useful. This is no place for a man. And don't forget the tea.'

He didn't answer the midwife directly, but as he stood he said to Rose, 'I'll bring the water up shortly and then I'm staying with you till it's born.'

'You are not.' The midwife's voice was sharper now. 'I've never heard owt like it in all me born days. You'll stay downstairs like any other man and I'll call you once it's all over and I've got Rose cleaned up. All right?'

'No, it's not all right.' Glancing back down at his wife, he said softly, 'Would you like me to be here with you, lass?' and at Rose's nod, added, 'That's that then.'

As he left the bedroom he could hear Kathy muttering under her breath but it didn't bother him an iota. All he was concerned about was Rose and he knew she would want him to be at her side during the birth of their child. She'd had moments of panic about the confinement for weeks now, and the dire tales some of the old wives hereabouts took great delight in relating didn't help. They never mentioned births that went as smoothly as clock-work but let them cotton on to a horror story and they couldn't get enough of passing it on. If Rose had had a mam or a close female relative she could have talked to, it wouldn't have been so bad, he thought as he got a big pan of water on the hob. As it was, she only had him to discuss her fears with and he'd spent many an evening holding her in his arms and reassuring her all would be well. Not that he had any clear idea of what exactly was involved in having a bairn, but he'd done his best.

When he returned to the bedroom with the hot water and a cup of tea, Kathy didn't mention him leaving again but her attitude made it clear she was far from happy. He sat beside the bed, holding Rose's hand and wiping the sweat from her brow now and again, murmuring words of love and encouragement as the pains intensified still more. When she began to push she clung to his hand as though it was a lifeline and he wondered how much more she could take. Stupid, perhaps, but he hadn't expected the birth to be so painful or such hard physical work; how women did it over and over again was beyond him, but Kathy seemed to think all was well and progressing as she expected.

He saw the midwife look between Rose's legs before sliding a towel under her bottom as she said, 'Another couple of pushes and you'll be holding your babby, Rose. Come on, lass, nearly there now.' And sure enough a minute later Rose gave a long drawn-out groan and the baby slid into Kathy's waiting hands, immediately giving a mew of a cry and then another.

'You've done it, lass, you've done it,' David whispered as he bent and kissed his wife. Kathy deftly cut the umbilical cord and put a clothes peg on it, before giving the baby a quick wash which made it squawk and cry in earnest. Wrapping it in a clean towel, Kathy handed the child to Rose, whose tired face was alight with happiness.

'It's a little lassie an' right bonny an' all.' Kathy glanced at David as she added almost apologetically, 'I dare say it might be a lad next time.'

He hadn't wanted a boy. He could think of nothing more perfect than a miniature Rose and he had told her so in the past. Knowing Kathy wouldn't understand he just smiled and thanked the midwife for all she'd done before leaning down and kissing Rose again. 'Our bairn, lass. She's here at last and she's beautiful.' Like her mam.

'She's so perfect, Davey.' Rose was cradling the baby close, staring into the tiny face with an expression of wonder. The baby had quietened immediately she'd been placed in her mother's arms as though she was exactly where she wanted to be.

'Aye, she is.' David found he was fighting back the tears, emotion overwhelming him at the look on Rose's face. Only the presence of Kathy stopped him breaking down. Nevertheless, his brown eyes were misty as he reached out and stroked the small downy head with the lightest of touches.

'Well, I need to get you cleaned up and the bed sorted, lass. Give the babby to Davey.' Kathy was back to her bossy self. 'Take the bairn downstairs so I've got room to do the necessary,' she added briskly to David as Rose handed the infant to him. 'I can't be falling over you up here.'

This time David made no protest, kissing Rose once more before he walked out of the bedroom, holding their precious bundle as though the baby was the finest Dresden china. Once in the kitchen, he sank down into his old comfy armchair to one side of the range, captivated by the little person staring at him with milky blue-grey eyes.

Some of his pals at the shipyard who'd got bairns had warned him that they all looked like skinned rabbits when they were born, red and wrinkled and blotchy, but his daughter wasn't like that. She was truly beautiful, he thought. One tiny hand, the fingers so delicate and the nails so minute he could scarcely believe they were real, reached out of the cocoon as the baby gave a big yawn, exposing little pink gums.

'I'm your da,' he whispered, the tears he had kept at bay so far now rolling down his cheeks. 'And I'll always love and protect you for as long as I live. It won't matter if you're all grown up in the years to come and you think you don't need me any more, I'll still be here for you, me an' your mam. We're going to be so happy, the three of us. Do you know that? We might not be rich or live in a palace but this little house will be filled with love for you. You're going to heal all the past for your mam, I know that, you and me between us, all right?'

The baby yawned again and then surveyed him unblinkingly as though she understood every word.

'And if some brothers and sisters come along for you to play with we'll love them too, but if that doesn't happen it won't matter 'cause we've got you and you're everything. Do you know that? Everything.'

He could hear voices upstairs and then the sound of Rose laughing. He smiled. He loved it when she was happy. Sometimes he would act the fool just to make her laugh. She hadn't had much joy in her life before she had met him, but he intended to fill her world with it in the coming years. He knew he was the luckiest man in the world to have Rose as his wife and now – he looked down at the baby again – now he had the icing on the cake.

Some bairns were playing in the back lane beyond the yard and as the sound of their voices filtered through the open kitchen window, he settled more comfortably into the armchair. His daughter was fast asleep now, small rosebud lips pursed and tiny eyelashes resting on porcelain skin.

He didn't think he had ever been so happy in his life.

Chapter Two

'You look as rough as a badger's backside, man. Had a few jars last night, did you?'

'On my wage with a wife and bairn to keep? Chance'd be a fine thing. No, the babby's teething and we've had a few bad nights, that's all.'

'Aye, well, I did warn you when you were set on rushing Rose up the aisle that it wouldn't be all billing and cooing, didn't I? An' to fall for a bairn before the ink was dry on the wedding certificate weren't none too bright either.'

'I've no complaints.' David grinned at his best friend, pulling the thick woollen scarf that Rose had knitted him tighter round his neck against the bitterly cold wind coming off the sea. The Sunderland shipyard where they worked as welders – Bartram's – was the most exposed yard in the town being right on the seafront, unlike the other nine yards dotted along the banks of the Wear. When the men at Bartram's did a night shift in the winter months it wasn't unusual for them to wear two coats over a couple of jumpers, along with a balaclava and scarf, but David wouldn't have dreamed of working anywhere else. Bartram's was a real family yard. Everyone knew everyone else and the feeling of camaraderie was strong. It was safer than some of the others like Doxford's or J. L. Thompson's too; they were known as the 'blood yards'. Accidents still happened at Bartram's, of course – all the shipyards were dangerous places where conditions were dire and safety precautions non-existent – and since he'd been taken on as an apprentice at the age of thirteen he'd seen some things that had kept him awake at night, but you just had to get on with life, didn't you, he thought to himself.

Nathaniel Alridge shook his head, punching David lightly on the arm. 'Aye, well, I still think you should be sowing a few wild oats at your age and breaking hearts along the way. You're only young once.'

David smiled wryly. 'To my mind you sow enough oats for the pair of us and then some. Gladys Shaw's mam was telling Rose that Gladys has been crying into her pillow every night for the past weeks over you.'

Nathaniel shrugged. 'I never made any promises. You know me.'

'Aye, I do.' Nathaniel had a well-deserved reputation as a ladies' man. Even when the two of them had been knee high to a grasshopper playing in the back lanes and alleyways, the lassies had made a beeline for him. They found his thick crop of dark blonde hair, piercing blue eyes and wide smile irresistible.

All except one lass, David corrected himself. His Rose

had never taken to Nat, not from the first day he'd introduced her to him a short while after he and Rose had met. Funny that. She was always polite to Nat, and she hadn't raised any objection when he'd wanted him as his best man at their wedding, but she didn't like him nonetheless, he could tell. He'd once made some laughing remark that it was fortunate he'd seen her first before she saw Nat, and she had stopped what she was doing and put her arms round him and, her face deadly serious, had said that he was ten times the man Nat would ever be. She'd been baking at the time and he'd been sitting at the kitchen table watching her, and when he had pulled her onto his lap and started making love to her, the fruit scones had burned.

His mouth quirking at the memory, David said, 'You know I've never had a way with the lassies like you, besides which Rose is enough for me and always will be. I thank me lucky stars each night she looked the side I was on, man. I still can't believe me luck.'

Nathaniel made no comment to this. The two men were crouched on a top saddle tank doing some welding, and he turned his head so his face screen hid his expression. It amazed him that his friend had never guessed how he felt about Rose, but he knew he hadn't. Davey was an open book, he thought with a feeling of scorn. If he'd suspected anything he would have had to bring it into the open, that was what Davey was like.

Rose . . . Nathaniel pictured her in his mind's eye, his body hardening. Thick chestnut-red hair, heavily lashed clear green eyes, small nose and a full mouth set in a heart-shaped face that was so beautiful it made a man ache. She had taken his breath away the first time he'd seen her. She still did.

She had been sixteen when Davey had introduced them and as innocent as a lamb. He'd had several girls by then and could recognize those with experience a mile off. Davey, on the other hand, had never so much as walked out with a lass before, and then he'd gone and reeled in a corker like Rose. It was still a mystery to him what she saw in his friend and if he could have lured her away from Davey he'd have done so like a shot, best pal or not. But for some reason Rose only had eyes for Davey.

'You still seeing that lass from Baxter's sweet shop, Millicent, wasn't it?' David asked after a minute or two.

'Mildred, and no. We'd only seen each other a couple of times and she wanted to invite me to Sunday tea with her mam an' da.' He had seen Mildred more than that as it happened, and the last time they'd walked out he'd had her on the bank at the back of the engine works near South Rocks. He'd lost interest after that.

David shook his head. 'Poor lass. Another one who'll be crying into her pillow over your ugly mug then.'

Nathaniel glanced at his friend, grinning at the back-handed compliment to his good looks as his gaze ran over David's short stocky body and rough features. He knew Davey had never minded him getting all the lassies and he didn't understand that either.

The men's conversation had been conducted at the top

of their voices; from when the buzzer sounded at seven-thirty in the morning all hell was let loose. Riveters, caulkers and others working on their respective jobs meant the noise was deafening, but neither David nor Nathaniel noticed the din any more, not after six years of it. At nineteen years of age they were hardened veterans.

In the next moment the dinnertime buzzer cut off the noise like magic. Men downed tools and made for the canteen, pushing and shoving and laughing as they went. David and Nathaniel had a system which worked well. David would collect two bowls of soup and two puddings and make his way to one of the tables to save them seats. Nathaniel would join the longer queue for the main dinners. These were served out of large boiler-like containers – one for the meat, one for the vegetables, and potatoes from a third, with gravy being poured out at the end of the line onto each meal from a massive tin jug held by Ada, the supervisor of the canteen and something of a dragon.

A couple of men nicknamed the 'sand dancers' were standing in front of Nathaniel when he joined the queue. With Bartram's being situated in an exposed position on the south dock, sand was brought in by the tide each day and the sand dancers had to shovel it away. It was an unrelenting and back-breaking task. One of the men turned and glanced behind him, and seeing Nathaniel, nodded to him, saying, 'Hey, Nat, how're you doing?'

Nathaniel nodded back. 'Fair, Terry. Fair.'

'Fancy coming down the Shipwright after work for a

few jars? Jed Owen's missus had another bairn at the weekend, a little lad after their seven lassies and he's celebrating. Tell Davey he's welcome an' all although I dare say he'll be high-tailing it home to Rose as usual. Mind, if I had one like her at home I'd be doing the same. Missed out there, didn't you, lad,' he added with a sly grin at his pal standing next to him. 'Bonniest lass for miles and she picked our Davey.'

Nathaniel's prowess with the ladies was known and somewhat resented in some quarters, not least because of the cockiness that accompanied the tales of his exploits.

'I reckon you might be losing your touch, Nat. What say you?'

Nathaniel's feelings for Rose were a constant thorn in his flesh and this, added to his earlier thoughts, tightened his mouth. He had a desire to smash his fist into the gormless face in front of him, but instead made himself shrug and smile. 'Don't worry about me, Terry, I get more than enough,' he said, adding nonchalantly, 'Was that your missus I saw in the Grey Horse Saturday night with a group of lassies from the pickling factory? Having a right old time they were with a bunch of sailors from one of the cargo boats.'

The smile was wiped off Terry's red-veined face. His wife, a huge blowsy woman with a foul mouth and a liking for gin, regularly frequented the less salubrious public houses in the East End with her cronies in the evenings, leaving her husband and their brood of unwashed ragamuffins to fend for themselves. Terry was half her size, and it was whispered that when he objected to her antics she used her fists on him. Certainly it wasn't unusual to see him sporting a cut lip or a black eye. The Grey Horse was a notorious public house and generally referred to as a knocking shop.

Terry visibly swelled, drawing himself up as far as his five foot nothing allowed. 'What're you getting at?'

Nathaniel's handsome face was the picture of innocence as he smiled at the bristling little figure. 'Getting at? Nowt, man. Just wondered if it was your Nora, that's all.'

'Leave it.' Terry's pal nudged him. 'He's just trying to wind you up. Don't give him the satisfaction.' Glaring at Nathaniel, he manhandled Terry in front of him, prodding him forwards.

When Nathaniel got to the table where David was seated, David stared at him. 'What was all that about, with Terry Wood? Looked like he was miffed about something?'

Nathaniel sat down. Sliding David's plate across to him, he picked up a spoon for the soup. 'Oh, that little runt, he's got a big mouth, that's all. Made some crack about you being henpecked,' he added slyly, hoping to ruffle David's complacency with the lie. 'I reminded him what he landed himself with at home and he didn't like it.'

David shook his head. 'You needn't have bothered on my account, Nat. He can say what he likes. He's jealous, that's all. Me an' Rose have got something special and the likes of Terry Wood can't understand it.'

It was said serenely and for the second time in as many minutes Nathaniel wanted to punch someone. Smug beggar, he thought viciously.

'But thanks, man,' David said warmly, wondering for a moment if he'd offended Nathaniel by not being grateful enough from the look on his friend's face. 'I appreciate you looking out for me.'

Nathaniel forced a smile. 'What else are mates for?'

David nodded, smiling. Nat might be a Jack the lad with the ladies, he thought, but no bloke could hope for a better pal. He just wished Nat would find a nice girl he could settle down with. He felt as though he and Nat had grown apart in the last little while. He was a married man now with a family and responsibilities, whereas Nat still went down the pub most nights and drank a good bit of what was left from his wage after he'd given his mam his board. A steady lass would give Nat stability, a purpose in his life. He had said the same thing to Rose a few days ago and she'd shrugged her shoulders.

'Nat's not the marrying kind, Davey. He's not like you. Don't you know that yet? You're as different to him as chalk to cheese, thank goodness. As soon as Nat gets what he wants from a girl, he's on to the next one. It's the chase he likes. Personally, I'd feel sorry for any lass foolish enough to think he'd change his ways just because of a wedding ring.'

He'd felt duty bound to protest and defend Nat at the time, but secretly, after he'd thought about it, he had accepted that there might be more than a grain of truth in what Rose said. He didn't understand why she was so down on Nat though, especially because his friend went out of his way to get on with Rose. Nat always brought a little something for her when he called at the house. When they were in season, there wasn't a week that went by that Nat didn't present her with a single rose wrapped in fancy paper. 'A rose for a Rose,' Nat would say, smiling, but although she always thanked him David could detect an edge to his wife's voice.

He shook his head mentally and sighed at what he saw as the contrariness of the fairer sex. He would never understand the way women's minds worked if he lived to be a hundred. Look at his own mam, for one. Just because Rose had been brought up in the workhouse and her mother hadn't been married, his mam had been dead set against him marrying what she'd termed 'workhouse scum'. His face darkened. He'd never forgive her for that. His mam had turned his da and sister against Rose too. Real nasty, his mam had been and in the end she had forced him to choose between Rose and his family. And who the hell was his mam to turn up her nose at anyone? His sister had been born six months to the day after his mam and da had got wed, he'd found that out when his mam and one of the neighbours were having a barney.

Lost in thought, he barely noticed what he was eating and when Nathaniel leaned forward and said, 'Penny for 'em?' David realized some minutes had gone by.

'They're not worth a penny, man. Just thinking about me mam and our Phyllis. The pair of them were shopping in the market the other day and looked straight through Rose apparently. Like she didn't exist. Rose had the bairn with her an' all. You'd think me mam would want to see her own grandchild, wouldn't you, especially with Phyllis and Jack not having any and them having been married for six years now.'

In truth Nathaniel had mixed feelings about the state of play between David and his parents. When it had transpired that David's mam had taken against Rose he'd hoped the bad feeling would cause a split between his friend and Rose, because David thought a lot of his mam. At the same time Nathaniel had wrestled with the desire to go round to the house and tell Mrs O'Leary she wasn't fit to lick Rose's boots. He hadn't, of course, but he still harboured a faint hope that the friction would eventually drive a wedge between man and wife although to date that showed no sign of happening. Relaxing back in his seat, he said, 'It's their loss, man. Your mam will need you before you need her.'

'Aye. Aye, I know that, but still' – David hunched his shoulders – 'it's not fair on Rose. She's never had a family with a mam an' da and brothers an' sisters and it would've been nice if we could all have got on. She had a rotten time of it being brought up in the workhouse.' He ate the last spoonful of his baked jam roll and custard before adding, 'Rose always says all she wants is me an' the bairn, mind you.'

'There you are then.' Nathaniel pushed out his chair with the backs of his knees as he stood up. 'Time to get back.'

'She wants a houseful of bairns, does Rose,' David said as he trotted along at his friend's side. 'An' she's a right good mam to Betsy, and a grand cook. I eat like a king.'

'Aye, I know.' *You've said so enough times.*

'Keeps the house as clean as a new pin and she's a dab hand at making a penny stretch to two. I don't know how she does it but she can make a piece of brisket melt in the mouth, an' her pastry knocks me mam's into a cocked hat. And I thought Mam was a good cook.'

As David continued to extol his wife's virtues Nathaniel got to the point where he wanted to yell at him to shut up. If anyone knew how perfect Rose was, he did. If only he'd seen her first. It wasn't a new thought but one that haunted him night and day. He would have made sure Davey didn't get a look in then.

As David's best pal, he got to see Rose on a regular basis and although it was bitter-sweet he couldn't imagine not seeing her. David invited him round to the little two-up, two-down terrace he and Rose rented in Sunderland's East End a couple of times a week for dinner. He was Betsy's godfather after all, a role he exploited to the full.

Of late, it was becoming increasingly hard not to betray himself when he was in her presence though, and he often wondered if Rose had an inkling of his feelings. On the whole he thought not. As far as she was concerned he was simply her husband's lifelong pal and that was that. Sometimes he had the feeling she didn't see him as a man at all, which was the hardest thing to bear. He was used to lassies responding to him with giggles and shy, uncertain smiles, even the married ones, but Rose had never been like that. He couldn't make her out – he had never been able to – and it excited him as much as it frustrated him.

He was glad when they reached their place of work, even though the climb up the staging to reach the top saddle tank was more difficult in the snowy weather. It was a tremendous height and there were no safety nets, but he was used to that. Heights had never bothered him and even if they had he would have had to get used to this side of the job pretty fast. It was piecework at the shipyard – you were paid by how much you did – and he, like most of the men, was more concerned with earning a good living wage than the conditions he worked in. All the individual trades looked after their own interests and were fiercely parochial, but it had always been that way, and as a welder he could make better money than average which was all he cared about.

The noise was in full throttle again and when they reached the tank David and Nathaniel began work immediately. It was just the two of them inside it – they usually worked together if they could – and they had only resumed welding for five minutes or so when it happened. The wooden manhole cover on which David was standing cracked and broke, and before he could jump clear he'd partly fallen through and was clinging on to the rim, his torso and legs dangling over the drop to the bottom tank some seventy feet below.

Instinctively, Nathaniel dropped to his knees and stretched out, grabbing David's hands at the wrists as he stared into his friend's terrified eyes.

Nathaniel was tall at over six foot, and well-muscled, weighing considerably more than his friend. They both knew he could pull David up and through the hole to safety. David's face was already expressing his relief when an image of Rose flashed across the screen of Nathaniel's mind, causing him to freeze. He hesitated for a split second.

David's fingers were clutching the frayed cuffs of Nathaniel's jacket. When Nathaniel let go of David's wrists, jerking back and away as he did so, David's hold was broken. He gave a high, blood-curdling scream as he fell, hurtling down between the double skin bulkhead to land on the top of the tank below.

Nathaniel sat back on his heels, staring at the hole where David had been a moment before. His head was spinning and a feeling of nausea spiralled up into his throat. After a long moment he nerved himself to peer through the hole. He could see David's body, still and lying at a strange angle, and men running to the scene of the accident.

He swallowed hard against the bile in his throat, unable to move for a moment or two, but it wasn't until he had climbed down from the top saddle tank and one of the other men confirmed David was dead that he brought up the contents of his stomach where he stood.

He was conscious of a couple of men taking him along

to the canteen and getting him a cup of tea and then others gathering around, one patting his arm and several talking in low troubled voices. Everyone knew that he and David were best mates and had grown up together and furthermore David was well liked. One or two workers began to curse and swear, reeling off the number of accidents that had occurred in the last years, the majority of which had been caused by falls from staging or girders or rudders. Bartram's might have a better track record for serious incidents than most other shipyards, but even so men lost their lives every year working in the plant.

The men were shushed into silence as the foreman approached. It didn't do for management to catch wind of complaints. When Mr Ferry sat himself down beside Nathaniel the other men dwindled away. Even for a death the work didn't stop.

Ralph Ferry, a big red-faced man, sat shaking his head before he said, 'It's a damn shame, lad. A damn shame. His wife's recently had a bairn, hasn't she? This'll hit her hard. Look' – he hesitated, licking his lips – 'I've got to go and break the news to her. I don't suppose you'd come with me? A friendly face, like? I'll see to it you don't go short in your pay packet.'

Nathaniel moved his head slightly. 'Aye, I'll come.' He was wondering what was the matter with him; after the initial shock of what had happened he felt numb. He had killed a man. Not just any man, but *Davey*, his best pal. He'd killed him and yet he didn't feel anything.

'Thanks, Nat, I appreciate it.' The relief in the foreman's voice was palpable. It was part of his job to carry out these visits, he knew that, but it didn't make it any easier, and for a young lass and mother to be told she'd lost her breadwinner a week before Christmas . . .

Clearing his throat, he stood up. 'Finish your cuppa, lad, there's no rush. We'll go in a few minutes, all right? Does the lass's mam live near or a sister maybe? Someone we could call in on before we go who'd come and be with her?'

Nathaniel shook his head. 'There's no one. She— Rose was brought up in the workhouse and her mother died in there when Rose was still a bairn.'

'What about the in-laws?'

Again Nathaniel shook his head. 'They don't get on. In fact, they haven't spoken since Davey and Rose got married.'

'Dear, oh, dear. So the lass is all alone in the world? Is that right?'

Nathaniel met the man's eyes. Quietly, he said, 'I'll look out for her, the bairn an' all.'

'Well, that's right good of you, lad. There's not many who'd say that at your age. He had a good pal in you, did Davey.' The foreman clapped him on the shoulder and then said, 'I'll be back shortly but like I said, there's no rush.'

Nathaniel sat perfectly still after the man had walked away. Feeling was coming back and with it a trembling deep inside. The echo of Davey's scream as he fell was piercing the numbness, that and the look in his friend's eyes in the last second.

He hadn't meant to do it, not really, he told himself. It wasn't like he had planned it or anything. He'd lost his grip on Davey's wrists, that was all. He hadn't been able to hold on to him. Accidents happened all the time at the shipyards, everyone knew that, and that was all this was – another accident. And Davey would want him to look after Rose, of course he would. Her and the bairn, his goddaughter. He hadn't caused the manhole cover to give way, it hadn't been his fault. It could just as well have been him standing on it, after all. This was just fate, all this, it was meant to be.

He continued telling himself the same things over and over again as he drank his tea, but however much he tried to ignore it a faint echo of that terrible scream reverberated in his head.

Chapter Three

Rose wiped a floury hand across her brow as she smiled at her daughter. Betsy was chewing on a hard piece of bread she'd baked in the oven, and the baby's cheeks were bright red from the teething that was causing her such discomfort. Nevertheless, as the child caught her gaze she grinned the toothless smile that always melted Rose's heart. It still amazed her, the consuming love she felt for this tiny piece of humanity she and Davey had created. During the later months of pregnancy when she'd begun to feel the baby moving inside her she had known the love she felt for it was beyond anything she could have imagined, but when her daughter had been born and she'd held her in her arms for the first time Betsy had become her world.

Sliding the jam tarts she had made into the oven, she cleared the kitchen table of the debris of baking and then brewed herself a pot of tea. Betsy was beginning to grizzle – it was time for her feed – and after taking the tarts out of the oven to cool Rose poured herself a mug of tea and then settled comfortably into one of the two old dumpy armchairs in front of the range with the baby on her lap. Once Betsy had latched on to her breast and was sucking avidly, Rose's glance wandered around the kitchen, her eyes taking in the whitewashed walls, painted kitchen cupboards in a bright shade of yellow and the scrubbed stone flags on the floor. She loved this room, she loved the whole of her little house. She was so lucky.

The kitchen was warm in stark contrast to the snowy December day outside, and although it was only just after one o'clock it could have been twilight, such was the dimness of the light. She drank the cup of tea she'd placed at her feet before she'd sat down and by the time she had finished Betsy was sound asleep, her downy head lolling and one small plump hand still resting on her mother's breast.

Carefully, so as not to awaken the child, Rose adjusted her blouse and then closed her heavy eyelids. The last couple of weeks she'd been walking the house with Betsy most nights, trying to keep the baby quiet so that Davey could have his sleep, bless him. The thought of her husband brought a smile to her lips. Several times Davey had got up and made them a pot of tea before reaching for Betsy, saying he would take a turn with their daughter. She couldn't think of another man hereabouts who would do the same. He was so good to her.

She must have dozed off, the rhythmic tick of the kitchen clock on the mantelpiece over the range hypnotic, because when a knock sounded at the back door she came to with a start. Betsy was still fast asleep and she got up with the baby in her arms and laid her in her pram in a corner of the kitchen before going to the door, wondering who was calling on her with the weather so bad. Likely one of the neighbours on the scrounge for something or other; Mrs McKenzie next door had already 'borrowed' a cup of sugar and a jug of milk this week.

She opened the door with a polite smile on her face which froze as she surveyed Nathaniel and the man standing just behind him. It was this individual who said, 'Mrs O'Leary? Could we have a word?'

'Wh–what about?'

Nathaniel cleared his throat. 'It'd be better if we came in, Rose. All right?'

The fear that had gripped her when she had seen the men's solemn faces was choking her now. Something had happened to Davey; it was the only reason Nathaniel and this man would be knocking at her door at this time in the afternoon. When she and Davey had first got together she'd worried herself sick about him being involved in an accident at the shipyard, but as time had gone on she'd relaxed more about it.

Opening the door wide she stood to one side and the two men walked past her into the kitchen, taking off their caps as they did so. As they turned to face her, Nathaniel's companion said, 'The name's Ralph Ferry, lass. I'm David's foreman. I think you ought to sit down for a minute.'

She remained exactly where she was, staring at them. 'What's happened? Is Davey all right?'

'Mrs O'Leary—'

'Is he? Is Davey all right?'

'There's been an accident, Rose.' It was Nathaniel who spoke as the foreman twisted his cap round and round in his fingers. 'It's bad. Look, sit down and—'

'How bad?' She must go to him, why was she wasting time talking to them like this? 'Where is he?'

'I'm sorry, lass.' Ralph shook his head as he spoke. 'He's gone. He took a bad fall and well, there was no chance. He didn't suffer, it was instantaneous.'

'No.' All colour had left her face but she was ramrod straight. 'No, it's not true. You're mistaken, he couldn't—' She took a deep heaving breath. 'He's careful. He's promised me he's always careful.'

When she swayed, both men moved as one but it was Nathaniel who steadied her, taking her weight as he half-carried her over to one of the armchairs in front of the range. Even in these moments of acute stress he was aware of the silky softness of her hair brushing his cheek and the thick shadow of her eyelashes on porcelain-fine skin. His voice slightly unsteady, he murmured, 'It's OK, it's OK,' as he lowered her into the seat and then squatted down in front of her, chafing one of her hands between his. 'Just breathe, that's it, nice and steady.'

She hadn't fainted but she'd come close, and now as Rose opened her eyes she stared at Nathaniel vacantly for a moment before withdrawing her hand and whispering, 'I'm all right.'

'It's the shock,' he said softly. 'Take a few minutes.

Look, I'll put the kettle on. Lean back and shut your eyes.'

Rose didn't protest; in truth she was feeling most peculiar. She felt hot and sick and Nathaniel's voice seemed a long way off. She heard him talking to the foreman in a low voice and the man saying something in return, but it wasn't until she heard the back door open and close that she opened her eyes to find she and Nathaniel were alone.

'He had to go back to the yard – I said I'd stay with you for a while,' Nathaniel said in answer to her stare. 'Now sit still till you've drunk something, it'll make you feel better.'

Davey, Davey, Davey. His name was reverberating in her head. He couldn't be dead, not her Davey. She closed her eyes again, feeling as weak as a kitten. He was so full of life, so exuberant and funny; only this morning he'd had her in fits of laughter over their breakfast, imitating Mick Duffy from three doors down when he'd had a few, singing 'When Irish Eyes are Smiling'. No one could make her laugh like Davey.

It was a minute or two before Nathaniel touched her arm; she opened her eyes as he said, 'Here, I've put plenty of sugar in, for the shock I mean.'

She took the cup and saucer from him. 'Thank you.' Swallowing hard, she whispered, 'What happened?'

'Rose, don't think about that now—'

'I want to know.'

He stood looking down at her for a moment. 'Like Ferry said, he fell.'

'What from? How? Did you see it?'

He nodded. 'We were working together on a saddle tank and the manhole cover gave way. He – he didn't stand a chance, it was a seventy-foot drop or more.'

Oh, Davey. She stared at Nathaniel, her sea-green eyes huge in her white face. 'Is it true what the foreman said? He didn't suffer?'

'I promise you.'

'How do you know?'

'Rose, I'm sure, all right? It happened so fast he wouldn't have known a thing.' Nathaniel rubbed his hand across his face, remembering that scream. 'Not a thing,' he repeated.

Slow tears brimmed in her eyes and then began to roll down her cheeks, and as her breath caught in her throat she began to sob. Taking the cup and saucer from her Nathaniel set it down and then kneeled in front of her, gathering her into his arms. Almost immediately she jerked away, saying through her tears, 'It – it's all right, I – I –'

He leaned back on his heels, saying softly, 'Don't be daft, lass. Cry it out. I loved him too, remember, and if you can't cry in front of me it's a poor do.' Holding her, touching her, it was intoxicating, heady. He went to take her in his arms again but she was too quick for him, rising to her feet as she said, 'Betsy, I must see to Betsy,' as the baby began to stir and whimper.

He let her move away, and once Betsy was in her arms said, 'Here, give her to me while you drink your tea,' taking the child before she could protest. As she stood hesitating, he said more firmly, 'Sit down and drink your tea, Rose,' and felt a little thrill of satisfaction when she obeyed.

He stood jogging the baby against his chest as he watched Rose, and when she set down the cup and then fetched a handkerchief out of her skirt pocket and scrubbed at her eyes, it took all his willpower not to reach out and touch her hair. She was so beautiful – even distressed like this she was more beautiful than any girl he'd known. Davey would never have been able to hold a woman like this for long, she would have tired of him eventually and broken his heart. At least the accident had spared him that pain. And it *had* been an accident, he hadn't engineered the manhole cover breaking after all, he told himself, and if he'd tried to haul Davey up who was to say that they both wouldn't have fallen to their deaths?

'I'll take her now.' He came to himself to see Rose reaching for Betsy and as he handed the child over, she murmured, 'You have to get back, we'll be all right.'

He was about to answer, 'No, I'll stay,' but in truth Ferry *would* expect him to return shortly, so instead he said, 'Can I fetch one of the neighbours for you?'

'No, I'd rather be on my own.' It was said in a manner that brooked no argument.

'I'll come back later then.'

'No, you don't have to, really.'

Quietly, he said, 'It's not a question of having to, I want to.' And when she looked as though she was going to protest further, he held up his hand. 'Davey would have expected me to see to you and the bairn, Rose. You know he would.'

She stood biting her lip but she couldn't argue with what she knew was the truth. Instead she said, 'There is one thing you could do, if you wouldn't mind? His mam an' da will need to be told and you know how things stand with them and me.'

Nathaniel nodded. 'Of course.'

'And – and thank you for coming with the foreman to break the news.'

'He was my best pal, of course I'd come.'

The words were respectful and full of concern, but as she raised her head and met his eyes just for a moment she caught something in his gaze that made her freeze. She had seen it before on occasion when she'd caught him off guard, a hunger, an almost ravenous flash of something dark that made her feel as though he was stripping the clothes from her body where she stood and seeing her naked. It was gone in an instant as his lids veiled his eyes, and when he looked at her again the sapphire blue gaze was clear and friendly, but this time she was more sure than ever that she hadn't imagined it. The very first time she had met him nearly two years ago she'd glimpsed it. It had been enough to unnerve and unsettle her even though he'd never put a foot wrong or said a word out of place. Suddenly she couldn't wait to get him out of the house, her voice feverish as she muttered, 'I must see to Betsy, she's due a feed,' as she walked past him and opened the back door.

'I'll see you later then and I'm sorry, I'm so sorry, Rose.'

He was still talking as she shut the door after he'd stepped into the yard, and for a moment she stood with her back to it, breathing deeply. And then the knowledge that Davey was dead, that their life together was gone and all the plans they'd made for the future were as nothing swept over her anew. She fell to her knees, clutching Betsy tightly against her breast, and as the tears choked her and Betsy began to cry it was as though an abyss had opened at her feet and she was falling into it.

Chapter Four

The funeral was over. It had been a good turnout, someone had said, considering it was Christmas Eve.

Rose shook her head as she sat staring into the flames of the fire. 'A good turnout.' What did that matter? But it had been said as though she should draw comfort from it, and the vicar had reiterated the same sentiment when he'd remarked that she must be gratified her husband was so clearly respected and liked by his fellow workers and the folk hereabouts.

Tears stung the backs of her eyes and as she stood up she said out loud, 'None of that, no more crying.' Tears did no good, besides which she'd cried enough the last few days to fill the ocean. She had kept telling herself that once the funeral was over – which she had been dreading – she would be able to take stock, to start thinking about the road ahead. Well, it was over and it had been even worse than she'd anticipated. Davey's family hadn't said a word to her nor had they come back to the house, all of which she'd expected, but as they'd left the graveside she had heard Davey's mother say to Phyllis that Davey would still be here now if he hadn't married her and had to work so hard. 'Men take silly chances when they're under pressure,' she'd said loudly enough so everyone could hear. Back at the house the mourners had made short work of the refreshments she'd provided, bought with the rent money, but the neighbours had been good, lending her cups and saucers and plates, and Mrs McKenzie had helped her to wash up afterwards and then returned the borrowed crockery whence it'd come.

The thought of her neighbours' kindness was weakening, affecting her far more than Davey's family's hostility, and brought more tears. After a grim childhood in the workhouse she'd had an early introduction to how cruel and unfair people could be and had become accustomed from a very young age to expect bitter rejection and rough treatment from those who thought themselves better than her. She knew Davey had been saddened by the attitude of his family and his mother in particular, but in truth their refusal to accept her had only bothered her because it had upset him. She'd told him many times she was tougher than she looked and it didn't worry her, but he wouldn't believe her. *Davey, oh, my lovely Davey . . .*

The sound of Betsy's grizzling in her cot upstairs was a welcome distraction, and when she walked into her daughter's little room, the moment the baby saw her she stopped whimpering and smiled. A rush of feeling, so strong that it brought the breath catching in her throat, swept through Rose, and for a moment nothing else in the world mattered. She bent down and lifted her child from the snug nest and immediately Betsy cuddled into her. The room was bitterly cold – for the last few days there had been ice on the inside of the window as well as outside – but Betsy was warm and flushed from her cocoon of blankets topped by a small eiderdown Rose had made when she was pregnant.

Since she had given birth to Betsy, Rose had found herself thinking about her own mother more. All she had been told by the officious workhouse matron was that her mother had been unmarried and barely fifteen years old when she'd had her, and that she had died just eighteen months later. It must have been so hard for her giving birth when she was little more than a child herself, and then her life being cut short when she was so young and after enduring the workhouse. Unbeknown even to Davey, she had talked to her mam in her mind, telling her she loved her and that she hoped she was happy where she was. Now she whispered, 'Help me, Mam. I need you. Tell me what to do.'

Downstairs she changed and fed Betsy after lighting the lamp. It was nearly five o'clock and dark outside but she was trying to eke out the last of the oil. Their coal bunker in the back yard was nearly empty too, and she had little food in the house. The refreshments for the simple wake for Davey had taken all the money she had, but she had known it was expected that she provide something. Not to have done so would have been considered disrespectful to his memory. No matter that she was at her wits' end, the proprieties had to be maintained, she thought bitterly. As it was it had been a dry wake; she simply hadn't been able to afford any beer or whisky which she knew wouldn't have pleased some folk.

Betsy was gurgling to her teddy bear in her pram, and as Rose stood staring out of the window into the swirling dancing snowflakes, she let herself imagine what today would have been like if Davey was here. He would be arriving home in the next little while with a small turkey for their Christmas dinner like he had done the year before, his brown eyes a-glow because they would be having some time together.

Last Christmas Eve they had gone to midnight mass, walking through snowy streets arm in arm, but they had spent the morning of Christmas Day in bed, making love and talking about names for the baby she was expecting. It had been a wonderful day; the only blot on the landscape being when Nathaniel had called round in the evening with a present for her – a single hothouse rose in a fancy box tied with ribbons. She shut her eyes, her gaze inward now. There was something about Nat she couldn't come to terms with no matter how hard she tried for Davey's sake. He made her flesh creep.

The sharp tap at the window brought her eyes snapping open and there he was. He grinned at her, his eyes narrowing when she didn't smile back. He had opened the back door before she got to it, walking in as though he had the right to enter at will. He had had the same arrogant, proprietorial attitude at the funeral earlier today, she thought tensely and it had made her feel uncomfortable and embarrassed but she hadn't wanted to cause a scene, not when they were burying Davey. Now though, as he dumped an armful of packages on the table, she said stiffly, 'Nat, what are you doing here?'

He straightened, taking his snow-covered cap off and banging it against his leg. 'Brought you a few bits, that's all, and Ferry asked me to drop Davey's settlement money in. He thought it'd come in handy, it being Christmas.'

She had been told that as a gesture of goodwill the company were giving her a month's pay although, as the letter she had received a few days ago had stressed, they believed the accident had been caused by Mr O'Leary not taking due care and attention. When she had asked Nathaniel how a manhole cover giving way could be blamed on Davey he'd shaken his head and said, 'It's always the same, lass. It's never the company's fault. You can't fight 'em, it's just how things are.'

As he took an envelope out of his coat pocket and placed it beside the packages on the table, he said, 'They want you to sign for it, Ferry said.'

She stared at him for a moment. She wanted to tell him to go and not to come back but he was Davey's friend and he'd been good to her over the last week, visiting Davey's parents and helping her arrange the funeral. She hadn't asked for his assistance with the latter but somehow it had just happened, along with him walking to and from the church with her and sitting beside her during the service. The funeral had taken the little nest egg she and Davey had tried to put by for a rainy day even though it had been the cheapest coffin the undertakers had had, with one horse and an open cart delivering it to the churchyard.

Ignoring the fact that he clearly wasn't welcome, Nathaniel began to unwrap the packages he had brought, his voice matter-of-fact. 'I thought you could use a few groceries over Christmas, lass. I dare say you haven't been shopping what with the funeral an' all. There's half a ham here and some vegetables and I picked up a chicken for tomorrow, it being Christmas Day. There's milk and a quarter of tea and—'

'You shouldn't do this.' It had come out sharper than she had intended. Moderating her tone, she added, 'It's very kind of you but there's no need really. I can manage.'

'Davey would have expected me to look after you and the bairn.'

Nathaniel had said the same thing several times over the last week and she hadn't argued, but this time she shook her head. 'You've done enough already. I'm very grateful but I don't want you spending your money on us.'

He shrugged. 'I've no one else to spend it on and that' – he pointed to the envelope on the table – 'won't go far. Ferry said they've paid the same as the last four weeks but it won't last long, you know that.'

'It's fine really. It will tide us over the next week or so while I think what to do.'

His eyes narrowed. 'What do you mean?'

She couldn't discuss this right now, not on top of the funeral today. 'Nat, I'm really tired. Thank you for your support and everything you've done but I just want some time by myself tonight. I – I hope you understand.'

His face had stiffened and it was clearly with some effort that he said, 'Of course, you must be exhausted, but you shouldn't spend Christmas alone. I'll come by tomorrow and—'

'I won't be alone. I have Betsy.'

'She's a baby, Rose. You need people to talk to, company.'

'Betsy is all I need.' Her voice was quiet but carried an unmistakable message.

His temper rose, but telling himself to go steady he replied in a tone as quiet as hers had been. 'Like I said, you must be exhausted and no one can think like that. I'll leave you to have an early night.' He paused a moment, as though waiting for her to say something, and when she remained silent he pulled his cap on his head and walked to the door, opening it and stepping into the snow-covered yard without another word.

She waited until he had gone into the back lane before quickly crossing to the door and locking it, sliding the bolts across the top and bottom for good measure. It was the first time since she and Davey had moved in that she had locked and bolted the door – no one did, it was unheard of – and once she had done so she stared at it, shocked at herself. Did she really think she needed protection from Nathaniel? She didn't have to think about the answer and with it came the realization that she was frightened of him, that she had always been frightened of him deep down but when Davey was alive she had buried the panic and unease because, as Davey had been fond of saying, Nat was like a brother to him.

A little cry from Betsy broke in on her thoughts and she lifted the baby from her pram, settling her on the clippy mat in front of the range propped up with a couple of cushions where she happily played with her wooden rattle. After making herself a pot of tea, Rose sat down in one of the armchairs, staring at her daughter. Betsy would grow up without her father now. She would never know the da who'd adored her. She couldn't bear it, she couldn't. Her poor bairn. And why had this happened to Davey when there were lots of bad men out there, men who couldn't give a fig about their families?

She wallowed in misery for a few minutes, but then in spite of herself the look of delight on Betsy's face at the sound the rattle made brought Rose out of the pit of despair. Whatever it took, she would provide for her daughter and keep her safe, she told herself fiercely. It was up to her now. When she had met Davey she'd been working as a kitchen maid for the grand sum of two shillings and sixpence a week, but there must be better paid work she could do? In a factory perhaps, or cooking and cleaning for one of the big houses Hendon way? No one would employ a woman with a babe in arms but maybe Mrs McKenzie would be prepared to take care of

Betsy during the day if she came to a monetary arrangement with her? It would benefit them both.

The provisions that Nathaniel had brought were still on the table. After finishing her tea, Rose put them away before opening the envelope. The notes and coins added up to just over three pounds, although she knew that Davey had brought home well over a pound a week. She shook her head at the meanness. The rent was three shillings and ninepence a week and she'd have to buy more coal for the range soon. It was their only means of warmth and having hot food and drink. Nathaniel was right; this money wouldn't last long.

She felt a moment's blind panic, her heart racing, and told herself to calm down. There was a way out of this, there had to be. Davey would expect her to find it.

Somewhere in the distance she could hear carol singers, their voices thin and far away at first but then growing closer. She'd always loved carols but tonight she found them depressing, emphasizing the fact that the rest of the world were getting on with their lives as though Davey had never existed. She put her arms round her middle, swaying back and forth and stifling the moan in her throat so as not to upset Betsy.

She pulled herself together after a few moments, sitting down on the clippy mat and playing with Betsy until the baby's last feed at eight o'clock. Once she'd put her to bed she retired herself, worn out physically, mentally and emotionally. She slept the sleep of exhaustion for a few hours but then awoke before dawn, missing the warm bulk of Davey beside her and worrying about the future. Betsy had had her first two teeth break the gum together three days before, and since then had slept well. It had been the first little milestone that Davey would never see, and it had been bitter-sweet.

By the time the bells rang out heralding Christmas Day in Holy Trinity Church some streets away, Rose had embraced several possibilities. Working in a factory or a shop or laundry would all involve Mrs McKenzie being able to have Betsy for which she would have to pay her something, and she wasn't sure whether she would be earning enough to make ends meet as it was. There was also the option of turning the front room into a bedroom and taking in two lodgers. It would help with the rent although she'd have to take in washing and maybe approach the factories round about for some outside work that could be done at home, other-wise she'd never manage. Perhaps she could move Betsy's cot into her bedroom and take in more lodgers? She hated the idea of strangers in her home but then they wouldn't remain strangers very long, she told herself ruefully.

Once she was up and dressed she found that the tap in the yard had frozen solid, as it had done every morning for the past week, and by the time she'd pushed several pieces of burning paper up the spout and got the water trickling it was beginning to snow again. She was about to go indoors when Mrs McKenzie's son appeared in her back yard and after a perfunctory 'Merry Christmas', told her his mother had slipped on the ice late the previous night on her way to the privy and broken her leg. 'Gonna be a long job, Dr Randall said,' he added gloomily. 'Broken in three places it is.'

Rose sent her condolences but her main thought was that she could expect no help with Betsy from Mrs McKenzie now, so that narrowed down her options.

It was mid-morning when Nathaniel made his appearance and as soon as the knock came at the back door Rose knew she'd been expecting it. Betsy was having a nap and she'd just sat down at the kitchen table with a cup of tea, so when she saw his gaze move to the mug she felt duty bound to ask him if he wanted a hot drink.

'Wouldn't say no.' He'd walked straight in after knocking again and her voice had been tight, so when he said in a soft tone, 'You all right this morning, lass?' she merely nodded before walking to the teapot keeping warm on the range and pouring him a cup while he divested himself of his cap and coat.

He nodded his thanks, taking it from her and then sitting down at the table where he said, still in the soft voice, 'It's customary to say "Merry Christmas" but I think in the circumstances that's pointless. How are you feeling? Did you get some sleep?'

She sat down on the opposite side of the table. 'Yes, yes, I did.' She was aware he had a couple of packages that he'd put on one of the four hard-backed chairs along with his outdoor things and was desperately hoping they weren't for her.

That hope was dashed when he reached for them, saying, 'I got you and Betsy something.'

'You shouldn't have done. I told you yesterday you've done more than enough since – since Davey—' She couldn't continue, her voice reflecting the sudden pain that had gripped her afresh. She just couldn't believe she wouldn't see him again.

He waited a moment and then said, 'I'd already got these before. It'd be daft not to have them. I'd told Davey.'

She didn't know if that was true. He was staring at her in a way that made her feel his eyes were emitting a sharp and piercing light that went right through her clothes, right through her skin. She swallowed hard and took a gulp of tea to ease the constriction in her throat.

'Here, open Betsy's first.' He passed her the larger of the packages and then leaned back in his seat again, straightening his broad shoulders and raking one hand through his thick hair.

Carefully she put down her cup and just as carefully she slowly opened the package wrapped in fancy paper. It was a doll and clearly expensive, with beautiful clothes and a porcelain painted face topped with a mass of chestnut-brown hair the same colour as her own. It wasn't a toy for a baby but a much older child, she thought, as he said, 'There was one with blonde hair but I liked this one better,' his voice deep and meaningful.

She kept her eyes on the doll in her hands as she said quietly, 'It's lovely, Nat, thank you.'

He didn't speak as he slid the other parcel towards

her. She unwrapped it even more slowly and when the silk scarf in a pale shade of green with dusky-pink roses embroidered on it was revealed, she took a deep breath. 'I can't accept this.' She raised her eyes and his gaze was waiting for her.

'Of course you can.' He smiled, his brilliant blue eyes fixed on her face. 'I told you, Davey knew what I'd got you.'

'No, I can't, really. It's far too expensive.'

'Don't be silly, Rose. It's just a small Christmas present to cheer you up, that's all.'

Did he think anything – *anything* – could 'cheer her up', the way she was feeling? Besides which, that remark gave the lie to the fact that he'd bought the scarf before Davey died, or was she being overly suspicious? Whatever the case, she couldn't accept it, not now Davey was gone. Everything had changed, didn't he realize that? A man didn't buy a single woman presents of this nature, not unless she was a sister or aunt or mother. He must know that. Her voice sounding prim even to herself, she said, 'It wouldn't be right, not now. It's beautiful and it's kind of you but I can't take it.'

'I chose it especially, with the roses an' all.'

He sounded hurt and for a moment she wavered. Was she reading more into this, into his behaviour as a whole, than was there? He *was* Davey's best friend, after all. Not only that but he was young and handsome and could have any lass he wanted. But then she remembered the remark about the doll's hair; it could be nothing, of course it could, but there was always something like that with Nat. Some seemingly casual comment or a look that made her feel uncomfortable. Her mind made up and her voice unusually firm, she said, 'I'm very grateful but I can't accept it, Nat. You must see how it would look to other people.'

'I couldn't give a monkey's cuss about other people.'

She looked at him, prepared to argue her case, but under his fixed stare her heart started to pound against her ribs.

'I bought it for you and it's yours. Burn it, put it in a drawer and forget about it, it's up to you – but it's yours.'

His voice was flat and steady and his face revealed nothing but Rose knew he was angry. Not a sad angry which might have caused her to attempt to make amends and appease him, but rather an incensed fury that caused her to shrink back in her chair.

Almost immediately his whole persona changed yet again, his expression one of pain. 'Remember I loved him too, lass, all right? I know what you're going through, and you've the bairn to tend to an' all. I just want to help if I can, what else are friends for? I understand you're not thinking straight at the moment so we'll leave it at that. My mam sends her regards by the way and says if there's anything she can do you've only got to ask. You're not alone although it might feel like it.'

He'd made her feel ungrateful and confused. She didn't know how to answer and so she said nothing, and after a moment or two Nathaniel began to talk about inconsequential things – the church service he and his family had attended that morning; his mother preparing the food for all his brothers and sisters and their families who were coming for Christmas dinner and the bedlam that would ensue, and so on. She listened quietly, speaking mostly in monosyllables when she had to and wishing he would go.

He didn't take his leave until after Betsy had awoken and she had fetched the baby downstairs, and even then it was reluctantly. She stood straight and stiff as he said goodbye, holding Betsy tightly to her, and when he reached out and took the baby's hand in his, jogging it up and down, she had to summon all her willpower to remain still.

The rest of the day crawled by, filled with memories of the last Christmas Day with Davey, and as the snow thickened and the light vanished earlier than usual the kitchen was lit only by the glow of the fire. Normally she loved this time when Betsy had her late-afternoon nap and the kitchen was cosy and quiet, but since the accident the ability to find joy had melted away. And now there was Nathaniel too, always hovering at the back of her mind and making her jump at her own shadow.

Prompted by this last thought, Rose locked and bolted the back door and then closed the curtains. Sitting down in one of the armchairs by the range, she closed her eyes. At some point over the last hours she'd come to the decision that the only way forward was to take in lodgers. The front room was bare except for the three-piece suite she and Davey had bought; they had been saving to buy a chiffonier and a nest of tables at some point in the future. She could sell the suite and buy two single beds and a wardrobe from the Emporium in High Street East with the proceeds. They specialized in second-hand furniture and as long as the beds were reasonable, they would do. She could move Betsy in with her and buy two single beds for that room with the money from the shipyard, along with bedding. If she didn't have enough cash, she'd have to pay off the remainder week by week. It cost more that way but that couldn't be helped. She could take in washing too to supplement her income. She would manage. Somehow she would make ends meet, she had to.

She must have fallen asleep because she awoke with a start a little while later to knocking on the back door. She didn't move or make a sound, her heart beginning to slam against her chest, because she knew who it was.

The handle of the door was tried a few times, and then Nathaniel's voice came, deep and angry: 'Rose? Rose, are you in there? What's going on? Open the damn door.'

She put her thumb in her mouth, biting down hard and praying Betsy wouldn't wake up and begin to cry.

He knocked a few more times and then all went quiet but she still sat in the darkness for some minutes more before getting up and lighting the lamp. Davey had been her rock but not only that, he had given her his name and respectability along with a new life, that of wife and mother, and he had loved her. Oh, how he'd loved her. He had told her so every day and it had had the effect of causing the wounds of her childhood and early youth to fade as she'd settled into her new role. For the first time in her life she had felt safe and treasured.

Her eyes darkened as she looked at the locked and bolted door and her stomach turned over.

Now everything was different, terrifyingly different, and the future had gone from being something to look forward to and dream about to something grim and dangerous, because Nathaniel was always going to be there. Immediately the thought came she told herself not to be so silly. She was panicking and there was no need to. Nathaniel was a man, just a man, and even if he did like her in 'that' way as she suspected there was no need to be scared of him. She was Davey's wife – widow, she corrected painfully – and Nat had been his best friend since childhood. Like Nat had said himself, he loved Davey, and that in itself was protection for her. Wasn't it?

From his vantage point in the back lane Nathaniel saw the light come on in the kitchen and he ground his teeth, his eyes narrowing. He'd known she was in there, damn it, so why hadn't she answered the door? He'd been taken aback when he'd found it locked but then in the next instant he had told himself that she was a woman living alone, and a beautiful one at that, so maybe it was just as well. But he'd expected her to let him in once he'd called to her.

He debated whether to go back and bang on the door until she opened it but decided against it in view of the neighbours. It didn't take much to get folk gossiping and he was well aware he needed to be canny in the circumstances. He stood for a while longer in the quiet cold night, big fat snowflakes settling on his cap and the shoulders of his coat, and his gaze fixed on the kitchen window. All day he had been thinking of her and it had fair driven him mad at his mam's with everyone so jolly and the bairns running around yelling and screaming.

After a few more minutes he tore his eyes away from the faint glow of the window and turned the way he had come, his stride long and quick as he walked, his hands thrust in his pockets.

What was it about Rose that so tortured him? he thought bitterly. He prided himself that he knew all about women; from when he was barely out of short trousers the lassies had thrown themselves at him and he couldn't help but have them, not when they laid it out on a plate. What man would refuse? But he had never loved any of them. In fact he hadn't believed in the concept of love – only lust. Lust was honest and real, earthy, whereas love was some fantasy dreamed up by poets and suchlike, a silly daydream for bit lasses with their rubbishy penny periodicals. Aye, that's what he had believed until Davey had introduced him to Rose.

He reached the end of the back lane and stepped out into the street beyond, which was deserted, although lights shone from behind curtained windows and as he passed one house there was the sound of riotous singing within. Christmas Day and here he was tramping the streets while everyone else was having a high old time, and all because of her. But it was early days. He nodded to himself. And sooner or later it was going to dawn on her that she was alone in the world with a bairn to support and no bread-winner. The memory of a dead husband wouldn't pay the rent or keep her warm in bed at night. She needed him. A faint smile touched his lips. She hadn't realized it yet but she needed him, and come hell or high water he was going to have her; he wouldn't let anything or anyone stand in his way, not this time. But for now he'd go back and have a few jars before he went to bed. Since the accident he wasn't sleeping well but some beer and a couple of whiskies would take him to a different place where that scream didn't echo in his ears when he lay his head on the pillow.

Chapter Five

It was the first Monday in January. India was holding celebrations to mark the succession of Edward VII as Emperor but in Britain the snow and blizzards made that hot exotic country seem as though it belonged to another world. New Year's Eve had come and gone amidst the usual Northern revelry and subsequently life had settled into its humdrum pattern for most folk. But not for Rose.

She'd had invitations from one or two of the neighbours to join them on New Year's Eve, along with Nathaniel's mother, but had declined them all. Instead, once Betsy was in bed, she had spent the last night of the old year writing little cards advertising rooms to let which were now displayed in several shop windows. That very morning she'd been along to the Grand Emporium in High Street East and spoken to the manager, a kindly middle-aged little man. He had come to the house a short while later accompanied by an assistant driving a horse and cart, made her an offer on the three-piece suite and taken it away there and then. He'd told her he was doing a house clearance the next day and would have two single beds for sale which he'd hold for her, and that another two would be sure to turn up soon.

Taking the bull by the horns and doing something positive about her situation had helped a little, and now, in the deep twilight of a winter afternoon, Rose sat at the kitchen table making a list of further things to do. At the very top was sourcing work she could manage at home and once she had the two rooms for the prospective lodgers set up and ready she intended to make enquiries. She glanced across at Betsy who was sitting on the clippy mat playing with her rattle and the rag doll Rose had made her for Christmas; the most important thing was making sure her child was kept safe and well and that they were together.

She had just fed Betsy some mashed-up potato and gravy – she had started weaning her after Christmas and now breastfed her only half as much – and then sat the child in her highchair with a hard crust of bread, when the knock came at the back door. She locked it every day when it began to get dark; it gave her time to prepare herself for Nathaniel's visits rather than him being able to march straight in, although once or twice he had surprised her by calling round in his lunch hour. She'd done everything she could think of to discourage him apart from being downright rude but he seemed to have the hide of a rhinoceros. With some difficulty she had maintained a polite but cool attitude, although she never asked him to sit down or have a cup of tea now.

Nevertheless, as sure as eggs were eggs, he'd be back the next day, smiling and charming and outwardly friendly.

No, that last wasn't quite fair, she told herself as she walked across the kitchen, her stomach churning as it always did when he called round. He *was* friendly, but there was that something beneath the surface too.

He had hammered on the door again before she could unlock it, and as she opened it he pushed past her so roughly he almost unbalanced her in the process. 'What the hell is this?' He brandished a card in her face. 'What do you think you're playing at? Are you trying to make me mad or what?'

She stared in shock. The handsome face was puce with rage and he was shaking.

'Well?' He glared at her. 'Answer me.'

She was totally taken aback but her body was like a ramrod now at his tone. She took the card from him without speaking and saw it was one of the advertisements she'd placed in the shop windows. Her voice cold, she said, 'I would have thought it is quite obvious what this is.'

'Don't take that tack with me.'

Now she was glaring back but aware of Betsy in her highchair she kept her voice low as she said, 'Would you please leave, Nat.'

'The hell I will.' He grabbed the card from her and tore it in two, throwing it on the floor. 'A lodger!' He spat the word. 'You alone in this house with a lodger, you must be mad.'

'I am not mad and as it happens I intend to have four lodgers.' She was trembling inside and hoped it didn't sound in her voice. 'How else do you think I am going to maintain this house and feed us both?'

'Not by prostituting yourself.'

'*What did you say?*' Her nails were digging into the palms of her hands and her breath hissed through her teeth as she said, '*How dare you.*'

'Oh, I dare, Rose. I dare, and I tell you something else, there is no way another man is coming over this threshold and into your bed, let alone four of the beggars.'

He must be deranged. The thought came and it actually moderated her reply as she said, 'I am talking about taking in four lodgers who will be sleeping in the front room and Betsy's old room, and that is all. Betsy and I will be in my room.'

'Don't be so naive. Looking like you do they'll eat you alive.'

'Lots of folk take in a lodger or two—'

'You're not lots of folk.' He took a deep breath, visibly attempting to gain control. 'Look, I've already told you I'll look after you and the bairn, haven't I?'

'You can't, you must see that? You've been very kind since Davey died, but I have to find some way of paying the rent and making ends meet.'

'I'll see to all that.'

Again she said, 'You can't. You've got your own life to live and—'

'What if I want my life to be with you?' He took hold

of her shoulders in one swift movement. 'I didn't want to say this so soon but I love you and I want to be with you.'

Her recoil was immediate and instinctive. As she wrenched herself free she took a step backwards, her eyes huge in her white face. 'Stop it.' She took a shuddering breath. 'Just go.'

'No, I won't go. Look, you want a lodger. Fine. I'll move in and pay you whatever you want. You managed on Davey's wage so you'll manage on mine.'

Was he mad? 'Davey was my husband so we managed together.'

'And I'm prepared to marry you, Rose, after a suitable time has gone by for appearances' sake.'

'I don't want to marry you, I don't want to marry anybody.' She backed across the room and as she did so Betsy began to whimper, sensing something was wrong. 'I can take in lodgers and perhaps washing and we'll get by, Betsy and me.'

'You'll take in lodgers over my dead body.' His face was dark with frustration and fury. 'I mean it, no one is coming into this house apart from me, both now and in the future. I'll kill you and her an' all' – he glanced at Betsy – 'before I let that happen. Do you want that on your conscience?'

'You wouldn't, you wouldn't hurt Betsy.'

'Only if you make me.' He reached out to her again, grabbing her wrist and pulling her violently towards him, and as he did so anger boiled up in her, swamping the fear and panic, and she slapped him hard across the face.

Whether it was the slap or the nearness of her as he held her against him she didn't know, but suddenly the last of his control had gone. Clutching her to him, he pinned her arms to her sides and forced her head back, taking her mouth in a savage kiss. She struggled desperately, aware that Betsy was now screaming for all she was worth, and her body writhing, she brought her knee up between his legs with a force borne of terror.

He emitted a strangled scream and collapsed to his knees, his hands clutching his private parts, and before he could recover she yanked open the kitchen drawer and grasped the carving knife, holding it in front of her as he lurched to his feet. She expected him to come at her again or shout and curse, so when he stood, half-bent over and gasping as he said, 'I'm sorry, I'm sorry,' it threw her for a moment.

He raised his head, a sheen of sweat on his brow and his face still contorted with pain. 'It's all right. I mean it, I'm sorry. I lost my head for a moment, that's all. It's over, don't look like that.'

She stared at him, the knife still held in front of her. 'Get out of my house.'

He took a couple of long breaths, gingerly straightening and wincing as he did so. 'I've frightened you and it wasn't supposed to be like this but you made me so angry, you must see that? Look, see to her.' He gestured towards Betsy who was still yelling and crying.

She didn't lower the knife, nor did she move.

'Rose, I care about you and I want to look after you

and the bairn, is that so wrong? It's what Davey would have wanted—'

'Don't say that! Don't you talk about him.'

Her voice was so shrill it made him jump and cut off his words in mid-flow. He stared at her, his chin jerking up out of his collar in a nervous movement that was uncharacteristic of him. He'd gone about this all wrong, he knew that, but seeing that card in the newsagent's window had sent him crazy. She shouldn't have done it; how had she expected him to react at the thought of another man – possibly four from what she had said – living in this house with her? His anger was beginning to boil again but he tried to rein it in as he said, 'You understand I won't allow you to have lodgers? I'll come and live with you here and pay you whatever you like, but no one else is, Rose. I mean it. I'd kill the first man who tried.'

She could see he meant it, something so dark was looking out of his eyes that it sent a shiver down her spine. Nevertheless, she kept her gaze steady and her voice firm when she said, 'You can't tell me what to do or how to live my life. I want you to go now and never come back.'

'You don't mean that,' he said with the arrogance she always associated with him, 'and even if you do it's not going to happen. I told you, I love you.'

'And yet you've threatened me and my daughter?'

'You made me do that.' His tongue drew a quick line over his upper lip. 'All I want to do is love you and take care of you and I've told you I'll marry you, haven't I? Damn it, I could name any one of a handful of women who'd bite my hand off for an offer like that.'

'Well, go and ask one of them then.'

'I want *you*, Rose. And I will have you, make no mistake about that. I won't let anyone or anything stand in my way.'

Part of her couldn't believe this was happening; the other part was saying she had always known there was something fundamentally wrong with him, something deep and dangerous. She believed him when he said he could have any number of lassies. Davey had always said they flocked round Nat like bees to a honeypot, so why was he so determined to have her? She didn't believe he loved her; love didn't threaten and intimidate the object of its affections or try to use force.

Betsy's cries had reached a new pitch and now she said, 'I want to see to my daughter, Nat, and I'll ask you again, please leave.'

'All right, I'll go.' He stood facing her, tall and handsome and still amazingly sure of himself as he said, 'But I'll be back and in the meantime think about what I've said because I mean every word. We're young, we've got the whole of the rest of our lives before us and I can love you as you've never been loved. We'll move down South away from here and everyone who knows us and make a new life – no one need know Betsy isn't mine. We can be a family and when more bairns come she'll have brothers and sisters to play with.'

Rose felt her stomach pulling itself tight as if away from something unclean. 'Davey will always be Betsy's da.'

The blue eyes flickered but all he said was, 'We'll see.'

She watched him as he walked to the door but remained quite still, and when he opened it he turned, saying, 'The path's all mapped out, Rose, and if you know what's good for you, you won't try and fight me and make me angry again. Most women would be down on their bended knees thanking me for what I'm offering you, think on that.'

When the door shut she watched him from the window and once the tall figure had turned into the back lane she dropped the knife into the sink and flew to the door, locking and bolting it with shaking hands before hurrying across to Betsy and lifting her out of the highchair. The baby's face was red and wet with her tears, and as she cradled the little body against her, Rose began to pray. 'Help me, God, help me, show me what to do. Please, please, show me what to do . . .'

Chapter Six

Rose spent a sleepless night going over and over every word Nathaniel had said and by the morning she had come to the conclusion that she would have to leave Sunderland as soon as she could. It would mean saying goodbye to the home she and Davey had shared and all the happy memories it contained, but she told herself she would take Davey with her in her heart. For the life of her she couldn't see any other way out of this nightmare. She believed Nathaniel when he said he would harm Betsy if she followed through on her plan to take in lodgers. She didn't care about herself, but from the way he had spoken and even more the look in his eyes she knew he would use Betsy to control her if she didn't put some distance between them. All her earlier suspicions about Davey's best friend had been realized, but she had never imagined quite how unbalanced he was. Whether he really believed he was doing what Davey would have wanted in taking her and Betsy on she didn't know, but in one way it didn't matter. She had to disappear.

Betsy awoke at the crack of dawn and the day began, but all the time Rose's mind was buzzing with what she had to do. At some time during the long night she had decided she would go and see Mr Todd, the manager of the Emporium, and tell him her situation had changed and she had to leave the town immediately; she would ask him to buy the rest of the furniture in the house and any bits and pieces like the clippy mats, saucepans and crockery and so on. She would need every penny she could get. Fortunately she still had a large portion left of the money the shipyard had sent, along with the cash from the sale of the three-piece suite, but that wouldn't go far. She knew where she was going to make for, though, so that was a start. Not long after they'd got wed, Davey had taken her to Gateshead one Saturday afternoon so she could experience a train journey for the first time. The Gateshead East and West stations were close to the town's shopping centre as well as the riverside industries, and they'd had a wonderful time looking at the shops and eating a cream tea in a little restaurant they'd found. She'd already suspected she might be pregnant with Betsy and she had told Davey over their sandwiches and cream cakes, and, careless of onlookers, he'd reached across and kissed her full on the lips, his eyes shining. Yes, Gateshead held good memories. She nodded to herself. She'd take a temporary room somewhere and start looking for work as soon as she got there. A live-in position as a housekeeper perhaps, or working in a boarding house cooking and cleaning. Anywhere she could keep Betsy with her.

She found she couldn't eat any breakfast; her stomach felt as though it was tied in a knot. She was just waiting for Betsy to wake from her morning nap and get ready to go and see Mr Todd when there was a sharp rap at the back door. It was still locked and bolted, and as she peered out of the kitchen window her breath caught in surprise. Davey's mother was standing there, her black coat and hat dusted with snow. She opened the door, staring at the grim-faced woman on the doorstep.

Vera O'Leary looked at the girl she loathed and detested, the chit who'd stolen her lad and turned him against her. Her flat round face gave nothing away as she said, with no preamble, 'I've come to talk to you,' and when Rose stood aside, she marched into the kitchen carrying the faint smell of cabbage with her, before turning and facing her daughter-in-law.

Totally out of her depth, Rose said tentatively, 'Won't you sit down?'

Her sturdy legs planted slightly apart, Vera surveyed her without speaking before her eyes flicked round the kitchen. To her disappointment it was as clean as a new pin, the range blacklcaded, the fender gleaming and the stone flags on the floor scrubbed. Her gaze fastened on the pram in a corner of the room and in answer to the unspoken question, Rose said quietly, 'Betsy's sleeping in her cot upstairs.'

Davey's brown eyes had always been as warm as hot

chocolate but Vera's were as dense and dark as bullets as she stared coldly at Rose. 'It's about the bairn I've come.'

'Betsy?' This was the first time the family had acknowledged her existence and shock had Rose stammering as she said, 'Wh–what about her?'

Before Rose's lips had settled on the last word, Vera was speaking. 'You'll have to get work now, won't you.'

For a wild moment Rose thought Davey's mother was offering to have Betsy while she went out to work, but then she was swiftly disabused of this idea when the woman went on. 'It's no place for the bairn now, here with you. She needs a proper home and a mam an' da. You won't be able to keep this place going and provide for her.'

The two women faced each other across the kitchen, one figure small and squat and the other tall and willowy. Rose didn't repeat her offer for Davey's mother to be seated nor did she make any retort, but she waited, knowing more was coming.

'Our Phyllis and Jack are prepared to take the bairn on and bring her up as their own as long as you clear off somewhere and keep away for good.'

'What?'

'You heard me. The bairn would have a good home and be brought up proper, and there'd be me an' Harold an' Jack's mam an' da an' all, as well as Jack's sisters and brothers and their families. She'd have cousins to play with–'

'They wouldn't be her cousins. Jack is no relation to Betsy and neither is his family.' Rose heard herself speaking the words and marvelled at how calm they sounded considering how she was feeling inside.

'The bairn wouldn't understand that.'

'So let me get this right.' Rose, her voice still level and quiet, said, 'You are suggesting that my daughter would be brought up never knowing anything about her real parents?'

'Not quite.' Vera's gaze was narrowed. 'When she was old enough she'd be told she is my son's child.'

'And me? Her mother?'

Whether Vera was fooled by Rose's apparent restrained demeanour or whether she didn't understand the cruelty of her next words wasn't clear. 'She'd be told you were dead, of course.'

Now Rose's voice did rise as she said, '*Get out of my house.*'

'Don't you come that tone with me, madam. You'd do well to think about what I've said. It'd leave you free to make your own life and knowing you, it wouldn't be long before you had another poor fool to support you – but even the most smitten man'd be chary about taking on some other man's bairn.'

'I said get out and don't come back.'

'You.' Vera's face was ablaze with the force of her hate. 'You workhouse scum, morals of an alley cat like all your kind. Bad blood runs in your veins, m'girl, and blood always outs. You reeled my David in before he knew what was happening and once you'd got your hooks in him he was done for. And that poor bairn of his, being left with the likes of you. God alone knows what'll become of her.'

Rose had always considered herself a gentle person but now she had an almost overwhelming desire to fly at her mother-in-law. Instead she opened the back door, her voice quivering as she said, 'I can't believe my Davey came from you, he was everything you're not, good and kind and loving. He was ashamed of you, do you know that? Disgusted and ashamed. As for me, I'd rather see my child homeless than living under a roof where she'd come into contact with you. I'm sorry for Phyllis that she can't have bairns, but I'm even more sorry for her that she's got a mother like you.'

The colour had left Vera's face now but the bitterness and hate twisted it into something ugly. She swept past Rose out into the yard, turning once outside. 'I'll see me day with you, girl. If there's any justice, I'll see you brought low and in the gutter where you belong—'

She was still talking as Rose shut the door in her face.

Rose went to see Mr Todd in the afternoon. Once Vera had left she had cried herself dry, but had felt better once she had washed her face and fetched Betsy down from her morning nap. Nevertheless, she decided to wait until after lunch before venturing out. The Emporium manager had been very understanding, not asking any awkward questions and promising he would call round in two days' time if that was convenient? They had agreed a time and she had left the shop with Betsy in her arms, the snow being too deep to take the pram out.

Once home again and with the door locked and bolted, she had sat feeling totally spent, her thoughts racing. She had no doubts about leaving the town. Vera's visit had only strengthened her determination to put as much distance between Nathaniel and herself and Davey's family as she could, but it was the sequence of events she had to get clear in her mind. Mr Todd was coming to the house at eight o'clock in the morning on the day they'd arranged, and he was bringing his horse and cart and an assistant. She needed to be packed and ready to leave, for the sooner she could catch the train into Gateshead and find somewhere to stay, the better. Once he had paid her she could leave the key with him and go; he could drop it in to Mrs McKenzie as he left. One thing was for sure, Nathaniel mustn't find out what she was about to do.

He came just after six o'clock. She had fed Betsy, who was now sitting in her highchair playing with her rattle, but had been unable to eat anything herself, her stomach feeling out of sorts. As she opened the door he smiled his charming, boyish smile and it crossed her mind that no one would believe her if she told them how he'd been with her the night before.

'Here.' He handed her a box of chocolates tied with a pretty ribbon. 'A peace offering.'

She forced a smile. 'You didn't have to do that.' She had been rehearsing what to say but now he was here it was harder to follow through.

'I wanted to. I like buying you things.' His smile widened. He hadn't known what to expect tonight but she was more reasonable than he'd hoped. He'd admitted to himself that he hadn't handled things well the day before but she had provoked him with this ridiculous notion of taking in lodgers. He'd had to make it clear he wouldn't tolerate it. 'Can I come in?'

'Of course.' She stood aside and watched him as he sauntered across to Betsy, his hand resting on the baby's downy hair for a moment before he turned to face her. Everything in her wanted to snatch Betsy up so he couldn't touch her again, but she kept her face smiling and her voice calm as she said, 'About yesterday?'

Before she could continue he held his hands up, palms facing her. 'I didn't want to get angry with you, Rose. Do you understand that? But you must see that men coming into this house isn't an option? Like I said, if you feel you want a lodger I'll move in and we'll sort something out, but regardless of that I'm not going to let you and Betsy starve, now am I?'

His voice was soothing, soft. She stared at him, her skin prickling. 'I've been thinking about what you said.'

'Oh aye?'

'I want some time to come to terms with it all. It's only been a couple of weeks since the accident and I've not been sleeping well. My mind's befuddled.'

72

'Of course it is,' he said eagerly. 'That's natural.'

'So can I have a few days to get my head straight, till the weekend perhaps? Then you could call again and we'll discuss things.'

His expression darkened. 'You're not going ahead with this lodger idea in the meantime?'

'No, I can promise you that. I went to the other couple of shops where I'd put cards and had them taken out of the windows.' This had the advantage of being true. On the way back from the Emporium she'd realized this would add credence to what she was going to say to Nathaniel.

He was smiling again. 'Good. You need protecting from yourself, I can see that. I only want to take care of you, of both of you,' he added swiftly, glancing at Betsy for a moment. 'And I'd be good to you, Rose.'

His eyes lingered on her mouth for a moment and again her skin prickled as though a fly was crawling over it. She nodded – words were beyond her.

'I'll come back Saturday then, how about that? And I'll bring a bottle with me. We can toast the future, our future.'

She found it unbelievable that he could talk like this when it was only two weeks since they had buried Davey.

Her expression must have revealed something of what she was thinking, because in the next breath, he said, 'And Davey, of course. We'll toast Davey and what he meant to both of us, but I know he'd want us to look ahead and not dwell in the past.'

She was so sick of him parroting out what he insisted Davey would have thought or wanted that she had to lower her eyes quickly, in case she gave herself away. Quietly she said, 'Till Saturday then.'

'Aye.'

He stood for a moment more just staring at her and when he would have said something else she walked to the door, opening it and forcing another smile as she said, 'I need to put Betsy to bed now.' As though on cue the baby flung her rattle on the floor and started to grizzle.

'Right.' He pulled his cap more firmly over his forehead. 'Will you need more coal or food before Saturday?'

'No, we're fine.' *Go, just go.*

Her body inwardly cringed away from the bulk of him as he passed her and stepped outside into the cold frosty air, but as he reached out and touched her cheek for a moment she remained perfectly still.

She stood in the doorway until he had opened the little gate at the end of the yard and entered the back lane, returning his wave before she shut the door, her heart thudding as though she had run for miles. After turning the key in the lock and sliding the bolts across, she walked over to Betsy, lifting her out of the highchair and holding her close.

'You'll grow up knowing exactly who your da was and how much he loved you,' she said with a soft fierceness. 'And I'll never give you up, no matter what happens.' She would die before she let anyone take her child away; whatever it took she would keep them together. She wasn't stupid, she knew it wasn't going to be an easy road, but the toughness of her formative years in the workhouse had prepared her for this, she told herself. Some girls of her age had been spoiled and cossetted their entire lives but she'd always had to stand on her own two feet – until she met Davey. Then, for the first time, she'd felt loved.

She settled Betsy on her lap for her last feed and as the baby began to suckle she pictured Davey in her mind: his blunt, good-natured face, his easy laugh, the way he'd look at her as though she was the only woman in the world – and she had been, for him. She knew that. Had he known what his love had meant to her? She doubted it, for how could you explain to someone who had been brought up in a family, a respectable family with a mother and father, how the stigma of the workhouse penetrated your mind and soul? How the matron had daily reminded her and the other bairns like her that they'd been born in sin and as such were unclean, shameful? The lowest of the low, even among the inmates of the workhouse.

She took a deep shuddering breath, the sick feeling that had been with her since childhood and which had faded on marrying Davey gripping her again. Past slights and humiliations flashed through her mind and she gave a little whimper deep in her throat before telling herself to stop thinking. It was Vera O'Leary who had stirred this all up and she wouldn't give Davey's mother the satisfaction of bringing her low. She *wouldn't*. Davey had given her his name, she was Rose O'Leary now, not Rose Potts, a bastard child to be scorned and ridiculed, and

Betsy had been born within the sanctity of marriage and in the sight of God. Her bairn would never be called workhouse scum or be spat at by other children or made to feel worthless. She would make sure of that. Whatever faced them in the future, she would make sure of that.

Chapter Seven

Rose sat staring out of the window of the train, Betsy fast asleep on her lap. She wasn't seeing the countryside though, her thoughts blinding her to the view as the train puffed along. *She'd done it.* She sat as stiff as a board, the anxiety that had gripped her from the moment she awoke making her ramrod straight. Right until the train had left the station in billows of smoke she'd expected Nathaniel to materialize and attempt to haul her back to the house. But everything had gone like clockwork.

She took a deep breath, consciously relaxing her rigid shoulders. Mr Todd had arrived promptly at eight o'clock and they had agreed a price for the remaining contents of the house, along with Betsy's pram. She'd agonized over that. Betsy would have been able to sleep and play in it, and it would also have served to carry their bags, but with the snow so deep in parts and the manoeuvring it would take on the train she'd reluctantly decided to leave it behind. Instead she had fashioned a kind of carrying pouch for her daughter out of a blanket which tied round her own shoulders and waist and left her hands free for their bags. She had included Nathaniel's presents in the items she was selling; just looking at the doll and scarf made her flesh creep and the doll wasn't suitable for a baby anyway. She would buy Betsy another one when she was older.

Mr Todd had baulked at having the responsibility of leaving the key with Mrs McKenzie, but as he had cleared the house quickly and efficiently it hadn't delayed her much. Once she had been ready to leave, she had popped the key, along with Nathaniel's box of chocolates, round to her neighbour. She had kept her explanation brief, merely saying she had to go away for a while and she didn't think she would be returning to Sunderland, and when Mrs McKenzie had asked a few questions she had parried them and left as quickly as she could.

'. . . isn't she.'

Rose suddenly realized the plump, middle-aged woman sitting opposite her on the train had spoken and she hadn't heard a word. Flushing, she said, 'I'm sorry?'

'The bairn. Bonny little thing, isn't she.'

'Aye, yes, she is.'

'Your first?'

'Yes.'

'Meself I had ten but when the last one was stillborn I told my Ken enough was enough. Your hubby not travelling with you then?'

The woman's brown eyes were bright with interest and Rose saw her glance take in the two cloth bags at her feet. She had already decided what to say if anyone asked and the lie came easily. 'No, he needs to work but I'm visiting relatives in Gateshead to show them the baby.'

The woman nodded. 'By, they'll love her, lass.'

Rose smiled but didn't reply; she didn't want to talk and looked out of the window again. She didn't know much about Gateshead other than that it was like most North-East towns and its industry centred on the river, with the inevitable rope and chemical works, slaughter-houses, ironworks and so on. Davey had read her a description of the Tyne once when the newspaper had done an article about a Mr Richard Heslop. It had tickled Davey what Mr Heslop had written:

> *There's chemicals, copper, coal, clarts, coke an'*
> *stone*
> *Iron ships, wooden tugs, salt, an' sawdust, an'*
> *bone*
> *Manure, an' steam ingins, bar iron an' vitrol,*
> *Grunstans, an' puddlers (Aa like to be litt'ral)*

'Now that's proper poetry,' he had said, grinning. 'None of your mushy talk about love at first sight an' suchlike.'

'But you believe in love at first sight,' she'd protested.

'Aye, I do since I met you, but that's personal like, not to be shared with every Tom, Dick and Harry by writing it down and letting folk read it. No, Heslop's got it right in my book.'

'You're a philistine,' she'd said, laughing, only to squeal

as he'd caught hold of her and pulled her onto his lap, thereby finishing the conversation as he'd made love to her.

Her full lips tightened with pain, and like she did a hundred times a day, she thought, *Davey, oh, Davey.* The more she had gone over Nathaniel's words the night he had kissed her, the more convinced she was that far from wanting to keep Davey's memory alive, Nathaniel seemed determined to erase it. The way he'd talked about moving down South and letting people believe Betsy was his was chilling, and there was Davey's own mam proposing that their child be brought up by Phyllis and Jack and that she be told in the future both her parents were dead.

'You all right, lass?'

Her fellow passenger had spoken again and wiping her face clear of expression, Rose said quickly, 'Yes, I'm fine. It was just a bit of a palaver getting our things together and catching the train, that's all.'

'Oh aye, it's easier when they're a bit older. I had two sets of twins under five at one point, now that was a game and a half, no mistake. On the go from dawn to dusk I was, and then Ken'd come in from work and cause high jinks if his meal wasn't on the table. I told him he might work down the docks but I'd swap his job for mine any day. But that's men all over and I have to say he's not a drinker, I'll give him that. Whereas my sister's man . . .'

Over the next little while Rose let her fellow passenger natter on, finding she only had to say the occasional word or two. It was twelve miles by train to Gateshead, but they stopped at various little stations on the way – East Boldon, Brockley Whins, Pelaw, Felling – before arriving at Gateshead East station. This was situated a short distance south-east of the High Level Bridge and had been reconstructed sixteen years earlier when two generously proportioned side platforms and a substantial building containing all the station facilities had replaced the previous inadequate premises.

Betsy awoke as the train chugged into the station in billows of smoke but settled quite happily in her home-made carrier with a hard crust of bread to chew on. Rose felt very small and very insignificant as she left the train holding the bags; everyone else seemed to know exactly where they were going and were in a hurry to get there. She emerged from the station into Wellington Street and stood looking about her for a few moments. It was already gone noon and would be dark by four o'clock and she had to find somewhere for them to stay before then.

She noticed a few horse-drawn cabs waiting a short distance away and as she watched, one of the passengers from the train climbed into one and the horse trotted off. It dawned on her that cab drivers would know the town better than anyone. She walked across to the remaining cabs and as she did so a middle-aged driver took his pipe out of his mouth and said, 'Where to, lass?'

She swallowed nervously. 'I'm sorry to bother you but I just wondered if you knew of somewhere I could rent a room for a short while? Not – not a hotel or anywhere expensive.'

The man had a rough, weather-beaten face and he stared at her for a moment. 'Just you and the bairn, is it?'

She nodded. There had been something in his voice that made her say, her tone defensive now, 'My husband was killed in an accident at the shipyard he worked in recently.' She knew what he was thinking – a woman on her own with a baby? Likely she was an unmarried mother who was no better than she should be.

'Oh aye? Which shipyard was that then?'

'Bartram's in Sunderland. He had a fall the week before Christmas.' It was unfortunate she couldn't repeat the story she'd told the woman on the train about staying with relatives to deter just this sort of speculation, she thought, her face flushing. People always assumed the worst.

She was about to turn away when the man said quietly, 'That was bad luck, lass. Them shipyards are dangerous places.' He stared at her for a second or two more and then seemed to come to a decision. 'Look, my sister runs a guest house near Saltwell Park but there's not much doing usually through the winter months. I dare say she might have a room but it'd be payment in advance, mind.'

'Yes, of course.' Rose hesitated. She didn't want to spend precious money on a cab when she could walk or take a tram. 'How far is it?' she asked awkwardly.

Hubert Dodds prided himself on being a good judge of character and he'd bet his last farthing the bonny little piece in front of him was a respectable lass even though she was on her own with a young'un. The story about the husband dying rang true, but it seemed odd she didn't have any family to help. Still, it was none of his business, although he dare say Beattie would want to know the ins and outs before she agreed to take the lass in. With this in mind, he said, 'I'll take you there, no charge. It's only right to make sure I haven't sent you on a wild goose chase with the bairn an' all.'

Rose's face flooded with fresh colour. 'No, it's fine. If you just give me directions—'

'Lass, I've a daughter about your age and I wouldn't want her tramping the streets with a bairn and bags and no one to give her a hand. Come on, hop in.' So saying he took the bags out of her hands before she could protest further and then helped her into the interior of the cab that smelled of leather and pipe smoke with faint undertones of horse, replying to her flustered thanks with a brief smile. Aye, she was a nice little lass, he was sure of it, he thought as he climbed into his seat. He just hoped Beattie agreed with him. She was prim and proper, was Beattie, and if she felt the story about the husband wasn't true, that'd be the end of that. Perhaps he shouldn't have opened his big mouth in the first place – the missus'd be sure to tell him that when he related the events of the day – but the lass had looked so lost and forlorn. The vicar had preached about the Good Samaritan only this last Sunday, he'd remind Elsie of that if she gave him any grief.

It was beginning to snow again, just the random

feathery flake blowing in the wind, and as Rose sat in the cab she felt panic rise up in her throat about what she was going to do if the cab driver's sister had no vacancies. Betsy was sitting on her lap and gazing out of the window with rapt fascination, and as the horse clip-clopped along Rose prayed silently, pleading with God to help her. Betsy would need to be fed and changed soon. Of course most people would say she was mad to leave Sunderland, especially with a child to look after, and maybe she was, but although it was probably reckless and foolhardy she didn't feel she'd had any choice. Not after what Nathaniel had said and done. He wasn't normal. She shivered, but it was nothing to do with the bitterly cold day. All the years that Nathaniel had been Davey's best pal and yet Davey hadn't known him, not really. It was frightening.

Beattie Harper stood on her doorstep listening to her brother's explanation of why he had brought a young lass with a baby to her door, and as he finished she glanced towards the cab. 'You'd better bring her in so I can have a word with her but I'm making no promises, mind, and I'll thank you not to do the same in the future. This is a guest house, not a boarding house for any Tom, Dick or Harry, as you well know.'

'She only wants somewhere for a short while.'

'Does she indeed? And why is that then?'

Hubert shuffled his feet sheepishly. 'I don't know.'

Beattie gave him an exasperated big-sister look that he

remembered well, before saying, 'Bring her in then, but you'd better wait in case she's not suitable.'

'What am I supposed to do with her then?'

'I don't know but you should have thought of that before you spoke of me to a complete stranger, shouldn't you. And leave her bags in the cab for now.'

That didn't bode well. Hubert opened his mouth to say more, looked into his sister's lined face with its thin cheeks, thin lips, thin eyebrows and thin grey hair pulled so tightly back from her brow that it looked painful, and changed his mind. Muttering something under his breath that finished with 'Christian charity', he walked over to the cab and opened the door. Apologetically, he said, 'She wants to have a word before she'll say if a room's free.'

Rose nodded that she understood but her chin jerked up as she climbed out of the cab with Betsy in her arms. She hadn't been able to hear their conversation, but then she hadn't needed to; it was clear from the cab driver's sister's face that she was far from pleased and had probably assumed the worst about her.

Beattie was waiting in the front room as Rose and Hubert came into the house, and her voice was crisp as she called, 'Come through and shut the front door behind you, please, Hubert.'

Preparing herself, Rose entered the room with her head held high. She had nothing to be ashamed of, whatever this woman was thinking. She was faintly aware of a pleasant smell of lavender and beeswax, of several two-seater brown leather sofas and a couple of occasional tables, and an enormous aspidistra on another table in front of the bay window, but all this was at the periphery of her vision. She stared at the tall thin woman in front of her and said quietly, 'How do you do?'

It wasn't often Beattie Harper was surprised, but the beauty of the girl and the dignified way in which she held herself had taken her aback somewhat. This did not show in either her face or her voice, however, when she said, 'How do you do, Mrs . . .'

'Shelton. Mary Shelton.' It was highly unlikely Nathaniel would trace her to Gateshead, but just in case, she'd decided to assume another name for the time being.

Beattie inclined her head. 'I'm Mrs Harper. I understand from my brother that you're in need of temporary accommodation, Mrs Shelton?'

'For a short while, yes.' Betsy was sucking her thumb as she turned her head this way and that taking in her new surroundings and was quiet for the moment, for which Rose was thankful. 'I explained to your brother that my husband was killed in an accident the week before Christmas, Mrs Harper. I have no family and my husband was estranged from his when he died, consequently I need to find work to support myself and my daughter.'

Beattie's eyebrows rose. 'Forgive me, Mrs Shelton, but surely it would have made more sense to stay where you were and look for work there?'

'I tried but there was nothing, besides which I felt it would be helpful to get right away from the memories and all. My daughter and I have to make a life for

ourselves now, and somewhere different is a new beginning.'

'I can see that, but still . . .'

Betsy had satisfied her curiosity and was now beginning
to wriggle and whimper. Rose hitched the baby up in her
arms a little. She knew what the reaction would be if she
said her husband's best friend had made unwelcome
advances to her. They would think she had encouraged
him in some way – it was always the same in things of
that nature. It was never the man's fault. Just last year
in the shop at the end of their street the wife of the
proprietor had caught him on top of the eighteen-year-old
assistant in the storeroom at the back of the premises,
and despite the girl saying he had attacked her and him
having scratches on his face, everyone had decided the
girl was a bad lot.

Keeping her voice level now, Rose said, 'It was my
decision and I'll have to live with it, for right or wrong.
As I said, I could expect no help from my husband's
family and there was nothing to keep me in Sunderland.'

'I see.' Beattie felt there was more to this than met the
eye. She looked at her brother, a long look which said
only too clearly she was far from pleased with him. That
was the thing with men, she thought waspily. A pretty
face and a fine ankle and they were putty in a certain
type of woman's hand. Not, to be fair, that she thought
the girl in front of her was a hussy, but there was something she wasn't saying nonetheless.

'Your brother said you might have a room to rent short

term, but of course if that is not the case I perfectly understand.' Rose had seen the look and thought she knew exactly what the woman was thinking.

'Did he say I always take payment in advance?'

'Yes, he did.' Rose looked straight at the landlady and her voice was crisp when she said, 'I can assure you that I have not left Sunderland owing rent or having any other debts, and I can pay you whatever you ask right now.'

Behind her Hubert shuffled his feet; he was more than a little embarrassed. 'Of course you can, lass. No one is suggesting anything different.'

His sister sent him another look that would have felled a lesser man, but behind her stiff facade she was thinking quickly. She was satisfied in herself that the woman in front of her was respectable enough, even though she hadn't got to the bottom of things, and she rarely had a guest during the winter months so a little extra money for a week or two wouldn't come amiss. Added to which, she could hardly send her out into the cold and with the weather worsening with a small baby to take care of.

Making up her mind suddenly, she said, 'Well, now that's clear I see no reason why I can't offer you a room, Mrs Shelton.' Glancing at Hubert, she said, 'Go and bring Mrs Shelton's luggage in while I put the kettle on. I think we could all do with a cup of tea.'

Hubert wasn't about to argue. As he scurried into the hall, Beattie said, 'Sit down, Mrs Shelton. I'll show you the room after you've had a hot drink – you must be tired after your journey.' Betsy's squirming and whimpering having reached a new pitch, she added, 'Is the child hungry?' and when Rose nodded, continued, 'Sit here and feed her and I'll see to it that you are not disturbed. Come along to the kitchen at the end of the hall when you're ready.' And so saying she left the room, closing the door behind her.

Rose sank down onto one of the sofas, her legs feeling weak with relief that they had somewhere to stay. Slipping off her coat, she undid the buttons of her blouse and put Betsy to the breast. It was snowing more heavily outside, and again thankfulness flooded her that they'd found shelter. What the room was like or how expensive it was didn't matter right at this moment. She'd escaped. They were safe.

Chapter Eight

Over the next day or so Rose realized that she could have done a lot worse than a room in Mrs Harper's establishment. The house itself was a two-storey, semi-detached residence in a tree-lined avenue, and as far removed from the narrow terraced streets in the centre of Gateshead as Buckingham Palace to the East End of London. Apparently Mrs Harper had married well, and on her husband's untimely death at the age of thirty-five had been left with a small nest egg in the bank and the marital home bought and paid for, but a need to earn some kind of income to enable her to continue living in the house she loved. Hence her taking in paying guests, normally through the summer months.

She was charging Rose three shillings and sixpence for the room, one of five bedrooms the house boasted, and this included a cooked breakfast and a supply of coal for the fire in the small blackleaded fireplace which kept everything as warm as toast. The room was spotlessly clean and furnished with twin beds, a wardrobe and a chest of drawers, and two small easy chairs set either side of the sashed window. A large square of carpet covered most of the floor and Mrs Harper had even provided a cot for Betsy, but the most amazing thing, as far as Rose was concerned, was the innovation of a bathroom complete with a lavatory at the end of the landing. When she'd first opened the door and stepped inside she'd stood in awe for some moments.

Of course she knew this standard of hitherto unimaginable luxury could not continue for long and that it was a brief glimpse into how the other half lived; she had to find work and fast. But what? Her landlady was not a chatty soul, and she'd exchanged only a few words with her over breakfast every morning, which was served in solitary splendour in the large dining room which held four tables each with four chairs, but Rose decided she would try and pick Mrs Harper's brains about the possibility of jobs in the area. There might be something available in larger guest houses, or even hotels or private houses.

She brought the subject up on Sunday morning as Mrs Harper served her bacon and eggs, but the landlady stared at her doubtfully, shaking her head. 'You'll be hard pushed to find anything in that realm where you can take the child, Mrs Shelton. Have you references?'

'No, no, I haven't. I never expected to find myself in this position, Mrs Harper.'

'Quite so. Well, I know of an agency in the town for women where you can register your name and they see if they have got anything that suits. Perhaps you could try there? Of course, the factories and laundries would be no good, and I would say shop work is out too. I know you wanted to leave Sunderland but I really think you would have been better staying there where maybe friends or neighbours would have been prepared to help with the child.'

Rose made no reply. She didn't expect Mrs Harper to be in sympathy with her without knowing the full facts, and she doubted she would look on her favourably if she knew about Nathaniel. No smoke without fire – how many times had she heard that about folk in the past? You didn't have to be guilty of anything to have mud stick.

'The newspapers and some of the shops advertise positions in Gateshead too, but as I said, with the child . . .'

Again Rose said nothing. She felt Mrs Harper wasn't fond of children; she and her husband had travelled and entertained often and Rose had got the impression that a family had never been on their agenda. Which was fair enough, she supposed. Certainly the landlady had shown no interest in Betsy whatsoever. And that was fine, of course it was, but it would have been nice to think she might be able to leave Betsy with the landlady for an hour or two while she looked for work. But something would turn up, she told herself bracingly as she finished her breakfast quickly, before Betsy started to stir in her cot upstairs. The baby was teething again and she'd been walking the floor with her in the early hours to keep her from crying and disturbing Mrs Harper, but at least this meant that by eight o'clock, when breakfast was served, Betsy was ready to go down for a nap. Yes, something would turn up. It had to.

By the end of January her optimism had faded and she was sick with worry. She had visited the agency Mrs Harper had spoken of, but the woman behind the desk had made it plain she could place her somewhere ten times over but not with a child. A housemaid; a companion-maid; a nursery maid in a big house on the outskirts of Bensham – the list had gone on but Rose had noticed each position had the word 'maid' in it, and she wasn't sure if she wanted to go into service. Anyway, as the lady had made clear, it wasn't an option for her, and she had left the agency somewhat dispirited but telling herself there were always the newspaper advertisements and cards placed in shop windows. She followed them all up, even the most obviously unsuitable positions like 'laundry checker' or 'female bar staff required', but to no avail. In fact she nearly came to blows with one sour-faced man who was looking for a machinist in his small clothing factory when he suggested she should put Betsy in the workhouse for a while until she was 'in a fit state to provide for a bairn'.

It was on the last Friday in January, after another fruitless visit, this time answering an advertisement in the local paper for a cook-cum-housekeeper at a vicarage, that Rose was given a ray of hope.

The morning was numbingly cold and a strong wind was blowing that spoke of more snow as she left the establishment on the south side of Midge Holmes. She had only been in the house a matter of minutes; the clergyman's wife had taken one look at Betsy and declared Rose was quite unsuitable for the position. As she walked down the front garden path, Betsy snuggled into her chest, she thought longingly of the pram she'd had to leave in Sunderland. It would have kept the baby warm and dry and protected from the north-easterly wind. She'd wrapped Betsy up as best she could but still her little nose was bright red with the cold.

She'd just opened the gate leading on to the lane she'd walked down five minutes before when she heard someone behind her. Turning, she found the small maid who had opened the door to her initially hot on her heels. Her voice little more than a whisper, the young girl said, 'I hope you don't think I'm poking me nose in, but you come about the job, didn't you?'

'The cook-cum-housekeeper position, yes.'

With a quick glance behind her, the girl muttered, 'I've gotta be quick, the mistress won't like me talkin' to you, but I wondered if you knew about the hirings at the beginning of every month at Birtley market? First Monday they are. Course, it's not called the hirings any more, not like years ago, but a lot of the country folk hereabouts, farmers an' the like, still go there if they want labourers an' stable hands, an' women to work inside an' all. Me sister, our Dolly, was left with a bairn when her intended skedaddled after putting her in the family way, scum he was. Anyway, she got taken on by a farmer over near Whickham. The thing is' – the girl's tone became apologetic – 'they're not so particular at the hirings, if you know what I mean.'

Rose nodded. She wasn't about to explain that she was a widow; the girl probably wouldn't believe her anyway and she didn't want to appear as though she thought herself better than the maid's sister. 'Thank you, I didn't know about it, no.'

'Aye, well, I'd try your luck there, in front of the Pig and Whistle, all right?' The maid bent forward, tweaking the blanket away from Betsy's face as she said, 'Aw, she's a bonny little thing, isn't she. I can see why you wanted to keep her.'

Rose was saved a reply as a voice sounded from the doorway: 'Bernice? What do you think you're doing?'

The girl straightened without looking round. 'I've gotta go but take it from me, you wouldn't want to work here anyway. He's all right but she's a tartar.' She made a face and then turned, her voice prim as she called, 'Coming, Mrs Howard.'

Rose thought about what the little maid had told her on the tram on the way back to Summerfield Avenue. She decided she wouldn't tell Mrs Harper what she intended to do. The hirings didn't sound altogether respectable – at least, someone like Mrs Harper might not think so – but she couldn't afford to be choosy. The train fare to Gateshead, the rent for the room, the tram rides she'd taken looking for work and having to buy something to eat in the evening had all bitten into her small stash of money at an alarming rate. She was frightened. She glanced down at Betsy snuggled on her lap. And she'd begun to dream about her earlier life in the workhouse again, dark nightmares that caused her to wake in the middle of the night whimpering with terror. Suddenly it didn't matter what people might think of her if they saw her standing with Betsy at the hirings; the only thing that *did* matter was securing a roof over their heads.

At some time during the night she awoke in a panic realizing she hadn't asked the maid what time the hirings began. After worrying about it till daybreak she decided she'd just have to leave for Birtley as early as she could on Monday morning.

Saturday and Sunday passed slowly with flurries of snow now and again which prevented Rose leaving the house, worried as she was that Betsy would get chilled and catch a cold. She was praying that the worst of the snow would hold off until after she had been to the hirings. She felt sick when she thought about it, of standing with Betsy hoping someone would employ her and everyone assuming the worst about her, but she had no choice. The workhouse was forever on her mind now, much as she told herself she would never willingly walk into its dreaded confines. But could she let Betsy starve instead? She was in no doubt that Mrs Harper's opinion on the matter would be along the same lines as those of the man at the clothing factory; the landlady had made it clear a couple of times that their staying at the guest house was purely temporary, and Rose felt that this particular fount of the milk of human kindness was rapidly running dry.

She was awake before daylight on Monday morning and after peering anxiously out of the window was relieved to see it wasn't snowing yet. She expressed some of her milk into a little cup and let a rusk dissolve in it before she woke Betsy for her breakfast. Her breast milk alone didn't satisfy the baby now. Betsy was a little grumpy at being woken but ate her breakfast, finishing with a top-up of breast milk after which Rose bathed and dressed her and then got ready herself.

At eight o'clock she was downstairs in the dining room although her stomach felt as though it was in a knot and she didn't know how she was going to eat, added to which she'd had to bring Betsy with her as the baby wouldn't settle. She forced her meal down quickly while Betsy contented herself chewing on a crust of toast, and after telling Mrs Harper she was going after another job in the town she left the dining room before the landlady could ask any questions.

Within five minutes they had left the house and were walking along Summerfield Avenue. It was bitterly cold but the sky was high and blue, a weak winter sun shining on the banked-up snow either side of the pavement. She had left their belongings in the room; she would come and collect them later if she was fortunate enough to find a position somewhere.

It was eleven o'clock when Rose arrived at the small market town of Birtley. She had caught a tram to the outskirts of Gateshead but had walked the last couple of miles along lanes deep in snow, and her boots and the bottom of her skirt and coat were sopping wet by the time she walked into the market square. She saw the Pig and Whistle public house immediately, a large white-washed and thatched building with a battered sign of a pig prancing with a whistle in its snout.

The market place was a large open square and mostly cobbled, bordered on three sides by buildings of various kinds. It seemed to be divided in two from what she could see; on the far side there were a number of stalls selling vegetables, meat, flour and yeast, tea, sugar and other food, along with pedlars plying their wares from trays hung round their necks holding tapes and ribbons and trinkets. Closer to the Pig and Whistle it was clearer, just two farm carts standing side by side, both with middle-aged women selling baskets of eggs, cheese, cream and butter, and milk from large churns which they doled out to customers who had brought their own jugs and bottles.

The space immediately in front of the public house was empty apart from several men of various ages who were standing talking or sitting on the pub's low stone wall, and a robust young woman with red cheeks who eyed Rose up and down as she walked towards her. When she was close enough, Rose said, 'Is this where you stand for the hirings?'

'Aye.' The woman looked to be in her early thirties or late twenties, and she didn't smile as she said, 'Wouldn't bother if I were you, not with the bairn.'

'Aw, give over, Maggie.' One of the men sitting on the wall had heard what she'd said, and now he addressed himself to Rose as he added, 'You've got as much right to be here as anyone, lass. Don't take no notice of her.'

'You can shut up an' all.' The woman rounded on the man. 'Worst day's work I ever did, marrying you.'

'You were keen enough at the time. Couldn't get me down the aisle quick enough if I remember.'

'That was when you were working for Farmer Tollett an' I thought you were set up for life with the cottage an' all.'

'Not my fault he sold up and the new bloke had five sons to do the work. Blood's thicker than water.'

'Huh.' The woman hitched up her ample breasts, pulling her shawl more tightly round her. Turning back to Rose, she said, 'What you after?'

'I'm sorry?'

'What sort of work are you hopin' for?'

'Anything,' Rose said truthfully.

'Live-in?'

Rose nodded.

The woman's hard eyes narrowed. 'Got caught out with the bairn, did you? Some bloke do a runner?'

'No, my husband died.'

'Right.' She might as well have said 'That old story', from her tone. 'What about family, couldn't they help?'

'No,' said Rose shortly, turning away.

'Hoity-toity. Strikes me you haven't got anything to be uppity about. Still, with a face like you've got there's always one way to earn a few bob.'

'*Maggie*.'

This time the woman took notice of her husband and after a muttered 'I was only sayin'', became silent, probably realizing she had gone too far.

The exchange had confirmed Rose's fear of what everyone would be thinking and she stood in silent misery, not looking to the left or right, her cheeks scarlet with humiliation. Thankfully Betsy was fast asleep but sooner or later she would wake up and need feeding and possibly changing. It had been foolish to come here with her but what else could she have done? If Mrs Harper had been a different kettle of fish she could have asked her to mind Betsy for a while, but she could just imagine how that request would have gone down.

At one point before the church clock at the back of the square behind the buildings struck twelve o'clock, a farmer had come and talked to two of the men who had gone off with him after a minute or two. By then Rose felt like a block of ice. She had long since stopped being able to feel her feet and her hat and coat offered little protection from the piercing wind that had sprung up.

Betsy woke up just after midday and immediately began to cry, whether from hunger or cold or a combination of both, Rose didn't know. After trying to pacify the baby for over half an hour she was becoming increasingly desperate.

It was then that her previous interrogator, her voice conciliatory now, came over and said, 'If you want to see to the bairn, old Seth, the pub landlord, won't mind. He's got a snug in the back he only opens at night for the card players, but if you buy a hot toddy or somethin', he'll let you use it for the bairn, all right? He's a good sort, Seth.'

'Th–thank you.' She was so cold her teeth were chattering.

Old Seth turned out to be as amiable as promised, and once ensconced in the small room off the main pub that smelled strongly of stale beer and tobacco smoke, Rose fed and changed Betsy. She had ordered a bowl of soup and a roll from the landlord, and once Betsy was calmer, Rose drank most of the soup, leaving a little and some fragments of bread which she turned into mush in the bowl and then fed to the baby, knowing her breast milk alone wouldn't satisfy Betsy for long.

After wrapping Betsy up again as snugly as she could she left the sanctuary of the little room and stepped outside. The wind had picked up still more while she had been inside and now the sky was darkening, the sunshine of the morning a distant memory.

Maggie and her husband had disappeared; whether they'd been taken on by someone or had just gone home due to the worsening weather Rose didn't know. Only two men remained and herself.

The two men stood quietly together, chatting now and again but mostly silent, and although Rose caught the occasional glance they sent her way she didn't speak. After the brief sojourn in the warmth of the pub room it seemed even colder and Rose hoped the snow would hold off a little longer. Betsy had been peering out of her cocoon watching the comings and goings in the square for a while and eventually fell asleep again, which was a blessing. There were fewer folk about now, and Rose had just promised herself that when the church clock struck three o'clock she would admit defeat, when she noticed a man walking towards her, his eyes fixed on her face. He was a large man in every sense of the word, tall with a protruding stomach and ruddy be-whiskered face, his clothes somewhat grubby and unkempt.

'You lookin' for work?' He spoke when he was still some yards away, his voice surprisingly high for such a big man.

Rose nodded. 'Yes, yes, I am.'

'Live-in?'

She nodded again.

'I want someone in the house, cookin' and cleanin' and the rest. Me mam died a few weeks afore Christmas.' His gaze took in Betsy, still fast asleep in her nest. 'How old's the bairn?'

'She's seven months.' She expected him to ask more about Betsy and mentally prepared herself, so when he merely said, 'When can you start?' she blinked in surprise.

'I own the mill at Rowlands Gill. You heard of it? Vickers is the name. Arthur Vickers.'

'No, no, I haven't.' And then she added quickly, in case she had offended him, 'I don't come from round these parts, you see.'

Again he asked no questions beyond saying, 'So, you want the job? I can't pay much, three bob a week, but you an' the bairn'll have all the grub you can eat and a roof over your heads. I doubt you'll get a better offer. It'll be just in the house you're needed, I've got a lad who comes and helps me in the mill. No place for a woman, a mill.'

She stared at him, not quite sure why she was hesitating, and a number of seconds elapsed before she said, 'Yes, yes, please, I want the job.'

'I want someone straight away.'

'Aye, yes, that's fine.'

'Where's your things?' He glanced at her feet.

'At – at my lodgings in Gateshead.'

'Gateshead?' He frowned. 'Well, I suppose I can take you there afore I turn for home. Long way round, mind. You got much?'

'Just a couple of bags.'

He nodded. 'I've sold all the sacks of flour I brought with me so there's plenty of room in the cart. We'd better be making tracks then, it's going to come down soon, I can smell it.'

So saying he turned and made off across the square and after a moment Rose followed him. He stopped at a horse and cart tethered at the far end of the square. The back of the cart was covered in a film of white and there were several hessian sacks in one corner. 'You an' the bairn all right there?'

'Yes. Yes, thank you.' She scrambled up and settled herself behind his plank seat just as the first of the snow-flakes began to fall.

'Hold on then, it can get a bit bumpy but better than shanks's pony, eh?' Once he was in his seat, after untying the reins, he clicked for the horse to move off.

Rose, her heart thudding fit to burst, watched the disappearing view of the square as she cuddled Betsy close. For better or worse another stage of her life was beginning but as the miller had said, she and Betsy would have a roof over their heads and full stomachs, and it sounded as though she would be the sole mistress of his house which was far better than having to take orders from another woman. This would work out, she would make it work.

PART TWO

Out of the Frying Pan

1904

Chapter Nine

The last eighteen months had been quiet ones on the whole for Rose as the housekeeper of Vickers Mill House. The forming of a new militant movement to gain the vote for women – the Women's Social and Political Union – had passed her by, along with Marie Curie, a French scientist, becoming the first woman to win a Nobel Prize. Arthur Vickers never bought a newspaper when he went into town for the simple reason that he couldn't read, and even if he had heard of these events, he wouldn't have reported them back to Rose. He believed women should know their place, which was serving men, and it was foolish to give them ideas above their station.

The house was quite separate from the mill. It was set some fifty yards away in a small incline, and had its own yard as well as a square area of grass where the chickens had their run and coop. In the whole time she'd been at the house, Rose had only seen the lad who came from the nearest hamlet every day apart from Sunday to help Arthur in the mill – just twice, and then from a distance.

Arthur had made it plain on her first day that she was not to set foot in the mill, not that she wished to. Keeping house and caring for Betsy and seeing to the chickens suited her just fine.

Her initial time at Mill House had been spent washing and scrubbing and polishing. It had transpired that Arthur's late mother had been an invalid for a number of years before her death, and the whole house had been filthy, covered in grime and dust and mouse droppings. Once she had put the huge stone-floored kitchen to rights, a major task in itself, she had started on the living room and then the dining room, although Arthur had told her this was never used. Nevertheless, she couldn't bear to leave it in the state it had been in. Two of the four bedrooms, the two she and Betsy now slept in, hadn't been occupied for decades and there had been mould on the furniture as well as the walls and ceiling, but Arthur's late mother's room, along with Arthur's too, had not been much better. For twelve weeks solid she had worked from dawn to dusk getting things straight, but once she'd finished the house and its contents were transformed.

She had washed every scrap of bedding and linen, every curtain, and beaten the numerous clippy mats covering the floors to within an inch of their lives. She'd scrubbed and waxed and polished the furniture, and although Arthur hadn't commented she was pleased with the results. Under all the filth and mould of years most of the contents of the house were of good quality, and the kitchen – her favourite room – with its beamed ceiling, enormous open fire with bread ovens either side, long wooden table and chairs, oak dresser and two cushioned settles standing against whitewashed walls, was a pleasure to work in.

The privy and wash house were outside in the flag-stoned yard, and when she'd first opened the door to the former she had gagged. It had taken a whole day to bring it up to scratch but now she kept it clean and fresh with daily ashes down the hole in the plank seat, and insisted the miller take the contents to the dung hill in a nearby field once a week, where a local farmer spread it on his crops. She always threw two or three handfuls of lime down the hole after it had been cleared, but tried not to use the privy for an hour or so to give the smell a chance to clear.

Rose hadn't left the confines of the house and its grounds at all since the day she and Betsy had arrived, nor did she have any wish to do so. Although she told herself there was no chance of Nathaniel finding them, the fear of it always hovered in the back of her mind. It was for this reason she had been careful how much she'd said to Mrs Harper on the day she'd left the guest house. With Arthur waiting outside in the horse and cart she'd admitted she was going to be a housekeeper for the miller, but had intimated he had elderly parents living with him at the mill. It sounded more respectable than admitting she was keeping house for a single gentleman. Not that the miller was a gentleman in any sense of the word; in fact, she'd soon realized he was a brutish, uncouth indi-vidual. She'd been vague about the location of the mill when Mrs Harper had asked, merely saying it was in the country. The less the landlady knew, the better.

She had been there for ten weeks before Arthur had made advances to her one fine April morning. She'd been hanging the washing on the line in the yard, and he'd come up behind her and grabbed her bottom with his big meaty hands. Rose had screamed, at the same time whirling round and slapping him across the face with enough force to cause him to take a step backwards. 'Don't touch me.' Her voice had been a low hiss but he couldn't doubt she meant every word. 'If you do anything like that again, I'm leaving.'

'Oh aye?' He'd stared at her, his hand to his cheek. 'An' where would you go, m'lady, with the little'un? You've got a good going-on here an' don't you forget it.'

'And don't *you* forget that you've got an even better going-on since I came here. The place was a pigsty – animals wouldn't have lived the way you were.'

His lip had curled. 'Don't come the high an' mighty with me, not you. You think I believe that cock an' bull story about your husband dying in an accident? Some bloke left you with a bellyful, that's the truth of it. I wasn't born yesterday.'

'If you think that why did you offer me the job?' Even as she said the words it dawned on her exactly what Arthur Vickers had been expecting, even before he confirmed it.

'I need someone to clean an' cook an' I was tired of having to go into town to get my other needs met. I expected you to be more obliging, the position you're in.' His tongue had slid over his thick lips. 'Look, I'll give you extra for it, all right? Can't say fairer than that.'

It was only her love for Betsy that had prevented her from leaving then and there. February and March had been bitterly cold with hard frosts and snowstorms, and that particular April morning had been the first time she had been able to peg the washing outside to dry, but already the sky was clouding over. She didn't want to be homeless again and tramping the countryside looking for work. She let none of that show in her face, however, when she said, 'Let's get one thing straight right now. I'll continue to get the house to rights and then I'll look after it as though it was my own. I'll wash and cook and clean and make a penny stretch to two, but one thing I won't do is warm your bed. Do you understand me? And while you're talking about money, you haven't paid me for the last four weeks.'

'I told you, business has been poor.'

'And *I* told *you*, I don't mind waiting for a bit but I won't be made a fool of.'

Arthur Vickers stared at the girl he'd imagined would be a pushover. A young lass like her with a bairn, he'd thought she'd go down on bended knee for him giving her an' her flyblow a roof over their heads. True, she'd already got the place better than it had ever been and she was a fine cook; his mam hadn't been a patch on her, God rest her soul. Mary could make a tough bit of brisket melt in your mouth and her cakes and pies were the best he'd ever tasted. He liked his grub, he didn't mind admitting it, and he'd eaten like a king the past few weeks, but this other thing – why couldn't she see reason? She'd opened her legs willingly enough for the man who'd given her the bairn, why not him? His tone wheedling now, he said, 'No one'd know, if that's what's troubling you. Come on, Mary, be reasonable.'

'If you want me to stay this is the last time we discuss this. If not, I'll leave today.'

She meant it, damn her. He rubbed his bristly chin with a floury hand. And he knew in hiring her he'd got the best of the bargain, even if it meant he still had to go further afield to get serviced. He shrugged. 'Have it your own way. You're not my type anyway. I prefer a lass with a bit of meat on her bones.' The brothel he frequented had several big women and one in particular, Nell, knew lots of tricks to keep a man coming back for more. Shame she had a face like a mare's backside.

'And for your information I *was* married and to a man in a million.'

He shrugged again. 'No odds to me.'

Since that time he hadn't troubled her again, although when the weather had been bad and he hadn't been able to get into town for a while she was aware of him watching her when he didn't think she knew and often he would be rubbing himself, his loose-lipped mouth working and his beady eyes half-closed. She had made up her mind that when Betsy was a little older she would leave Mill House and try and find a job elsewhere, and to that end she had saved every penny of her wage – when Arthur saw fit to pay her. His stock excuse was that business was poor although she didn't altogether believe this. But in the meantime she and Betsy were living in a lovely house and Betsy was growing up healthy and well with fresh country air to breathe and wanting for nothing. Arthur had agreed that she could cut down some of his mother's old clothes to make little dresses and other things the child needed as she grew – in lieu of a few weeks' wages, though. He did nothing for free.

Arthur went into town once a week with the cart loaded with sacks of flour, some of them seconds, and he never came back without having sold it all from what she could make out. The horse and cart had to pass the house before it reached the mill and on numerous occasions she had made it her business to look down on it from an upstairs window. When she had challenged him about it he'd insisted he took fewer sacks into town than he'd used to and had to charge a reduced price. He made a great show of coming into the kitchen on market day and counting out his supposed takings minus any food he'd bought for the week, but she suspected he'd got another cash box hidden somewhere in the mill where he deposited the bulk of his earnings. He resented paying her the wage they'd agreed that first afternoon eighteen months ago, she knew that, and he often dropped little hints that she should be grateful for having a roof over her head and enough food to eat. And she was grateful, but more for the fact that hidden away as she and Betsy were there was little chance of Nathaniel finding them, especially under her false name.

But now it was the height of summer and Betsy had had her second birthday a month ago. The occasion had been bitter-sweet for Rose. On the one hand she delighted in the fact that her child was as bright as a button and developing as she should; on the other she grieved that Davey would never see these milestones and how beautiful his daughter was. Betsy had her chestnut hair but Davey's brown eyes, and she was enchanting.

The July day had been a hot one and after she had finished her chores Rose had taken Betsy for a walk in the meadow close to the house, where they'd spent a happy hour or two picking wild flowers which now reposed in a vase on the kitchen windowsill. Arthur, on the other hand, was in a foul mood. The lad who came to help him in the mill had broken his arm some weeks ago, and with the extra work he'd been forced to do Arthur had been unable to pay his usual visits to the brothel in town that he frequented. He was rising before dawn and rarely finishing at the mill before ten at night for his supper, after which he usually drank a bottle or two of home-made blackberry wine and staggered off to bed.

Betsy had been asleep for some hours when Arthur came in that night, and Rose saw immediately that his disposition had not improved. Flinging himself down into his carved armchair at the head of the long kitchen table, he scowled at his supper of meat roll and pease pudding, even though Rose knew it was one of his favourite meals. He always insisted on a hot supper, come winter or summer, along with a hearty cooked breakfast, lunch and dinner, but she didn't mind the work involved. She enjoyed cooking and although he never paid her any compliments she knew she was a good cook.

For some minutes he shovelled the food into his mouth without speaking, before belching loudly and pushing the empty plate away. Silently she removed it and placed a fruit pudding in front of him before once again busying herself washing dishes. She never ate supper herself and didn't enjoy any meals in Arthur's company; his table manners were non-existent and he made her feel sick.

He glared at her when she picked up the empty pudding bowl, gesturing towards the flowers by the kitchen window. 'If you've got time to waste getting them, you're not doing enough round the house.'

She knew he had been spoiling for a fight for days and regarded him with cool disdain. Remnants of the meal he'd consumed were sticking to the bristles on his chin and round his thick-lipped mouth and he made her inwardly shudder. Calmly, she said, 'The house is spotless and you know it.'

'Huh.' He had drunk most of the bottle of wine she had placed on the table next to his plate and now finished the last of it. Getting to his feet he walked over to the cupboard where he kept his drink and took out the bottle of whisky he'd brought back with him on market day, opening it and pouring a good measure into his glass before picking up the bottle and disappearing into the sitting room, muttering under his breath.

Rose breathed a sigh of relief. He was a thoroughly unpleasant individual at the best of times but she'd found that when he was in his cups he was worse.

She tidied the kitchen and put the porridge to soak for breakfast in one of the big copper pans. These had been dull and grimy and encrusted with old food when she'd arrived at the house, but now hung in gleaming splendour either side of the fire above the bread ovens. She sighed with pleasure as she glanced around the room. She sometimes pretended that this was her home and that Davey would be walking in from work in the evening, his homely face alight with love for her and Betsy. She had begun to do this when she had realized that the memory of what he looked like was fading. It had panicked her, and she now made a conscious effort to picture him in her mind every day. She was determined that when she left Mill House she would revert to her real name again; she didn't want Betsy to lose Davey's surname for good.

Once everything was as it should be she climbed the stairs to bed, checking on Betsy before going into her own room. The little girl was fast asleep and by the moonlight that lit the room as bright as day, Rose could see Betsy's thick lashes curled like dark smudges on her cheeks, her tumble of chestnut curls spread out on the pillow. She was so bonny, Rose thought, gently stroking a curl or two from the small forehead. So perfect. As long as Betsy continued to be healthy and happy and safe she could endure living in close proximity to Arthur for another few years until her daughter was old enough to start school. Then she would find them a couple of rooms somewhere in a town and work during the day when Betsy was at her lessons. It would all come right, she was sure of it.

Tucking the linen cover more securely round the small shape – Betsy was inclined to fall out of bed – she stood for a moment longer, drinking in the sight of her child. One day she would show Betsy her marriage certificate when the time was appropriate, so her daughter would know for sure that her parents had been married, but for now that didn't matter. She had been unwilling to produce it for Mrs Harper and then later Arthur Vickers because it stated her real name, and if it was a choice between anonymity or respectability she'd go with the former, certainly until she left this place.

Leaving the door to Betsy's room open in case the child called for her in the night, she went next door to her own bedroom and got ready for bed. The warm summer twilight had given way to darkness in the last few minutes and she lay for a while thinking and planning for the future before drifting off to sleep, one hand under her cheek and her hair spread out on the pillow much the same as Betsy's had been.

Arthur Vickers sat for another hour or so downstairs slumped in his armchair and staring morosely into the empty fireplace. He was angry, angry and frustrated, and the more whisky he drank the angrier he became. Mary'd made a monkey out of him, he thought bitterly. Here he was keeping her and her flyblow well fed with a roof over their heads and yet she acted like she was untouchable. Well, someone had touched her all right and the bairn was living proof of it. It'd been weeks since he'd got any relief from Nell and his body was crying out for it. He couldn't go on like this much longer and why should he? Aye, why should he?

He swore harshly, then sat grinding his teeth as he worked himself up into a flaming temper, his hands clenched into fists. Half the bottle of whisky was gone and after a while he poured himself another glass, staring round the room with bleary eyes. He'd bet his last farthing that she'd never lived in a house like this one before, but was she grateful? Was she hell. She had a good going-on thanks to him but you'd never know it from the way she treated him. No other man would put up with it and he was blowed if he was, not any more. It was time she learned who was the master in this house.

He lurched to his feet, his head muzzy but the need of his body inflamed by his sense of injustice.

Aye, he'd show her all right and what was she, after all? Scum from the town, that's what. If she'd been a decent lass she wouldn't have been stood at the hirings selling herself, now would she. Her family had turned her out when she'd got herself a bellyful, that was the truth of it.

He climbed the stairs slowly and when he was standing

on the landing he quietly shut the door to the child's bedroom. He didn't want her coming in and interrupting what he was about to do. Mary pandered to the bairn too much as it was and that was another thing that would change if he had anything to do with it. Spare the rod and spoil the child, that's what the good book said and it was right an' all. His father had taken the belt to him when he was a nipper and it hadn't done him any harm.

When he entered the bedroom he stood for a moment looking down at her, his tongue running over his lips. She'd brought this on herself. He'd offered to pay for it in spite of forking out money every week as it was – he ignored the fact that he hadn't actually paid her for some time – but she'd acted the outraged maiden. Well, no more. If he'd had any sense he'd have done this months ago.

He was already as hard as a rock with anticipation, and unbuttoning himself he pulled down the covers and yanked her nightdress up over her thighs as he climbed on top of her.

Rose was dreaming. Even in her sleep she knew it wasn't real, but that didn't matter. She wanted to stay in the dream where she was safe in Davey's arms and he was smiling down at her, his brown eyes alight with love. But then his arms weren't gentle any more. They were rough, pulling at her nightdress, and whisky-soaked breath hit her full in the face.

She reared up in terror, fully awake now as a hard

weight descended on her. Her legs were being forced apart and as she struggled and then screamed, the flat of a man's hand slapped her violently across the face, jerking her neck so that she felt as though her head had been torn off.

Muttered obscenities and the rank smell of male sweat added to the horror of what was happening, and on the periphery of her mind she realized her screams had woken Betsy, who was crying and calling for her. In spite of the crippling pain in her neck and the sheer weight of him that was squeezing the breath out of her chest she continued to resist, kicking and biting and pummelling at his thickset body for all she was worth. Even when she felt him enter her she didn't give in, and when he tried to adjust his position to grab her hands, she managed to twist and wriggle out from beneath him – but before she could escape he'd caught her again, pinning her on the edge of the bed now as he attempted to enter her once more.

Betsy's cries were frantic and it was this, her child's distress, that gave her a burst of superhuman strength. From somewhere she found the power to push at him so ferociously that – perched as he was on the edge of the bed straddling her – he lost his balance and went catapulting backwards with a crash that shook the house.

Her only thought was to get to Betsy before he came at her again. Whimpering, she scrambled off the bed and fled out of the room. Once on the landing she saw he must have shut the door of Betsy's bedroom before he came in to her. Opening it, she almost knocked her daughter off her feet – the toddler must have been on the other side – and scooping the hysterical infant into her arms, she murmured, 'It's all right, it's all right, hinny, Mam's here.'

She had been expecting him to follow her but as Betsy's sobs died away all was quiet. She waited a full ten minutes before cautiously opening the little girl's door again. Everything was completely still.

It took her a while to settle Betsy back in bed but eventually the child was asleep, her rag doll tucked under one small arm. Rose stood by the side of the bed for some time after that, wondering whether to investigate further or just stay where she was. She hurt all over and the muscles and tendons in her neck were screaming, the ache between her legs where he'd forced himself into her making her want to wash herself to get rid of any particle of him.

The utter silence in the house after what had happened disturbed her. Picking up the heavy brass candlestick from the windowsill of Betsy's room, she ventured cautiously onto the landing, ready to use it as a weapon if he was trying to trick her.

In the moonlight streaming into the room between the open curtains she saw his legs first from the doorway, and then, as she tentatively crept further forwards, she saw what had happened. The miller was lying on his back, the way he must have landed, and he'd fallen into the small fireplace with its portcullis fender. One of the pointed lead finials had pierced his skull, judging by the dark pool of blood surrounding his head.

Steeling herself, her heart pounding so hard it actually hurt, she inched closer until she reached the body. His eyes were open and unblinking, his mouth agape in what almost looked like surprise. He was dead. Rose made a small incoherent sound in her throat.

She stood staring down at him for a full minute, frozen with sick terror as she realized what she had done. But she hadn't meant to kill him, she whimpered in her mind. She had just been trying to get him off her. Her stomach heaving, she fought against the nausea, the faintly metallic odour of blood mingled with stale sweat and alcohol making her giddy.

How had she come to be in this position? she asked herself frantically. Twenty months ago she'd been happy, content in her role of wife and mother and wanting nothing more out of life. She could go down the line for this and then what would become of Betsy? She had to do something, but what? What could she do?

Chapter Ten

It was morning. After shutting the door on her room the night before she had come downstairs and put the big black kettle on the range, heating enough water to fill the old tin bath whereupon she'd scrubbed herself raw, using the blue-veined soap to wash away every trace of the miller. Then she had made a pot of tea and when the tears came she hadn't tried to stop them. Some while later when the shock and panic had diminished she'd been able to think more clearly. She had to make plans.

The mill was reasonably isolated but still had the occasional customer buying direct from Arthur, usually seconds from what he'd told her in the past. She never had any contact with these callers, and she hadn't met Arthur's assistant face to face, so she doubted if anyone could recognize her. Furthermore, she'd come to the house under her assumed name so even if Arthur had mentioned her it would be as Mary Shelton. How soon Arthur's lad would be coming back to work she didn't know, but one day in the near future he would turn up and she had to be long gone by then.

As a soft summer dawn stole across the sky she made some decisions, and by the time Betsy woke up at just after seven o'clock she knew exactly what she had to do.

She spent the day quietly with her daughter. Her neck was paining her so much she could barely look to left or right and she had multiple bruises on her arms and legs and a huge one on her cheekbone where the miller had hit her. It was the agony in her mind that was the worst thing though, and a minute-by-minute battle.

Once Betsy was in bed she forced herself to begin what she intended to do although the thought of it made her skin crawl. First, she moved everything of hers from the bedroom to the living room, and then carried all the contents of Arthur's room into what had been her bedroom so it appeared as though that was where the miller slept. She tried to ignore the body but it was hard. Already big bluebottles were beginning to buzz around, no doubt attracted by the blood.

Once she was satisfied that the room looked as it should, she fetched the whisky bottle – now only a third full – and placed it open on the little table by the bed with the glass in which she poured a little whisky. Then, her stomach turning over, she directed her attention to the miller himself. He was still obscenely unbuttoned, his penis, now a small shrunken thing, lying in its nest of pubic hair. Nerving herself, she pulled his trousers down to his ankles to make it look as though, in his inebriated state, he had fallen while attempting to undress himself.

She had to leave the room at this point and, running down to the kitchen, brought up the contents of her stomach in the stone sink.

It was another ten minutes before she could go upstairs again, and after checking both what had been Arthur's room and then her own, she closed the door on the body, satisfied she had done all within her power to make the death look like an accident. Which it had been, she told herself once she was back in the kitchen and shaking so violently that she had to sit down. That was what she had to remember. This wasn't her fault. He had attacked her and she had only been trying to defend herself, although whether a court of law would see it that way she didn't know and she certainly wasn't going to take the risk of finding out.

The next thing she had to do was harder. She had already checked the contents of Arthur's cash box in the house and as she had expected it was practically empty, holding a couple of shillings and a few pennies. By her reckoning over the last eighteen months he had only paid her half of what he owed her, and that meant she was due at least five pounds that she had worked for. And she *had* worked, she told herself fiercely, especially in the first few months getting the house in order. The place was a palace compared to what it had been, and its owner had been looked after like a king in every regard but one. He'd employed her as his housekeeper and as such she had worked her fingers to the bone, but prostituting herself had never been part of the bargain, at least as far as she was concerned.

She ran her fingers over her belly. The soreness between her legs was worse today and she was bleeding slightly from his rough handling of her, but the rape was nothing in comparison to the fear that he might have impregnated her. She kept telling herself this was unlikely – he hadn't finished what he'd set out to do – but she wouldn't know for sure until her next monthly. But she couldn't think of that now, she had to go to the mill as she had planned once the day was over and she could be sure no one would be calling for flour. Somewhere the miller had a hoard of money, she was sure of it, and she needed every penny she was owed.

The day had been as hot as the one before it and even now, at eight in the evening, the air was warm and muggy. She wanted to search as best she could while there was still light, besides which Betsy always slept solidly for the first few hours after she had been put to bed. If the child awoke at all it was always in the middle of the night.

When she was standing in the paved yard of the mill she stared up at the building which had the sails at the back of it. The evening was quiet – even the birds seemed to have stopped singing – and it added to the faintly eerie feeling that had gripped her. She wanted to run back to the house, to where it was familiar, but time was of the essence. Arthur's lad could return any day now.

Telling herself there was nothing to be frightened of,

she walked past the brick piers that supported the mill and then the large cart that was standing near the central post, half full of sacks of flour. Everything was covered in a film of white. After a thorough search of the ground floor she climbed the almost vertical wooden ladder to where the great millstones and other equipment were. Stacks of hessian sacks of raw grain dominated one wall, and as she stood looking around she heard a rustling in one corner and a large rat popped its head out before scurrying away. She shuddered. She didn't mind mice but rats were altogether different.

She spent a long time exploring this part of the mill and the light was beginning to fade when she nerved herself to move a heap of empty sacks in one corner, prepared to leap away if a rat jumped out. There was no rat but underneath the sacks was an old box with a rusty broken lock. She took a deep breath, her heart beginning to race. It was heavier than it looked and after trying to move it she gave up and simply lifted the lid, still wary of rodent activity close by, and then sighed with disappointment. It seemed to be full of old books and papers but she delved right to the bottom to make sure. Her curiosity piqued as to why the miller would hide the box, she opened one of the volumes and then gasped with shock. It was a picture book, made up of photographs of naked men and women performing various acts. All the books and papers were the same, and one even concentrated on young girls and boys. Sickened, and feeling contaminated by having found them, she closed the lid of the box and put the sacks back on top of it.

By now the light was almost gone and she was exhausted to the very depths of her being. The terrible events of the night before and sorting out the bedrooms and so on had drained her reserves, and after brushing the floor with an empty sack to hide any trace of her footsteps, she made her way back to the house and collapsed on the sofa in the living room, fully dressed and with her shoes still on. Perhaps there was no money? She had cleaned every inch of the house over the last eighteen months, even spring-cleaning the attic to rid it of the numerous mouse nests and other debris, and she was fairly sure that if the miller had had a hidey-hole she would have come across it. By her reckoning he would have thought exactly the same, hence her search of the mill. But she must be wrong. If he did have a hoard of money he had hidden it well, whether here or in the mill, and although someone might find it one day it wouldn't be her. And no one could need the five pounds or more that she was owed like she did.

It was hard to get comfortable on the sofa – her neck was paining her and her multiple bruises were throbbing and aching – but eventually she must have fallen asleep because when she suddenly came to, it was from a dream. A vivid one. She had been in a small building and there'd been money all around her on the floor, half-crowns and shillings and even sovereigns. And in the dream she had been saying, 'I knew it, I knew it,' and she had been filled with an almost ecstatic delight.

She sat up, groaning as her stiff neck and joints protested, and then sat in a daze of tiredness. It wasn't yet light but she needed to go to the privy. Reluctantly she swung her feet to the floor and walked through to the kitchen and then into the yard beyond. It was here that there came over her a strange feeling, a host of butterflies suddenly fluttering in her stomach as she looked across the yard to the wash house. The brick-built structure held a copper boiler with a fire underneath, two deep galvanized tubs with a dolly to agitate the clothes and a box mangle, and the tin bath she'd used the night before. She only ever took a bath on market day when she was sure Arthur wasn't around, and to her knowledge he had never used it – he barely even washed at all – and yet more than once she had caught him coming out of the small building with what she could only describe as a furtive expression on his face. Had her subconscious been trying to tell her something as she'd slept?

Her heart racing, she went back indoors and lit the oil lamp that normally sat in the middle of the kitchen table. She had to search now, before Betsy woke up and the day properly began.

When she opened the door of the wash house she stood for a moment or two in the doorway, holding up the lamp. The ceiling and walls were whitewashed and the floor was stone-flagged. Where could someone hide something in here? It had no nooks and crevices like the house and the mill but then that meant that no thieves would be interested in looking here, which was just the way the miller would think.

She checked round the boiler first and then the tubs, even moving them to see if the slab beneath was disturbed. That only left the box mangle, a long brute of a thing that she had a fight with every wash day. The box was filled with stones and travelled backwards and forwards over the rollers around which the clothes were wound. At the end of its progress in each direction it tipped to allow the rollers to be removed. Turning the wheel was hard work because the box was so heavy. There was nothing wedged under the mangle itself – she could see through the slotted wood – but to search thoroughly she needed to drag it aside, which was easier said than done, and she was sweating before she had finished.

She could see straight away that one of the slabs had been disturbed, and again she had to use all her strength to heave it aside. A small portion of the earth in the middle of where the slab fitted had been scooped away and she could see two little bags tucked deep in the hole. Trembling now, she lifted first one and then the other out. They were heavy and the contents jingled.

The dawn chorus was beginning, and she didn't stop to look in the bags, stuffing them into the deep pockets of her apron. She replaced the slab and then manoeuvred the mangle inch by inch back into place. All the times she had fought with this beast on wash days and she had never known what was beneath it, she thought when it was finally back in position.

The faintest blush of pink was stealing across the morning sky as she hurried back to the house, feeling as though the Devil himself was after her – but then she'd met him the night before last, she told herself bitterly. Betsy was still sound asleep, curled into a ball like a little dormouse, and going downstairs again she made herself a pot of tea and then sat down at the kitchen table. She undid the cord on the neck of the first bag and tipped the contents out, staring at the coins it had contained. There were a number of sovereigns as well as a mixture of other coins, but nothing under a sixpence. The second bag held even more.

She drank a cup of tea as she was feeling shaky, and then counted up. Ninety pounds, fourteen shillings and sixpence. She sat back in the chair, her hand to her throat. He had stowed away all this money, a small fortune that would buy a three-roomed cottage in Sunderland, and yet he had baulked at paying her the three shillings a week they'd agreed. She had transformed his home, cooked four substantial meals a day for him and tasty ones at that, in spite of the cheap cuts of meat and motley vegetables he bought reduced on market days; she had washed and cleaned and kept everything spotless, and he had pretended he couldn't afford to pay her wage.

He'd been a mean, lecherous, horrible man. She nodded to the thought. Those mucky pictures . . . And he had been inside her, a man like that. But she couldn't dwell on it, it weakened her and she couldn't afford to be weak. She and Betsy had to leave here today. Her bags were already packed and there were just a few things of Betsy's to add to them and then they could be gone. She'd make sure there was no trace of them for anyone to find first though. She was sure folk knew the miller had employed a housekeeper, the lad from the village for one, but who was to say when she had left?

She looked at the pile of coins on the table. She knew Arthur had no siblings and no close family of any kind. He had mentioned a second cousin in Australia once but had intimated that he was a bad lot and could well be dead for all he knew. There was no one to inherit the mill and house and his possessions, and likely once word got out that the miller was dead the contents of the house would disappear who knew where.

She swept the coins back into the two bags and stood up. She was going to take this money for her and Betsy – it would give them a security in the days ahead that she had never imagined having. She didn't know what the future held – she could even be pregnant from his attack on her – but she did know one thing for sure. Money meant food and drink and a roof over their heads, and more importantly, it kept the spectre of the workhouse at bay. No one was going to help her except herself and this was a chance in a lifetime. And when her conscience troubled her, as she knew it would, she would look at Betsy, her precious daughter, and know she had done the best for her. Nothing else mattered but keeping

Betsy safe and close to her, and if she had to answer for this act on Judgement Day so be it, but in the here and now she had no doubt about what she was doing. Men preyed on vulnerable women – look at Nathaniel and then the miller – but she could make this money work for her. She wouldn't waste a penny. But for now she had to concentrate on putting as much distance between this place and themselves as they could before nightfall. Before she left she'd make sure the chickens had plenty of food to tide them over until someone found them, and old Bess, the horse, was all right out in the field close to the mill.

Walking into the sitting room, she tucked one pouch into each of her two bags, thinking it wise to separate them. The few pounds she'd been able to save while working for the miller she had already put in her purse. She stood for a minute, her heart racing. She'd made her decision for right or wrong. Now she had to live with it.

Would Davey have agreed with what she was doing? The answer brought her chin lifting, and in reply to the accusing voice in her mind, she said, 'But you're not here, are you? And I've got to do what is best for me and Betsy now.'

She ran a hand across her brow, telling herself she was daft to talk to thin air, but hearing the words out loud had emphasized how much she had changed since Davey's death. She was a different person now, she had to be, and she wouldn't apologize for it either. Nathaniel had acted as though she was his property, the miller too, and she would never again put herself in a position where a man could do that. This money had given her two precious things – power and independence – and it was up to her now to capitalize on it.

Chapter Eleven

Nathaniel stood staring at the man in front of him, the excitement tingling through his veins not showing in his face. All these months of looking for her and now at last something. Keeping his voice steady and even, he said, 'And you say this woman with a child that stayed with your sister for a few weeks was called Mary Shelton?'

'Aye, that's the name she gave, all right.' Hubert's voice was wary. 'And she said her husband was dead, killed in an accident, so I don't think it's your wife, lad.'

It was Rose. He knew it. 'It was about the time she upped and disappeared and there's not many who look like Rose,' he said quietly. 'I've been looking for her and the bairn ever since.'

'And you say you'd had a row?'

'Aye. She'd got it into her head that I was carrying on with another woman. Some poisonous old biddy in our street had told her so but I swear there was nothing in it. Before I met Rose I'd courted this woman's daughter and the whole family took umbrage when I finished with her.'

Hubert surveyed the young man who had been asking around about the lass he knew as Mary Shelton. One of the other cab drivers had told the man to have a word with him as he remembered a young woman and baby who fitted the description getting into Hubert's cab well over a year ago. She'd stood out, he'd said, a beautiful young lass travelling alone with a little'un.

Hubert gnawed on his lower lip for a moment. This young man seemed genuine enough and he was certainly good-looking; he could imagine the women would go down before him like ninepins, but by the same token he could well have been carrying on behind his wife's back. 'It would take a lot for a young lass to up and leave her home, lad, especially with a babby. You sure there was nothing in what she'd been told?'

'Would you fool around if you had a missus like her?'

No, he wouldn't, but then everyone was different and this fellow had an arrogance about him somehow.

'Look, Rose and the bairn are my life. I've been half mad these last months.'

This time there was a definite ring of truth in what he said and Hubert felt somewhat reassured. Women were emotional creatures at the best of times and whether the lad had been messing around or not he clearly loved the lass.

'If you'd just give me your sister's address so I could go and talk to her, I'm sure she'd be able to tell me enough to know whether it was Rose or not. That's all I'm asking.'

'And you say you've been looking for her since she left?'

'Aye, I've been to hell and back, man.'

'Well, I have to say that a woman's place is with her husband, and for the bairn to grow up without a da isn't right whatever way you look at it.' Hubert sighed. He wished he'd never picked the lass up in the first place and got involved in this.

'I can pay you.' Nathaniel reached into his pocket and brought out his wallet. 'Whatever you want.'

'Put your money away, lad. I don't want it.' Hubert looked into the clear blue eyes and what he saw there made him sigh again and say, 'Look, I'll take you to me sister's but even if this lass turns out to be your missus – Rose, you say? – well, if it is her she didn't say where she was bound for when she left there, all right?'

Nathaniel breathed out slowly, his relief evident, and again it caused Hubert to warm to him. It wasn't right for a lass to leave her husband and take away his only child, whatever he'd done. Marriage vows were sacrosanct, and if every woman took off after a tiff where would the world be?

There was a fatherly edge to his voice now when he patted Nathaniel on the shoulder and said, 'Don't fret, lad. You'll find them, I'm sure of it, and likely she's regretted leaving many times and will be all the more ready to let bygones be bygones and come home. Just make sure you treat her right and reassure her about the future when you find her.'

Patronizing old fool. Nathaniel smiled, bringing his

charm to play as he said quietly, 'I will that and thanks – thanks, man.'

Once in the cab he sat back in the seat, his hands clasped between his legs and his stomach turning over. He'd taken the day off work to come to Gateshead, sending a message to the shipyard to say he'd got the skitters. The foreman wouldn't be best pleased but he couldn't help that. He couldn't have gone in, not after what he'd learned last night.

A group of them had gone down the Queen's Head to meet an old pal who'd left the shipyards and gone into the navy and was home on leave. It had been the usual sort of night, boozy and loud, but in a quiet moment the sailor, Percy Murray, had come and sat with him and asked after Rose, knowing that Nathaniel and Davey had been best pals since childhood. 'His wife ever come back to these parts?'

Nathaniel had shaken his head. Any mention of Rose brought a physical pain.

'Strange do that, wasn't it, her taking off the way she did after Davey copped it. Me mam was going to see her sister in Gateshead the day Rose must have left because she saw her on the train with the bairn and bags and what-have-you. Thought it strange then, me mam did, but she didn't think the lass was leaving for good.'

For a moment Nathaniel had been unable to speak, just staring stupidly at Percy, and he'd had to moisten his lips before he could say, 'Your mam saw Rose on the train?'

'Aye, that's right.' Percy had taken a swallow of his beer before he'd gone on: 'Hard to miss, wasn't she, Rose. Stunner if ever I saw one. Anyway, me mam said Rose got off the train at Gateshead and she saw her getting into a cab outside the station, so she must have had somewhere to go. Perhaps family? It was a week or two before me mam found out from one of the neighbours that Rose'd sold up and skedaddled. You don't expect that, do you? Not with a bairn and all.'

'No, you don't expect it.' He'd never forget the night he'd found her gone. He'd arrived at her door with a bunch of roses – hothouse blooms, cost him the earth they had – and found the house in darkness and locked up. He'd waited for a couple of hours in the back lane, thinking she'd gone out somewhere, and had finally decided to knock on the door of her neighbour, Mrs McKenzie, to see if she knew where Rose was.

It had been an age before the old lady had come to the door on crutches, and then he'd thought she'd lost her marbles when she'd said Rose had left for good. 'Sold everything she has,' Mrs McKenzie had said, sounding slightly put out. 'I'd have bought the dresser off her if I'd known she was going, lovely thing it was, but old Todd at the Emporium took everything.'

'But – but that's not possible,' he'd stammered, his stomach dropping down into his boots. 'She wouldn't do that.'

'Possible or not, that's what she's done, laddie. Brought the key round for me to give to the rent man and he won't be best pleased. Likes a bit of notice, he does, if someone's moving.'

'Where's she gone?'

'Your guess is as good as mine. She just said she won't be coming back, that's all. Cagey she was, come to think of it.'

'But – but she's not left the district? I mean, she's still living round here somewhere?' He hadn't been able to believe it.

'Like I said, your guess is as good as mine.'

He hadn't been able to get anything else out of the old woman and had walked away after a few moments, his head spinning and a feeling of nausea making his legs weak. He remembered he'd sat down in the snow in the back lane – for how long he'd never know – and cried like he hadn't done since he'd been a bairn. And then a feeling of rage had brought him to his feet. How dare she think she could do the dirty on him and leave without telling him? Skulk away like a thief in the night? He'd take it out of her hide when he found her, and find her he would. She couldn't have gone far, not with the bairn and all. Likely she'd rented another place in a different part of town, or taken a couple of rooms somewhere, that'd be cheaper with the bairn. Damn it all, what was the matter with her? He'd offered her everything, hadn't he?

The rage had kept him going for a week or two while he had searched the immediate area and then further afield, asking everyone he knew to keep an eye out for her and even going into local shops and pubs and cafés. He had gone to see Davey's parents in the end although he hadn't expected they would be able to shed any light on where Rose was. That was when Vera O'Leary had told him she'd been to see Rose and why. Like a bolt from the blue everything had made sense. Rose hadn't run away from him, he had told himself, but from the threat of Davey's family trying to take Betsy from her. She had said herself her mind was befuddled and she wasn't sleeping properly, and Davey's mam had made her even more confused and anxious. He could have throttled the woman. He'd lost his temper completely, telling Vera some home truths that had left her white and shaking before he'd finally stormed out of the house, banging the door behind him.

From that day, however, his belief in himself, which had taken a knock when he'd found Rose gone, had returned. Vera had frightened Rose away and all he had to do was to find her and everything would be all right. She would become his. It was meant to be. The problem was, he hadn't allowed for the fact that she seemed to have disappeared into thin air and no one had seen hide nor hair of her. Until last night.

He came out of his thoughts as the cab pulled up outside a large semi-detached house in a very pleasant tree-lined avenue. There were no bairns playing outside here, he noted, no swinging on ropes from lamp posts or kicking empty tin cans for a game of footie. The street was quiet. Every house had a small area of neat front garden enclosed with black iron railings, and each front door was freshly painted. There was a card in the window of this one which read: 'No rooms vacant' and a 'Guest house' sign hung from a polished brass bracket on the wall.

Hubert had jumped down from the cab onto the pavement. He was full of misgivings, knowing full well that Beattie wouldn't like him bringing Mary's – or Rose's, he supposed he ought to say now – husband to the house. He opened the door of the cab, his voice over-hearty as he said, 'Here we are then, lad, although how much me sister'll be able to help you I don't know.'

'That's all right.' Nathaniel climbed out as the horse stood swishing his tail in the warm morning air. It was only ten o'clock but already it was getting hot. 'I'm just grateful for anything she might know.'

'Aye, well, I doubt she'll be able to spare you long. Looks like the guest house is full and she'll be busy.'

The front door wasn't locked and Hubert opened it. Nathaniel followed him into the hall as he called, 'Hello? Anyone here?'

Hubert had no sooner spoken than a thin, severe-looking woman came bustling out of what must be the kitchen at the end of the hall, wiping her hands on her apron. Her smile faded as she saw the two men. 'I thought you were one of my guests. What are you doing here, Hubert?'

'Just want a word, lass, that's all.' Hubert's voice was meek and apologetic and Nathaniel assumed, rightly, that the man was somewhat intimidated by his frosty-faced sister. 'This here gentleman is looking for Mary Shelton, or Rose as it seems now she's called. He's her husband and—'

Beattie's glance went to the front room, from which came the sound of voices. Breakfast was finished and some of her guests were sitting having coffee in there. She didn't want them being party to this conversation. Glaring at her brother, she said, 'Come through to the kitchen.'

Nathaniel followed Hubert down the hall and into a large kitchen. A scrubbed table was piled with dirty dishes and it was clear Beattie had been washing up when they had interrupted her. Feeling he would have to use all his charm to thaw the woman out, he stitched his most appealing smile on his face and stepped forward, holding out his hand as he said, 'The name's Nathaniel Alridge, ma'am, and I'm sorry to bother you but I wondered if you could just spare me a minute or two? I would deeply appreciate it.'

There weren't many women who could resist Nathaniel when he wanted to win them over and Beattie was no exception. Her astonished brother saw her face soften as a tinge of pink stained her cheeks, and she was definitely flustered when she said, 'Of course, Mr Alridge. I – I was just clearing up after breakfast. I have a full house and the mornings are always hectic. Would – would you like to sit down?' She was wiping her hand on her apron again and then shook Nathaniel's, her blush deepening.

'I won't keep you, Mrs . . . ?'

'Harper. Beattie Harper.'

'I won't keep you, Mrs Harper, but I understand from your brother that you were kind enough to help a young woman with a child some time ago? I think that lady could possibly be my estranged wife. May I explain?' He had decided on this story on the train. A husband held more clout than a friend.

The three of them sat down, and Nathaniel launched into his explanation of wronged husband once more. 'I had no idea that Rose was going to take it into her head to run off,' he finished after a minute or two. 'You can imagine my shock when I came home from work to find her gone without a note or anything to explain. I was beside myself.'

He had taken off his cap and ran his hand through his thick fair hair in a gesture of frustration, his blue eyes holding Beattie's. She swallowed and nodded sympathetically.

'All I want to do is to find her and my child and bring them home so we can put all this behind us. I want to make her happy, Mrs Harper. Can you understand that?'

Hubert thought his sister was going to swoon.

'But of course I have to find her first and I wondered if there was anything at all you could tell me that would help?'

'I would if I could, Mr Alridge, but Mary – Rose – didn't say where she was bound for, merely that it was in the country. How far away I don't know, but I wouldn't think it would be too many miles because the miller came to pick up her things in a horse and cart.'

'The miller?' said Nathaniel quietly, his heart beating faster. 'She was going to work for a miller?'

'Yes, that's right. For a miller and his elderly parents I understood, as their housekeeper. The mother was getting too old to keep house and they needed help. From what I saw of the miller he was no spring chicken so I dare say his parents would have been in their seventies, perhaps older.'

How many mills could there be in this neck of the woods? Nathaniel thought, his spirits soaring. However many there were, it wasn't like residential properties. He'd find her, no doubt about that. It might take some time but he'd find her. He rose to his feet, smiling as he said, 'Thank you, Mrs Harper. You've been a great help and I won't keep you any longer.'

Beattie was all smiles as she saw them out, and once in the street Nathaniel turned to Hubert. 'Thanks again for your help. It's narrowed down the search somewhat. I don't suppose you know of any mills not far from here?'

Hubert didn't answer for a moment. In truth he was feeling uneasy again about the young man he had brought to his sister's house. The way this Alridge fellow had got Beattie eating out of his hand had brought his earlier suspicions about him to the fore. Likely he *had* been playing around with this other lass his wife had been told about, and maybe she hadn't been the first either. A lass didn't leave her home in the midst of winter with a babe in arms on a whim. He had always been of the opinion that no one should come between man and wife, but on this occasion he found he didn't want the bloke to find her. He shrugged, unsmiling, and said, 'Can't assist you there, I'm afraid.'

The fair brows drew together, hooding the eyes. 'I thought cabbies knew most places?'

'In the town, aye, I could take you anywhere you want to go but not the country, and that's where Beattie said the lass was heading.'

The blonde head came forward, the piercing blue eyes narrowing to slits. 'I meant it when I said I loved her.'

There was something threatening about him now and Hubert stiffened. 'Like I said, nowt comes to mind, all right?'

After a moment Nathaniel nodded. 'Fair enough, I dare say I can ask around. What do I owe you for the cab fare?'

'I told you, it's on me.' Taking this man's money would have felt like accepting thirty pieces of silver and he wished he'd followed his first inclination and kept quiet about this lass ending up at Beattie's.

'Ta, thanks. I'll be on my way then.' Having said that, Nathaniel didn't immediately start walking, not until the cab driver had climbed up into his seat, clicked his tongue at the patiently waiting horse and they had moved off. Then he walked slowly down the street, his mind buzzing. A miller, and one who lived in the country. That could mean anything. It could be a stone's throw from the outskirts of Gateshead or further afield but whatever, he would find her. He'd had months of searching the streets of Sunderland in any spare time he had, thinking he'd caught sight of her in this place and that only to be disappointed, and sometimes jumping off trams when he spotted a chestnut-haired woman with a child in the distance. There were times when he'd wondered if he'd end up unhinged. And all because of Vera O'Leary, damn her.

The temper that seemed to erupt from some deep cavern inside him more frequently in the last eighteen months had him breathing hard, his hands clenched into fists. He made himself relax his fingers, one by one, and then breathed in slowly through his nose, exhaling a few times as he told himself to calm down.

He took off his cap, raking back his hair which always flopped down over his forehead, before pulling it on again and striding forward more quickly. He would find her and then everything would fall into place. And maybe it was better this way, with a number of months between him tracking her down and her managing on her own with the bairn. If she'd been a skivvy for this miller and his parents it wouldn't have been a bowl of cherries, especially with the old folk. His da's parents were dead but his mam's were still alive and right cranky devils.

Aye, she'd likely be more than ready to fall into his arms by now and once she was his, he'd give up the other lassies. None of them meant anything. He made a sound deep in his throat that signified the scorn he felt for the females he'd had. The last one, Nancy Newton, had been the wife of a miner, a lad he'd been at school with, and when he knew Adam was on the late shift he'd enjoyed many an hour with Nancy, teaching her things Adam had never dreamed of in the bed department. And she'd been a willing pupil, by she had, until she'd fallen for a bairn; whether it was his or Adam's, who knew, and he cared still less.

He marched on down the street and as he passed a couple of young lassies in summer dresses, he registered their interest in him. They'd be easy, like Nancy and all the others, and he knew if he turned round and looked at them they would be staring after him, all bold innocence and girlish curiosity. It happened all the time, and normally he would have given them the eye just to see them giggle and flutter their eyelashes but his heart wasn't in it today. At last he had a lead on Rose, and whether it took days or weeks or months he would find her. And when he did – his mouth thinned and the handsome face took on a steely quality – she would be his.

Chapter Twelve

Rose climbed down from the carrier's cart and lifted Betsy onto the pavement, and as the elderly driver handed her the two bags she thanked him again for the lift. She'd met him on a country lane after making slow progress initially after leaving the mill; Betsy's little legs had dictated the pace and the further they'd walked the heavier the bags had felt. He'd pulled up beside them, smiling as he'd said, 'You look done in, lass. Dunno where you're headed but I'm on the way to Consett if that's any help?'

She had never heard of Consett but had replied that she was on her way there and would be very grateful for a ride in the cart. He'd moved a few sacks and boxes to make a space for them and they'd been on their way again. Betsy had fallen asleep almost immediately, lulled by the rocking of the cart, and Rose had soon found that Eustace – as he'd introduced himself – was a gregarious sort of fellow who could talk the hind leg off a donkey. Once she'd told him she was going to stay with friends but had never been to Consett before, he'd been delighted to relate the merits of his birthplace to a captive audience.

'Nowt but a backwater, Consett was, when I was a nipper,' he had told her, 'but now we're a thriving town with a steelworks that's the envy of the North. All thanks to one man, I reckon, and that's William Jenkins. He took over the Consett Iron Company some thirty-five years ago now, and it was him that turned it around. He was a force to be reckoned with, was old Jenkins, and not scared to stick his neck out, unlike some. He was forward-thinking, you see, that's the thing, and more than that he was for the workers. You won't hear a bad word said about him in Consett, God rest his soul. Looked after his men, he did, and it made for a happy workplace. Course, you still get the housewives complaining about the red dust from the works that gets into every nook and cranny, my missus included, but like I say to her, it's that red dust that puts food on the table and clothes on folk's backs. I'm right, aren't I? Eh, lass? Aye, I'm right.'

The question was rhetorical. The old man didn't want an answer, just someone to listen. Rose was more than happy to do that. Everything she could learn about Consett before she arrived, the better.

'Happiest days of my life when I worked for Mr Jenkins, I tell you, but a steelworks isn't the place for old men, more's the pity. Eighty, I'll be, come Christmas, can you believe that?'

Rose said no, she couldn't believe it, and then listened again as he nattered on. 'Grand town hall we've got on the corner of Middle and Front Street, holds a thousand people, and there's the Cooperative Hall an' all, and some fine shops and eating places. Seen 'em all come in my time. We were just a little village on the hillside, miles from the sea, but now there's umpteen churches and schools and the like, and the town's growing all the time. A body could do worse than settle in Consett, take it from me.'

Rose agreed with him. As the cart trundled along and the rich scent of dog roses and flowers without number perfumed the still air, she thought she could see herself living in Consett. It wasn't as big as Newcastle or Sunderland but it was far enough away from the latter and Nathaniel. She had toyed briefly with the idea of heading way down South, perhaps even as far as London, but had found the pull of her roots in the North East was stronger than she'd imagined. She could see herself feeling like a fish out of water in the South, and it was going to be hard enough to make a new life for herself and Betsy as it was.

When she caught her first glimpse of Consett she saw that the iron- and steelworks dominated the skyline with the town sloping away beneath it. The works looked to be huge and, perhaps naively she admitted, she hadn't expected such a massive area to be taken up with an array of industrial buildings.

Eustace stopped the horse for a few moments. 'There she is,' he said as proudly as though he'd built it all himself, brick by brick. 'Still wet behind the ears, I was, when I got a job at the company. Derwent Iron it was called then, and we earned every farthing of our wage, I can tell you that. I was there from the first day it opened and the lads today have it easy compared to what we did. Mind, we were glad of the work. There wasn't much doing round these parts afore that, but it was like stepping into hell itself when they set me on in the blast furnaces. The heat an' smoke an' dust an' noise couldn't have bin worse if old Nick himself was in charge. Two hundred an' thirty tons a week we produced, better than any hereabouts. Me an' my pal, Abe, had to bring the coke an' ironstone an' limestone to the blast furnace in barrows, an' you had to be fit 'cause them barrows held a ton of stuff. I hated 'em. It weren't too bad if you got a barrow with good wheel rims, but if they were worn away it made 'em right beggars to move. Twelve-, eighteen- or even twenty-four-hour shifts we did then if need be, but usually it was six in the morn till six in the evening, and vice versa. The furnaces always had to be kept going, you see, that was the important thing.'

Rose looked at the wizened old man. He appeared so frail and shrunken, it didn't seem possible he'd once done such hard physical work. 'You must have had breaks, though?' she said, as he clicked his tongue to get the horse moving again.

He chuckled wryly. 'Breaks, lass? We had no set time for them, not like the lads today. Food an' drink was taken as and when we could manage it. Keepin' everything ticking over was more important than us. We were expendable, you see, and them up top reminded us of it if we forgot. Aye, them early days at the works weren't no picnic.'

'Is your friend, Abe, still in Consett?'

'Abe?' He was silent for a moment. 'He copped it a few years after we started at the works. Gassed he was. Left a wife an' two bairns. There were plenty like him an' all, gassed or burned or whatever.'

'Oh, I'm sorry,' Rose said softly. More widows like herself.

'Long time ago now, lass, but we'd bin best pals since we were no older than your little'un – and for him to go like that.' This time the pause was longer. 'Took me a good while to get over it, I don't mind admitting. Mind you, better to go quick like Abe did than linger like some poor devils, never able to work again and good to neither man nor beast, especially if they were the breadwinner. It'd be the workhouse then, the whole family going in. The houses were tied, you see. Abe's wife was lucky, her mam an' da took her an' the two bairns in. Dunno how they managed cause her mam an' da lived in Puddlers Row with just a single room up and down an' a ladder to get from one room to another, an' they still had three bairns at home when Abe died. Still, you do anything for family, don't you.'

'Yes,' Rose had said quietly. 'You do anything for family.'

The old man had fallen silent after that, probably lost in memories of when he and his pal Abe were young, and it hadn't been long before they had reached the town itself.

She had told Eustace that she was meeting her friends outside the town hall, deciding that was as good a place as any to get her bearings. Now, as the horse and cart disappeared into the distance, she stood looking about her, Betsy clutching her skirt but happy enough following her long sleep in the back of the cart.

Rose glanced down at the small head with its riot of chestnut curls, and as she did so, Betsy looked up at her and smiled. Her big brown eyes with their thick lashes were so trusting it made Rose's heart ache. What was she doing dragging her daughter to yet another new place? she asked herself, but then what choice did she have? She'd been so happy when Betsy was born, knowing her child would have a secure family home and lots of love, something she herself had never experienced growing up in the workhouse. She'd imagined her path was set for life – having more bairns in the years ahead and being a good wife to a man who loved her. And then, in just one day, everything had changed. Davey was gone and she had to be mam and da to their precious daughter.

Shaking herself mentally, she became practical. She had to find somewhere to stay for a while until she got the lie of the land. Not another guest house like Mrs Harper's, something more impersonal. A hotel or an inn. She didn't want to face any questions or probing into her background, especially after what had happened at the mill.

Without any clear idea where she was going she began

walking, a bag in each hand and Betsy still clinging to her skirt. They'd only gone a short distance when she saw an inn, the Bee Hive. To the side and front of the building there was a mini market going on, a few women in shawls and bonnets sitting by their baskets of potatoes and other vegetables, nattering away in the sunshine. A number of stalls were scattered here and there and she stopped in front of one, buying a small bag of treacle toffee for Betsy. They sat on the low stone wall fronting the courtyard of the inn for a while; then, deciding to take the bull by the horns, Rose picked up the bags and with Betsy in tow, made her way over and through the big brass-studded door of the premises and into a large oak-beamed room. It was mid-afternoon and most of the tables were empty, but a couple of old men with fox terriers at their feet sat nursing pints of beer by the empty fireplace, and a smart-looking gentleman was sitting at the bar talking to the buxom barmaid.

As she stood hesitating by the door, a small rotund man with a bulbous nose came out of an archway to the left of the bar and seeing her, walked over. 'Can I help you, lass?' he said, his eyes lingering on her bruised cheekbone for a moment.

'I'm – I'm looking – I wondered if you had a room vacant?' she stammered, feeling out of her depth as both the man at the bar and the barmaid stared at her.

'A room, is it? For just you and the bairn?'

She nodded, expecting more questions, but he merely looked her up and down, though not unkindly, before he said, 'I only have three rooms – we're not a big place as you can see – and two of them are occupied, the best two. I've a smaller one free.'

'Could I see it?' She'd pulled herself together now and her voice was stronger.

'Right you are. Come with me. Here, let me carry them for you,' he added, taking the bags from her before she could protest. 'The stairs are steep, you'll have to hold onto the bairn.'

She followed him through the archway he'd come out of moments before into a gloomy corridor, an open door a few feet away revealing a kitchen where a woman and a younger girl were working at a table. 'That's me wife an' daughter,' he said conversationally as he led the way to where a flight of stairs disappeared upwards almost totally vertically. She could see now why he had taken the bags. Gathering Betsy in her arms, she climbed the stairs carefully, steadying herself with the stout handrail, and emerged onto a fairly wide landing which had light streaming into it from a window at the far end. The landlord walked past two doors and stopped at a third, opening it with a key he took from a large bunch hanging on a brass ring attached to his trousers. He stood aside for her to precede him into the room. Although it was small as he'd warned, holding a three-quarter-size bed, a single wardrobe and a small table with a china bowl and jug on it, Rose liked what she saw. There was a patchwork quilt, bright yellow curtains at the window and a thick clippy mat to the side of the bed. The floorboards were clean and polished and everything seemed fresh, and although the whitewashed walls were devoid of any pictures or a mirror, the room seemed homely and welcoming.

'It's a bob a night, cheaper if you stay for a week. We don't do breakfast – the wife likes a lie-in – and the evening meals start from five through until the wife says she's had enough. She'd always rustle up a sandwich or soup for lunch for you and the bairn, though. She does the same for any guests.'

'I'll take it.' Rose put Betsy down, reaching into her pocket for her purse. 'How much do I owe you for the week?'

He grinned. 'By, lass, I wish all our guests got their money out as quick as you. Let's see. You an' the bairn'll have to share the bed and there's not room to swing a cat in here for her, is there. Shall we say four bob for the week? Just don't let on to me other guests – they're paying top whack but like I said, their rooms are bigger. I'll take the jug with me and fill it so you an' the bairn can freshen up, and bring a towel shortly, all right?' He pocketed the four shillings she handed him, adding, 'The privy's downstairs and we lock up at midnight, but I daresay you an' the bairn'll be in the land of nod afore then. If you want something to eat of an evening up here once you've got her off, I dare say we can manage that.'

Rose smiled. 'You're very kind.'

'Kind, you say? I'll tell me regulars you think that when I have to turf 'em out of a Friday night when they've got paid and drink themselves silly. The name's Wilbur, by the way, Wilbur Croft, and the wife's Tessa.'

'Rose O'Leary, and this is Betsy.' It was good to use Davey's name again.

He crouched down, smiling at Betsy, who promptly buried her face in her mother's skirt. 'Don't seem two minutes since our Amy was that age,' he said as he straightened again. 'Now she's courting one of the Consett Iron lads and getting bits for her bottom drawer.' He handed her the key before walking onto the landing and passing her bags to her. 'I'll be back with the water and towel in a minute or two. You want me to send our Amy up with a tray in a while? Bread, cheese, ham, something like that? Coffee for you, milk for the little'un?'

Again she said, 'You're very kind,' but now there was a lump in her throat. He was so nice, so normal. She'd forgotten what it was like to be around people who were normal after all the months at the Rowlands Gill mill.

'You can settle up for any food and drink at the end of your stay,' he said before shutting the door. 'We don't always do that but I know an honest face when I see one.'

She stared at the door after he had gone. *An honest face.* What would he say if he knew she had ninety pounds in her bags that she had taken from a dead man? She sat down with a plump on the bed, her bruises and the pain between her legs worse suddenly. They would say she had killed him if anyone found her but she hadn't, she hadn't killed him, not really. It had been an accident.

She had pushed him off her but he had hit his head on the fireplace himself. It wasn't as though she had intended what had happened, although after the way he had attacked her he had no one to blame but himself. He'd been a horrible man, mean and dirty and loathsome. She began to tremble, and it was only Betsy coming to tug on her skirt and saying, 'Mammy, dolly?' that prevented the panic from taking hold.

She fished the rag doll she had made Betsy for her first Christmas out of one of the bags where she had tucked it for safety before leaving the mill. Betsy was inordinately attached to the doll although it was definitely the worse for wear now, and she hadn't wanted to risk it going astray. Sitting the child on the bed with the rest of the treacle toffee and her beloved plaything, she swiftly unpacked the bags, stuffing them and the pouches on top of the wardrobe. She'd paid Arthur to get a pair of shoes for Betsy some months ago but these were now too small, and as she took them off the child's feet the little toes were red and cramped. One of the first things to do was to buy Betsy another pair, and perhaps a dress for best; the clothes she had made for her would do for everyday wear for a few months more. She could manage herself although her boots were on the verge of developing holes in the soles; she'd see if she could get them mended over the next day or two.

Passing Betsy her other toy, a small teddy bear, she watched for a few moments as her daughter gabbled away in a language all of her own to the doll and the bear, jumping them up and down and playing a game of her own making. She was such a happy child, Rose thought with a feeling of deep thankfulness. The events of the last twenty months didn't seem to have impinged on her zest for life at all.

A knock at the door brought her out of her reverie and she opened it to find the landlord with the jug and towel. No sooner had he departed than another knock heralded his daughter with a tray holding a small crusty loaf, pats of butter, a generous wedge of cheese and several slices of ham, with steaming coffee for her and milk for Betsy.

'Me da said to bring this up.' Amy smiled at her as she came further into the room. 'If you move that jug and bowl I'll put it on the table, shall I?' That done, she turned her attention to Betsy. 'Ooh, she's bonny. How old is she?' she said to Rose, smiling at Betsy, who – to Rose's surprise – beamed back instead of hiding her face as she was wont to do. 'Look at that hair and them eyes – you'll have all the lads coming round when you're older, won't you, hinny.'

'This is Betsy and she's just turned two,' said Rose, feeling slightly overwhelmed by the girl's exuberance. Amy clearly was a bubbly sort.

'She's lovely.' Amy grinned at her, her pretty face with its snub nose open and friendly. 'I love little lassies. Me sister, Daisy, she's got three and all under five. Keeps her on her toes, I can tell you. I go round when I can and take the oldest two out for a bit to give her a break. Good as gold they are with me, bless 'em. I've told Frank, that's my intended, I want four boys and four girls. I think eight's a nice number, don't you? Me mam only had our Daisy and me, and Daisy's seven years older so we didn't play much as bairns. She thought I was a nuisance, half the time, but we get on grand now.'

As Amy came up for air, Rose said quickly, 'Thank you for the tray. I think Betsy was getting hungry.'

Taking the hint, Amy said, 'Well, I'll leave you to it, shall I, but if you want something don't be afraid to ask, you being on your own, like.'

She was obviously burning with curiosity, unlike her father, and Rose sighed inwardly. So much for her hope that staying in an inn would be less intrusive than a guest house.

Once Amy had left, Rose sorted out a small plateful of food for Betsy but before beginning on her own, she looked up at the top of the wardrobe. She was going to have to find a hiding place for the pouches if she didn't want to take them with her when she left the room. Or perhaps she could deposit the money somewhere? The town must have a bank? She had never been inside such an establishment but then she had never had ninety pounds before, she thought with a slight touch of hysteria. For today, though, she would stay put in this room rather than venturing out again. A good night's sleep and everything would fall into place.

She looked at Betsy tucking into her food with gusto and smiled. Her daughter was safe and that was enough for now. Tomorrow was another day.

Chapter Thirteen

Over the next days, several things did indeed fall into place. Rose wasted no time in depositing most of the money in a bank in Front Street, not far from the inn, keeping a little for expenses. The young cashier who'd served her had immediately called for the manager when Rose had mentioned the sum she wished to place in the new account, and once ensconced in his office he had proved most helpful. She'd told him that her husband had met with an accident at work and the money was a payout from the company concerned, and he had enquired no further. He'd talked her through the procedure of opening the account, made sure she filled in the paperwork correctly and had given her a cheque book, after which he had ordered coffee for them both and a glass of lemonade for Betsy. All in all it had been a pleasant experience rather than the ordeal she'd prepared herself for, and she had left the premises reflecting what a difference money made to the way one was treated.

After leaving the bank she had gone directly to the

shops and bought Betsy a new pair of shoes, a little smocked frock and matching cardigan, and some underwear. Betsy had been thrilled with the shoes, refusing to take them off and looking down at them so often on the way back to the inn that she had fallen over twice.

With nothing to do but take care of Betsy, Rose did a lot of thinking on her daily walks with the child and during the time in their room at the inn. To some extent she was back in the same position she'd been in when she had agreed to become housekeeper for the miller – albeit now with a considerable amount of money in the bank. It would still be difficult to find any sort of work with a child in tow, but neither did she want their nest egg to dwindle away, which would happen if she didn't provide an income for them. But doing what? She had no training for anything besides cooking and cleaning and keeping house, but after Rowlands Gill mill she didn't want to put herself in a similar position again, even if she could find a housekeeping job in Consett which was highly unlikely. From now on, she decided, wherever she and Betsy called home, she wanted to shut the door at night secure in the knowledge that it was just her and her daughter in the house. Until Nathaniel's advances towards her she'd never thought much about the danger men represented to a woman on her own, but now after the rape it was on her mind most of the time. Her physical bruises were fading, but she knew something fundamental had changed within her. She wanted as little to do with the male sex as possible.

Since staying at the inn and despite her intentions to keep herself to herself she had become friends with Amy, for the simple reason that it was impossible not to. The young girl was irrepressible and full of life, with a sunny nature and a genuine desire to see the best in folk. Furthermore, she had taken to Betsy and Betsy to her, and when Amy suggested that Rose and Betsy accompany her to her sister's house so the children could play, Rose hadn't liked to refuse. She had told Amy about Davey being killed at the shipyard and that she had left Sunderland because a certain man had made it plain he wanted her and wouldn't take no for an answer, resulting in an altercation and her bruised face, but had given the impression she had come to Consett straight from her home town.

Amy had listened sympathetically before saying, 'You're so beautiful, Rose, that's the thing. I can't imagine any man *not* wanting you. My Frank did a double take on Sunday afternoon when he called round to take me out and you and Betsy were just leaving for your afternoon walk.' This was said without guile – Amy knew Frank was devoted to her. They were childhood sweethearts and neither of them had looked at anyone else. 'Not that your beauty excuses how this man behaved, of course, especially with your husband having just died and everything. He must be a right nasty piece of work to carry on to the point where you felt you had to leave Sunderland altogether.'

Rose had said yes, he was a nasty piece of work, and

then changed the subject. That had been a couple of days ago, and now she, Betsy and Amy were on their way for the proposed meeting with Daisy and her children. The afternoon was hot with a slight breeze, but the fine particles of red dust from the iron- and steelworks still floated in the air. The town itself was built to the east of the huge sprawling complex but the company was the life-blood of the inhabitants of Consett and it dominated the area.

A maze of railways brought raw materials such as limestone and coal into the town, and on the hillside to the west of the ironworks were enormous slag heaps, vast man-made mountains. Amy told Rose the company had umpteen pits of its own as they walked towards Daisy's, filling her in on the locals. 'It's mostly miners and steel men in Consett,' she said as they swung Betsy between them, each holding one of the child's arms. 'Our Daisy lives in Steel Street, which is a step up from Blackleg Row and Consett Terrace and round them parts. One-down-and-one-uppers they are, and when scarlet fever's about an' whooping cough and the like, it's always them folk who get it worse. What can you expect with a standpipe for water and the open drains right at the backs of the houses? Lonnie, Daisy's husband, was born in Puddlers Row and when he come round courting her our da told him he'd better fix his sights higher 'cause he wasn't having a daughter of his living in one of them houses. Steel Street is nice, though, and they've got the park at the end of it. That's where I usually take the bairns when

I have them. Better than playing in the gutter or in the back lanes, a park, isn't it, and the bandstand's lovely.'

Rose nodded. She found that was usually all that was required of her in the company of Amy, who was the proverbial chatterbox.

On her daily walks she had explored much of the town, trying to work out where was the best area to rent a property. She agreed with Amy that the older houses in the streets that had first been built by the Derwent Iron Company for their employees decades ago seemed unsanitary and smelly, the open brick channels for waste that ran at the back of the dwellings emptying into large gullies close to the habitations. Now, at the height of summer, the streets reeked, and the privies in the back yards added to the smell.

'When Daisy takes the bairns round to see Lonnie's mam an' da she tries not to use the privy,' Amy continued as they turned into Harvey Street. 'She'd been used to ours at home and she nearly died the first time she went there when they were courting. It's all midden privies in Puddlers Row and thereabouts, and three or four privies empty into one ashpit that's not even covered. She won't let the bairns play out there either 'cause when the scavenger's cart comes they barrow the filth out onto the back lanes or streets and bits fall off.' Amy wrinkled her nose. 'Course, where the company own the houses they clean the ashpits, but private owners are supposed to do it themselves and in some of them the ashpits are always overflowing. Me mam says Puddlers Row and Consett

Terrace and the rest of 'em round there ought to be knocked down and the company fork out for new housing. Me da says fat chance.'

They continued to chat as they walked, Amy pointing out streets she considered better than others. Rose had told her that she wanted to rent somewhere and that she'd had a payout from her husband's company after the accident to tide her over for a month or two. Amy had already offered to ask Daisy if she knew of someone who could mind Betsy during the day when Rose found work.

Rose was grateful, but she didn't like the idea of leaving her daughter with a stranger, however reliable the woman was purported to be. She'd told herself she was being silly, but she couldn't help it. She had a fear of letting the child out of her sight for a second, and the older Betsy got the stronger it became. She hadn't confided this to Amy because she knew the girl wouldn't understand. Bairns played out in the streets and back lanes even before they could walk, older children looking after the younger ones and wiping snotty noses or pushing them about in old prams. Even as the thought crossed her mind they passed a group of little ones, a protesting baby being mothered by two small girls who couldn't have been more than three years old, while three slightly older lads played with some round shiny pebbles in the gutter. They were all barefoot and dressed in not much more than rags but seemed happy enough, the two little 'mothers' taking turns in jogging the unfortunate infant so violently on their knees it was a wonder its head didn't fall off.

They passed a market on the way to Steel Street and Rose stopped at one stall to buy some teacakes to take to Daisy's, and a big round oat biscuit for Betsy to eat as they walked. The child had a couple of mouthfuls and then handed most of the biscuit to her mother, frowning as she said, 'Don't like.'

It was unusual for Betsy to refuse anything and Rose took a tentative bite herself, only to grimace in disgust. Amy tried it and shook her head. 'They've added too much chalk.'

'Chalk?'

'Oh aye, add some chalk to the flour and it goes further. What are the teacakes like?'

Rose broke one in half, giving some to Amy and popping a morsel in her own mouth. They were nothing like the teacakes she made.

'Not too bad,' said Amy, 'not like the biscuit.'

'I think they're awful.' Rose looked down at the bag. 'Do you think Daisy will want them?'

'Oh aye, with three little'uns. The thing is, you can never be sure what you're getting at the market. Some of the stallholders take shortcuts if you know what I mean, 'cause their stuff has to be cheaper than the shops. Gives 'em more profit.'

'But not if folk don't go back to them. I wouldn't go back to that stall, would you?'

Amy shrugged. 'Depends how hungry folk are, I suppose.'

'Just because they can't afford shop prices they shouldn't get poor quality.'

Amy giggled. 'Hark at you, beating the drum. Perhaps you ought to set up a stall, lass, eh?'

It was meant as a joke, but as Amy spoke it was as though a light had gone on in Rose's mind. Davey had always gone on about how good her food was and that she knew how to cook a piece of brisket so it tasted like best steak and how to make delicious broths and stews with mediocre ingredients. Her cakes and scones and gingerbread were a patch above, too, if she did say so herself. She had money sitting in the bank, she could use some of that to set herself up but of course she would have to find somewhere to rent first so she had the use of a kitchen. But she could do this, she knew she could.

For the first time in a long while she felt a frisson of excitement quicken her breath, and her emotion must have shown on her face because Amy said, 'What? What is it?'

'What you just said, I think I could do that, Amy, if I found somewhere to rent so I could cook the food and take it to a stall. It would mean I could prepare everything at home and have Betsy with me and then come to the market with her. It's perfect.'

Amy stared at her doubtfully. They had stopped walking and Betsy stood between them, looking enquiringly up at her mother. 'It'd be a lot of work, lass, and you could get loads left at the end of the day an' have to sell it for next to nothing.'

'That might happen at first but I'll give good value for

money and I certainly won't add chalk to my flour to make it go further.'

'You're so young. Most of them stallholders are getting on a bit.'

'Not all of them.'

'And how will you get your stuff to the market once you've cooked it?'

'The same way as those others do, I suppose. On a handcart or something?'

'What about in the winter when there's a foot of snow?'

'*Amy.*'

'I'm only saying, that's all, lass.'

'This is the answer to what I can do, I know it is. I've been praying for something that means I can keep Betsy with me all the time and I could, doing this. I'd be my own boss in a way, wouldn't I.'

'But for a bit lass . . .' Amy's voice trailed away. 'You don't know anything about running a market stall.'

'Everyone has to start somewhere. The thing is, Amy, since Davey died I've felt like I'm drowning in deep water and trying to fight a current that wants to drag me under. I can't explain it but I need to do this, however it turns out. If I try and fail so be it, but I'll do everything within my power to make it work.'

Amy was shielding her eyes from the bright sun and now she smiled. 'All right, I won't say another word if you're set on it but I'd get somewhere to rent close to the market. That way you won't have such a drag with your stuff.'

Rose nodded. She would if she could. She knew a number of houses in Consett were owned by the Consett Iron Company who kept them for their workers, but there were private landlords too and folk who took in lodgers and so on. Now she knew the way forward she'd start looking for somewhere straight away.

They continued to Daisy's house which turned out to be a two-up, two-down terrace with a small back yard. Daisy herself was an older and somewhat wearier version of her younger sister, but she had a ready smile and quick wit and after a while Rose felt as though she'd known her for ages. After a cup of tea and a teacake, Rose and Amy took the two older girls and Betsy to the park where they played happily for a couple of hours, but all the time, whatever she was doing or saying, Rose was thinking about the market stall. She would be doing something she loved, she told herself, which was halfway to making a success of anything, and she wouldn't mind how hard she worked or the number of hours she had to put in. She would be independent, answerable to no one but herself.

Once they had taken Daisy's girls home, they walked back to the inn in the late-afternoon sunshine, Amy regaling her with the wedding dress she and her mother were already making in any spare time. 'It's bonny,' Amy said dreamily, 'and Daisy's three are going to be my bridesmaids. They'll look so sweet in pink, won't they? Me da wanted me to wait till I was eighteen to get wed but I've persuaded him for next spring when I'm seventeen. Like I said to him, there's no point in waiting if you know you've got the right one and I've loved Frank since he started at my school when I was nine. Him and his mam an' da and brothers had just moved here from Hedley on the Hill cause his da was starting at the iron-works, and I saw him that first day and I just knew. He said he felt the same. We were inseparable after that and although my mam an' da and his used to take the mickey, we've stood the test of time, haven't we? He still makes me go weak at the knees every time I see him.'

Rose smiled. Amy was nothing if not dramatic.

'Honestly, he does,' Amy insisted. 'Was it like that with you an' your husband?' And then realizing she hadn't been exactly tactful in the circumstances, she added, 'Oh, sorry, lass, sorry. Me big mouth running away with me.'

'It's all right. No, it wasn't really like that with me and Davey, at least, not for me. He said he knew right away I was the girl he wanted to marry but I took a bit more time. I'm naturally cautious, I think,' she said almost defensively, feeling suddenly she'd let Davey down in some way. 'But we got married within a few months of meeting so I suppose it was quick. His parents thought so anyway.' She grimaced. 'They didn't like me.'

'No?'

'Well, it was more his mam. And the others followed suit, for a peaceful life, Davey said.'

'Ah.' Amy nodded like a wise old sage. 'She was jealous, I bet. Some mothers are like that with lads. I'm lucky, Frank's mam is grand and we get on like a house on fire.

Better than with me own mam sometimes although I'd never tell her that, bless her, but she can be right bossy, especially us working together.'

Once back at the inn Amy disappeared to the kitchen, only to appear again a few minutes later with soup and rolls on a tray for Rose and Betsy. 'Mam kept it from lunchtime,' she explained. 'She thought the bairn would be tired after playing with our Daisy's lassies and want an early night.'

Tessa was right. Betsy ate the rolls and soup half asleep and was soon tucked up in bed. Rose sat looking at her daughter for a long time, stroking the small forehead and just drinking in the sight of her child. How Davey would have loved seeing Betsy grow up, she thought sadly. When she'd been pregnant he'd admitted he'd like a little lass he could spoil and who would be a daddy's girl.

Rose sighed. So much had happened since the accident but now she felt the future was clearer. She had a plan. She would pay for however many days she needed here at the inn while she looked for somewhere to rent – that wasn't a problem – and she would find out how you went about having a stall at the market too, and search out where the cheapest ingredients for her food could be bought. Every farthing would matter.

She needed to keep as much of her nest egg in the bank as she could, but of necessity there'd be furniture to buy, along with equipment for the kitchen and so on. She'd purchase a couple of linen aprons and mob caps too; it was important to be tidy especially if you were selling food. She'd make sure she was clean and present-able at all times.

Her heart began to thud harder with excitement. Amy might have been jesting when she'd suggested the market stall and she'd clearly been dubious about the success of such a venture, but that didn't matter.

Rose drew in a long, deep breath. She needed an under-taking like this, something that she could pour her heart and soul into, leaving her little time to think about the miller and what had happened at Rowland's Gill mill. During the day she tried to banish the dark thoughts of what she had done, but through the long night hours they came to haunt her, disturbing her sleep and causing her to wake more tired than before she had gone to bed.

She stood up and walked over to the window, looking out into the courtyard below as her mind wandered. When she had been old enough to leave the workhouse, the master had arranged a job for her as a kitchen maid at a big house near Mowbray Park. The cook there had been full of old sayings and proverbs, and one she remem-bered was 'Big oaks from little acorns grow'. Right at this moment she felt like a little acorn, but she intended to grow, as much for Betsy as herself. She wanted to give her daughter a secure home and good food, shoes on her feet and clothes on her back. That wasn't too much to ask, was it? At least in the workhouse she'd never had to go barefoot, like those little bairns today, but in truth she would have preferred that to carrying the stigma of the workhouse with her. Sometimes even now she felt it would be with her until she died, that it was in her very bones. When she was a young lass she couldn't imagine that any lad would ever look the side she was on; she'd felt that the mark of her beginnings was written across her forehead.

A large part of her love for Davey had been gratefulness.

The thought came sharply and without warning, shocking her. She stared blindly now, looking back in time. She'd loved Davey, she told herself painfully, of course she had. Maybe not as he had loved her, but then in any relationship one person loves more. That was natural. And yes, she might have been grateful to him and thankful that he didn't see her as second-rate or inferior, but she'd cared deeply for him, appreciating the good and kind man he had been. But for the accident she would have been content with him for the rest of her life.

Suddenly annoyed with the introspection, she clicked her tongue irritably. She'd made Davey happy and in so doing she had been happy too. What was wrong with that? This was all Amy's doing, going on about love at first sight and Frank still making her weak at the knees. And in truth she didn't want anyone to make her feel weak at the knees, she acknowledged fiercely. In fact she would hate it. To give a man that sort of power over her would be terrifying. She wanted nothing more than to be left alone to bring Betsy up as Davey would have wanted, that was all she asked.

Nevertheless, her thoughts had disturbed her and it took her a long while to fall asleep when she went to bed, Betsy curling into her like a small animal in a burrow, and when her dreams came they were more in the form of nightmares once again, dark threatening figures chasing her and shouting her name.

Chapter Fourteen

The following morning after her conversation with Amy, Wilbur knocked on the door of Rose's room. 'Amy tells us you're thinking of renting somewhere close to the market, lass, and if that's the case you could do worse than going to see an old pal of mine,' he said quietly. 'Runs a shop off Victoria Street as his main business, but he's got a couple of houses he rents out too. Always canny, Henry was. Even as a lad in short trousers he'd come to school with a bag of barley sugar or treacle toffee and sell some to the other bairns for a nice little profit. Anyway, he was in here for a pint or two the other night and mentioned one of his tenants had done a moonlight flit owing him several weeks' rent. Right browned off, he was.'

'And this house is close to the market?'

'Oh aye, I think so. You could go and see him and ask, anyway, say I sent you and can vouch for you if you like. He's all right, is Henry, and he'd ask a fair rent.'

So it was that at eleven o'clock Rose found herself

standing in Henry's shop. Wilbur had told her it was a grocer's but it seemed to Rose the shop stocked a little of everything. Outside under an awning boxes of fruit and vegetables were on display and there were more inside, along with shelves from floor to ceiling filled with jars of preserves, pickles, tea, coffee, sugar, confectionery, a tub of butter and another of cheese, ham, eggs, bacon – everything a housewife could possibly need and more besides. The man behind the long wooden counter that ran the length of the shop was weighing up a slab of butter for a customer when Rose entered holding Betsy's hand, so she stood looking about her. In one corner there were tools and pots and pans and other hardware items; in another, heaped on top of each other, sacks of flour and potatoes and even kindling wood, along with a box of candles, long bars of soap from which small pieces would be cut off to the customer's requirements, and a big container of packets of grate blacking.

Once the woman in front of her had completed her purchases Rose stepped forward. 'Mr Hartley?'

'Aye, lass, that's me. Henry Hartley at your service.' He had been wiping his hands on a piece of old towelling as he spoke. 'What can I get you?'

'Mr Croft, Wilbur Croft at the Bee Hive, said you might have a house available to rent. I'm staying there at the moment but I need a place of my own.'

'Is that right?' His hands had become still and now he dropped the rag on the counter, narrowing his eyes. 'Just you and the bairn, is it?' The inevitable question.

Rose nodded. 'My husband met with an accident and I decided to move to Consett for a new start. I – I intend to have a market stall once I'm settled. I'm – I'm a cook.' This last was pushing the truth a little but Mr Hartley didn't look too impressed by her. 'I have enough money to pay for however many weeks you want in advance,' she added hastily, 'and Mr Croft said to tell you he would vouch for me. I wouldn't leave owing you anything and—'

'Hold your horses, lass.' He smiled kindly now. 'I take it Wilbur told you what them blighters did? Me own fault, though. I didn't take to 'em from the start and I should have trusted me instincts. This' – he tapped the side of his rather large nose – 'never lets me down.'

Rose didn't know what to say but then as he looked down at Betsy and said, 'And what's your name, hinny?' the little girl buried her face in her mother's skirt. 'This is Betsy and I'm Rose, Rose O'Leary.'

'Well, Mrs O'Leary, the house in question is in Park Street, two-up, two-down and the rent's three bob a week. Dare say I could show you it later if you've a mind? The wife's out at her sister's now but she won't be long. Shall we say twelve o'clock?'

She remembered Park Street was close to the market that she and Amy had stopped at the day before. Her voice eager, she said, 'Thank you. Thank you very much, Mr Hartley.'

'Don't thank me yet, lass. It might not suit.' He reached into a glass jar on the counter and pulled out a small rainbow-coloured lollipop. 'Here, hinny.' Bending over the counter, he passed it to Betsy, who took it with a shy 'Thank you'.

An hour and a half later Mr Hartley was opening the front door of the little terraced house and Rose, carrying Betsy, was following him into the narrow hall. The small front room was immediately to her left and at the end of the hall was a kitchen with a tiny scullery which contained a pot sink with a cold tap. Hot water would have to be heated in the blackleaded fireplace boiler but that was all right, Rose thought as she looked around her. Upstairs were two square bedrooms, each one having a small fireplace. Situated across from the back door of the kitchen in the stone-slabbed yard was the brick-built privy, an ashpit with a large wooden lid containing the hole where one sat. A big tin bath hung in one corner of the yard and, in the corner opposite, a large wooden poss tub resided next to a small coal bunker. The house itself was devoid of furniture and there were no curtains at the windows, but the kitchen range was a good size and there was a bread oven on the other side to the boiler.

The house itself was none too clean and the range was filthy. It didn't look as though it had been cleaned in months, thick grease coating it and bits of mould growing here and there.

Mr Hartley saw her looking at it and he shook his head. 'Right dirty so-an'-so's this last lot were. The place was as clean as a new pin when they took it on. Me wife an' daughters always do a spring clean before we have a new tenant but it's never been as bad as this. They were going to come in and see to it over the next day or two, but if you wanted to do it to your own satisfaction you could have a couple of weeks rent free. Does that sound fair?'

Rose nodded. She would far rather clean the place herself and compared to what she'd found at the Rowlands Gill mill this was nothing. 'Thank you, yes.'

'You got your furniture in storage?'

'No, I decided to sell up when I left. It was easier that way.'

'Aye, I dare say. Come far, have you?'

'From Sunderland. My husband worked in a shipyard, that's where he had the accident.'

'Lethal places, sure enough. Well, lass, if you're looking for good second-hand stuff, there's a bloke in Store Street who'd sort you out. Jimmy Crawford. He has all sorts in his shop – furniture, linen, pots and pans, the lot, and there's no fleas or lice either, not like some. He'd likely have everything you need.'

Again she said, 'Thank you.'

'So I take it we've got a deal then? Like I said, I'll do a couple of weeks free and then you can pop the rent into the shop after that on a Friday evening. How does that sound?' He handed her the keys as he spoke. 'Any problems, you know where I am.' He bent over and ruffled Betsy's curls. 'You help your mammy get your home sorted, eh, hinny?' and with that he shook Rose's hand and was gone.

She stood in the kitchen for some moments more, slightly stunned by how quickly everything had happened. They had somewhere to live, or they would have when she had cleaned and scrubbed and bought everything they needed. She surprised Betsy by bending down and whisking the child into her arms whereupon she danced about the kitchen for a minute or two, Betsy squealing and loving every second. And for those brief moments she was happy.

Over the next days a transformation took place at 7 Park Street. Once she had cleaned every inch of the house, spending hours on the range alone, she tackled the two bedrooms, distempering the walls and ceiling in a fresh cream colour. Next she did the landing, stairs and hall, again in cream, which took several coats as everything had been a muddy brown colour. The front room and kitchen received a pretty yellow paint, the ceilings again cream, and after she had blackleaded the range and the fireplaces in the bedrooms and front room, she really felt she was getting somewhere. The privy was an unpleasant job, but by the time she'd finished it was clean, sweet-smelling and devoid of the army of spiders who had lived there.

Amy proved to be an enormous help. Every morning she took care of Betsy and after the first day Rose ceased to worry about leaving the child with her, knowing she was well cared for and happy. At lunchtime Amy and

Betsy arrived at the house with sandwiches and a bottle of lemonade, and then Amy went back to the inn to work and Betsy stayed with her mother for the afternoons.

Some evenings Amy turned up at the house and then took Betsy back to the inn with her and put her to bed, sitting reading in the room until Rose returned when it was dark. Other times Rose left it as late as she could before she returned to let Betsy go to sleep. It was a full ten days before Rose felt the house was ready to receive furniture and other items, and she and Amy spent a morning at Jimmy Crawford's second-hand shop which turned out to be like an Aladdin's cave. Amy had confirmed Mr Hartley's recommendation, saying Crawford's was a step up from other second-hand shops, and although he charged a little more Rose could see she was getting good value for money.

She bought a three-quarter-size bed for her bedroom and a single one for Betsy's, along with a wardrobe and chest of drawers for each and thick rugs to cover a little of the bare floorboards. The bedding she decided to buy new from a shop some doors away, topping the sheets and blankets with a pale blue eiderdown and matching curtains for her room, and the same for Betsy but in pink. She also got curtains for the downstairs rooms from this shop, but the two armchairs, small coffee table and large rug for the front room she bought again from Mr Hartley, along with a kitchen table and two long plank seats, a thick clippy mat, a dresser, numerous pots and pans and baking tins and other utensils and crockery.

She was horrified how much everything came to but needs must, she told herself, and she wanted to create a comfortable and snug home for Betsy.

There was one item in Jimmy Crawford's shop that was pure extravagance but she couldn't resist it – a wooden Noah's Ark for Betsy complete with chunky hand-made animals and little figures of Noah and his family. It would be a new home present, she told herself, and Betsy had never really had toys before apart from her beloved rag doll and teddy bear.

Jimmy Crawford and his son delivered everything the following day, positioning the furniture where Rose wanted it and carrying the beds and wardrobes and chest of drawers upstairs for her. The Noah's Ark Rose put on the coffee table in the front room, imagining Betsy's face when she saw it and the hours of enjoyment the little girl would have. They could sit in here together on winter evenings, she thought, herself perhaps reading and Betsy playing, just the two of them. And that was the way she wanted it for the future too; the mere thought of a man being around made her shudder. She'd started her monthly some days before so the weight of that worry was gone but if she thought about the rape and what had happened to the miller it made her flesh crawl. She had to make a success of her cooking, she *had* to – it meant everything, because it would give her autonomy.

Amy had offered to have Betsy for the whole day while Rose supervised the deliveries and got things straight, so on the way back to the inn that evening Rose bought two huge bunches of flowers and two enormous boxes of chocolates, to thank Amy for caring for Betsy, and also Tessa for sparing her daughter these last days without complaining.

She intended to move to the house tomorrow; she and Betsy could go shopping for supplies together and she had already asked the coal merchant to deliver enough coal to fill the bunker in the yard tomorrow morning. Everything was set. She had stopped at the market a few days ago and spoken to one of the stallholders who had directed her to the market overseer. He would arrange her pitch and she had already paid the nominal fee he required for the council and for the stall itself. He'd been a nice tubby little man with a bushy grey beard, who had informed her that while most of the stallholders paid for six- or twelve-monthly rights to secure their stall, she might like to start off paying monthly 'to see if it suits'. She knew what that meant. It was a kind way of saying he wasn't sure if she would make a go of it.

As she reached the inn with the flowers and chocolates, she stood for a moment in the courtyard before entering. Tomorrow would see the start of her new life and already she had a good friend in Amy. She had to put the past behind her and concentrate on the future, it was the only way to live. She could see herself settling in this steel town with its red dust and warm community. The other day she had been passing the forge, with its slate roof held together with sheep bones, and the blacksmith had stopped shoeing a horse for a few moments to talk to her, saying he'd seen her coming back and forth for a few days. She had told him she was going to have a stall on the market selling cooked food and he had promised he would come and sample some and tell his customers about her too. Whether he would or not she didn't know, but it had been nice of him to say so, all the same.

When she entered the inn Wilbur directed her through to the family's private quarters off the kitchen, and there she found Betsy playing with the toys that Tessa kept for Daisy's children when they called round. At the sight of her mother Betsy left the tower of wooden bricks she and Amy had been building and rushed to her, and after Rose had given Amy the flowers and chocolates she lifted the child into her arms, holding her close for a moment.

She was lucky, she was so, so lucky to have this precious, beautiful bairn. Betsy was all she would ever want in life. She would ask God for nothing more.

Chapter Fifteen

Nathaniel felt the familiar disappointment grip him. Foolishly perhaps, he admitted, he'd imagined he'd find Rose without too much trouble after talking with Beattie Harper, and to that end he'd taken a couple of weeks off work with the excuse that he'd damaged his hand in an accident at home. He knew it would mean the sack if he was caught out but finding Rose was worth the risk. Besides, he was good at what he did and he'd comforted himself that if the worst happened another shipyard would take him on.

He had been to umpteen mills with no Rose, but then yesterday he'd happened across an old man close to the hamlet of Highfield who'd told him about a mill at Rowlands Gill. 'Bin a mill there for donkey's,' the be-whiskered old fellow had told him, puffing on his clay pipe as he sat on the front doorstep of his small cottage at the edge of woodland. 'Vickers, that's the name, but if I remember rightly the son's never wed so I daresay it'll go out of the family when he pops his clogs.'

The sun had already been setting so Nathaniel had decided to spend the night at an inn he'd noticed a mile or two back, but now it was morning and he was standing outside the mill. The young lad who had come out of the building when he'd called had just informed him that the miller had died and there was no one in the house.

'I'm just clearing up the last of the flour an' stuff before the constable comes to secure the place,' the youth explained.

'When did he die? The miller?'

'Three weeks or so ago now.'

'So he lived here by himself? There were no elderly parents?' That's what Beattie Harper had told him, that Rose was going to work for a miller with elderly parents, so this looked like yet another dead end.

'No, he lost his mam back end of 1902 and his da had gone before that but he didn't live alone. He got himself a lass in shortly after his mam went, the old goat.' He winked lewdly.

'A lass? You mean a housekeeper?'

'If you want to call it that,' the lad said, grinning.

'What would you call it?'

'Well, I only saw her from a distance now and again but she was young and bonny an' had a babby, so I reckon old Vickers knew a good thing when he saw it. Word is he picked her up in Gateshead, and you can't tell me she was there just to keep house.'

Nathaniel stared at the lad. It was Rose, he knew it. It all fitted, but what the hell had she been doing coming to look after a single man living on his own? Quietly, he said, 'She might have been,' his soft tone belying the temper rising in his chest.

'Aw, come on, a young lass with a babby speaks for itself, don't it. She was no better than she should be, and Vickers liked 'em like that. You ought to have seen some of the pictures he'd got hidden away at the back of the mill when the constable came to search around. Make a sailor blush, they would.' He gave another sly grin.

'The constable?' Nathaniel stared at the spotty face. 'Why was the constable looking around?'

'Well, it was all a bit funny to tell you the truth and they wondered whether it really was an accident that took him at first. Him being found the way he was, in the bedroom with his head bashed in. Well, I say bashed in but they reckon now he was three parts to the wind and fell and pierced his skull on the fender in the fireplace, but there was no sign of the lass and her bairn, see? Nothing. They didn't know if it was a robbery or something, or if this lass was involved, but there were some nice bits in the sitting room, his mam's silver from her wedding an' such and nothing had been touched so they decided it was an accident after all. The lass could have upped and gone any time in the weeks beforehand 'cause I wasn't around, so' – he shrugged again – 'there it is.'

'What did she look like?'

'Well, like I said I didn't see her near to but I could tell she was bonny.'

'What colour hair?'

'Brown. Reddy brown I'd say an' a nice figure but like I said, she must have caught her toe when she landed herself with the bairn. Why else would a lass come to look after Vickers? He was no oil painting.'

She had prostituted herself to this Vickers bloke and yet she wouldn't let him look after her. Nathaniel's stomach was churning. She'd let young lads like this one snigger about her and all the time he'd been tearing his hair out trying to find her. He would kill her if he got his hands on her.

'Mind you, she'd have earned every penny with Vickers if them pictures we found were anything to go by. Made your hair curl, they did. Perhaps she'd had enough and took off and that's why he was drinking himself senseless. Like me da said, Vickers had lost his live-in whore.'

It was the last word that did it. With a sound like a snarl Nathaniel had his hands round the youth's throat, squeezing for all he was worth. They fell to the ground, the lad squirming and trying to claw at the hands strangling the life out of him, but Nathaniel was tall and strong with muscles like steel and the rage that had him in its grip made him twice as powerful.

It was over in a couple of minutes and as everything became still the morning was full of birdsong. Nathaniel sat back on his heels, staring at the lad's bulging eyes and protruding tongue. Part of him was aware that it was Rose he had been throttling but at the same time he hadn't been able to bear hearing her spoken about in that way. This scum had deserved all he'd got.

The red mist before his eyes was gone now and with it the roaring in his ears. He glanced about him, self-preservation kicking in. Who knew he had been coming here today? He hadn't mentioned it to anyone at the inn last night, had he? He cast his mind back, thinking about the meal and drinks he'd had before he'd gone to bed. No, he'd had a bit of banter with the barmaid when she'd served his meat pie but that was all. There was the old fellow he'd spoken to who'd told him about the mill but he was a couple of miles away and as deaf as a post; he'd had to shout his head off to make the old man understand.

He stood up slowly, his brain racing. He had to hide the body somewhere it wouldn't be found for a good while, if ever. Young lads were always taking off for pastures new and by the sound of it this one had lost his job at the mill.

He could let the river take him? No, what if the body caught in weeds or debris not far from here? He'd have to move it somewhere and bury it in a hole deep enough for animals not to dig it out.

Striding into the mill, he looked about him but there was no spade or fork to hand. Exiting quickly, he glanced towards the house some distance away and, running now, he sped towards it. When he reached the building he found the front door was locked but glancing across the yard he saw, to his great relief, a couple of old spades leaning against the wall of the brick-built privy which had probably been used to clear the muck from inside to take it elsewhere.

Panting, he grabbed the better spade and ran back to the mill. The lad had said that the constable would be coming back at some point and the last thing he needed was to come face to face with the law.

Heaving the body over his shoulder, he steadied it with one hand, and carrying the spade in the other, made off down the track at the side of the mill which led into woodland and beyond that farmer's fields bordered by hedgerows. Looking about him all the time and going as quickly as he could, he came out of the woodland after some few minutes and into a field of corn. He skirted this, still keeping his eyes peeled, and then walked through another field of crops and yet another. Puffing now, he saw ahead a further dense area of woodland beyond a field where cows were grazing. He was some distance from the mill now and, aware that all the time he was out in the open carrying the lad he was at risk of being seen, he made for the trees. By the time he reached the stone wall bordering the wood the sweat was running down his face in rivulets and the stink of cow pats on his boots was strong.

The drystone wall was chest high and he dropped the body and the spade into the grass on the other side before vaulting over himself. The only emotion he was feeling was panic. Once in the wood he walked for a minute or two along a natural trail made by animals, probably foxes and badgers, before coming to a halt in front of a grassy area in the midst of the trees. He lowered the body to the ground and, walking forward with the spade, prodded the undergrowth. There were clumps of bracken and brambles in parts as well as grass and wild flowers, and although they'd had no rain for weeks he thought he could dig a sufficiently deep hole and then cover it with natural vegetation again so it would be unnoticeable, not that anyone was likely to come here.

It took a long, long time. The roots of trees snaked into play now and again, and the sting of sweat in his eyes caused him to stop several times to spit on his handkerchief and wipe them. All the time he worked he was cursing Rose. This was her fault, all of it, damn her. If she had just fallen in with what he wanted rather than running away, he would have sorted Davey's mam for her. He would never have let that old crone take Betsy, surely she must have realized that? But no, she'd had to do a vanishing act and make him scour the country for her and what was the result? He'd been forced to shut that lad's stinking mouth.

Had she been this miller's mistress? The boy had been in no doubt of it. And whatever conclusion the constable may have come to, it seemed damn odd to him that the man had been found dead and Rose had done another flit. Had she let him paw her about and do some of the things the bloke's dirty pictures had portrayed? He could imagine what they were like. Had she enjoyed it? Encouraged him even?

He thought his head would burst with the pressure of the blinding rage gripping him. His ears ringing, he kept digging, adrenaline coursing through his veins.

He dug down so far he had a struggle to climb out of

the hole but once he had, he tipped the body into it and began covering it with earth. When he'd finished he trod the ground down and then lay the big clumps of grass and vegetation he'd been careful to remove with their roots intact on top. That accomplished, he scattered leaves and bits and pieces all around until he was satisfied that no one would guess a body was buried here. The grave was completely obscured and camouflaged perfectly to merge in with the rest of the glade.

The sun was high in the sky now – it must be well into the afternoon – and he found he was exhausted. He would have liked nothing more than to throw himself down and take a nap, but he wanted to get the spade back to where he had found it and then find a stream or river where he could wash himself and clean his boots and make himself presentable.

Once he reached the mill he approached it cautiously, mindful of the constable, but all was quiet and deserted. He replaced the spade by the privy, resisting the desire to try and force a window and get into the house to see where she had been residing for the last eighteen months or so. There must be nothing suspicious to alert anyone regarding the miller's lad, besides which every second he was here it was risky. Nevertheless, he walked round the house peering in the windows, thinking of her sitting there, eating, drinking, laughing, sleeping with another man. If the miller hadn't already been dead he would have liked to cut him up into little pieces, he thought savagely, his hands clenched fists.

The rage brought the pounding in his head to the fore again and he pressed his fingers against his temples, willing himself to calm down.

Once he was on the track leading away from the mill he walked swiftly before turning off into one of the numerous byways and lanes threading the countryside. There was nothing for it but to cut his losses for today and make for home once he'd cleaned himself up, but this wasn't the end of his search, not by a long chalk, he promised himself.

He found the perfect spot after a while, a crystal clear stream bordered by thick grass verges where the only company was the twittering of the birds in the trees overhead. He had a long drink of the icy cold water first and once his thirst was sated he stripped off all his clothes, washing himself from his head to his feet and then seeing to his boots. Once they were clean he brushed any debris from his clothes and pulled on his shirt and trousers, leaving his jacket and cap with his boots which were drying.

The sun was still hot and the grass was warm and scented with a hundred flowers, and as he lay stretched out the only thought in his head was how he was going to find Rose and Betsy now. But find them he would. However long it took, he would keep looking. She'd done the dirty on him with the miller and she had to pay for that, but after he'd taken it out of her hide and she was crawling at his feet, he'd make an honest woman of her. She didn't deserve it and some might say he was barmy, but he had to have her. Until he had her where he wanted her he'd know no rest.

It was thick twilight when he awoke and for a moment he wondered where he was before the events of the day came flooding back. He sat up, reaching for his jacket and cap and then pulling his now dry boots on. He felt no remorse about the miller's lad, nor would he.

Standing up, he realized he was hungry. He'd go back to the inn and have a meal and spend another night there, he decided, and he knew he wouldn't be sleeping alone. The barmaid had made it plain the night before that he only had to lift his little finger and she would oblige, and she'd been a pert piece. Aye, he'd have his fill of her tonight and then head for home in the morning and get back to work, but that didn't mean he'd given up. Far from it. Rose was still here in the North East somewhere, he felt it in his bones. Sooner or later he would come across her. He might even get a bit of money behind him and travel round looking for her – he could work his way when he had to. He was young and strong and Sunderland held nothing for him.

He began walking swiftly, his deep blue eyes glinting in the dying sunlight, and now he was thinking of nothing but the meal he was going to have at the inn followed by a night with the barmaid. The glade in the wood, the body of the young lad who lay beneath the earth, didn't weigh on his mind, nor did he give a thought to the heartache the boy's loved ones would endure in the weeks ahead when there was no sign of him.

It had been round about the time the nightmares about Davey had ceased that he had begun to feel the power in himself and realize how the attitudes and viewpoints of society kept people in mental chains. But not him. No, not him. You had to make things happen in life. Most folk were like sheep, weakly following what was expected of them, and they had no one to blame but themselves when they ended up miserable and disappointed. He was different. His mother had accused him of becoming hard recently but she didn't understand that you had to take life by the throat and shake it into shape; only then were you invincible. While you took notice of society's laws and morals, you were just one of the herd. He was above that. And the more he had understood he was special, the more the power inside him had manifested. He always got what he wanted. And he wanted Rose . . .

PART THREE

The Baker's Shop

1908

Chapter Sixteen

From where she was still snuggled under the covers, Betsy lay listening to the clatter of boots outside the house. The men were making for the ironworks, she knew that, which meant it wasn't six o'clock yet. It was dark outside and bitterly cold but she was as warm as toast in bed, although she knew the moment she poked her nose out of her cocoon the bedroom would be like an ice-box, last night's fire nothing but cold ashes in the tiny grate. The clippy mat beside the bed gave brief comfort from the freezing linoleum floor covering her mam had put down over the floorboards; although the lino looked nice, it always seemed colder than wood in the winter.

She shut her eyes again, revelling in the fact that it was a Saturday and there was no school. Not that she minded school, she admitted, in fact she liked it, and at least she could come home for lunch. Her two best friends, Flora and Sally, had to stay and they were always moaning that there was nowhere to eat the sandwiches and cold tea they brought with them because they weren't allowed to sit in the classroom. There was the porch, but the stone floor was freezing to sit on and the children who were lucky enough to sit on the pipes never moved until the bell went for class.

She liked her lessons and writing on her slate with chalk, and at morning and afternoon breaks in the winter everyone got a cup of hot cocoa; but though she loved playing with her friends, nothing compared to being at home with her mam or going to the market and seeing everyone. The market was like a big family where she knew all the stallholders by name, and even if they were grumpy with each other they never were with her.

Curling into a little ball, she thought about the day ahead. She knew how it would pan out – every Saturday was the same and she liked that. It would begin when her mam called her down for breakfast after she had stoked up the range and got their porridge ready. Her mam's porridge was lovely, thick and creamy, not stiff with salt like some folk had it. She'd hate that.

Then once they'd had breakfast and while she got dressed, her mam would lay the fire in the front room and in their bedrooms ready to light for when they came back from the market later on. She'd told Flora and Sally she always had a fire in her bedroom in the winter months so the room wasn't too cold when she went to bed, and they'd been green with envy. Their mam didn't read them bedtime stories either or settle them down with hot milk and a biscuit, but then they had umpteen brothers and sisters so she supposed their mam was too busy to do things like that. They were lucky to have each other to play with. She would have loved a twin sister. If her da hadn't died when she was a little baby she might have had a sister to play dollies with, but he had so that was that.

The smell of her mam's baking was reaching her even under the covers and she sniffed appreciatively. Her mam was always up and dressed and downstairs baking before she woke up, summer and winter, and she knew there would be boxes of scones and cakes and fruit loaves and sandwiches already stacked by the back door of the kitchen ready for when Matthew came. Her mam paid him to help her take all her wares to the market each day on his handcart. She was a bit frightened of Matthew even though her mam had told her he couldn't help the way he talked and looked, and that something had happened to him before he was born which had caused him not to be like other lads. Her mam said she had to be kind to him and she was, even when she couldn't understand what he was saying. Her mam seemed to know though, so that was all right.

She dug out Abigail, her rag doll, and Bruno, her teddy bear, from where they had worked down the bed in the night, and played a game in which she was the teacher and they were her pupils until her mother called her some time later. Climbing out of bed, her feet found her slippers and she pulled on the thick fleecy dressing gown her mam had bought her at the beginning of the winter, her old one being too small. She'd chosen this one herself and it was pink with flowers on. She knew she was lucky having a mam who bought her nice clothes; Flora and Sally had to wear their older sisters' hand-me-downs whether they fitted or not.

Rose looked up from the range where she was stirring the porridge as Betsy danced into the room, the doll and teddy bear tucked under one arm. 'Hello, hinny,' she said softly, relishing the sight of her daughter as she did every morning. And then as Betsy came for a kiss, she stopped what she was doing and whisked the child up into her arms, making her squeal as she nuzzled her face into her neck. Setting her down again, she watched as Betsy washed her hands in the bowl of hot water she had ready in the scullery, and then came running into the kitchen again.

They ate their bowls of porridge side by side and then Rose got up and put some rashers of bacon and pieces of bread in the big black frying pan, adding an egg each when the bacon and fried bread were nearly ready. Betsy ate well and loved her food but Rose often wondered where she put it – her daughter was sylphlike and looked as though a breath of wind could blow her away. She had worried about it in the early days but had come to realize that although Betsy looked delicate she was actually a tough little thing on the whole.

'Mrs Blackett said she'd bring me some storybooks her grandchildren have finished with last Saturday. Do you think she'll remember?'

Large chocolate-brown eyes set in a heart-shaped face

stared seriously at Rose. Adelaide Blackett had the green-grocer's stall next to theirs and adored Betsy, but at seventy-plus it was common knowledge she was becoming increasingly forgetful. Her two sons had been trying for some time to make her give up the stall but since she had been widowed at forty it had become more than just her livelihood. The companionship and camaraderie among the stallholders was strong and for that reason everyone had rallied round to support the old lady, helping her with setting up in the mornings, packing stuff away at the end of the day and making sure no one diddled her out of any money. Every Saturday Betsy spent most of her time with Adelaide, helping her weigh out her goods, taking the money and putting it in the cash box, or just talking to the old lady. Betsy didn't seem to mind the number of times the old lady repeated herself or got things mixed up, but then the same innate kindness and gentleness that had been characteristics of Davey were in his daughter, Rose thought fondly. There wasn't a nasty bone in Betsy's body.

'I don't know if she'll remember or not, hinny, but if she hasn't brought them don't say anything, will you. It might upset her if she thinks she's disappointed you.'

Betsy nodded solemnly. Even when Mrs Blackett called her by the name of one of her grandchildren and asked how her brothers and sisters were, or said she hadn't seen her for a long, long while and asked what she'd been doing, she didn't correct her. Her mam had told her Mrs Blackett's brain was tired. Not in the same way as

Matthew's, but it still meant she didn't think like other folk sometimes.

Mopping up the last of the fat from the bacon with a slice of home-made crusty bread, Betsy finished her breakfast. Before she got down, she said, 'Thank you for my breakfast. Please may I leave the table?'

Rose smiled and nodded. She wanted Betsy to grow up with good manners – it was one of the few things she was strict about – but the child never complained and rarely forgot what was required of her.

Once upstairs, Betsy dressed quickly, taking off her nightdress and pulling on her vest and flannelette knickers, her lace-trimmed petticoat, her warm red woollen dress with the embroidered flowers round the neck and her white-frilled pinafore. It was too cold to dawdle, and once her socks and boots were on she scampered down to the snug warmth of the kitchen, humming one of the songs she had learned at school as she went.

Within a minute or two her mam had finished laying the fires and Matthew was at the front door. Once he began to load his big handcart Betsy put on her coat and scarf and her blue woollen hat with a pom-pom on top. It was still only half-past seven and the December sky was heavy and low, a few wispy snowflakes drifting in the air. It had snowed every day the week before and the snow was still banked up high in places, but it was dirty now and uninviting. She liked it when it was fresh but when it got mucky it was just cold and slippery.

She glanced down at her new snug boots with their

sheepskin lining. They kept her feet as warm as toast. Poor Flora and Sally had holes in theirs that let the snow in, and they'd showed her their chilblains the other day which had looked so sore.

Betsy sighed. Flora had whispered that their granny who lived in Shotley Bridge had turned up last weekend with a new pair of boots for both of them, but their mam had made the twins take them off as soon as their granny had gone home and taken them to the pawnshop. She had been indignant on her friends' behalf, but when she had told her mother about it after she had got home from school, her mam had shaken her head and said, 'Poor woman.' She hadn't understood that. Surely it was Flora and Sally who were deserving of pity?

'Ready, hinny?' Rose came into the kitchen, tweaking the pom-pom on Betsy's hat and as the child grinned at her she thought, as she did many times, how lucky she was to have her. As sweet as a nut, that's what Amy and her parents always said about Betsy, and they were right. Poor Amy . . . Rose's smile faded. Since her friend had married her Frank she'd had one miscarriage after another, the last one being only two weeks ago. And there was her sister Daisy about to deliver twins. It was so unfair. Amy and Frank would be wonderful parents and they doted on Betsy even more than their nieces.

Matthew had already set off for the market, which was just a couple of streets away, and now Rose ushered Betsy out of the house in front of her and locked the front door. No one locked or bolted their doors in the community apart from her, she knew that, but she wouldn't have been able to rest if she didn't. As time had gone on the fear of Nathaniel finding them had lessened to a large extent but it was still there, hovering at the back of her mind and occasionally erupting from her subconscious in dark, troubled dreams. Often the mill would feature too. She had come to terms with the part she had played in the miller's death but it still weighed heavy, especially when she was tired. That whole episode in her life was like an ugly spectre sitting on her shoulder, and to ward it off she kept herself busy every waking hour, often falling into bed so exhausted that she was barely able to undress.

She managed the stall at the market six days a week, arriving before eight o'clock in the morning and leaving at three in order to collect Betsy from school. On school mornings she took Betsy to Amy and Frank's house in the next street, and her friend delivered the child to school for nine o'clock. Rose liked to pick Betsy up herself in the afternoons though, so that her daughter could tell her all about her day and they had some time together before tea.

Once Betsy was in bed, Rose began the first batch of baking for the next day. Biscuits, tarts, fruit loaves and jam rolls mostly. Other items, such as scones and cakes and bread, she liked to make fresh in the morning, rising at three o'clock most days. This regime meant Rose rarely had more than four hours' sleep, except for a Saturday when she fell into her bed as soon as Betsy was asleep and slept in on the Sunday morning. It was a punishing schedule but she'd got used to it, and the fact that her little business was such a success made the long hours worthwhile.

At the very beginning, she'd made no profit for some weeks and had actually lost money when she'd been left with baskets of food at the end of the day. She'd gifted this to Amy and Daisy and her neighbours. She knew it was because she charged more than other stalls with similar produce, but had felt she must start as she intended to carry on. However, anyone who did buy her goods always returned, and within three months she was having to bake more as she'd sold out before the end of the day. She sourced her ingredients as cheaply as she could but made sure the quality was good and that the flour was never bulked up with chalk.

Word had spread. By the end of the year she was earning enough for all their needs and was able to put money by each week. And so it had continued. Apart from customers to the stall, she had a number of other buyers. Mr Hartley always took a regular number of teacakes and gingerbread which he sold in his shop, and a couple of councillors' wives and one or two other influential dignitaries like a doctor's wife and the local vicar had a weekly order which Matthew delivered for her. The pigeon-racing club and cricket club were among her regulars and for the last eighteen months, demand had outstripped her ability to supply. Reluctantly she'd had to turn away business.

Rose was thinking about this as she walked with Betsy

to the market. An icy wind was cutting the air like a knife and the low grey sky promised that more snow was imminent. She'd had four years of manning the stall in all weathers, and worrying each day that Matthew would tip up the handcart with its deep wicker baskets covered with linen and send the lot into the road, as had happened more than once. She was fond of the majority of the stallholders and most she counted as friends; they supported each other and went out of their way to help one of their number who needed it, as in the case of Adelaide, and it was probably this comforting factor that had delayed her from doing what she knew was the next step. She needed to rent a shop with a flat above so she had her business and home under one roof. It was a big decision – she was the breadwinner and couldn't afford to fail – but she felt the last four years had laid a foundation that was sufficient to build on if she had her own premises and an assistant to help her.

They had reached the market and there was Matthew waiting by her stall with the baskets intact, thank goodness. Several stallholders were already setting up and the usual cheery banter and greetings ensued with Betsy being made a fuss of.

She would miss this little community, Rose thought later that morning as she watched her daughter with Adelaide. It was the nearest thing to a big family she'd experienced, but she had to consider what was the best in the long run for Betsy and herself. If she had a shop of her own she could open it once she had taken Betsy to school in the morning, and maybe leave it in the hands of an assistant for a few minutes when she collected the child in the afternoons. Living above her work would mean she could stay open as long as she liked, knowing Betsy was safe upstairs, and she could expand the business how and when she liked. No more standing in the market in weather like today. She glanced again at her daughter, whose little nose was bright red with the cold. No more tramping to and fro when it was pouring with rain or snowing, and trying to keep her produce dry when the wind blew the rain in the wrong direction.

Of course the rent for the sort of premises she had in mind would be much more than her present two-up, two-down house and the cost of the stall, but the advantages would be huge. It was time. She knew it was time and that she had been putting this decision off for far too long.

She came out of her reverie with a start as a deep male voice said, 'Excuse me, may I buy a few of those delicious-looking fruit tarts?' and realized a tall, a very tall, man must have been standing in front of the stall waiting to be served for some moments while she had been wool-gathering.

He was smiling, one dark eyebrow raised, and wondering what on earth he must think of her and more flustered than she would have liked, she said hastily, 'Yes, yes, of course, I'm sorry. How many would you like? They're a penny each.'

'Shall we say six?'

She quickly put the tarts in a paper bag, knowing she was blushing but unable to do anything about it. It wasn't just that she had been caught daydreaming; it was something about the man himself.

After she had handed him the bag and taken the payment, he thanked her but didn't move away. Instead, in a voice that held no accent as such but which, as a child, she would have described as toffee-nosed, he said, 'Do you make everything yourself?'

She nodded. 'Yes, sir.'

'Quite an undertaking. How often are you here?'

'Every day, except for Sundays, of course.' He was not only very tall but broad across the shoulders, and although not exactly handsome, he had a presence – that was the only way she could describe the male magnetism emanating from him to herself. His clothes matched his voice, being those that the upper classes wore, and his leather riding boots were polished to perfection. Wishing he would go, she lowered her head and re-arranged the tarts that were left, but when she looked up again he was still there.

'I'm sorry, I should have introduced myself. Alexander Bembridge, at your service.' He smiled again, revealing white, even teeth.

Hot now with embarrassment, she wondered if she should curtsy but decided not. Forcing a smile, she said, 'Can I get you anything else, sir?'

'Not today, thank you, but if these tarts are as delicious as they look no doubt I'll be back.' He stared at her face for a moment more as though he was going to say something else but then turned and walked away, and as he went she became aware that she was holding her breath and breathed out through her nose.

'Hobnobbing with the toffs, are you, lass?' Cissy, who had the stall on the other side, grinned at her as she spoke. 'Bit of all right, isn't he, Major Bembridge.'

'Major?'

'Aye. He's the son of William Bembridge. You know, the industrialist who's got that big estate outside Castleside and his finger in umpteen pies here an' there.' Seeing Rose's blank face, she said, 'No? By, lass, I thought everyone knew the name of Bembridge round here. Me sister was taken on there in the kitchens when she was a little scrap of nothing – she's forty-odd now – and the stuff she used to bring back on her half-day off that the cook had slipped her kept us going, me mam having been left with twelve of us when me da died. They've only got the one lad though, the Bembridges, and rather than following in his father's footsteps Mr Alexander went into the army. Caused a right to-do at the time, according to our Marge, but Mr Alexander stuck to his guns and his mam an' da had to accept it.' Cissy walked over to Rose, lowering her voice as she added, 'What was he saying to you anyway? I've never seen him in the market before.'

'Nothing really.' Rose liked Cissy but the woman was the biggest gossip in the market. 'Just asking when I was here, that's all.'

Cissy raised her eyebrows. 'Was he indeed?'

'Not in that way. He just liked the tarts he bought,' Rose said dismissively.

'I bet that's not all he likes.'

'He was merely being polite.'

'That's how it starts with the toffs an' the likes of us, lass, but they've got one thing on their mind and one only and it's not tarts. Well, it is in a way' – Cissy dug Rose in the ribs with a broad grin – 'not that you're a tart, far from it, but they look on all our sort as easy pickings.'

'Cissy, he was here for a minute or two, no more, and he was the perfect gentleman.'

'Like I said, that's how it starts with them and then afore you know it your knickers are off and your belly's full.'

'*Cissy*.' Rose was shocked and it showed.

'Aw, lass, you've bin married an' you've got a bairn, you know what it's all about.'

Unbidden, Nathaniel's face popped into her mind and now Rose nodded slowly. 'Yes, I know what it's about.'

'You're a bonny lass an' you cause a stir wherever you go but that has its own price,' said Cissy with the wisdom of her kind. 'If you'd bin born into wealth and riches it'd be different, you'd be protected then, but as it is you have to see their sort for what they are. The workhouses are full of young lassies who listened to a silver tongue and thought they were going to be whisked out of the mire and into a life of ease, and I dare say a lot of the young bloods haven't given a thought to their bairns born on the wrong side of the blanket. It's a man's world, lass, and even more a rich man's world.'

Rose's gaze had wandered as Cissy had been talking and she saw that Alexander Bembridge had stopped to talk to the market overseer some distance away. They appeared deep in conversation, and as she stared, Alexander suddenly raised his head and looked straight at her. Startled, she dropped her eyes, but was left with the impression that they had been talking about *her*, or was she just being paranoid after what Cissy had said? Whatever, it had unnerved her.

'Believe me, Cissy,' she said firmly, 'I'm not interested in Alexander Bembridge or anyone else. Silver tongues are like water off a duck's back to me.'

'Don't be too sure.' Cissy hitched up her ample breasts with her forearms as she spoke. A big buxom woman with a tribe of youngsters who some reported were not all her long-suffering husband's, she was known for liking a bit of slap and tickle with some of the other male vendors. 'Everyone likes a bit of flattery, lass, and to know that they're special. And that's what his type make you feel, special.'

There was a touch of bitterness in Cissy's voice, and as Rose stared at her she wondered if the rumours were true about Cissy and the chairman of the local councillors. According to the market gossip, the man, who was married with a couple of bairns, had made Cissy fall head over heels in love with him and then after a brief affair finished the relationship. Several months later Cissy had given birth to a bouncing baby boy that was said to be the spitting image of the man in question.

Quietly, Rose murmured, 'I don't want to feel special, Cissy. I just want to bring Betsy up the best I can.'

Cissy nodded and the warmth was back in her voice when she said, 'Aye, she's a grand little lass, Rose. Excited about Christmas, is she?'

Christmas was just a week away and tonight when they got home from the market Rose had promised Betsy they would decorate the kitchen and front room with paper chains and some other bits and pieces she'd bought. Unbeknown to Betsy she had ordered a small Christmas tree from one of the stallholders too. She smiled now, glad of the change of subject. 'She doesn't know yet but I've booked two seats for the pantomime at the Royal for Christmas Eve afternoon.'

'You won't be here then? There's always a lot of customers on Christmas Eve buying last-minute bits.'

Rose shook her head. She'd considered that but had decided this year she wouldn't work on Christmas Eve like she had done before. As Christmas Day fell on a Friday, it would mean she and Betsy would have four whole days together before she returned to work the following Monday after Boxing Day. Her bank account had again grown very satisfactorily this year, and what was the point in being her own boss if she couldn't choose when to spend time with her daughter?

'Aye, well, you know your own best, lass. Me, I'll be

here early and leave when the last customer goes. It'll be mayhem at home with my lot.'

Rose smiled again but didn't comment. In spite of her large brood Cissy wasn't exactly a maternal creature and had happily admitted in the past that she let the older children take care of the younger ones when she was at work. Her husband had a job at the ironworks and worked shifts, so it seemed to Rose that the bairns mostly brought themselves up.

Another customer stopped at the stall and Cissy made herself scarce, but the meeting with Major Bembridge had disturbed Rose and for the rest of the day she felt unsettled. Later that night as she lay in bed she found herself going over the incident, picturing his rugged face and deep-set grey eyes before she realized what she was doing and gave herself a mental talking-to. She would probably never see him again, nor did she want to, she told herself firmly. And even if he was interested in her – which could be purely her imagination – she didn't have to worry about it. There had been lots of men over the last four years since she had been in Consett who had made it plain that given an ounce of encouragement they would like to take her out, but that encouragement had never been forthcoming, and the last person she'd consider as a suitor would be a member of the upper classes. She agreed with Cissy – that would be prone to disaster from day one and no good could come from it.

Nevertheless, she found it difficult to fall asleep in spite of her exhaustion, a restlessness gripping her that saw her down in the kitchen at two in the morning drinking hot cocoa as she gazed up at the criss-cross of paper chains dangling from the ceiling that she and Betsy had made that evening. She needed to get on with the next stage of her life, that was the problem. Once she found suitable premises and set up her business she'd have too much to do to waste time on idle thoughts, and she had no need to be anxious anyway. Nothing had changed, everything was just the same as it had been yesterday and the day before and the ones before that. It was, *it was*.

Chapter Seventeen

'It's Christmas Eve, Mam.'

'Aye, I know, hinny.' Rose smiled down at her daughter. She'd just gone into Betsy's room to wake her up for breakfast, but as soon as she had opened the door the child had sat bolt upright in the bed, obviously having been awake for some time, her shiny chestnut curls tousled about her elfin face.

'I can hang my stocking up tonight for Santa.'

'You can indeed, but before that I've got a surprise for you so why don't you come down for breakfast and I'll tell you what it is.'

Betsy was out of bed like a shot, and pulling on her dressing gown she followed her mother downstairs. Once in the kitchen she quickly washed her hands in the scullery and then wriggled herself onto the bench at the kitchen table, her face expectant. As Rose deposited her bowl of porridge in front of her, she said, 'What's the surprise, Mam?'

Rose had been looking forward to this moment for

weeks. 'Well,' she said softly, 'I thought there might be a little girl that I know who would like to go to the pantomime this afternoon, but of course I could be wrong?'

Her answer was Betsy flinging herself on her as she screamed with delight. 'Really? Really, Mam?'

'Really, my pet.' Disentangling the child, Rose kissed the top of her head. 'Now eat your porridge, and we've got bacon and sausages and black pudding today because it's Christmas Eve.'

The look Betsy bestowed on her was so blissful that Rose had to laugh. She had already lit the fire in the front room so it was warm in there, and once Betsy had finished her breakfast and got dressed, they played for most of the morning with a doll's house she had bought her the year before, the Christmas tree in a corner – which they'd decorated with tinsel and glass baubles and tiny silver bells – casting a festive glow over the room.

For the first time since Alexander Bembridge had come to her stall at the market, Rose felt relaxed. In spite of telling herself she was being ridiculous, she'd been on tenterhooks every day expecting he might appear. She was probably making a mountain out of a molehill after what Cissy had said, and the chances were that he didn't like her in *that* way at all, but nevertheless she knew she had been as jumpy as a cat on a hot tin roof. But now she had four days with Betsy and she intended to make the most of them.

She couldn't wait to see Betsy's face on Christmas

morning when she saw what Santa had brought her – a little shop with real scales, a beautifully dressed baby doll, a number of storybooks and games, and a big jar of all Betsy's favourite confectionery including the whipped cream bonbons and lemon squirts she was particularly fond of. It was going to be a lovely Christmas.

After lunch they got ready for the pantomime, Betsy hopping about like an excited cricket and quite unable to stay still while Rose did the child's hair and put a new velvet ribbon on her ponytail of curls.

It was snowing again as they left the house, big fat flakes that warned of more to come. Betsy skipped along at her mother's side as though she was on springs, causing several passers-by to smile understandingly. When they reached the Royal Theatre they joined the crowd of people in the foyer of gilt-edged mirrors and dark red velvet, Betsy's eyes nearly popping out of her head at the splendour of it all.

Rose stood in the throng of excited children and indulgent parents and grandparents, holding Betsy's hand. Her daughter's first pantomime. How Davey would have loved to be here. She always brought him naturally into conversations with Betsy so he wasn't a stranger, but of course the child had no memories of her father herself. When Betsy had started school she had asked why she didn't have grandparents and aunties and uncles like the other bairns, why it was just the two of them. She'd explained that her own parents were dead and that Davey's lived a long way away along with their other relations. For the time being Betsy had been content with that. It helped that Amy and Frank had taken on the role of auntie and uncle, and Amy's parents were fond of Betsy too and treated her much the same as they did Daisy's bairns. They'd been invited to the inn for Christmas Day dinner and tea along with Amy and Frank and Daisy's family.

An usherette with a jaunty pillbox hat and smart uniform which clung to her curves was taking people's tickets and directing them into the theatre, and as they joined the queue, a voice said, 'Mrs O'Leary. What a surprise. You're going to the pantomime too?'

Her heart stopping, she turned to see Alexander Bembridge with a boy and a girl about Betsy's age behind her. Bairns. He'd got bairns, was her first thought, and in spite of herself she felt a keen sense of disappointment and vaguely being let down. It made her voice stiff when she said, 'Hello, Mr Bembridge,' inclining her head with a polite smile.

'These are my godchildren, Rosaleen and Nicholas, who I get to spoil at regular intervals when I'm home on leave. Their father is my oldest friend.'

Godchildren. They weren't his. She smiled at the pair of them, saying, 'This is Betsy, my daughter. I think she must be about your age.'

It was the little boy who said, 'I'm six and Rosaleen's five,' as he stepped forward, holding out his hand. 'How do you do?'

His sister followed suit, and as Rose shook their hands she wondered what their godfather thought of Betsy, who was hiding behind her skirts. 'What beautiful manners,' she said to Alexander. 'I'm afraid Betsy is shy with strangers.' The two children were dressed beautifully too, the girl in particular who was wearing a red velvet coat and hat with a white fur trim and carrying a white fur muff.

Alexander crouched down and smiled at Betsy. 'Have you been to the pantomime before?'

Betsy shook her head.

'Then you are in for a treat. It's Mother Goose this year and can you keep a secret?'

Betsy nodded solemnly.

'Those eggs of hers are real gold. Think of that.'

'Really, Uncle Alex? Are they?' Rosaleen spoke up, her eyes wide.

'Most certainly,' said Alexander as he straightened. Rose caught the conspiratorial look that passed between his godson and himself, like that of two adults indulging a child, and thought how close they must be and how grown up the little boy appeared.

The foyer had been emptying as they talked and now Rose said, 'I think it's about to begin,' wanting nothing more than to end the conversation.

'We've got a box, would you care to join us?'

He must have noticed that the tickets she was holding were for the stalls. Her voice stiff again, Rose said, 'Thank you, but no,' and to the children, 'I hope you enjoy the pantomime.'

'Perhaps a drink in the interval then?'

'We really must take our seats.' She knew it was rude to avoid answering him but for the life of her she didn't know what to say. What if someone she knew saw her associating with him? They'd immediately jump to the wrong conclusion. 'Goodbye,' she said politely, guiding Betsy before her to where the usherette was waiting by the door into the auditorium.

As they entered the dimly lit interior her heart was still racing nineteen to the dozen. For him to be here today and not only that but making a point of speaking to her too. As for the invitation to join him and the children in his box, well, it was absurd. Surely he must have known that?

Down in the orchestra pit the musicians were tuning up as the usherette showed them to their seats, and almost immediately the lights faded, much to her relief. She was vitally aware that somewhere above her, looking down, Alexander would be able to see her and she felt as tense as a coiled spring. It was only Betsy grasping her hand in excitement as the orchestra began the opening tune and the tasselled drapes swished apart that brought her out of the maelstrom of her thoughts. This was Betsy's day, she told herself, suddenly feeling angry with Alexander Bembridge for intruding on it and taking her attention away from her daughter. She wanted to enjoy every moment of it with her.

Betsy gasped in wonder, glancing up at her mother with shining eyes as the pantomime began – a whirl of colour erupted on the stage and the compère introduced the story. The outlandish costumes, vivid make-up and wigs of the performers all added to the spectacle, and gradually Betsy's rapt delight in the proceedings cast a spell over Rose too so that she almost forgot about Alexander Bembridge. Almost.

When the interval came, the usherette walked down the front of the stalls with a little tray attached to her neck by ribboned cord holding drinks and ice creams. Some folk had left their seats and gone into the foyer or to the bar area, but quite a few were still in the auditorium now the lights had come on again. Rose went and got Betsy a bottle of juice and an ice cream which she ate in her seat, chattering about the huge goose and the big gold eggs and the magician until the lights dimmed again and the second half of the show began. It was only then that Rose realized just how tensely she'd been holding herself, expecting any moment a hand on her shoulder and a repeat of the invitation to join Alexander and his godchildren for drinks.

As the show came to an end and the encores finally gave way, they donned their coats and then joined the throng slowly filing out of the auditorium. Betsy was still feverishly excited and red-cheeked but Rose found herself responding to the child's chatter with only half her mind. The other half was focused on the possibility that she might run into Alexander again as they left the theatre.

They were halfway across the vestibule when she saw him. It wasn't difficult – he towered above most of the men present. He was scanning the crowd and as he caught sight of her he smiled and nodded and then proceeded through the doors of the theatre into the street. She hesitated, but the sheer volume of people leaving carried them forward towards the exit and as they walked down the steps of the theatre she saw it must have been snowing heavily all the time they were inside, and it was still coming down.

He was waiting for her, standing to one side of the stream of folk, flanked by his godchildren. 'Mrs O'Leary.' He raised his hand as he called and several people turned and stared for a moment.

Highly embarrassed, Rose considered ignoring him but feeling that he was quite capable of calling again and not wanting to make matters worse, she took Betsy's hand and made her way over to where he was standing.

'So,' he said to Betsy as they reached him, 'what did you think of Mother Goose? Would you like one of her big golden eggs to take home?'

Betsy shook her head. 'It would make her sad if one of her eggs was stolen.'

'Well yes, yes, it would, I hadn't considered that.' His smile included Rose but she didn't smile back, hotly aware of the interested glances they were attracting. Everything about Alexander Bembridge, even the way he held himself, stated that he was from the top echelons of society, so what – people would be thinking – was such a man doing talking to someone like her? 'You're clearly a kind and thoughtful little girl, Betsy.'

As Betsy dimpled at him, Rose said coolly, 'We really

must be making our way home, Mr Bembridge,' her voice warmer as she said to the two children, 'Have a lovely Christmas.'

'Let me offer you a lift, Mrs O'Leary. I've got my carriage over there.' He turned and gestured with his hand and she saw a large carriage parked a little way down the street with a coachman standing impassively by the two horses.

'No, no, thank you. It's not far.'

'Please, I insist. Even a short walk in this weather is prone to mishap, the pavements are treacherous.'

'Really, I couldn't trouble you unnecessarily.'

Her voice had been firm but his was firmer when he said, 'If you or the child turned your ankle and were laid low for Christmas I would never forgive myself.'

This was ridiculous. What was the matter with the man?

'If I see you safely to your door I shall be able to enjoy my Christmas dinner all the more, Mrs O'Leary, rather than wondering if some ill has befallen you.'

His eyes held hers and in spite of herself she found she couldn't look away. A deep twilight was falling and with the snowstorm, perhaps no one would notice if she rode with him in the carriage? Almost immediately she countered this with, don't be silly, of course folk would notice and tongues would wag if she arrived at the house in his company. A fine carriage like his stopping at her doorstep would be noted for sure.

'Shall we?' He gestured again towards the waiting

coach and horses, and telling herself that if she persisted in her refusal it would only prolong the awkwardness, she inclined her head in defeat. Short of being downright rude, she had no option.

The coachman was holding the door of the carriage open as they approached, and once the three children had scrambled up the steep steps, Alexander's hand at her elbow assisted her inside. Betsy's eyes were like saucers as she took in the plush leather seats and quilted sides and roof, and as Rose sat down beside her, opposite Alexander's godchildren, he joined them, sitting between Rosaleen and Nicholas with an easy air that was all at odds to the way she was feeling.

Once she had given her address to the inscrutable coachman the door closed and the next minute they were off, Betsy clutching her hand tightly and staring out of the window in rapt fascination as the shops and house windows glowed through the falling snow.

Alexander broke the silence when he said quietly, 'I was sorry to hear about your husband, Mrs O'Leary. It must have been difficult for you with a little one to care for.'

She was startled into looking straight at him. So he *had* been making enquiries about her to the market manager. She hadn't imagined it. 'Initially, I suppose, but we do very well on our own now.'

There had been a pointedness to her reply but he merely smiled genially. 'I don't doubt it. You are clearly a very resourceful woman and I'm sure business must be

booming if those tarts were anything to go by. Where did
you learn to cook like that?'

'I've just always loved it, that's all.'

'Well, you have a true gift. Some of our army cooks
could do with a few lessons from you. They say a soldier
marches on his stomach but if that was true I'm afraid
we'd be a poor lot overall. Still, one can get used to
anything if it's necessary.'

But it hadn't been necessary, not for him. He had
chosen to go into the army against his family's wishes.

Her face must have given her away because he leaned
forward slightly. 'What is it?'

She thought about prevaricating for a moment but then
found herself saying, 'If something is unavoidable, I
suppose that is true.'

'But that wasn't the case for me?'

She hoped the darkness in the carriage was hiding her
blushes. Now she did prevaricate. 'Was it?'

He laughed softly. 'You should take up fencing. You
would be very good at it.'

She stared at him. He didn't seem in the least offended.

He opened his mouth to say something more but before
he could, his goddaughter had tapped his arm saying,
'That man, Uncle Alex, why is he dancing like that?' Tram
cars loaded to the hilt with Christmas shoppers had passed
them, and the pavements were equally crowded, but now
they all looked to where Rosaleen pointed and saw a man,
still with the red dust of the ironworks on him, doing a
kind of Irish jig as he lurched on and off the pavement.

Quite seriously, Alexander said, 'He's just full of the festive spirit, sweetheart, that's all. He's happy that it's Christmas,' and as his gaze met Rose's he smiled and she smiled back.

'He's drunk.' Nicholas's voice held a bitterness that was all at odds with his age. 'Like Father gets sometimes.'

'*Nicholas.*' Alexander didn't shout but there was steel in the reprimand and suddenly Rose could see how this man could control the soldiers beneath him.

The atmosphere in the carriage had changed completely and as Rose felt Betsy move closer in to her she put her arm round the child. Rosaleen had turned from the window to stare at her godfather and Nicholas had sunk back in his seat, hunching his shoulders and clearly trying not to cry. After a moment Rose saw Alexander reach out and take the boy's hand, and as Nicholas looked up at him, he said very softly, 'Your father needs all your support and help. Remember we talked about that? This will pass but for the time being you need to be strong for your mother and sister. I wouldn't ask this of you if I wasn't sure you were man enough.'

The small boy gave a tremulous smile and nodded, and Rose was relieved to see that the coach had turned into her street and a moment later had drawn up outside her house. The coachman jumped down almost before the horses had stopped and opened the door, and Rose handed Betsy to him before alighting herself. Before she'd had a chance to say her goodbyes, Alexander followed her out of the carriage, and as the coachman climbed back into his seat he stood with her on the pavement. 'I need to explain.' His voice was soft and low. 'If you will permit me? Nicholas does not normally behave in that way and I would not wish you to think ill of him.'

'Really, there's no need.'

'Nicholas's father was with me eighteen months ago on a posting to India. There was some local unrest but nothing serious, mere skirmishes here and there, but then one night a mob attacked the Hindu quarter and we were sent to restore order. Different religions and not least the caste system makes for a volatile combination at times. Lawrence and two of his men were chasing a group of natives who had attacked a young mother and her children and they followed them onto the rooftops. A terrace gave way and they plunged some ten or fifteen feet to the ground. Lawrence's men sustained nothing more than cuts and bruises. Lawrence broke his back. He'll be in a wheelchair for the rest of his life.'

'That's awful.' She stared at him, aghast.

'He's only been out of hospital a few months but he's finding it hard, hence the drink. There have been a couple of' – he hesitated – 'difficult incidents at home which unfortunately Nicholas has witnessed, one with the children's mother. Lawrence is penitent afterwards but the whole situation is damnable.'

She didn't know what to say.

'I'm sorry, I wouldn't have spoken this way but for Nicholas saying what he did. I felt I must give an explanation of the circumstances. Nicholas is very fond of his mother and he hates seeing her distressed. Of course he loves his father too but Lawrence was away for large chunks of time before the accident, so the bond is not the same.'

'I understand,' she said quietly, 'and you really didn't have to explain, Mr Bembridge.' Should she be calling him Major Bembridge? She didn't know and didn't like to ask.

'Yes, I did.' What was it about this woman that had captured him from the first moment he had laid eyes on her? She was beautiful of course, but he knew other beautiful women and had slept with quite a few, but she – she was different. His eyes were riveted on her face and he felt as though he could stand here for the rest of his life just looking at her. She had a quiet strength about her, a composure and natural dignity that he'd rarely come across before.

Rose was feeling anything but composed, the beating of her heart threatening to suffocate her. He shouldn't be standing here talking to her and looking at her like that; she had already noticed the curtains in the house across the street twitching. Somehow she managed to say evenly, 'Thank you for seeing us home and Merry Christmas. I must get Betsy in the warm.'

'Of course, of course.' He glanced up into the sky as though he had only just noticed the falling snow, and then his gaze rested on her again for a moment before he looked down at Betsy and said, 'I hope you have a lovely Christmas and Santa Claus brings you everything you want, Betsy, but just in case he forgets something with being so busy tonight, you can go to the shops after Christmas with your mother and buy a present for yourself.' He had put his hand in his pocket as he had been speaking and now pushed a coin into Betsy's little fingers.

As Rose began to protest he smiled and said softly, 'Merry Christmas,' before turning and climbing into the carriage.

She didn't wait for it to trundle off before she opened the door and went inside, but once she had shut it she stood listening for a few moments, her head whirling. Who would have thought she would run into him again at the pantomime of all places? And with his godchildren? He hadn't spoken of a wife or sweetheart and surely if he had either they would have been with him today helping with the children? And then she mentally shook her head at herself. What did it matter if he had a wife or sweetheart, for goodness' sake. It was none of her business.

'Mammy, look.' Betsy held out her hand and in it was the coin Alexander had pressed on her. It was a gold sovereign.

Rose stared at the coin and then at Betsy's bright eyes. It was far too much for a small child; he must have given it in error. And then she sighed. She could be wrong but she doubted if Alexander Bembridge did anything in error. She was going to have to be on her guard in the future because if he imagined that a ride in his grand carriage and a gold sovereign could turn her head he had another think coming. The last man in the world to get involved with in any shape or form would be him.

'Who was that lady and little girl, Uncle Alex?' As the coach turned for Castleside, Nicholas, his demeanour back to normal, moved to the other side opposite Alexander and his sister so he could see out of the window better.

'Just friends of mine, Nicholas.'

'She's very beautiful, isn't she,' piped up Rosaleen. 'Like the fairy queen in the picture book you gave me for my birthday. I liked the little girl too. Can she come and play with me one day?'

'Of course she can't,' scoffed her brother. 'When we go home it would be much too far away for Betsy to visit. Wouldn't it, Uncle Alex?'

'I'm afraid so.' Alexander smiled at his goddaughter. 'But I'm glad you liked Betsy, Rosaleen.' In an effort to distract them, he added, 'What did you enjoy most about the pantomime?'

'The pretty ladies,' Rosaleen said immediately, earning a snort of contempt from Nicholas.

'You can see ladies in nice dresses any day of the week. What about the magician? You liked him, didn't you?'

Rosaleen nodded. 'But not as much as the ladies.'

'For goodness' sake. They only danced and sang.'

'I don't care. I liked them best.'

Alexander let them argue amicably as the coachman

encouraged the horses into a light trot. His mind was filled with the image of the woman he'd just left, the woman who had occupied his thoughts for days. He had made a conscious effort not to return to the market. It had been a pure fluke that he'd strolled through it that day. If Ebony hadn't thrown a shoe necessitating him finding the nearest blacksmith he would never have met her, and he knew no good could come from his interest in her. She was a young working-class widow with a small child; his parents would have a fit if they learned of any association between them, besides which he was only home on leave occasionally. But she had bowled him over – that was the only way he could describe how he felt to himself. Certainly no other woman had had such an immediate and intense impact on him. He couldn't dwell on it, he knew that, and it would be easier once he was back with the regiment. But first he had Christmas and the New Year to get through. It was going to take all his patience and then some to cope with things at home.

He groaned inwardly. One of the reasons he had persuaded Lawrence and Estelle and the children to come to Highfield Hall over the festive period was to try and offset his mother's almost obsessional desire to match-make. With Lawrence in the state he was in, his mother had conceded that a quiet Christmas and New Year was best, but that hadn't stopped her inviting the Conways and the Charlton-Smythes for a few days and both families had unmarried daughters. But he *had* been concerned, deeply concerned, about his friend's state of mind, he reassured himself as a pang of guilt made itself felt. The letter Estelle had written to him in secret last month had been desperate and he knew she was beside herself about the effect the situation was having on Nicholas. The boy was angry with his father and although he could understand that, he had to try and nip it in the bud and help him understand. Nicholas was intelligent far beyond his years but he was also an impatient and spirited little boy and even at six years old suffered fools badly. Rosaleen had a much sweeter and gentler nature, like her mother. He supposed if he was being honest Nicholas was the spitting image of his father in nature as well as looks, which was why the two clashed. Lawrence had never been one to make allowances for another's shortcomings.

He gazed unseeing out of the window into the whirling snow.

Whatever, it was a damn mess and for the life of him he didn't know how to put it right. Lawrence's time in the army was over and, like himself, it was the only thing his friend had ever wanted to do. They had met at prep school and been close companions ever since, going to university together and getting their commissions on the same day.

It wasn't long before the carriage was bowling between the iron gates and onto the gravel drive which led to Highfield Hall itself. Alexander's grandfather had had the house built to his own specifications, and he had been a man with a keen appreciation of beauty in all its forms. The drive was wide and could take four coaches abreast, and the manicured gardens and sculptured trees were even lovely in the winter with a coating of snow, but the house was magnificent. It was made of mellow stone with two huge wings either side, and as the drive widened out into an enormous forecourt and Alexander looked at his home he experienced a sense of pleasure. This hadn't always been the case. In the couple of years when he had been at loggerheads with his parents about joining the army, the whole estate had felt more like a prison. A luxurious, beautiful and comfortable one, but a prison nonetheless.

Now as the massive front door was opened, a footman came hurrying down the curved steps to where the carriage had pulled up just in time to open the door allowing Alexander to descend, whereupon he helped the children down one by one. It was quite dark by now but the snow and not least the brilliance of the lights shining from many of the windows in the house lit up the area like day.

'They are waiting for you in the drawing room, Mr Alexander, for cocktails before dinner, and Nanny has the children's tea ready in the nursery.'

Cocktails before dinner. Here we go, Alexander thought. No doubt the ladies would be in their finery and outdoing each other to shine – the Conways and the Charlton-Smythes, that was. They had all arrived for Christmas that morning, and he had been immensely relieved he had booked the pantomime for Nicholas and Rosaleen and could legitimately leave everyone to it after lunch. He had seen Lawrence to his suite of rooms in the east wing first, smiling wryly when his friend had remarked that being an invalid did have certain compensations at times. Lawrence disliked high society almost as much as he did.

Once inside the grand hall, where a number of glass chandeliers sparkled like stars, Alexander said in an aside to the footman, 'Tell my mother I'm going to change before I join them, would you?' Taking his godchildren by the hand, he walked them up the magnificent staircase to where their nanny was waiting.

When he had waved them off he went to his own quarters which were at the back of the house overlooking the sweeping grounds and pleasure gardens, which in turn led to carefully controlled woodland and a large lake with a sprawling summerhouse and boathouse. In the summer his mother liked to have garden parties there. She was a great one for entertaining, he thought a trifle cynically. They had their own farm on the estate which kept them supplied with everything they required but this was tucked well away from the main house so no animal noises or smells invaded his mother's delicate senses.

His father's valet, who also looked after him when he was home on leave, had laid out his evening clothes on his bed, and now he changed into the formal attire his mother insisted on for dining even when it was just the three of them. 'One has to maintain standards at all times' was one of her stock phrases and he'd heard it since his childhood.

He had been a trial to his poor mother, he thought ruefully as he checked his reflection in the mirror. She had come from the very top of the upper class, having connections with royalty, and had married beneath her to some extent when she had met his father, but it had been a love match. They were still in love thirty-five years later and his father worshipped the ground his mother walked on. He knew they would have liked more children after him, but when it hadn't happened unfortunately his mother had poured the full extent of her maternal smothering on him.

The harshness of the thought made him feel guilty, not an uncommon occurrence where his mother was concerned. When he looked back over his life thus far he always seemed to have been rebelling against her in some way or another, and of course his father always supported her no matter what. It was good they were so devoted to each other on the one hand, and on the other it irritated him to death at times, but he had to admit that the feeling between them was what he wanted when he chose his own life partner.

He turned from the mirror but instead of going straight downstairs walked over to the large bay window. He drew back the heavy velvet drapes which the maid had closed earlier. The snow was falling more lightly now and the scene in front of him was a winter wonderland, its pure beauty making him catch his breath.

Rose O'Leary. He'd had no idea she even existed days ago, so how come she was filling his every waking moment? When he had caught sight of her today no power on earth could have stopped him approaching her, even though he knew it was madness. His dark brows drew together in a frown. What was her history? All the market manager had seemed to know was that she and the child had arrived in Consett some years ago. But from where? How could he find out more about her? Did he *want* to find out more when any relationship between them was impossible?

The answer was instantaneous and he groaned inwardly. She had shaken him to the depths of his being and the ironic thing was, she was completely unaware of it. Not only that but she had made it clear she wanted nothing to do with him, and he couldn't blame her. What the hell was he going to do? If he hadn't seen her again today he might just have been able to put out the fuse that had been lit inside him when he first saw her in the market, but now it was too late. He closed his eyes for a moment, and again he asked himself, what was he going to do?

The answer to this in the immediate here and now came in the form of the footman knocking on his door and calling, 'I'm sorry, Mr Alexander, but the mistress wonders how long you will be?'

'I'll be down in a minute.' He breathed in and out slowly a few times, telling himself to relax. He had this evening to get through and it wouldn't be easy with his mother's eagle eyes watching his every move with the girls she'd lined up for him downstairs. The slightest interest on his part would have her hearing wedding bells, he knew that. Thank goodness Lawrence was here to take the edge off the evening, but that in itself was another problem; he would have to make sure his friend curtailed his alcohol consumption for Estelle's sake as much as anything. Lawrence hadn't been physically violent with her but the old saying that you always hurt the one you love was certainly true in his case, and words could do more damage than any blow.

Resigning himself to a tense and stressful evening, he left his rooms, and as he descended the staircase he could hear that someone – probably one of the Conway or Charlton-Smythe girls – was sitting at the grand piano in the drawing room playing a Christmas carol while the rest of the assorted company joined in. As he opened the drawing room door to the strains of 'God Rest Ye Merry, Gentlemen' and a host of bright faces turned towards him, he forced a smile to his lips. He had never felt less merry in his life.

Chapter Eighteen

'Now let me get this right, lass. You say you want to take on old Cunningham's bakery shop, is that right? Just you. On your own?'

'Yes, that's right, Mr Preston. I've been told you own the premises along with the gentlemen's outfitters next door.'

'Aye, I do. I do sure enough but . . .'

Rose waited a moment and then said, 'But?'

'A bakery, lass, is hard work, and Cunningham only just managed to keep his head above water afore he up and died. The rent isn't cheap, I'm warning you now, not with it being in Middle Street which is a prime location if I do say so myself, and of course there's the living accommodation above.'

'I know, that's why I want it.'

Albert Preston stared at the young woman on his doorstep. It was five o'clock on New Year's Eve and inside the house his wife and daughters were getting ready for the neighbours coming round later. He'd shut up the gents' outfitters early and had been home just a few minutes. 'How did you hear about the shop being available? Cunningham only died two days ago.'

'Wilbur Croft told his daughter, who told me. I understand Mr Cunningham was drinking there on Tuesday night when he had his heart attack. It was a terrible shock for everyone.'

'Aye, I dare say.' Privately Albert thought that if Stan Cunningham had spent less time at the inn and more at his bakery his business would have benefited, but it didn't do to speak ill of the dead. Stan had been different when his wife and two sons were alive, but when the cholera took them umpteen years ago he'd changed.

'I wanted to come and see you before anyone else approached you about the premises, Mr Preston. I've had a stall on the market for the last few years but I know the time is right for me to go to the next stage.' He was still looking at her doubtfully and now Rose said, 'I can pay the rent in advance, however many weeks you require.'

Albert shook his head uncertainly. 'Look, come in a minute, you can't stand there getting snowed on, and we'll discuss it, all right?'

'Thank you. Thank you so much.' As Rose stepped into the hall of the large terraced house, a woman came bustling out of the kitchen at the far end bringing with her the smell of baking. On catching sight of Rose, she said, 'Why, it's Mrs O'Leary from the market. I'm right, aren't I, lass? What on earth are you doing here on New Year's Eve?'

As her husband quickly explained the reason for Rose's presence, Ruth Preston ushered Rose into their front room where a bright fire was burning in the blackleaded fireplace. 'Warm yourself, lass,' she said kindly, before turning to her husband and adding, 'Mrs O'Leary will make a go of the bakery if anyone can. Remember that cherry shortbread you liked so much at Christmas? That was hers. I'll go and make a cup of tea while you discuss details,' and so saying she beamed at Rose before leaving and shutting the door behind her.

Albert's voice was wry when he said, 'Well, it looks like you've got yourself a bakery, lass, if you want it, but you ought to come and see the shop and the living accommodation too before you decide. The rent's monthly and I was charging Stan Cunningham a pound. That all right with you?'

'That's fine,' said Rose eagerly. 'When can I see it, Mr Preston?' It was cheaper than she had expected considering their living accommodation was included.

He smiled. 'You're keen, lass. I'll say that for you. Now ordinarily I'd say in the morning but with it being New Year's Day an' all, and considering we've got a bit of a do going on here tonight and I might well be nursing something of a thick head, shall we say tomorrow afternoon about two o'clock? How does that suit?'

'That's wonderful.'

'I'll meet you there then,' he said, just as his wife came in with a tray of tea and biscuits.

Half an hour later Rose was walking back towards

Amy and Frank's house, where she had left Betsy. Her mind was buzzing. This was going to work, she knew it was. It had come just at the right time and although she wouldn't have wished poor Mr Cunningham to die like that, a bakery becoming available was nothing short of a miracle. Mr Preston had explained that the contents of the shop and the furniture in the flat upstairs had all been bought by Mr Cunningham and so his nearest relative, a sister, would inherit them, but he was sure the sister would be quite happy for her to make a reasonable offer. She wouldn't want the contents of the flat – she had her own furniture – but to be able to buy the bakery paraphernalia lock, stock and barrel would be marvellous.

She looked up into the millions of snowflakes falling from a laden sky. They'd had a brief respite from the weather for a few days after Christmas and a thaw had set in, only to freeze over the last twenty-four hours making the pavements treacherous with black ice – and now with the snow, walking was fraught with danger. Once Christmas Day was over at the inn, she and Betsy had snuggled in together at home, her daughter playing with her new toys most of the time. When she hadn't been playing with Betsy she had sat and read a couple of the books she had borrowed from the reading and recreation rooms at the town hall. It had been in an effort to keep her mind from wandering and returning to the subject of Alexander Bembridge, as it had the annoying habit of doing given half a chance.

It was because of Alexander that she'd decided to

extend the period at home for a few days, rather than returning to the market after Christmas as she had originally planned to do. She thought he might well pay a visit there on the pretext of buying more of her wares before he returned to the army.

The whole situation weighed heavy. Not because she was intimidated by him, but more that thinking about him caused a fluttering in her chest she could well do without. She kept telling herself that she was being ridiculous, but there was something about him that drew her like a moth to a flame and she had never experienced that before. Of course, it could be that he was different to the working-class men she came into contact with every day, but it was more than that too.

She sighed as she began walking again. She didn't need this complication in her life, she really didn't, but perhaps it was only a problem if she let it become one? And she might never see him again. For all she knew he had no intention of coming to the market or trying to see her again. He came from a different world to her after all, and in spite of what Cissy had said, he didn't strike her as the sort of man who would try to take advantage of his position. But maybe she was being naive?

Anyway, all in all when Amy had called round to tell her about the bakery it seemed the answer to her prayers. She'd be able to move house and finish at the market, and as far as he was concerned she would have disappeared. This strange, disturbing and tenuous thread between them would be broken. He had his army career and would be away from home for large parts of the year, and the likelihood was that their paths would never cross. After all, Cissy had said she'd never seen him in the market before, and folk like the Bembridges didn't mix with the working class except in their role of employers.

When she arrived at Amy's house she spent a little time there, telling her friend and Frank what had happened, and was touched when they both immediately offered their services to help her with the move. She had been invited to the inn for New Year's Eve with Amy and Frank but had declined. It had been nice to spend Christmas Day there and Betsy had had a lovely time playing with Daisy's girls, but she didn't want to keep her up to see the New Year in, besides which the jollity and almost frantic merriment that went on during this night at the end of the year always made her feel she was on the outside looking in. It was strange, but she felt less lonely quietly sitting at home with Betsy asleep upstairs than being in a crowd of people who would be drinking, singing and dancing. Last year she had raised a glass to Davey as the kitchen clock had struck twelve, telling him she loved him and missed him and that Betsy was growing up strong and healthy and he would be proud of her. She purposely didn't let herself think about Nathaniel or the miller or her life in the workhouse, believing that it was right to enter the new year with good thoughts and not bad.

Once Betsy was in bed that evening, Rose found she

couldn't settle. It wasn't just the forthcoming meeting with Mr Preston and all the potential for the future it held that was making her restless, she knew that, but she didn't want to examine her feelings too closely. She went into the front room and tidied Betsy's toys; it was cosy and warm, a decent fire still burning in the little grate. Sinking down into one of the two armchairs the room possessed, she gazed about her. Little had changed since the day she and Betsy had moved in. The two armchairs upholstered in pale green damask; the large shop-bought rug in autumn colours and the olive green curtains at the window still pleased her. She hadn't wanted the heavy dark colours that most people favoured or mahogany furniture, and she certainly didn't want to crowd the room. Betsy's doll's house stood on the coffee table in the bay of the window with her other toys stacked next to it in a big wooden box that Rose had painted the same creamy pale yellow as the walls. Part of her would be sad to leave this little house where she and Betsy had been happy, but she would make their new home the way she wanted it.

When the knock came at the front door just before nine o'clock she knew she had been expecting it. She sat quite still for a few moments and then when it came again, got up slowly, her heart racing. *Of course, it might not be him.* Even as the thought came she dismissed it. It was Alexander Bembridge. No one else would come to the front door rather than round the back, New Year's Eve or no.

When she opened the door he was standing on the pavement and because of the two steps leading from the house his head was on a level with hers. 'Why, Mr Bembridge.' Somehow she managed to keep her voice steady and infuse a slightly surprised note into it.

'Hello.' His voice was husky and deep.

Out of the corner of her eye she could see a horse and trap tied to the lamp post a little further down the street and inwardly sighed. Her neighbours were going to have a field day with this. 'How can I help you?' she said coolly.

If he answered that truthfully she would bang the door in his face, he thought with dark humour. Gathering himself, because the sight of her had rocked him, he said, 'I wondered if I could have a word with you?'

For a split second she considered saying no and shutting the door or keeping him standing outside. If she did the former he was quite capable of knocking again, and the latter was keeping him in full view of the houses opposite. With no softening in her face or manner, she said, 'You had better come in for a minute with the weather being so inclement.' There was a thick coating of snow on his hat and the shoulders of his greatcoat.

'Thank you.' As she stood aside he passed her into the hall and she caught a whiff of the faintly lemony, delicious scent she had smelled before at the pantomime when he was close. It made her stomach muscles tighten and her heart beat faster.

After closing the door she led the way into the front room, her senses screaming. Indicating one of the armchairs, she said, 'Won't you be seated?'

Again he said, 'Thank you,' but then made no effort to sit down. He stared at her, and on the perimeter of his mind he was conscious of the fact that the room reflected the woman who lived in it – it was unusual, light, warm, charming.

'You said you wanted to talk to me?' Funnily enough his obvious discomposure was having a calming effect. 'Can I get you a hot drink, Mr Bembridge?'

'Alex. Please call me Alex.'

She blinked. 'I don't think—'

'Please.' His voice was very soft and as their gaze held, hers wary and unsure, his full of something that she recognized but would not put a name to, he said, 'I know I shouldn't have come here, I really do know that and I have fought against it, believe me, but' – he spread his hands in a helpless gesture – 'I leave for the regiment the day after tomorrow and I couldn't go without seeing you. It's as simple as that.' And then he shook his head at himself. 'That's a stupid thing to say, isn't it, because this isn't simple at all.'

'Mr Bembridge—'

'Alex, please.'

He seemed to fill her little room. Clearing her throat, she said, 'I don't know what you expected when you came here tonight but you are right, you shouldn't have come. If I have somehow misled you into thinking—'

'No.' He interrupted her vehemently. 'No, you haven't misled me.'

'Then why have you come?'

'Because I couldn't help myself, and please believe me, I have come with no expectation at all.'

He was such a big man, he seemed to be towering over her and, her voice weaker than she would have liked it to be, she said, 'Please sit down and I'll make a hot drink before you leave.'

For a moment she thought he was going to say more but instead, after one tortured glance, he sank into the armchair she had indicated.

She was all fingers and thumbs in the kitchen but eventually she had prepared a tray with cups of hot chocolate and slices of the rich Christmas cake she had made. When she walked into the room he leaped up to take the tray from her and as their hands touched fleetingly she felt the impact like an electric shock.

'It's all right,' she said as calmly as her racing heart would allow, 'but if you would lift Betsy's doll's house off the little table there, I'll put the tray on it.'

Once they were both seated, the table standing between them, she passed him the hot chocolate and a piece of cake. She noticed his hands were shaking and again his discomfiture eased her agitation a little. He ate a mouthful of cake and then said, 'This is delicious, perfectly delicious.'

'Thank you.' She waited until he had finished what was on his plate before she spoke again. 'I'm sorry that you felt you needed to come all this way on such a cold night, Mr Bembridge, but you must understand it is pointless, surely?' Even now the horse and trap tied up outside would be attracting the sort of interest and speculation she could well do without. The old wives hereabouts would jump to the worst conclusion and make a meal of any gossip, and unfortunately there didn't need to be a grain of truth in it for mud to stick. 'It would have been better for you to stay at home.'

And all Alexander could answer was simply, 'I know.' If she had been a different kind of woman he might have harboured some hope that one day she would consider looking favourably on him outside of marriage. He could have bought her a house or a cottage somewhere, a substantial property with a lovely garden for the child, and he would have remained faithful to her all his days. He wanted permanence with her, he knew that, and he would have considered her his wife. He had told Lawrence this when he had confided the reason for his distractedness over Christmas, and his friend had been frankly horrified.

'That would be an impossible situation, Alex. You must know that? And hear me out because I'm not necessarily thinking of you here. What about any children of your union? What label would the world put on them? But I agree that a formal marriage would be even worse, certainly for her. If she is as beautiful as you say she is the men might make allowances, but not their wives. They would destroy her. You must know deep down that the best thing, the *only* thing, to do is to stop this going any further? Return to the regiment and keep away for a long time. Time works wonders, or that's what everyone keeps telling me, anyway.' A touch of bitterness had coated his words despite the smile that had accompanied them. 'If you persist in this, you will ruin her life as well as your own, old friend.'

Remembering Lawrence's concern, Alexander stood up and walked across to the bay of the window to put some space between himself and Rose before he said what he had to say. Turning, he stared at her in silence for a long moment. 'I do realize that we come from different worlds and that any relationship between us would not be easy, but the truth of the matter is that I'm in love with you.'

Rose could feel the colour flood her cheeks and for a moment words failed her. His directness was unnerving. Gathering herself together, her voice low, she murmured, 'You don't know me at all so you cannot say that. We have only met twice.'

'Nevertheless, it is true. I'm not talking about mere attraction, but love. I have never felt like this before.'

Rose shook her head. She was more frightened of herself and the effect his declaration had had on her than Alexander. Something had leaped in her when he had spoken, something deep and primal. But this was madness, she knew that. He'd said himself that they came from different worlds, and the immense chasm between those worlds would be virtually impossible to bridge, even if she wanted to.

She had fought long and hard to get to where she

was now. She was content with her life. Her business, Betsy, her friends – it was enough. She didn't want a man, any man, taking that hard-won control away and the thought of physical intimacy terrified her. She couldn't help it but it did. She had told herself many times that Davey's gentle lovemaking hadn't been like the rape, that intimacy could be a beautiful thing in the right circumstances, but the trouble was she didn't believe it any more.

He watched the play of emotions flit across her face and wondered what she was thinking. She was a woman of mystery – he had been able to find out very little about her – but without a doubt there had been some kind of great trauma in her life. Without knowing how he knew, he was certain of it. Of course, it could be that the death of her husband had left her grief-stricken, but he felt it was more than that.

Rose took a deep breath, choosing her words carefully. 'I'm flattered that you imagine you love me but as I said, you don't know anything about me. What you feel *can* only be attraction, nothing more.'

'And you?' he said softly. 'Do you feel an attraction towards me?'

She needed to lie and kill this thing stone dead. It had come out of the blue and it was dangerous because it had already destroyed her peace of mind. She raised her head and stared at him but then the silent appeal in his dark eyes robbed her of speech. Their gaze locked for long moments, and when she spoke it was a little whisper, so low he could barely hear her. 'I can't do this, I can't. I – I want you to leave.'

'Please, don't be distressed.'

Now her chin came up slightly, her voice firmer when she said, 'Please go.'

'Are you frightened of me?' She didn't speak but her green eyes answered him, and he said urgently, 'Don't be, please don't be. I wouldn't harm a hair of your head.'

She hadn't imagined he would. It wasn't that kind of fear that was gripping her.

'Look, I have handled this badly, I am aware of that. Turning up here unannounced, what must you think of me?' He ran a hand through his thick dark hair in his agitation and for a fleeting moment she wondered what it would feel like beneath her fingers.

'I wish you no harm, please believe that if nothing else. It was just that I couldn't leave without telling you how I feel. I shall be away some time, you see, and I wondered if perhaps we could correspond? Get to know a little about each other?'

'I don't think that would be wise.'

'No, it wouldn't, but would you write all the same? As friends, purely as friends if that is what you wish. I ask for nothing more.'

She shook her head. 'I shall be moving soon, Mr Bembridge, and—'

'Moving?' The note of alarm in his voice would have been funny in other circumstances. 'You are leaving Consett?'

'No, I am not leaving the town but I plan to open a bakery so—'

Again he interrupted her. 'On your own?' And then, realizing she might take offence at his incredulity, he said hastily, 'I think that is admirable and having tasted your goods I am sure it will be a great success.'

She inclined her head. 'Thank you. But clearly I shall be very busy so . . .'

'Yes, of course, I understand.' After an ensuing few seconds of silent embarrassment he walked across to the chair at the side of which he had placed his hat and greatcoat. 'Please forgive me for disturbing you this evening and may I wish you a Happy New Year and every success with the bakery.'

Again she said, 'Thank you. Let me see you out.'

After opening the front door she stood aside for him to pass her and as he did so he paused for a moment, looking down at her. 'May I ask just one more thing of you before I leave? What is your name, your Christian name?'

He was so close she could see the black bristles on his cleft chin and a tiny nick where he must have cut himself shaving. The blood thundering through her veins, she said faintly, 'Rose. My name's Rose.'

'Rose.' He turned her name into a caress. 'It suits you, if I may say so. A winter rose, the most beautiful and delicate kind.'

She didn't move or reply, her large green eyes with their thick black lashes set in skin so fine as to appear like a child's staring at him, her mouth slightly moist.

He had never felt such burning desire as that which raced through him now, making him as hard as a rock, and he turned swiftly away before he took her into his arms and kissed her until she succumbed to his love-making. He didn't look back as he left the house and once he had climbed into the horse and trap he saw she had shut the front door.

He sat for a moment, breathing hard, his eyes shut, and for the first time in years he uttered a prayer. 'Let this be. Somehow, let this come to fruition,' he said to a God in whom he had not believed since he was in the army and had witnessed what men could do to each other in the name of religion. 'I'll do whatever it takes and I'll take on the lot of them' – his social circle, his friends and family, and especially his mother – 'if You mellow her feelings towards me.'

In spite of the disaster the evening had been, something had clarified in him nonetheless. She was the one for him. Now all he had to do was to make her understand he was the one for her, but he had no illusions about how hard that was going to be. It would be months before he was home on leave again and he just hoped the bakery she'd spoken of would keep her too busy to notice if any other men appeared on the horizon.

He ground his teeth, frustration and helplessness knotting his insides. He was a thirty-two-year-old man but he could have been a callow schoolboy still wet behind the ears, the way she affected him. He had got no encouragement from her tonight, not a word or the slightest softening in her attitude, and yet— His heart beat faster. He would swear on oath that behind that reserve and iron-clad will of hers she was attracted to him. He had known too many women in the past not to recognize the signs. He nodded to himself, remembering what had been in that last look of hers when they had stood so close they were just a breath apart.

After a minute or two he was calmer, and he clicked to the horse to start trotting down the snowy street. It was too early for revellers to be out yet, but behind closed curtains lights shone and he heard the occasional sound of piano-playing and laughter, or a child calling. Normal, everyday sounds, but tonight they caused him to feel like the loneliest man in the world. This was an alien environment to him, these working-class streets of terraced houses and small back yards packed side by side where folk lived cheek by jowl, but tonight he envied the occupants.

In deference to Lawrence his mother hadn't arranged her usual New Year's Eve ball at the house, but there was still a small soirée to get through and one of the Conway sisters in particular had made it plain that she would be more than willing to warm his bed. He didn't doubt for a moment, however, that Gwendoline's ultimate plan was to get him to marry her. He had heard from Lawrence that she'd made a name for herself with her carryings-on with some of the young bloods in London, and her parents had clamped down on her escapades, whipping her back to their estate in the country. They were anxious to see her walk up the aisle before she brought the family name further into disrepute, but according to what Estelle had learned from Gwendoline, the girl was champing at the bit to get back to London. Who better as a husband than an army man who was away most of the time and would leave her to her own devices, but with the respectability of a wedding ring on her finger?

He was on the outskirts of Consett now and as he left the town behind the tranquillity of the white landscape and the falling snow calmed him. He was in the devil of a mess, he admitted to himself, and he didn't know which end was up, but for the time being he could do nothing more. He had to return to the regiment and that was that, and to be fair, normally he couldn't wait to get back to his army pals. The social scene his parents enjoyed so much held no appeal for him, neither was he a hunting and shooting and fishing man like his father. Strange really, when he had chosen the army as his career, but the killing and shooting of defenceless animals and birds disgusted him. His father had never understood that and he knew he had disappointed him on numerous occasions.

The forecourt was brilliantly lit by lights from the windows in the house when he reached Highfield Hall, and he saw one of the stable lads waiting under a massive cedar tree, no doubt at the instructions of his mother. He'd intended to check on Ebony, his stallion, who had stumbled on some ice and strained one of his forelegs the day before, but now he reluctantly handed the reins to the lad and watched him lead the horse out of sight to the stable block at the back of the building. The front doors of the house opened in the next instant, more light flooding down the steps onto the forecourt.

'Don't tell me,' he called to the young second footman standing on the threshold as he walked towards him. 'They're waiting for me. Right?'

'Just so, sir.'

'Have the ladies finished their repertoire of music and recitations yet?'

'I couldn't rightly say, Mr Alexander, but there have been a number of renditions throughout the evening.'

'So it must surely be near suppertime? Please tell me it's near suppertime, Franklin.'

The footman tried to conceal his grin and failed. It was well known among the servants that the young master was as different from his parents as chalk from cheese. Everyone liked Mr Alexander. 'Shortly, yes, sir.'

As Alexander entered the warmth of the house, he heard what was almost certainly Gwendoline's voice lifted in song from the drawing room. She had an exceptionally fine voice, he'd give her that. It was unfortunate that in his mother's eyes such an accomplishment in a well-bred young lady was highly desirable, along with speaking a little French – and having a pedigree as long as his arm, of course.

As the footman opened the door to the drawing room, Alexander stood for a moment unnoticed on the threshold. The Christmas decorations were still in place, the magnificent tree in a corner of the room glittering as if loaded with jewels and adding its own sparkle to the splendid glass chandeliers overhead. His gaze swept over the rich scarlet and gold velvet sofas and chaise longues dotted about the vast room, the exquisite Louis XV style walnut and marquetry centre tables – a favourite with his mother – and other carefully selected furniture. Dominating one wall was the great stone fireplace in which crackling logs were piled high and shooting forth blue, yellow and red flames, a couple of his father's wolfhounds asleep on the Persian rug in front of it. It was all a picture of sumptuous opulence and grandeur, and the rich dresses and lavish jewels of the women present added to the scene.

Most of the assembled company, whether standing or sitting, were watching Gwendoline at the grand piano and she, in particular, lived up to her surroundings. Her dress glittered like a galaxy of stars and her fair hair was piled high with jewelled combs, their brilliance reflected in the necklace and bracelets she wore. As he stared at her she looked up, noticing him in the doorway, and smiled.

Suddenly, on the screen of his mind, there was a snapshot of a small snug sitting room and of the beautiful woman it contained, of a child's doll's house and the modest fire burning in the gleaming blackleaded fireplace.

He knew with all his heart where he would rather be.

Chapter Nineteen

Nathaniel lay propped against the heaped pillows on the bed, his arms behind his head, watching Maria as she stoked up the fire in the bedroom and then added another log to the crackling flames. The room was stiflingly warm, too warm for him, but Maria liked it hot. In more ways than one, he thought to himself, his gaze wandering over the voluptuous naked figure of the woman now sauntering over to him.

She reached the bed, bending over and kissing him long and hard on the lips. His hands came from behind his head and he cupped her heavy smooth breasts, feeling the nipples responding instantly to his touch. She moaned softly before straightening up and smiling sensually. 'I fetch us another bottle of wine, yes?'

He nodded and she trailed her fingers over his forehead before reaching for her black satin robe. As she pulled the belt tight and flicked back her long, dark hair, Nathaniel reflected that no one would have guessed she was approaching forty. Thirty, more like. Or even mid-twenties.

It had been one of Maria's late husband Alfonso's brothers who had told him her real age. She had been furious at the time, not just because Luigi had revealed her secret but because Alfonso's brother had been trying to warn Nathaniel off, threatening him that if he didn't leave Maria alone it would be the worse for him. It had taken Nathaniel a while to reassure her that he didn't give a monkey's cuss about her age or that she had lied to him. And in truth it didn't matter to him. Alfonso had left his wife very nicely off when he'd succumbed to a heart attack eighteen months ago. She owned the inn that was also her home, and the blacksmith's premises next door, as well as several cottages in the town of Chester-le-Street which were rented out and brought in a nice little income. She was sitting pretty. Alfonso had been an astute businessman by all accounts. Once his little empire was flourishing he had brought two of his younger brothers over from Italy to work in the kitchen of the inn, maintaining that family made the most loyal employees. He had been twenty-five years older than his wife, and according to Maria, useless in bed. She'd certainly been ripe for him, anyway, Nathaniel thought. Ravenous, in fact.

As Maria left the bedroom he sat up straighter and reached for his wine glass on the small table at the side of the bed, draining the ruby red liquid inside and smacking his lips. She knew all about wine, did Maria, probably because she had lived in Italy until she and her husband had come to England when she was just twenty-one. She'd told him all about her home country, the good food, the wine, the heat and endless days of sun under blue, blue skies. They knew how to live, did the Italians, she had said. Not like the cold English. Not that she found him cold, not in bed.

He had originally intended to stay no more than a couple of months in Chester-le-Street. He had come to the town because someone had told him on his travels that a woman answering to his description of Rose lived there and was working in a grocer's shop near the train station. The woman concerned hadn't been Rose but he had taken a room at the inn while searching her out, and Maria had needed a barman at the time, her previous one having fallen foul of the cholera and passed away just days before Nathaniel's arrival in the town. Within two weeks he had been warming Maria's bed every night and life had been so comfortable he had stayed longer than intended.

He set the wine glass back on the table, his eyes narrowing. Aye, he'd stayed nine months now. Too long. It was high time he moved on. He wouldn't have stayed this long in spite of the comforts of life with Maria if it hadn't been for the pleasure he took in knowing just how much it got under the skin of her brothers-in-law. Dolts, the pair of them, but he enjoyed lording it over them and rubbing their nose in it. He knew they imagined he was after getting Maria to marry him, and if things had been different he might have done just that. He'd be in clover sure enough and Maria would marry him tomorrow, he knew that. She'd dropped enough hints over the last few months. He'd become a wealthy man by some folk's standards if he wed her, and he could probably have put up with her possessiveness and neurotic need of him if it meant a life of ease. If she was his wife he wouldn't stand for her tantrums anyway – she'd soon learn who was master. But marrying her had never been an option because there was Rose. Always Rose.

He slid out of the too-soft bed with its heaped thick blankets and inches-thick eiderdown and walked across to the bay window. He pulled the drapes slightly to one side and stood looking down into the dark street below. It was snowing and at two o'clock in the morning no lights pierced the blackness. The inn was situated in Front Street to the south of the town, not far from the grim confines of the Union Workhouse. Chester-le-Street was more spread out than some of the places he had been to over the last years. Most of the township population was concentrated in the built-up area around where the inn was and a second pocket of houses and buildings to the south-west, and he had searched them carefully in his first weeks of arriving in the town, asking his usual questions and taking nothing for granted. Someone as beautiful as Rose with a young child would have attracted interest and speculation, but no one had seen or heard of her and eventually he'd had to admit defeat.

'Where are you?' he breathed softly, gazing out over the white rooftops. 'Where did you go and what did you do?' Many times over the long frustrating years he'd wondered if she had, in fact, fled South, maybe even to the capital, but something in his gut told him Rose was still in the North of England. He felt it in his marrow, that was the only way he could describe it to himself. And it was this same feeling that told him she was alive and well.

There had been numerous occasions when he had caught sight of a woman and child in the distance and for a brief, wildly intoxicating moment or two, had thought he had found her, only to be disappointed yet again. But far from discouraging him, these instances had urged him on. He *would* find her, he told himself now for the hundredth time, and when he did, no matter what the circumstances were, he would make her his. He would do whatever it took. They were meant to be together and she wouldn't escape her destiny; he had bought her ten times over with what he had sacrificed over the last years of searching and living a nomadic lifestyle. Not that life had been unpleasant and he had always found some kind of work when he had wanted it, like here at the inn. His appearance opened doors for him, especially with the ladies. He knew that and he used it.

Maria's return brought him turning from the window. She was carrying a tray with a bottle of wine and a platter of cold meats and cheese and bread, and she smiled at him as she surveyed him standing stark naked in front of her. 'I thought you need to keep your strength up,' she said, nodding to the tray. She put it down on the big oak chest at the end of the bed. Walking across to him she slid her hands down his chest and then stroked his penis in her fingers. 'The little man has work to do.'

Rather than becoming aroused as her fierce, almost primeval sexual desire was wont to make him, he felt a surge of irritation. Freeing himself, he picked up the bottle of wine and poured a glass before getting into bed, his voice cool as he said, 'I'm tired, Maria.' They'd been at it for the last two hours, after all. What did she expect?

She stared at him and although her voice was low when she spoke he knew her temper was rising. 'You have been thinking about her. I know this. Zis woman.'

When he had first arrived in the town and had taken a room at the inn he had made the mistake of asking Maria if she knew of anyone matching Rose's description. He hadn't used the lie about an estranged wife. From the first moment Maria had looked at him he had seen the open desire in her dark eyes and he'd thought she might be a pleasant dalliance for a while. Instead he'd said the woman he was looking for was the wife of his brother.

'Don't start.'

Her jealous rages were another thing that made him think it was time he left Chester-le-Street. He only had to glance at another woman and Maria was beside herself, but of late she had challenged him about Rose more often, as she did now.

'I start, I start.' She had her hands on her hips, her eyes blazing. 'This woman, this bad woman who ran away from her husband, why does not he search for her, eh?'

'I've told you, my brother is taking care of their bairns.'

'You say this but I do not believe. I think *you* want her. You say her name in your sleep. Rose. Rose.' She spat on the floor. 'I spit on her name.'

'Cut it out, Maria.'

'What is she to you? Your sweetheart, your' – her voice faltered for a moment – 'your wife?'

'I'm not married, for crying out loud. You know that. And she's my sister-in-law.'

'Even if this is true, you still want her.'

'I'm not having this again. I'll sleep in my own room tonight.'

As he put the glass of wine on the little table by the bed she was at his side before he had a chance to fling back the covers, throwing her arms round his neck as she lay across him. 'No, you no leave me. You stay.'

Swearing under his breath he tried to put her from him but she was like a limpet as he attempted to free himself, covering his face with frenzied kisses. When he eventually shoved her off him it was with enough ferocity to send her flying onto the floor with a thud that must have jarred every bone in her body. Rather than lying in a crumpled heap though, she struggled to her feet and then came at him, her hands like claws as they raked his face before he managed to restrain her. He shook her, much as a terrier would shake a rat, his voice a growl as he bit out, 'You're mad, that's what you are. Stark staring mad.'

'Don't leave me.' Now she was crying hysterically, still fighting him. 'Stay, you stay.'

'I'm only going to my room.' He had kept the room on for appearances' sake although every night for the last few months he had slept in Maria's bedroom. 'We both need time to calm down.'

'*No, no.*'

'Quieten down, woman. Do you want to bring Marcelo and Luigi here?' Alfonso's two brothers had rooms in the attics of the inn away from Maria's bedroom and the guest rooms, but with the row she was making he wouldn't be surprised if they heard her ten miles away.

'I no care.'

'Well, I do.' He wasn't opposed to taking the pair of them on but he preferred to do it fully clothed and with a weapon in his hand. As her crying rose to a new height he lost his temper, slapping her first across one cheek and then the other, making her head jerk like a puppet's. The shock was enough to silence her. She collapsed against him in the next moment and he lifted her up and deposited her on the bed none too gently.

She wriggled out of her robe, looking at him through streaming eyes, her arms outstretched towards him. 'You stay with me. I scream and scream if you leave, I swear it.'

Inwardly cursing the day he had ever succumbed to her charms, he climbed back into the bed and took her into his arms as she flung herself at him. She continued to sob, but quietly now. Nathaniel stared over her head at the flickering shadows on the far wall of the room he had always privately thought was more in keeping with a brothel than anything else. The scarlet satin sheets and eiderdown on the bed, the gold and red curtains at the window, the gaudy rugs and various gold lamps with beaded tassels and bobbles hanging from the embroidered shades, had taken him aback the first time he'd seen them. The more he had got to know Maria though, the better he had understood that the room suited her perfectly.

She was pressing herself against the length of him now, wriggling slightly. She liked to be naked and was proud of her body. She and Alfonso had been childless and so there were no stretch marks or sagging skin to mar the olive smoothness of her firm flesh.

'I sorry,' she whispered softly, her long fingers playing with his thick blonde chest hair. 'You still love me, yes?'

The usual question after one of her damn tantrums and spoken in the high, little-girl voice that she adopted at such times. It had long since lost the power to cajole him.

He didn't answer, and she twisted so that she was looking up into his face. 'Do not be angry with me, my Nathaniel.' She always called him Nathaniel, never Nat. 'I love you so much, you know this.'

He wondered what she would say if he told her he had decided to leave in the morning but he wasn't taking the risk of another screaming match. Instead he kissed her forehead, hoping it would suffice.

Maria moved so that she was astride him, her full breasts swinging as she began to pleasure him. 'I cannot live without you,' she murmured, bending forward for a second and licking the blood from a scratch her nails had wrought on his face. 'I would not want to. You understand?'

It wasn't the first time she had spoken in this way and he was aware of the veiled threat behind the words. It didn't bother him. If he left and she did away with herself that was up to her. He had known for weeks that the allure of her body was waning and he was tired of her demands. If she did but know it she had lasted longer than any of his other women, mainly because living at the inn with all the benefits it afforded had appealed to him for a while. He'd found he liked the freedom of a life on the road but it wasn't always easy or comfortable.

Mind you, he thought, as he grew hard beneath her ministrations, he might as well make the most of tonight, for who knew how soon he'd next find such an obliging companion between the sheets. Maria allowed him to do anything to her. He'd take advantage of that one last time. She was nothing but a whore at heart, they all were, these women who fell into his lap like ripe plums. Only Rose was different.

Once he'd had time to think rationally after he had disposed of the youth at the mill, he'd come to the conclusion that the lad had been talking rubbish, probably because of sexual frustration. He didn't believe his Rose had been the miller's mistress. She was pure, clean. All right, she'd been married, but that was because Davey had rushed her into it before she'd had time to think. She'd been little more than a child and Davey had taken advantage of that. It had all become clear the more he had thought about it. Rose had done her duty as a wife, Betsy was living proof of that, but she was still unawakened sexually and in that sense virginal, even chaste. It would be him who brought her to life, who taught her about the delights of the flesh. They were meant to be together and Rose knew that deep down. But for Vera O'Leary frightening her by threatening to take Betsy, she would have been his years ago. Somewhere she was waiting for him, expecting him to find her. He even heard her calling him at times. He didn't know what had gone on at the mill but Rose wouldn't have let another man handle her and he felt the miller's supposed accident was tied up with that.

Maria was panting, the light of triumph in her eyes that she had aroused him, and suddenly he didn't want to see her face any more. He turned her over roughly so that her face was pressing into the pillows and she was lying on her stomach. She wanted to be treated like a whore, they all did, even though they might cry and protest when he gave them what they asked for. He parted Maria's rounded buttocks with his hands, hearing her gasp as he entered her. He knew he was hurting her but that was part of his pleasure and her punishment that she wasn't Rose.

Chapter Twenty

Rose stood looking around the back of the bakery where all the food was made before being taken through to the front of the shop. She was exhausted but the two huge ovens, the bath tins, the wooden tables and all the other equipment were now clean to her satisfaction, along with the tiled floor which she'd scrubbed numerous times. Stanley Cunningham hadn't been too particular about his working conditions, that was for sure, although the front of the shop had been dirt-free. Stanley's sister had told her that after his wife and bairns had died she had come twice a month to give the living accommodation above the shop a 'going over', but Rose had spent a good few days in there too, scrubbing and washing and painting walls and ceilings. But now everything was ready for them to make their move from the little house they had lived in for the last few years. Amy and Frank were going to help her move all their furniture and belongings in the next day and then her new life would begin.

She felt a frisson of nerves and excitement shoot

through her and took a deep breath. She had learned from some of the other shopkeepers in Middle Street that the bakery hadn't been doing too well in recent years. There had been days when Stanley didn't open – 'He claimed he was sick but to my mind it was a sickness that came from the bottom of a bottle of whisky' had been said or intimated by more than one person, along with the fact that his bread had been made with more chalk than flour and some of his cakes and biscuits had been nigh on uneatable. She knew she would have to fight against the bad reputation the bakery had, and to that end she had decided to change the look of the front window. She had asked a local carpenter to fashion a three-tiered wooden stand which would fill the whole space and on which she would display fresh loaves of bread and buns, fancy cakes, pastries and biscuits, and big slabs of fruit and ginger slices. He'd also made a large sign to stand outside the shop door stating, *New owner, only the best flour and ingredients used*, and above that, in big, bold black letters, *The Crusty Loaf Bakery*.

Amy had asked her why she hadn't used her own name – 'Rose's Bakery' or even 'O'Leary's Bakery' – but she felt uncomfortable about that, even though she would have liked to see her name on the new shop sign. Nathaniel Alridge was always at the back of her mind, and although reason told her that if he did come to Consett he'd probably find her anyway, advertising her whereabouts by broadcasting her name didn't seem wise. She told herself over and over that Nathaniel had probably met a lass and was married with bairns by now, and that it was silly, even immodest, of her to think he was still interested in her, but nevertheless, the fear was always there.

Forcing her mind away from the past with all its heartache and pain, she took a long, deep breath and glanced round the bakery one last time. She would make a success of this even if she had to work twenty-four hours a day, she told herself fiercely. And she would hold true to what the sign stated, even if it meant her profits were less than they would be if she doctored the flour or used inferior ingredients for her cakes and pastries. She was already thinking that once she had become established with a regular clientele she might make broth as well as her baking wares. A basin of broth and a couple of crusty rolls made a fine lunch or dinner, and Davey had always loved her mutton or beef broth, saying it was the best he had ever tasted. But then he wouldn't have dreamed of saying otherwise, bless him.

Davey . . . The name brought with it the familiar feeling of guilt and self-reproach that had plagued her since she had admitted her attraction to Alexander Bembridge. She had never felt such fierce desire for Davey, never trembled at the thought of him or ached to see him. Theirs had been a comfortable, gentle kind of loving, at least on her part. Nothing like the feeling she had for Alexander, which only confirmed she had been right to send him away and make it plain she wanted no contact with him in the future. Alexander would possess her mind, spirit and body, she sensed it. It made no difference that they had never even kissed or had any contact of the flesh; what she felt for him was as raw and powerful as if they had known each other all their lives. It was dangerous; it would turn her into someone she had no intention of becoming.

She pressed her fingers to the sides of her temples as though she could force the thoughts away, those weakening thoughts that took charge of her mind the same way he would take charge of the whole of her if she was stupid enough to succumb to the temptation he represented. *But she wouldn't.* She let her hands drop to her sides. No, she wouldn't. She wanted none of it. She hadn't imagined she could be more frightened of anyone than Nathaniel, but meeting Alexander had shown her there were different kinds of fear.

A tapping at the shop window brought her snapping out of the whirling darkness and she came through from the rear of the building to see Amy and Frank, with Betsy between them, standing outside grinning. A rush of thankfulness for Amy cleared her head. She had never had a friend like her before, someone of her own sex who was there for her one hundred per cent and would do anything for her, no matter what was going on in their own life. Betsy adored her 'Auntie Amy' too, and she and Frank, Amy's parents, and Daisy and her family, had become their extended family, family they could rely on.

Life was good. As she walked to the door of the shop and unlocked it she nodded mentally to the thought. Yes, life was good and as long as she didn't let herself harbour thoughts about Alexander Bembridge, she could see it was only going to get better.

The next few weeks were ones of hard work and a certain amount of frustration at the chariness of folk trusting that the bakery was different under her ownership. Rose made sure she was in bed every night at ten o'clock because she was up at three to begin the first of the day's baking. Betsy attended the Consett Church of England school, and although Amy had offered to take her each morning, Rose liked to do it herself. Once she was home again she would dress the shop window and the shelves inside the shop and open the door to customers at nine-thirty sharp.

For the first couple of months Amy and Frank, along with Daisy's family, once again benefited from the amount of food left at the end of each day. Rose kept a certain amount back to be sold the next day as 'stale bread' at less than half the price, and some she would make into bread puddings or sell as 'crumb' to the local butcher three doors along to bulk out his sausages. But slowly, by the time spring raised a tentative head and the snow and ice of winter became a distant memory, word of mouth had spread and sometimes there was even a small queue in the morning waiting for the door to open. By the summer she was thinking about employing an assistant to help in the front of the shop so she could bake more, as she was regularly running out of bread and cakes by mid-afternoon when she fetched Betsy home from school. It would also mean she didn't have to close the shop for half an hour or so while she collected the child.

The very day she put an advertisement in the shop window Amy arrived at lunchtime in floods of tears. It transpired Daisy's husband had been killed in an accident on the way to work that morning when several cows that were being herded through the town to fresh pasture had taken fright and bolted. In its panic one had kicked Lonnie in the chest when he'd tried to help the cowhand restrain them, and the doctor thought the blow had stopped his heart beating. Apparently he'd fallen like a stone.

'It's not even like it happened with an accident at work,' Amy had sobbed after Rose had put the closed sign on the door and taken her upstairs to the flat to make a cup of tea. 'Daisy might have got something then to tide her over a bit. You know how tight things are for them anyway with the five bairns an' all.' Daisy's eldest three girls were at school but the youngest two, twins called Sarah and Katy, were only six months old. 'I've said I'll have the twins in the day if she wants to go out to work – it's the only way she's got a chance of keeping the house on – but like she said what can she do, she's not trained for anything, and there's no work for lassies round here anyway. She could go back an' live with me mam an' da but with the bairns it won't be easy, and you know how her an' Mam rub each other up the wrong way if they're together for more than five minutes. Me mam will interfere with the bairns, she can't help herself. She always thinks she knows best and it drives Daisy barmy.'

Rose nodded. Daisy and her mam loved each other but rarely saw eye to eye about anything. 'How about if Daisy came to help out here in the shop?' she said after a moment or two when she had worked out in her head what she could pay Amy's sister. It would have to be more than she had intended to pay for an assistant because Daisy would have the rent and household expenses as well as the children's clothes and shoes and what-have-you to find. Initially she had thought a young girl fresh from school who she could train up would be ideal, but she couldn't ignore Daisy's circumstances and not help.

Amy stared at her, eyes wide. 'Really?'

'Aye, yes, of course. If you could have the twins she can bring the other three with her every morning and either her or me can take them to school and collect them at night. They can come home here and play with Betsy until we shut shop, and then Daisy can come and pick up Sarah and Katy from you. Are you sure you're happy to have the twins every day, though?'

Amy nodded. 'I'd love it to be honest. Frank doesn't want me to work outside the home but with the miscarriages and everything I feel like it's a prison sometimes.'

'Oh, lass.' Rose hugged her. Amy didn't often talk about what she'd been through, she just soldiered on.

'I'm going back to see her later and if she's in a fit state I'll mention what you've said. She was in shock earlier when I said about her going out to work – I don't even know if she took it in properly. Mam's taken the twins to hers and one of the neighbours was sitting with Daisy but I don't want to leave her too long.'

They talked a little more and then Amy left. After she'd seen her out, Rose took the notice out of the window. Poor Daisy and poor bairns. Lonnie had always made a lot of his girls and the three older ones worshipped their da. Why was life so unfair sometimes?

Daisy came to see Rose the following day. By the time she left, it had been agreed that she would start work in the shop the day after Lonnie's funeral. She confided that they had always lived from hand to mouth, something Rose already knew, and that apart from the rent money and her housekeeping for the next week, she had nothing. Her parents had told her that they would stand the expense of the funeral, so that was one worry off her mind. 'I feel bad about it 'cause I know the money will have to come out of the bit they've put away for their old age, but they insisted.'

'Of course they did,' Rose said. 'That's what families are for. They love you. They want to help.'

Daisy burst into tears yet again at that. She had cried on and off since she'd stepped over the threshold. Fortunately their house was owned by a private landlord and not the Iron Company so there were no complications that way. Rose had told her she could pay twelve shillings a week which was generous, and it would leave Daisy nine shillings a week for everything else once the rent was paid. This had prompted more tears because Daisy had expected less. 'And of course you can take home bread and cakes each day,' Rose promised, knowing that money would still be extremely tight with five children to clothe and feed. Lonnie would have earned much more, but of course he was a man and it was accepted that men were the breadwinners. A woman's place was tending to her own hearth and before she was wed earning a little to give to her parents as their due for caring for her for umpteen years. Where widows in Daisy's circumstances fitted into this social decree wasn't clear, but then there was always the workhouse, Rose reflected angrily. That's what people would say to someone in Daisy's position. It was a man's world, especially a rich man's world, and everyone just seemed to accept it. She had raised eyebrows by taking on the bakery, she knew that. The market stall was more acceptable – lots of old biddies took their allotment or garden produce to market to earn a few pennies – but a shop was aiming too high for a woman. It took her out of the normal, leaving her in no man's land. Aye, she knew what people thought all right but she didn't care as long as they bought from her.

The thought brought her up short, making her realize how much she had changed in some respects in the last years. In the workhouse she had been taught that women like Emmeline Pankhurst and the Suffragette movement in general were evil – tools of the Devil to overthrow God's natural order. Well, she didn't believe that any more. Neither did she believe that a loving God would approve of the horrors that went on in the workhouse and elsewhere. No, it was man who had engineered such things. The Board of Guardians at the workhouse had been made up of influential and wealthy men in the town, and she remembered many visits when they would come and survey the inmates as though they were unpleasant bugs under a microscope. And if anyone dared to question the order of things the old trite phrase of 'It is the way things are and have always been' was trotted out. Well, it didn't *have* to be the way things were.

Daisy was a little calmer by the time Rose waved her goodbye. She had sent Amy's sister off with a basketful of food – crusty rolls, a slab of long oblong shortbread with cherries in the centre and crystallized sugar sprinkled on the top, pastries and cakes. She watched as Daisy trudged down the street, her shoulders bowed and her head down, and her heart went out to her. They had been such a happy little family and in one fell swoop everything had changed. She knew how that felt better than anyone. But Daisy would survive, the same as she had survived. Northern women were strong, they had to be; it was the same for all their sex in this male-dominated environment the world had become. The image which men – especially working-class men – had of the 'little woman' at home had to change. Emmeline Pankhurst and her followers were right.

She thought about Daisy all afternoon and when she went to fetch Betsy from school she saw Amy, who had come to collect Daisy's three older girls and filled her in on what they had agreed. 'Cor, lass, it was a good wind that blew you into our lives and no mistake,' Amy said, hugging her. 'Me mam an' da say ta an' all, by the way.'

Rose smiled but didn't say anything. She had got the distinct impression that Wilbur and Tessa Croft faintly disapproved of her taking over the bakery, but maybe they would change their minds now it was benefiting Daisy. They were old school, the Crofts, and when Frank had said he didn't want Amy working outside the home in spite of the fact that a little job of some kind, even just helping her in the shop, would have done Amy the world of good, her parents had backed him one hundred per cent.

Later that night as she lay in bed she found she couldn't sleep, in spite of being completely exhausted as she was every day by bedtime. She couldn't stop thinking about Alexander, going over everything he had said that last time she had seen him, picturing him in her mind's eye. She had done the right thing in refusing to correspond with him, it would have been a recipe for disaster, but . . . *No.* No buts, she chided herself in the next moment. Life went on. She had made her decision and it was the right one, and she must not doubt herself now. It would be madness to be thrown into the sort of turmoil she'd experienced after he had come to the house. She hadn't been able to eat for days and hadn't known if she was coming or going. The whole thing was ridiculous.

She must have fallen asleep at some point because she awoke with a start to find she had overslept and it was five o'clock. Although she prepared everything the night before and baked a certain amount of food she still had masses to do every morning and she raced around like a mad thing, dropping a tray of loaves fresh from the oven and burning two large fruit cakes. By the time she had taken Betsy to school and opened the shop she was tired and overwrought, and it didn't help matters that the weather had turned boiling hot, making the front of the shop unbearably warm.

It was mid-morning when the shop bell rang just as she was piling some ginger biscuits into a basket in the bakery to bring through to the front of the premises. She smoothed down her hair which she coiled on the top of her head in a bun when she was working, and checked that her apron was clean before walking through, only to stop in the doorway with a little gasp.

'Hello, Rose,' said Alexander Bembridge, for all the world as though they were old friends. 'I've just come home on leave and I thought I'd treat myself to some more of those fruit tarts . . .'

Chapter Twenty-One

That day in the summer set the tone for the future. Whenever Alexander was home on leave he would arrive at the bakery every day at some point, ostensibly to buy tarts or cakes. Daisy was in awe of him for a little while – he was one of the gentry, after all – but Alexander would tease and joke with her and soon she was his greatest ally. He would dilly-dally in the shop and often call back once or twice, saying he had forgotten to buy something but with a twinkle in his eye that made it hard to be cross with him. Almost every day he asked her out to dinner or suggested she take a walk with him once the bakery was closed, and although Rose refused it didn't seem to bother him at all. Christmas came and went, and when he presented her with tickets for the pantomime she thanked him coolly but said she had already bought some herself. He took this with his normal good humour, promptly passing the tickets to Daisy and then turning up later that day with four more tickets so she could take all her children. He was impossible, Rose thought. A law unto himself.

Daisy didn't help. 'I don't for the life of me see why you won't at least give him a chance and then decide if you like him or not,' she said on more than one occasion, until Rose broke down one day and said that she did like him and that was the reason she couldn't start a relationship with him. She poured out all her misgivings, and to give Daisy credit she did at least listen, before telling Rose she was daft.

In the spring, with business booming, Rose followed through on her plan to provide broth and hot meat pies along with the bread and cakes and so on. She rearranged the interior of the shop and added three small tables each with four chairs so that customers who bought hot food could sit and eat it on the premises if they so wished.

Alexander wished. It was the perfect excuse to linger even longer, and he made the most of it. He looked slightly incongruous sitting eating his broth or meat pie and crusty rolls among the working-class folk who frequented the shop, but he was a paying customer like everyone else and Rose felt she could hardly refuse to serve him. Besides, at heart she didn't want to. Secretly she found herself longing for the times he was home on leave when the days seemed brighter and the world a wonderful place. Perversely, though, this only strengthened her resolve to hold him at arm's length in spite of Amy and Daisy's exhortations to walk out with him.

Betsy had settled well into her new home above the bakery and their furniture had fitted perfectly into the slightly smaller space. Their sitting room was cosy and bright and the small kitchen was functional, and Betsy loved her bedroom overlooking the square of back yard outside. Rose had found some wallpaper with fairies and pixies on and had got it all ready before they moved into the flat as a surprise for the child. The room was large enough to accommodate Betsy's doll's house and other toys besides her single bed and wardrobe, and when she and Daisy's children got home from school they spent many happy hours playing together. Rose always insisted that Daisy and the girls had dinner with her and Betsy before they left each evening, and Amy fed the twins, so that when Daisy got home each night all she had to do was to get the girls into bed. Rose and Amy had put their heads together for ways of saving Daisy money and this was one of them, along with Amy and Frank having the little family round for lunch and tea every Sunday.

Eighteen months after Rose had taken on the bakery, she went next door to the gentlemen's outfitters one evening while Daisy managed the children. She wanted to have a word in private with Albert Preston before he shut up shop for the day. She got on well with Albert and whenever she popped next door to pay him the rent and have a chat, she made sure to take some of the shortbread he liked so much. He was just locking the door when she arrived on the doorstep, and once she'd explained that she needed to talk to him he ushered her through to the back of the shop where his tiny kitchen was and made them both a cup of tea. The upper floor of the premises was a workshop where his two sons were kept busy most of the time, and where he stored all the materials and other odds and ends.

Once they were seated on two hard-backed chairs he had brought through from the front of the shop, he looked quizzically at the young woman he had a great deal of respect for. She was a hard worker and he liked that. 'Well, what can I do for you, lass?'

Rose cleared her throat. She was more than a little nervous and had no idea how he would take what she was going to say. 'When we've talked before you mentioned that when you bought the premises next door it was an investment for your old age. Is that right?'

Albert nodded. 'Aye, that was the plan. Our Bart and Harry will take over here so that'll mean a steady income too. Me hands aren't what they were – arthritis, you know?'

'Well, I wondered if you'd ever thought about selling the bakery so you could have a lump sum in the bank behind you rather than the money you get from the rent each month? You'd have the income from this place, of course, but a lump sum would enable you to do whatever you want, travel, anything,' she finished lamely. He was staring at her in absolute amazement.

'Sell the bakery? To you, you mean?'

'Yes, to me.'

'Have you got that sort of money, lass?'

She nodded. 'I think so, depending on what you would ask, of course.'

'I don't know what to say.' He took a sip of his tea

and then winced. It was scalding hot. 'I've always had it at the back of me mind to sell at some point, to be honest. The wife's got a brother in Australia who's done very well for himself and he's written a number of times to ask us to go out there for a few months. He's her only sibling and she more or less brought him up when her mam died young. Broke her heart when he skedaddled off to the other end of the world, it did straight, but like I said to her, a man's got to follow his own destiny.' He shook his head. 'You've taken me by surprise, lass. Let me think about it, all right?'

'Of course.' It wasn't an outright refusal, which she had been afraid of. She had been thinking about it for the last six months. The bakery was doing so well that even with giving Daisy a rise in pay she had been able to add a considerable amount to the nest egg in the bank each month, and she'd had a word with the bank manager the week before and explained what she wanted to do. He had talked about a loan to make up any shortfall. She was an excellent customer, he had assured her, and the bank would do anything it could to further her business.

'And you're sure you want to do this, Rose? It's not going to put you in queer street? It's different meeting the rent each month to owning a place, you know.'

'I'm sure.'

Albert nodded and asked no more. Perhaps the rumours about the lass and the Bembridge son and heir were true after all? He'd told his wife he didn't believe that

Alexander Bembridge was Rose's fancy man, but for a young lass to have the sort of money behind her to buy a property . . . Well, it spoke for itself, didn't it. Still, it was none of his business – live and let live, that was his motto – but if folk got wind of it it'd add fuel to the flames for the gossipers. He suspected Ruth would be all for selling the bakery on; it'd mean they could go and see Ronald and his wife and bairns and pay their way while they were there, and still have a nice bit to come home to. He wasn't getting any younger and it would be enough to maintain the outfitters and his own house in the future. Aye, all in all, this could work out well for everyone.

Within a few weeks the deal was done. Rose bought the bakery for one hundred and thirty-five pounds. It meant she had to take out a loan of thirty pounds, but considering that she now owned her business and the little flat upstairs she was happy. She resolved to save every penny she could in the coming months. She would make it a priority to pay off the loan as soon as she could.

She would do it, she told herself on the evening the property became hers. And once the loan was paid off she would begin to save for the alterations she had in mind for the downstairs of the property. At the moment all the water for the bakery and the flat came from a tap in the back yard, but she intended to change that. And she wanted to build an extension too which would house an indoor bathroom and privy. Every improvement she made would benefit her and Betsy now and in the future. The present privy and the brick wash house which took up most of the yard could be knocked down and the whole of the area used for the extension. It was a shame there was no room in the flat for a bathroom, but it was what it was. And it was home, their home where they were happy together.

She had told Alexander what she intended to do on his last leave shortly before she had approached Albert Preston, and he had applauded her, saying she would never regret investing in bricks and mortar. As was the case in Consett, like every other town, she supposed, news about her buying the property off Albert had spread like wildfire, although he maintained he had kept it to himself. Certainly she had more than one person congratulate her about her acquisition of the bakery in the days that followed, but in her naivety she didn't think anything of it except that folk could be nice when they wanted to be. It wasn't until just before Betsy left off school for the Christmas holidays that she revised that opinion.

Betsy had been unusually subdued for a day or two but had insisted nothing was wrong when Rose had tried to question her. On this particular evening though, when she walked out of school surrounded by Daisy's girls, almost in the form of a barrier against the other bairns, Rose could see she had been crying. As they began to walk home in a little group, Rose took Betsy's hand. 'What's wrong, hinny? And don't say nothing. I know something's upsetting you. Tell me.'

Betsy left her gloved hand in Rose's but kept her head down. How could she tell her mam, her lovely mam, what the other girls had said, or how she had slapped Dora Finnigan across the face and had had to stay in at playtime? Even Flora and Sally hadn't stuck up for her, only Alice and Rachel and Violet, but that was probably because their mam worked for her mam, not because they didn't believe what the other bairns were saying. No amount of blinking would keep the scalding tears from falling and she walked blindly, wrapped in misery.

'Betsy?' When she didn't reply, Rose stopped, lifting Betsy's chin so the child was forced to look up into her face. 'What is it?'

The lump in her throat choking her, Betsy shook her head. She didn't fully understand what Dora and some of the other older girls had said but she knew it was bad.

Alice, Daisy's first born, who was the closest in age to Betsy, tugged on Rose's sleeve. 'It was Dora Finnigan and her gang again.'

'Dora Finnigan?' Rose knew Dora's mother, a small, thin-faced woman with sharp eyes who always hung about hoping for half-price bread at the end of the day, if and when she had any left. 'What has Dora been doing?' she said to Betsy, crouching down regardless of the snow and the bitter wind so her head was on a level with her daughter's.

Again it was Alice who replied. 'She was being nasty about you, Mrs O'Leary. They followed Betsy round the playground and when Betsy hit her, Dora told Miss Walton and Betsy had to go in. Playtime had only just started an' all. It wasn't fair 'cause it was Dora's fault but she's Miss Walton's favourite, everyone knows that.'

Rose stared first at Alice and then at Betsy. Straightening up, she said quietly, 'Let's get home and then we'll sort this out, all right?' Betsy was the gentlest of creatures; for her to hit someone she must have been badly provoked.

Once they arrived at the shop Rose told Daisy to put the closed sign on the door and they all went upstairs. She felt she needed Alice to get to the bottom of this, and it was only right that Daisy was present. Once the children had taken off their hats and coats and were sitting in a row on the rug in front of the fire warming their hands – all except Betsy who stood to one side, still looking at the floor – Rose said, 'I'll get us all some cocoa and biscuits in a minute, but first I need to know what Dora was saying. Betsy? Do you hear me?'

Betsy raised her eyes and looked at her mother, and such was the expression on the child's face that Rose put out her hand and pulled her daughter in to her. 'It's all right, hinny, it's all right.' But it clearly wasn't.

Glancing at Alice, who appeared to be the fount of all knowledge, she said softly, 'Can you tell me, Alice?'

Alice looked at her mother and as Daisy nodded her encouragement, the little girl said, 'Dora and her friends were saying that Mrs O'Leary—' She stopped, biting her lip.

'Yes?' said Daisy. 'Go on, pet. You're not going to get wrong.'

'They said that Mrs O'Leary has got a fancy man who bought her the bakery and that she's no better than Polly Stamp.'

Polly Stamp was a big, blowsy woman who lived in Pitt Lane and was known for accommodating any of the Consett Iron Company employees who knocked on her door for a bob a go. Like Betsy, Alice wasn't too sure why Polly Stamp was someone everyone tut-tutted about, but to link her name with Mrs O'Leary's wasn't good, she knew that.

Daisy looked at Rose. 'That didn't come from bairns,' she said grimly. 'It's their mams and das.'

For a moment Rose had frozen as Alice spoke, but now she said, 'Betsy, look at me, hinny. Dora and her friends are just silly little girls who don't know anything, all right? I bought the bakery myself with money I'd saved and what's called a loan from the bank which I have to pay back bit by bit. No one bought it for me.'

So this was what everyone had been thinking – that Alexander was her lover and he had set her up with her own business? That she was in effect a kept woman? The very thing she had feared when he had first shown an interest in her had come about, but strangely, rather than feeling crushed she found she was furiously angry. How dare their gossip and tittle-tattle upset her child like this?

'They – they said that you were bad,' said Betsy, finding her voice at last now it was out in the open. 'That's when I slapped Dora's face for her.'

'She did an' all,' Alice put in, admiration in her voice.

Dora and her gang were all big and well built, not to be messed with. 'She nearly knocked her over and Dora ran in to Miss Walton bawling her eyes out.'

'Who – who's Polly Stamp?' Betsy asked, drying her eyes. Her mam wasn't cross with her for hitting Dora and she'd said Dora was a silly little girl. Furthermore, she had caught the acclaim in Alice's voice and was beginning to feel better about it all. Her mam had said Dora didn't know anything and that she had bought the bakery herself, so Dora could put that in her pipe and smoke it and she'd tell her so in the morning.

'Don't worry your head about Mrs Stamp, hinny.' Rose kissed the top of Betsy's head. 'And don't worry about Dora either. I shall sort this out tomorrow, all right? And Alice' – she turned to Daisy's girls – 'thank you for being on Betsy's side in all this. You too, Rachel and Violet. You are good friends, all of you.'

The three little girls beamed and looked at her shyly.

'Now I'm going to make us all cocoa and I've got some ginger nuts and cheese scones to keep you going until we have our dinner.' She gave Betsy a hug and then walked through to the kitchen, Daisy following her. Daisy looked at her and then whispered, 'It's that Bridget Finnigan at the bottom of all this, lass. She's a nasty bit of work, always has been. Her and her cronies. Ethel McCabe's another one. You ought to hear their language when they get going, make a sailor blush it would. No one would heed anything they say.'

'Oh, they would, Daisy.' Rose turned to face her friend.

'Believe me, they would, but I'm not having Betsy upset like this.'

'What are you going to do, lass?'

'I'm going to make it clear that I'll be friends with whomsoever I please for a start,' Rose said grimly, 'and that I'm not answerable to scum like Mrs Finnigan. I don't want her served in the shop again, Daisy, nor Mrs McCabe and the rest of that bunch. If they come in when I'm in the back call me.'

Daisy nodded. She had never seen Rose look the way she was looking now. 'I'm sorry, lass,' she said helplessly.

'Don't be. Perhaps I needed something like this to wake me up but they'll regret it, Daisy, before I'm finished.'

Again Daisy nodded. She didn't doubt it. She was seeing another side of her gentle, kind employer and she wouldn't want to be in Bridget Finnigan's shoes when she next came into the shop scrounging for stale loaves and leftover cakes.

The next morning Rose delayed opening the shop and both she and Daisy took the girls to school. Rose left Betsy with Daisy and the other girls in the playground. The bell for going-in time hadn't rung yet and she wanted to find Betsy's teacher, Miss Walton, before it did. She walked through the building to Miss Walton's classroom. The teacher was standing with her back to the door writing something on the blackboard. Without knocking, Rose opened the door and said, 'Miss Walton?' with a steely voice.

The woman turned, her fat, red-cheeked face expressing

disapproval. 'Why, Mrs O'Leary,' she said with a stiff, oily smile. 'I didn't hear you knock?'

'That is because I didn't.'

Agnes Walton opened her mouth to say something, saw the glint in Rose's eyes, and shut it again.

'I have come to see you about an incident in the playground yesterday afternoon between Dora Finnigan and Betsy.'

'Oh aye. Well, don't worry about it, Mrs O'Leary. I gave Betsy a little talking-to and I'm sure she won't make the same mistake again.'

'Mistake?' Rose said icily.

'Betsy hit Dora or didn't she tell you that?'

'Yes, she did, and I commended her for it.'

'I beg your pardon?'

'Dora and her companions are twice the size of my daughter and they were intimidating her by following her around and making vile comments and accusations, Miss Walton. Were you aware of that?'

The teacher was becoming flustered. She usually adopted a superior attitude with the parents of the children in her care, but she sensed Mrs O'Leary wouldn't tolerate that. Of course, if half the rumours about her were true she had nothing to be high and mighty about. 'Well, no, but if Betsy struck the other girl—'

'So you didn't investigate the matter? Why was that?'

'I would have thought that is obvious.'

'Not to me.'

'Well, like I said, Betsy hit out—'

'In desperation, yes. Dora Finnigan is a bully, Miss Walton, in case you don't know. A nasty, spiteful little bully who uses words to wound and hurt, and I shall expect you to tell her to apologize to Betsy today for her behaviour. An apology from you to my daughter for your handling of this affair wouldn't go amiss either.'

'I – But – How dare you—'

The woman was spluttering and gasping now, her fat face beetroot red, but Rose in contrast was cool and composed. 'Oh, I dare, Miss Walton. I certainly dare. And let me tell you this, if this matter is not sorted out to my satisfaction I shall take it further. First to the headmaster, and then to the school board if necessary. Do you understand me? Dora Finnigan made inflammatory accusations against me to my young daughter and I shall involve whoever I need to in order to get this resolved.'

For the first time in her life Agnes Walton felt out of her depth. If Rose O'Leary really was Alexander Bembridge's bit of stuff then she was in with the toffs, and the Bembridges weren't people to get on the wrong side of. They were powerful and influential and had their fingers in plenty of pies. 'I – I will speak to Dora, Mrs O'Leary, and find out what went on.'

'I have told you what went on. I shall expect you to come down hard on this sort of behaviour without favour or prejudice. Have I made myself clear? And for the record, Miss Walton, I bought the bakery myself with no help from anyone, male or female, apart from the bank manager. Now, as he is seventy if a day and a highly respected member of the community, I trust the gossips like Mrs Finnigan won't point the finger at him for doing what is his job and assisting small businesses?'

The teacher blinked, the look on her face leaving Rose in no doubt that she had heard the rumours, maybe even knew what Dora and her friends had been saying yesterday. Daisy had told her that Mrs Finnigan was Miss Walton's aunt. The bell in the playground was ringing, and it was clear by the woman's expression that it couldn't be more welcome.

'I'll leave you now, but I shall expect you to do what I have asked, Miss Walton. Incidentally, any further harassment of Betsy will be laid directly at your door. You are paid to do a job and part of it involves making sure the children in your care are treated fairly and kindly, and that any sort of bullying is knocked on the head promptly. If you are not able to do this, then perhaps you need to question whether you have chosen the right career? Good day.'

She left the teacher with her mouth opening and shutting like a fish out of water and walked into the corridor. Children were pouring into the school, and as she caught sight of Betsy with Alice, Rose pulled them aside. 'I've sorted everything out with Miss Walton so forget about it now,' she said brightly. 'All right? Dora will apologize to you today and that will be the end of the matter.'

Betsy nodded. Her mam was wonderful. She wished now she had told her about Dora when all this had started a few weeks ago. She had gone to school in her new coat and Dora had called her stuck up and tried to snatch her woolly hat with the pom-poms, but it wasn't until Dora had started on about her mam that she had got upset. Alice had said that Dora was jealous of her because she was pretty and Dora had got a face like a sow's backside and to ignore her, but it was hard when Dora and her gang were forever surrounding her and saying things or trying to trip her up. She had seen Miss Walton watching once from her window and had thought the teacher might come out and stop the other girls, but she had just stood there, a slight smile on her face. Everyone was frightened of Dora, that was the thing, everyone except Alice. Alice had been lovely and she had made up her mind that she wasn't going to have Flora and Sally as her best friends any more but Alice instead.

'Now you have a nice day, hinny. You've all got your lunch bags?' Rose asked, glancing at Alice and her sisters too. 'Good. I'll come for you later as usual,' she said with a smile that belied how worked up she was inside. For her bairn to have gone through what she had because of her had cut her to the quick. She had said as much to Daisy, who had been vehement in her insistence that Bridget Finnigan and her sort were to blame, and although her head could see the logic of that her heart was another matter. She felt she'd failed Betsy, badly.

She walked back to the bakery through the snow that was beginning to fall, deep in thought, and once home asked Daisy to hold the fort for a while. A little while later she came down from the flat with a piece of paper in her hand. 'This is for the shop window,' she said, holding it out to her friend to read. 'What do you think?'

Daisy took it from her with a questioning look, and read out loud:

'To whom it may concern, and you know who you are. I have become aware of certain rumours circulating in the community and wish to state that I have bought this bakery with help from no one, and that I, and I alone, provide for my daughter and myself. I suggest that dirty-minded folk who assume otherwise should look to their own lives and stay clear of mine. Such people are not welcome to buy in this bakery from this day forth. To my other customers, it is business as usual.'

'By, lass.' Daisy raised her head. 'This'll put the cat amongst the pigeons.'

'I hope so, Daisy. I do so hope so.'

Daisy grinned. 'Nothing like taking the bull by the horns.'

'Or Mrs Finnigan by the scruff of her neck but this will have to do.' Rose smiled back, and then as they both laughed out loud she said, 'I think a cup of coffee is in order. What say you, lass?' Suddenly the day didn't seem so bad after all.

PART FOUR

Decisions

1911

Chapter Twenty-Two

Alexander sat at the dining-room table looking over the crystal and silver and huge bowl of hothouse flowers in the middle of the splendour, listening to his father pontificate about the recent disastrous general election. It had produced a remarkable tie, Liberals and Tories with two hundred and seventy-two seats each, which had done nothing to change party fortunes since the last election eleven months ago.

'Labour has been propping up the Liberals for months now, it's a damn disgrace,' his father was saying to Lord Rockingham, a friend of the family. 'And all over this People's Budget. Lloyd George and his lot are trying to push the government into equating robbery with democracy. The thing was thrown out by the House of Lords over twelve months ago but will the government listen? It's bad for the country, this squabbling, blast it.'

Alexander had heard it all before over the last couple of times he'd been home, and if he was honest he would admit he didn't give a damn, not tonight. He had hoped to be back at Christmas but that hadn't been possible and it was now the beginning of February. He hadn't seen Rose for over six months and had planned to dump his things and have a bath once he got home and go straight to the bakery before it closed, but he'd arrived to find one of his mother's social gatherings taking place with an important – to her – dinner party beginning at seven o'clock. Realizing he would have to wait until the following day he had tried to show good grace, but the conversation was grating on him. He wasn't a political animal by any means, but the fact that Lloyd George had proposed financing re-armament and the new old-age pensions through higher taxation of the propertied classes seemed fine to him.

He glanced around the table, at the men in their dinner suits and the ladies in their sumptuous dresses and jewels. The diamond necklace gracing the scrawny neck of Lady Rockingham would feed and clothe a working-class family for a year or two, he thought caustically, and here they were objecting that the new death duties Lloyd George had in mind might lead to economies on their massive estates.

'I agree, William.' Lord Rockingham, a fat, balding man in his sixties, nodded so enthusiastically his multiple chins wobbled. 'If the upper classes have to tighten the old belts it'll be to the detriment of tradesmen and the working-class people we employ, what? Bad form of Lloyd George, bad form.'

Had his mother's dinner parties always been as dire as this, or was he just noticing it more since being in the army, and especially since meeting Rose? The total belief in their superiority was staggering at times, like now.

'Left in the hands of the Liberals the country would go to rack and ruin,' a small man with a huge moustache piped up at the other end of the table. Alexander recognized him as the owner of umpteen coal mines in Northumberland and Durham, and he had never liked him. 'Look at the strikes we've had recently. What's wrong with miners working eight-hour shifts round the clock? It feeds the ridiculous number of brats these men father, doesn't it? Breed like rats, the lot of them, and live like rats too. No sense of decency or morality.'

'You're very quiet, Alexander.' Henrietta Conway, seated on his left, touched his arm lightly, smiling her cold, tight smile. She was still furious with him for snubbing her Gwendoline two years ago. She had done everything in her power to throw them together and she knew dear Arabella had too, and Gwendoline had been willing enough. If he had taken her on it would have saved all the unpleasantness that followed a few months later when the silly girl got herself entangled with a most unsuitable young man, an artist of all things. They'd had to buy the fellow off and whip Gwendoline abroad where she'd had the baby, and Godfrey had arranged for a farmer and his wife to bring the child up in some remote region or other of Greece. The whole thing had played havoc with her social engagements for a month or two and she had missed Charlotte Blenheim's wedding to Lord Golding, which had been *the* wedding of the year.

'I've been travelling all day.' Alexander was well aware he was out of favour with the Conways but he hadn't lost any sleep over it. When he had told his mother he would rather marry a dockside dolly than Gwendoline Conway because they at least were doing what they did to eat and keep a roof over their heads, she had thrown a blue fit, but he hadn't heard another word from her on the matter after that. He rather thought his father had had a word with his mother and filled her in about Gwendoline's less-than-discreet escapades.

'Of course.' Henrietta inclined her head. 'Silly me. I thought it was because you might have different views to the ones being expressed.'

'That too.' It would have been simpler to ignore her oh-so-genteel goading but he was sick of the lot of them.

'Oh, do tell.' And before he could say anything more Henrietta called down the table to his father. 'William, dear, I fear we might have a rebel in the ranks,' she said with a tinkling laugh. 'Alexander is up in arms – is that the right expression for an officer? – about our conversation tonight.'

Alexander saw his mother shoot Henrietta a glance that made him think it might be a while before the Conways were invited to one of her dinner parties again, as his father said, 'Really? Well, I always think some healthy disagreement is a good thing and I'm pleased to say my son has always had a mind of his own, Henrietta, as I think you know,' he'd added pointedly.

The matter might have finished there, but for Lord

Rockingham – who had an innate belief that he was always right – interposing. Fixing Alexander with a frown, he said, 'And what may I ask have you taken objection to, young Alex?'

It was for all the world as though he was a child having an unwelcome tantrum in the company of his betters. Ignoring his mother's imploring look, Alexander smiled coolly. 'No objection taken as such, Lord Rockingham,' he said easily, 'merely healthy disagreement as my father suggested. I remember Lloyd George's speech when he said that four spectres haunt the poor – old age, accident, sickness and unemployment – and that he intends to exorcise them. I applaud that, and the tax package laid down in the People's Budget. It's radical, yes, but necessary. A new supertax of sixpence in the pound levied on the ten thousand or so people with incomes over five thousand pounds isn't unreasonable, nor are the other changes. The Tories' condemnation that the budget is attacking the propertied classes is misguided. This is not an attack, it's a means of social reform, as is the talk about state pensions and unemployment insurance in the future. It means we are coming out of the Dark Ages.'

'The Dark Ages?' Lord Rockingham had got redder in the face the more Alexander had spoken.

'You don't think we are still existing in the Dark Ages when by accident of birth thousands of children are born into conditions you wouldn't dream of keeping your horses in? Mr Wynford spoke about his miners living like rats. Does a man of your intelligence really believe they choose to live in dilapidated hovels and spend their existence working underground with the risk of accidents and explosions like the one which killed nearly three hundred and fifty men and boys in Lancashire before Christmas? They do it so that their families can eat, and even then they have to live hand to mouth in impossible conditions.'

'Oh, come, come, Alexander.' Lady Rockingham shook her carefully coiffured head. 'Do you really imagine the lower classes can ever be different? My dear boy, you have to understand that in the main they are perfectly content in their ignorance. If one was to interfere in the way things are, who knows where it would end?'

'The only thing they understand is a firm hand.' It was the owner of the coal mines speaking again. 'What does the good book say – "Spare the rod and spoil the child"? Well, the poor are like children, and a good beating brings them to heel.'

Alexander's temper was rising. It was only his mother, after one quick glance at him, who prevented him letting rip at Enoch Wynford. Rising to her feet, Arabella said sweetly, 'Well, I for one have had quite enough of politics for one evening. Ladies, shall we retire to the drawing room and leave the men to their cigars and port? Alexander, could I have a moment of your time, darling?'

The ladies having dutifully filed through to the drawing room where coffee and mint creams awaited them, Arabella detained Alexander by slipping her arm through his until the drawing-room door had closed. Standing in the hall, she looked up at her son who was a good foot taller than her, but before she could speak, he said, 'Yes, all right, Mother. I know I should have just kept my mouth shut, but the rubbish they talk. "A good beating brings them to heel", indeed. The man's thoroughly objectionable.'

'I agree, darling. He is.' Arabella smoothed her dress before saying, 'I merely thought you might like to escape and have an early night after travelling all day, that's all I was going to say.'

Alexander looked down at his mother. Arabella Bembridge was still quite stunningly lovely at the age of fifty-five, her pale peaches-and-cream skin barely lined and her thick dark hair, although fading now, glossy and soft. Her grey eyes, so like his, smiled up at him, as he said, 'And of course, your consideration for my well-being would have nothing to do with getting me out of the room before I upset Father's cronies any further, would it?'

'Cronies?' Arabella wrinkled her little nose. 'That's such an army expression, Alexander. I prefer friends or companions.'

'Heaven help him if he considers Wynford a friend.'

'You know what I mean. And for what it's worth, I can't abide the man either.'

'But you invite him to your dinner parties.'

Arabella shrugged her smooth shoulders as she extricated her arm from his. 'I don't like half the guests who frequent this house, Alexander, but one has to make sacrifices. It might interest you to know that your father and one or two other men of influence in the district are putting pressure on Enoch to improve the living accommodation he provides for the men who work for him. But one has to tread carefully with such individuals.'

'I'd tread carefully with him all right, with my boot up his backside.' But Alexander was mollified somewhat. He dropped a light kiss on his mother's exquisitely styled hair. Her maid must have spent hours arranging it. 'Go and see to your little flock of followers,' he said indulgently, knowing she was queen bee in her social circle and loved it. 'I'll see you at breakfast.'

'Really, darling, you make me sound like a shepherdess,' she said, before turning after she had walked a step or two and adding, 'It's lovely to have you home, Alexander.'

He knew she meant it and on impulse he reached out and took her in his arms for a moment or two, hugging her carefully because of her elaborate dress as he said, 'I'm sorry I missed Christmas and New Year but it was unavoidable.'

'But you're here now,' she said softly, kissing him on his cheek as he let her go. 'And I'm going to get Cook to fatten you up a little. You're too thin.'

'Army food.'

Once she had disappeared into the drawing room he stood for a moment more in the hall. If what he wanted came to fruition she was going to be devastated, he knew that. There had never been a trace of scandal in the family. Mind you, he thought wryly, he was a long way off persuading Rose to walk out with him, let alone marry him. The last time he'd spoken to Lawrence his friend had reiterated all the reasons getting involved with her was a mistake, and if it was someone else in his position he would probably be saying the same thing. But this was different, *Rose* was different. Damn it, he had to see her. He took his gold fob watch out of its little pocket in his waistcoat and glanced at the time. 'Getting on for nine,' he murmured. It would be madness to go and see her at this time of night. Even if she answered the door she would be furious with him. He stood for a moment more, biting his lower lip, and then as Franklin came through from the dining room carrying a tray, he said, 'Tell one of the stable lads to bring the horse and trap round to the front, would you? No, on second thoughts, tell him to get it ready and I'll come to the yard in a minute.' He didn't want to advertise the fact that he was slipping out.

'Certainly, sir.' Franklin watched the young master take the stairs two at a time and disappear to his suite of rooms, before he walked through to the kitchen. The top hierarchy of the butler, the housekeeper and the first footman were still in the dining room dancing attendance on the guests, and two maids were seeing to the ladies in the drawing room, but the cook and the kitchen maids were bustling about and the valet was sitting having a cup of tea in front of the range. It was to him that Franklin said, 'Mr Alexander's told me to tell one of the stable lads to get the horse and trap ready.'

The valet narrowed his eyes. 'Oh aye? Did he say where he was going?'

'It's obvious enough, isn't it?' The cook had stopped what she was doing and now the three of them glanced one to another. From the butler down to little Toby, the youngest of the two stable lads, all the staff knew of the young master's interest in a certain lady in the town. It amazed them that the master and mistress hadn't caught a whiff of it, but Constance, Arabella's lady's maid, assured them they hadn't.

'Well, you'd better get to, hadn't you,' the valet said to Franklin. 'He won't like to be kept waiting.'

'He's gone to his rooms, to change I think, and then he's coming to the yard. He didn't want it brought round the front.'

Again they glanced at each other and it was the cook who said, 'He's taking a chance calling on her this time of night, isn't he? It's usually in the day.' When it had got back to them that the young master was frequenting a bakery in the town, the cook had gone to see her sister who lived a few doors down from the establishment. Her sister had confirmed that Mr Alexander was often seen in the premises when he was home on leave, sitting eating and drinking like everyone else, but that she had never seen him at night – although that wasn't to say he didn't call, of course.

It was a young widow with a bairn who'd taken the bakery on, the sister had said over a pot of tea, and she was a real bonny piece. Big green eyes like saucers, she had. She seemed respectable enough, but how a lass her age had come by the means to buy a business of her own, no one knew. This had been said with a knowing look, and although Alexander's name hadn't been mentioned it had hung in the air. Then, just a few weeks ago, the cook's sister had sent her a message saying she *had* to come into town on her half-day off, and there had been that notice in the window of the bakery. Well, Cook said on her return to Highfield Hall, you could have knocked her down with a feather. And she'd caught a glimpse of the lass in question and she was a looker all right, she could see what had captured Mr Alexander's fancy.

Not one of the staff believed anything but that the young master had bought the bakery for her – it was what the nobs did when they took a mistress, wasn't it, setting them up in their own place where they could visit when they felt like it – but it *was* surprising it wasn't a nice little cottage somewhere off the beaten track rather than a working bakery in the middle of town.

'It strikes me the lass is canny,' the housekeeper had said to the cook one day when they were discussing the matter in the housekeeper's sitting room over a cup of coffee. 'If he gets tired of her she's not left high and dry, not with a little business of her own and a nice income. Gives her that bit of security.'

The cook remembered this now and as the footman disappeared out of the kitchen door to the stables, she said to the valet, 'Has Mr Alexander ever mentioned the lass when you're looking after him? Given a hint, like?'

The valet shook his head. 'He's not here much, is he, and when he is he doesn't like "mollycoddling", as he calls it since he's been in the army. The most I do is lay his clothes out on his bed.' This was said with distinct disapproval.

'Aye, he's a rum un' all right.' The cook shook her head. 'But a proper gentleman, nevertheless. And clearly the lass has a bit about her. Not that that'd help her if the mistress caught wind of it. All the blue-blooded ladies she's paraded before the lad – there was that duchess a few years ago, wasn't there. You remember?'

'The one with a face like the back end of a tram? Aye, I remember her. More man than woman she was. Went out on the hunt with the menfolk and rode better than any of 'em.'

'Well, that French countess was lovely, wasn't she? You all said so.' The cook never saw much of the main house, not like the butler and the other staff who waited on the family and guests. Cook's domain was the kitchen and she was happy with that.

'Aye, she was a cracker.' The valet stood up. 'I'd better go and lay out the master's nightclothes and—' He stopped as Alexander walked into the kitchen, causing a bit of a fluster with the kitchen maids busy at the sink.

Alexander stopped in front of the cook. 'Another excellent meal, Cook. We could do with you in the army. Keep them all on their toes.'

The cook dipped her knee, blushing with pleasure. 'Thank you, sir.'

'I'm going for a drive to clear my head before bed. A little too much of Father's good wine, I fear.'

They watched him go out of the door into the yard just as Franklin walked back in. The young master said something and they heard Franklin laugh, and once the footman was in the kitchen and the door was closed, Cook said, 'What did Mr Alexander just say?'

'Only that he prefers the cold wind outside rather than the hot air being talked in the dining room.'

The valet clicked his tongue. He was old school and he didn't approve of what he termed the young master's over-familiarity at times, but then that was what the army did for you. It wasn't a profession for gentlemen like Mr Alexander, mixing with all sorts. He knew that the master and mistress had thought that if they gave their son his head in this he would soon find out he wasn't suited to army life, but on the contrary he seemed to have taken to it like a duck to water. Strange that, considering that as a young boy Mr Alexander couldn't even bear to watch the pheasants being shot on the estate.

'Cut along to the dining room and see if you are needed,' he said briefly to Franklin, and once the young man had gone, he looked at the cook. 'He's got it bad, I reckon,' he said glumly, 'the young master.'

She nodded and they stared at each other for a moment, before one of the kitchen maids dropped a big pan of hot water that had been soaking on the side all over the floor, thus bringing an end to further conversation.

Chapter Twenty-Three

Alexander was thinking much the same thing as he bowled along in the cold frosty air, the bitter wind slicing into his flesh. Overhead the sky was a dark velvet canopy with hundreds of bright twinkling lights, and somewhere in the far distance an owl was hooting. The night was calm and peaceful, but he felt anything but calm and peaceful inside. He wouldn't have believed a woman could have the sort of hold over him that Rose had. They had never embraced, he had never kissed her and yet she was in his flesh, his bones, his blood. All the time he had been out of the country in Leipzig as part of a team in Germany supporting two British Army officers accused of espionage, he had been thinking of Rose. The trial of Lieutenant Trench and Captain Brandon had been harrowing, and when they had been found guilty just before Christmas things had got even more difficult, with all leave being cancelled. But now he was here. He breathed in great lungfuls of air. Whether she would see him at this time of night was another matter altogether.

By the time he reached the street where the bakery was he was regretting the impulse to come, but not enough to return without trying to see her. He got down from the horse and trap, tying the reins to a lamp post and throwing the trap's thick tartan blanket over the animal, and then stood for a minute or two just staring up at the windows of the flat above the shop where lights showed behind the curtains. His heart was pounding like a sledge-hammer, and in spite of telling himself that attempting to speak to Rose was nothing compared to some of the things he'd encountered in his life as an army officer, it didn't help.

'Come on, man,' he muttered to himself after a while, 'it's getting later every minute. Knock on the damn door.'

He walked over to the front door of the shop and, his heart in his mouth, knocked three times. The sound seemed deafening to him in the deserted street and he winced, imagining her reaction. He knew he should have come tomorrow but it would be like every other time; there'd be Daisy trotting about and a bunch of other customers and he'd be forced to sit at a table if he wanted to see her at all, drinking soup or eating a pie he didn't want and looking like a lovelorn idiot.

It was a full thirty seconds before there was a light from the shop, and then he realized she was coming towards the door holding a lamp. He stared at her through the glass panel and could just make out the dark red of her hair and the pale oval of her face. When she unbolted the door and opened it, she stood looking at him for an endless moment, and in spite of himself he forgot every word of the speech he'd rehearsed on the way to see her. When she stood aside and said quietly, 'Come in,' he couldn't have been more astounded than if she had answered the door stark naked. He'd expected to have to argue his way in.

Still without speaking he followed her through the shop and into the bakery, and then up a steep flight of stairs at the end of the room and into the flat's sitting room. It was small and cosy, a coal fire burning in the hearth and a small tabby cat asleep on a rug in front of it. Rose gestured towards the animal. 'Betsy wanted a pet for Christmas.'

'She did?' He stood awkwardly just inside the room, the door still open behind him.

'She's called her Queenie. A grand name for such a little cat but of course she'll grow. She's just a kitten now.'

He nodded and then took the bull by the horns. 'I know I shouldn't have paid a visit at this time of night but I wanted to see you.'

'That's what you said on New Year's Eve two years ago when you came to my house. Tell me, Mr Bembridge, do you always do the things you know you shouldn't?'

He stared at her. Something had changed since the last time he had seen her. She was more . . . He couldn't find a word to describe how she was and gave up. Clearing his throat, he said gruffly, 'Where you are concerned I suppose I do.'

She smiled. 'Should I be flattered?'

She had mellowed towards him, that was what the change was. 'That's for you to decide,' he said, his eyes never leaving her face. Whatever this was, he was all for it.

'Well, as it happens I did need a word with you in private about something that happened while you have been away. It's' – he saw pink in her cheeks and realized she was blushing – 'it's somewhat embarrassing but I think it's only right you are made aware of it.'

He was instantly concerned. 'Are you all right?'

'Me? Oh, yes. Never better.' Which was the truth, Rose thought. The rumours had somehow cleared her mind and forced her to acknowledge that she was in love with this man. It was madness, of course, and it couldn't come to anything, but nevertheless she loved him. The whole sorry incident had also made her furiously angry at the injustice of it all, whilst bringing out an aggressiveness she had never known she was capable of. If she wanted to walk out with Alexander Bembridge then she would do so and folk could think what they liked – they did anyway. She wasn't going to live her life dictated to by the people around her, not any more, but if anyone said anything to her or to her child she would come down on them like a ton of bricks.

She looked at Alexander, trying to control the rush of emotion that had made her breathless when she had first seen him through the shop window. 'Come and sit down,' she said, indicating one of the two armchairs pulled close to the fire, 'and I'll get us a drink before I begin. Would you like coffee or cocoa or tea? I'm sorry I don't have anything stronger.'

'Coffee would be lovely.'

The small kitchen was through an archway off the sitting room and he caught glimpses of her as she prepared a tray, his heart racing every time he took in the sheer beauty of her. What on earth was she going to tell him? If anyone had hurt her he would swing for them, he thought in the army jargon that would have had his mother wincing.

She came in, served him his coffee and then sat down in the other armchair, before she said, 'I hope this doesn't disturb you but like I said, I feel you should know.'

He nodded. 'Please go on.' He couldn't take his eyes off her mouth. It was perfect, like the rest of her.

'It began when Betsy came home from school dreadfully upset one day. The other children had been saying things about me, things they must have heard at home.'

He sat forward in his chair, almost spilling his coffee. 'What things?'

'Basically that I had acquired the money to purchase the bakery from a gentleman, that he had "set me up here" was how it was put, I believe. That I was his mistress, and the bakery was in effect payment for services rendered.'

'Gentleman?' His face had blanched. 'They were talking about me? I have caused this distress to you?'

'The only people who caused this were the ones who gossiped, Alexander.'

It was the first time she had addressed him by his Christian name but he was too upset to notice. 'I should have realized. I am so sorry, please believe me. I wouldn't wish you a moment's pain because of me—'

'It's all right.' She stopped the flow of words gently. 'Really, it is. I went to the school and had a word with Betsy's teacher who, I understand, took the children in question to task, and I put a notice in the shop window too. I decided it was time to call a spade a spade.'

'A notice?'

She stood up and walked across to a small dresser, opening a drawer and taking out a piece of paper. 'I kept it after I took it out of the window. Here, read it for yourself.'

He read it with growing amazement and when he'd finished he raised his head.

She was smiling. 'Don't look so shocked.'

'I'm not shocked, not as such. More – Well, in awe of your courage.' He shook his head. 'And now I've come here tonight and played right into the gossips' hands. I'm sorry.'

'Don't be. I've decided I'm not going to live my life worried about what other folk think any more. I shall be friends with whomsoever I please.'

'And that includes me?'

Especially you. She didn't say this, however, merely nodding before taking a sip of coffee.

'Does friendship include having dinner together or taking a drive now and again when I'm home?'

She laughed, she couldn't help it. From looking crushed he was now positively delighted. 'As friends?' she said after a moment.

'If that is what you want.'

'It is.'

'Then I shall be content with that and value your friendship as the most precious thing in my life.' And then he paused. 'No, let me be honest. I always want honesty between us. I won't be content but I accept that is all you can offer.' *For the moment but by all that's holy he'd change that.* 'It doesn't alter my feelings, of course. You know I love you – worship, adore you. That will never change as long as I live.'

She blinked. 'Alexander—'

'I love the way you say my name.'

'I want you to know that if at any point you feel that our friendship has run its course I will understand. If you meet someone else who can offer you more—'

'I won't.'

'But if you do, that's all right.' It wouldn't be, of course, she'd die, but their relationship could only ever be a temporary thing, she knew that. If it became serious, if it ever got to the stage where he asked her to marry him and they became betrothed, she would have to tell him everything about her past and she couldn't face that. He would look at her differently, any man would. She had been raped and she had been responsible for another human being's death. Either of those things would tarnish her in his eyes and she couldn't bear that. But the fact that they came from different worlds would suffice as an excuse to stop their friendship developing into anything more. And it wasn't an excuse anyway, it was the truth. She couldn't fit into his world any more than he could fit into hers.

After a moment he said, 'I can't believe I'm sitting here like this drinking coffee with you, and you're not angry with me.' He raised one eyebrow on the last words, making her smile again. 'Can I come and see you tomorrow, after the bakery is closed, I mean? We could go for a meal somewhere perhaps? There's a particularly fine inn to the north of Castleside and another on this side of Lanchester. I could borrow my father's motor car for the evening.'

In spite of herself Rose felt a moment's panic. She had never ridden in a motor car before but he had spoken about it so casually. It was more evidence of the huge divide between them. Somehow she managed to collect herself and say with more composure than she was feeling, 'Thank you but I am not sure. I would need to see if my friend could come and sit with Betsy.'

'Betsy could come with us if you prefer? The Crown has a small room where one can dine in private.'

For a split second she wondered if he had dined and wined ladies there in the past. 'It would be too late for her. She has school in the morning.'

'Of course.' There was a small deprecating quirk to his mouth as he said, 'Forgive me. I'm not accustomed to children's routines.'

'Do you see much of your godchildren?'

'Nicholas and Rosaleen? Not as much as I would like. An army officer's life allows for little recreation and when I get leave I prefer to come home these days,' he said meaningfully. He was delighted when a faint tinge of pink touched her cheeks.

'And your friend, Lawrence? How is he?'

His face clouded over. 'He is finding it hard to adjust. Before the accident he could never be still for a moment, he was a man who always needed to be doing something, you know? Now he feels useless and a burden to his family. He isn't, of course, and Estelle still adores him which in the circumstances says a lot for her sweetness of spirit as he can be pretty foul at times. He's all but become a hermit on his estate in Scotland. They no longer entertain and rarely extend an invitation even to his parents to visit. He's an only child like me, and his mother is very distressed about the situation but every time they have tried to reach out to him it has made matters worse.'

'You're worried about him.'

He nodded. 'Lawrence is more than a friend, he's the brother I never had.'

'I'm so sorry.' The deeply sad note in his voice had touched her, and it was this that made her bold enough to say, 'Why don't you go and see him this leave? You might do him the world of good. Just knowing you wanted to see him would give him a lift.'

He was silent for a moment. Then he said, 'Would you come with me? You and Betsy? Estelle would love to speak to another woman, I'm sure, and Nicholas is away at boarding school so Rosaleen would be delighted to see Betsy.'

She stared at him, shocked.

'As friends, of course,' he said hastily, seeing her expression. 'And I would make Lawrence and Estelle aware of that.'

It wasn't that aspect of things that had shocked her, although maybe it should have, she thought ruefully, but she trusted Alexander that he wouldn't press his attentions on her. No, it was more the fact that he was proposing to introduce her to his friends, his social circle. 'I don't think—'

'Don't say no, not without thinking about it.'

'There's the bakery. I've taught Daisy a certain amount about the baking and so on and she's quite adept now, but she would never cope on her own.' She should have just said no, flat out, she thought in the next instant, without trying to explain herself. The whole idea was ridiculous.

'I'm sure there would be someone who could assist her for a day or two. We wouldn't be away long. Lawrence's estate is just over the border.'

'Alexander, I can't possibly go to Scotland with you.' She stared at him helplessly. How had they suddenly got to this stage? she asked herself bemusedly. One moment he had been grateful just to be invited in, and the next he was proposing she come away with him. Admittedly to see his friends, and also with Betsy in tow, but nevertheless.

'Why not?'

'Why? Well, it's perfectly obvious.'

'Not to me. When was the last time you took a break from the business?'

'I don't need breaks,' she said firmly.

'Yes, you do,' he said just as firmly.

'Whatever would your friends think if you arrived on their doorstep with a strange woman and child in tow?'

'I don't think you are in the least bit strange,' he said, grinning. 'Anyway, they know all about you.'

'They do?' She didn't know if that made it better or worse but rather felt it was the latter.

He nodded. 'They know I'm madly in love with a cold-hearted woman who won't give me a chance,' he said solemnly. 'They feel pretty sorry for me actually.'

She had no idea if he was being serious or not. 'Well, there you are then. They hate me already.'

'No one could hate you.' His voice had changed, becoming soft and husky. 'They'll love you like I do.'

'Alexander—'

He put down his cup and stood up, pulling her to her feet. She shivered as their hands touched but he made no attempt to take her into his arms, merely holding her hands. She was desperately aware of the height and breadth of him, of the clean intoxicating smell coming from him and the overall maleness that seemed to envelop her. She felt as though she was fifteen, sixteen again and meeting a man for the first time. But she wasn't fifteen; she was a grown woman with a daughter and a past. Oh, yes, and a past.

'Come to Scotland with me, you and Betsy. You said tonight that you have decided not to live your life worried about what other people think and that you'll be friends with whomsoever you please. Come to Scotland as my friend, Rose. Please. I know Lawrence is in a bad way and it would make all the difference if I have your support. It would be good for Lawrence and Estelle too, to have a diversion.'

She extricated her hands, turning, and with her back to him, said, 'Is that what I am? A diversion?'

'No, no, hell no. I didn't mean—'

She turned back to face him then and he saw she was smiling. This was madness, absolute madness, but for once in her life she wanted to be mad, to cast all her cares and responsibilities aside and do something stupid. And this was stupid, for him as well as for her. 'As friends?' she said softly.

'I swear it.'

'I'll have to see if Amy could come and help Daisy for a few days first.' She rather thought Amy would jump at the chance to get out of the house. The last miscarriage, just before Christmas, had been particularly traumatic. Amy had gone five months that time and they'd all hoped and prayed that at last there would be a bonny baby at the end of the pregnancy.

'Really? You'll consider it?' He had made the suggestion on the spur of the moment but hadn't dared to hope she would agree to it. This night was turning out better and better.

'I'll see what Amy says.' She glanced at the small wooden clock on the mantelpiece as it chimed. 'Alexander—'

'I know, I know, it's late.' He wanted to stay here in this little room for ever. He wanted to kiss her, undress her, take her to bed and make her his own— He turned abruptly and walked to the door, afraid of the strength of his feelings and his failing control. 'I'll go now but I'll be back tomorrow to find out what you have decided.'

'I'll see you out.'

Once they were downstairs in the shop he caught hold of her hands again, their gaze locking in the dim light. 'I meant what I said, Rose. I love, worship and adore you, and I've never felt like this before. In fact, I know now I've never been in love before. Since I met you I haven't looked at another woman, I want you to believe that. I understand there might be a hundred reasons why you don't want a romantic relationship with me, but I just want you to give me a plain straight answer. Do you care for me at all?'

After a moment, she said softly, 'I think you know the answer.'

'I hope I do.'

'But—'

'No, no buts, not tonight.' Lifting her hands upwards, he did not kiss them but pressed them against his cheeks for a moment. 'I'll see you tomorrow.'

She did not answer straight away. When she did, it was a murmur: 'This, our – our friendship can't come to anything. You do accept that, don't you?'

'Truthfully, no, I don't, and as I said before, I won't lie to you so although it's not the answer you want to hear, it's the only one I can give you. But don't worry about it now because I won't. My old nanny was a great one for believing in fate or destiny, "kismet", if you like. "What will be, will be," she used to say. "It's all in the stars, Alexander." It used to annoy me, quite frankly, especially if I was agitated about something and wanted her to be concerned too, but the older I've got the more I think that there's something in it. Some things are meant to be. Like my horse throwing a shoe and my coming to the market that day.' He smiled.

'That's a very comfortable philosophy,' she said quietly.

'Yes, I suppose it is.'

'I think we make our own destiny or "kismet".'

'I rather thought you might,' he said, laughter in his voice. He let go of her hands, turning and opening the front door of the shop and stepping down into the icy, deserted street, whereupon he made his way to the horse and trap and removed the blanket from the patiently waiting animal. Once he had climbed up into the seat, he waved to her where she stood in the shop doorway and then clicked at the horse to trot on.

Rose watched him until he disappeared in the darkness but didn't immediately go inside although the night was bitterly cold. Did fate really hold all the cards for a human life in her hands? she thought. If so, she could be monstrously unkind from birth. Why should one child be born into disease and poverty, and another into grandeur and riches? And if life was mapped out from an infant's first breath, did that mean there was no point trying to change things or better oneself? No, she didn't believe that. If she did she would still be back in Sunderland and probably tied to Nathaniel. Like she had said to Alexander, it was a comfortable philosophy, especially for the powerful and wealthy. It meant they could enjoy their existence without giving a fig for the injustice and misery that went on, especially for the poor. Was Alexander like that?

And then she immediately refuted the idea. No, no, he wasn't. She was over-thinking what he had said.

Slamming the door on her thoughts, she went back inside the warmth of the shop, the familiar delicious scents of bread and cakes and biscuits enveloping her.

Once back in the flat she checked on Betsy who was sound asleep, one small hand under her face and her chestnut curls spread out on the pillow. She was so beautiful it made Rose's heart ache, and again a stab of panic rent her through. Their life was secure and happy and predictable – what was she doing allowing Alexander into it? When it became apparent she was walking out with him the ensuing gossip might be kept behind closed doors – especially after her notice in the shop window and the fact that no one would want to get on the wrong side of the Bembridges, who wielded a great deal of influence – but nevertheless, it would still go on. What if Betsy was affected by it? Upset in some way?

She crept out of the bedroom and once in the sitting

room sank down into an armchair. Everything in her said it would be a mistake to go with him to Scotland, a mistake of momentous proportions, but she was still going to go. She shook her head at herself, making a small sound in her throat. She wanted a few days with him to remember for the rest of her life.

When Alexander reached Highfield Hall his mother's dinner guests were leaving in their cars and carriages. He waited until the last one had departed before he walked into the drawing room where his parents were discussing the evening over a cup of coffee, and his entrance caused them to look up in surprise.

'Alex?' His father stared at him, taking in that he had changed from his formal dinner suit into day clothes. 'We thought you had gone to bed some time ago. Is anything wrong?'

'Nothing's wrong and I didn't go to bed. I've been out, actually.'

'Out?'

His mother put in, 'At this time of night?'

'I drove into Consett to see someone, a friend, although she will become more than a friend if I can persuade her to look at me along those lines.' He had decided on the way home that he was going to tell them about Rose. While she had held him firmly at arm's length it hadn't been worth upsetting them, but now – 'I am in love with her.'

His father's mouth fell into a slight gape but his

mother's eyes narrowed. He knew that look. Her match-making look.

'I've known her for two years and loved her that long,' he said quietly, 'and I won't be dissuaded from pursuing her.'

His father went to say something but his mother stopped her husband by raising her hand and saying, 'William, ring the bell and ask for coffee and brandy for Alexander. Alexander, sit down. We will discuss this in a few moments. I take it we are at least allowed to ask a few questions considering you are our only child, and by all accounts are considering matrimony at some time in the future with this girl?'

'She isn't a girl. What I mean to say is, she is a woman, a widow with a young daughter,' he said as he sat down opposite them.

The footman appeared after he had dropped this bomb-shell and when William had dutifully ordered the coffee and brandy and the man had disappeared, Arabella again stopped her husband from continuing when William said, 'Why on earth haven't you mentioned this before and—'

'Wait, dear, please,' she said firmly.

Alexander knew it was because his mother didn't want the footman to overhear their conversation when he returned with the coffee, and in spite of himself he felt guilty at how she was going to feel when she knew the full extent of what he had to say. He didn't want to cause her distress or his father either for that matter, but Rose came first. He was damned if he was going to apologize for falling in love with her, or to try and keep their relationship secret.

Over the last couple of years he had had time to reflect on how he would proceed if she ever mellowed towards him, and it wouldn't be by insulting her and trying to keep her hidden away from his family and friends. He'd take them all on, every last one who dared to look down on her or criticize her because she came from a different class, and that included his parents, much as he loved them. He agreed with Lawrence that there would be those in his social circle who would be merciless in their derision and superciliousness, but this only concerned him in as much as it would affect Rose. They could always live abroad after they were wed; he could leave the army and he had an inheritance he'd never touched from his maternal grandparents. It would suffice to keep them and Betsy, and any children they might have, in relative comfort. Anything was possible if they were together. They could set up a small business, another bakery perhaps or a bistro.

A few minutes later, after his coffee had been brought in and the footman had left, his father said, a little testily, 'Am I allowed to talk now?'

'Of course, dear,' Arabella said before continuing. 'You say she is a widow with a young child? I'm not aware of anyone we know in that position who lives close to here?'

'You don't know her, Mother. Her name is Rose and she owns and runs a bakery in Consett.'

'Good grief,' said his father. 'Exactly how old is this widow?'

Alexander suppressed a smile. 'She's in her twenties, Father. That's all.'

Arabella's eyes hadn't left her son's face. Quietly, she said, 'I think you had better begin at the very beginning, Alexander, don't you?'

It took him a few minutes to relate it all and he kept nothing back, including the proposed trip to Scotland. To give his parents their due they didn't say a word until he had finished speaking, partly, he felt, because they were both in shock. At some point during his discourse his father had got up to stand with his back to the fire, his coat-tails pulled up, and it was from this position that he now said, 'You've lost your mind, m'boy. This whole thing is preposterous, surely you must see that? A working-class wench with a young child? It won't do. And you've said yourself you know nothing about her background. She calls herself a widow but to my mind that's doubtful. It's far more likely the girl got herself in trouble and—'

He stopped as Alexander jumped to his feet, his countenance dark. 'Don't talk about her like that, you don't know her.'

'And it seems to me you don't know much either.'

'I know enough to be sure I want to spend the rest of my life with her if she'll have me.'

'Oh, she'll have you, all right. She's played you like a violin, you damn fool. Can't you see what she's about?

A working-class wench with an eye to rising in the world and then you come along. Of course she wasn't going to agree to becoming your mistress when there was a chance that if she kept you dangling long enough you'd be foolish enough to offer marriage. I can't believe a son of mine could have been so damn gullible.'

'And I can't believe you are so narrow-minded and downright pretentious. You haven't even met her and yet you've blackened her name and labelled her little more than a whore. Now if you had said all that about some of the supposed ladies Mother has had up for inspection by me I could have understood it. I know that more than one of them has been handed from one man to another and enjoyed it, but because they come from "good stock", whatever that is, their whoring is brushed under the carpet. Every man in that room tonight has a mistress or two, apart from perhaps you, and the women are no better. It's well known that Lady Rockingham slept with half the court in her heyday and at least two of their children bear a remarkable likeness to their biological fathers.'

'That's nothing to do with this.'

'*It's everything to do with it!*'

They were facing each other now over the distance separating them like animals preparing to fight, their bodies stiff and expressing rage and their faces blazing with anger.

Arabella's voice cut sharply into the taut atmosphere. 'Stop it, both of you. Sit down and let us discuss this like rational human beings. I agree with Alexander, William. You cannot make a judgement on the woman's morals without having met her and without knowing the facts.' As the men took their seats again, glowering at each other, she continued, 'But even the facts as we know them so far are against any liaison with this person, Alexander, and I suspect you know this at heart. A mistress, kept discreetly, is one thing but a wife is quite another. Your life and hers would be untenable.'

'I don't agree.'

'Agree or not, that is the truth in the society in which we exist.'

'Then perhaps I shall remove myself from that society.'

William shot to his feet again. 'What does that mean?'

'The world is a big place, Father, and England and its archaic class system is only a tiny part of it. If this country won't accept Rose and me as a couple then I shall find somewhere that does. I have independent means thanks to Grandmama and Grandpapa, and a new life together where we are accepted purely on our own merits wouldn't be a bad thing.'

His father swore loudly, shaking his head. 'You're talking about Utopia and it doesn't exist, not this side of heaven.'

Arabella had gone white, and her voice trembled when she said, 'You would really do that? Leave – leave everything for this woman?'

'Her name is Rose, Mother. *Rose*. And yes, I would do that if I had to.' The look in her eyes was such that half of him wanted to go across and put his arm round her and comfort her; the other half, the stronger half, kept him sitting rigidly in his seat.

'I don't understand, this has come out of nowhere,' she said in a small voice quite unlike hers.

'No, not out of nowhere. I have loved Rose for two years and she has refused me that long, partly, I suspect, because she knew that what is happening now with you and Father would occur if she agreed to look on me favourably. I haven't mentioned her before because I didn't want to distress you if there was no hope she would change her mind.'

'And now you have hope.'

'Yes, I do. And let me tell you something else while I am about it. If Rose won't have me then I shall never take a wife, Mother. You have my word on that. I want no more prospective partners brought to this house like pedigree cows paraded before a prize bull—'

'Alexander!' His father's face was scarlet with temper. 'You go too far. Apologize to your mother.'

Arabella raised a hand to her husband once more before looking at her son. 'It wasn't quite like that,' she said quietly. 'I only wanted you to be happy, to find someone you could share your life with and have a family.'

'I know, I know, I'm sorry.' He knew she loved him, perhaps even more than she loved his father, and unlike a lot of women in her position in society she had never been a distant mother. A good number of his friends had only seen their parents once a day as children when they were brought down from the nursery before dinner for a while, but his mother had spent hours every day with him playing in the nursery or taking him for walks with their nanny. She had been affectionate too, hugging and kissing him and telling him how precious he was. He hadn't realized just how unusual she was in this respect until he had heard his friends talking about their childhood and youth, and now it softened him and he did go across to her, sitting down beside her and taking her in his arms whereupon she burst into tears.

'I'm sorry, I'm sorry,' he murmured softly, 'but I can't help how I feel about Rose any more than I can help breathing. And I am fully aware of all the reasons why a match with her would be difficult, I've had two years to brood on them after all, but it frankly makes no difference. I shall soon be thirty-five years old. Since meeting her I know I have never been in love before and I won't be again. If this doesn't work out then I shall go through life alone. But I intend to make it work, to persuade her to have me, and living abroad seems like the answer. It would cause you less embarrassment, and whatever you say to the contrary, Father, things are different abroad to some extent. We could be happy, I am sure of that.'

Arabella raised her head. 'I don't want you to disappear out of our lives, Alexander.'

'It wouldn't be like that.'

'Yes, it would and I couldn't bear it.' She dabbed at her eyes with a tiny lace handkerchief. 'If – if your mind is made up then we will present a united front as a family and weather the storm. You agree, don't you, William?'

William stared at his wife. From the first moment he had set eyes on her at a lavish ball being held for a number of debutantes, of whom Arabella had been one, he had fallen hopelessly in love, so he knew how his son was feeling about this woman. But his situation had been very different to Alexander's. Although her parents had wished Arabella to marry into the elite of society, they had at least both come from the upper classes and there had been no disgrace in her becoming his wife. She had been cossetted and protected as a child and young woman, and he had only been too pleased to continue in the same vein, and with her lineage she had never found herself the recipient of snubs or slights, just the opposite in fact. That would change if Alexander went through with this match. They would find certain doors closed to them and people would stop calling, and the London season would be a nightmare. Arabella had no real idea of what she was saying or the position she would find herself in.

'My dear,' he began, only for her to interrupt him as she had a habit of doing.

'I know what you are going to say,' she said quietly, 'and I am not quite so naive as you think I am, William. Certain of our acquaintances will no doubt be otherwise engaged for any dinner invitations we extend and we will find our own social calendar diminishing, but our true friends will hold fast. It will sort the wheat from the chaff. Of course everyone will have a perfectly lovely time discussing it until the next juicy bit of gossip rears its head, but that's only human nature. And to be honest there have been times of late, like tonight with that dreadful little man Enoch Wynford and even Lord and Lady Rockingham, when I confess I wished myself in another place entirely. Perhaps I am getting old, my dear, but really some of these people are quite objectionable, as Alexander pointed out.'

The last comment did not particularly warm William to his son. Everything had been tickety-boo until he had arrived home, and no doubt he would be off again in a few days to who knew where for months on end and it would be them who would be left to weather this storm Arabella had mentioned. Furthermore, as unpleasant as Wynford undoubtedly was, the man was reliable and astute when it came to any business dealings. The muscles in his cheekbones tightened and his voice was curt when he said, 'Nevertheless, Wynford and others like him need to be kept on side.'

'You keep them on side then, darling, but I shan't shed any tears if they choose to treat us as pariahs.'

'Look, I don't want you both to have to cope with that sort of thing. That's exactly why I am suggesting it would be best if I made my home elsewhere.' Alexander shrugged. 'That's if Rose and I get together, of course, which is by no means certain.'

Arabella smiled sadly. 'Darling boy, you have never known your own worth. Of course she will accept you and not for the reasons your father spoke of. I can understand she is full of misgivings too, it would be a huge change of life for her if she became your wife, but from the little you have told us about her it would seem she is a woman who carves her own destiny in this male-dominated world.'

Alexander stared at his mother. In all the many times he had thought about what the reaction of his parents would be if he told them about his love for Rose, it was his mother he had been most worried about. Her social life, her background, her connections had all served to make her the person she was, and he had imagined she would be shocked and furiously angry at his choice. And of course she was shocked, and he didn't fool himself that she wished things were different, but she had come through for him in a way that he had never envisaged. His father on the other hand was looking as though he could strangle him.

And it was his father who now said, 'This trip to Scotland to see Lawrence and Estelle? It's tantamount to declaring your intentions to the world. You do realize that?'

'Hardly, Father. They live in relative seclusion these days but even if that were so it suits me.'

'And how do you intend to get there?'

It was said aggressively and Alexander responded in like tone when he said, 'By train, of course, and then taxi to the estate.'

'So like I said, declaring your intentions to the world.'

'And like *I* said, I don't care about what people think or what conclusions they might draw.'

William made a sound in his throat that could have meant anything but he said no more. This whole affair was absurd and he didn't understand Arabella humouring the boy. He certainly didn't intend to. But there were ways and means to deal with this. Even if this woman was the love of his life Alexander would ruin them all if he tried to introduce her into polite society and he didn't intend to let that happen. But for now he would bide his time and put his thinking cap on; there were more ways to kill a cat than drowning it.

Chapter Twenty-Four

'She wants to meet you before we leave for Scotland. It's only natural, Rose. I haven't taken a young lady to Lawrence's before.'

Rose stared at Alexander. Nothing about this was natural, nothing, she told herself a trifle hysterically. In the space of twenty-four hours she was not only going to Scotland with him but now he wanted her to meet his mother. Did he have any idea how terrifying that was? 'You told them we are friends and that is the extent of our relationship?'

'Of course. I also told them I am in love with you and hope to persuade you to look on me more favourably in time.'

She shut her eyes for an infinitesimal moment. 'Then I can understand the summons,' she said tightly.

'It's not a summons, merely an invitation for tea this afternoon for an hour or two. Daisy can cope, can't she?'

'Of course I can.' Daisy had just returned from taking

the girls to school and was unashamedly listening. She had been delighted when she'd arrived at the shop first thing and Rose had told her about Alexander's visit the night before, saying immediately that she *must* go to Scotland with him and that *of course* Amy would be pleased to help her in the shop while Rose was gone. She had been even more delighted to find Alexander present when she got back a few minutes ago. She and Amy had been worried for some time that Alexander would give up his pursuit of Rose in view of her coldness towards him, but to give the man his due there was no sign of that. Just the opposite, in fact. The whole affair was like a story in the *People's Friend* or the *Lady*. So romantic. Love conquers all. She'd said this to Rose, who had shaken her head and replied tartly that stories were one thing, real life was another and the two should never be confused.

'It's nothing to do with whether Daisy can cope or not – I am concerned that your parents have got quite the wrong impression about what this trip entails,' Rose said stiffly.

'What does it entail?' he asked interestedly.

'It's for Lawrence's sake, and Estelle's too to some extent of course. Does your mother know that?'

'If she doesn't you can tell her so this afternoon.'

He was being deliberately perverse. 'I don't think it's appropriate for me to have tea with your mother, Alexander.'

'Dinner then? We leave for Scotland tomorrow.'

'My meeting them makes it seem' – she couldn't find the right words and finished lamely – 'serious.'

It damn well was serious and before this trip was over he hoped she would admit it. 'Not at all,' he said cheerfully. 'They know your position, they know my feelings, it's all out in the open, that's all.'

'What about your staff? What will they think?'

For a moment he was very much the son of his father when he said, 'What they do or do not think is of no consequence.'

'Some of them will have relations in the town,' she said quietly, 'customers of mine most probably.'

As though on cue the shop door opened and two women came in. Daisy saw to them but it wasn't lost on either Rose or Alexander that the women were far more interested in them than in what they were purchasing, and once outside the premises they both turned and looked back before scurrying away.

So it begins, Rose sighed, and with the thought came a stiffening of her back. 'Betsy and I will be ready after school at half-past three,' she said curtly, 'and now I have work to do.'

Alexander saw Daisy wink at him behind Rose's back but he kept his face straight when he said, 'Perfect. I'll be here on time.'

There were snowflakes in the wind as the car drew up at the foot of the Hall steps. Betsy had been as quiet as a lamb on the way to Highfield Hall, the wonder of riding in a motor car stilling her usual chatter. Rose knew how her daughter felt, but was determined not to show her own awe of Alexander's father's Rolls-Royce Silver Ghost and had kept up her end of the conversation on the way to the Hall; but she had fallen silent when the house had come into view. She had expected something grand but not this breathtaking palace of a place that was beyond beautiful.

The front doors of the house opened as the car pulled up and a footman stood on the terrace for a moment before he came running down the steps to open the passenger door, whereupon he assisted Rose onto the pebbled drive and then Betsy. Alexander joined them, taking her elbow as he walked her up the steps and into the hall with Betsy, still tongue-tied, clinging on to her hand.

The first thing that struck Rose as she entered the house was the warmth. There was a roaring fire set in a grand stone fireplace at the far end of the hall but she had no time to take more in because a butler had appeared, and he took their coats, hats and gloves. She was wearing the smart sage green costume that she had bought specially for her visit to the bank manager some time ago when in the process of buying the bakery, and Betsy was clothed in her Sunday best, a red velvet dress with lace collar and cuffs. She had thought they both looked very nice while they had been waiting for Alexander to collect them but now in the face of all this grandeur she wasn't so sure.

'Mother's arranged for us to have tea in her own drawing room,' Alexander said quietly as he took her elbow again. 'It's cosier than the main one.' He didn't add that he had requested this; he was well aware that the house and its contents would be overwhelming for her and he wanted to make this as easy as possible.

The young footman led the way through the hall and into a wide corridor, and halfway down this he knocked on a door before opening it and saying, 'Mr Alexander and guests, ma'am,' his face impassive as he stood aside for them to pass him into the room. As he closed the door the footman said, 'I will let the master know you are back, sir,' and Alexander inclined his head.

The room was lovely; the gold velvet drapes at the window perfectly matched the thick carpet, and the uphol- stered couches and several small armchairs were in a lighter shade. Like the hall it was as warm as toast cour- tesy of the blazing fire in the hearth, but all this was on the perimeter of Rose's vision. Her whole being was concentrated on the regal-looking woman who had risen as they had come into the room and was now walking forward with her hands outstretched, saying, 'Do come in and get warm, the weather is frightful again, isn't it. I'm Arabella, Alexander's mother, and you must be Rose. And this, of course, is Betsy.'

In truth, her first sight of the young woman her son was so in love with had taken Arabella aback. She had expected her to be attractive but the girl's beauty was striking; not only that but she held herself with the poise common to the upper classes rather than a working-class person. And then she silently reprimanded herself. She had to stop thinking that way if the girl was going to be Alexander's wife in due course, and she mustn't say or do anything to make Rose feel she was looking down on her.

'How do you do, Mrs Bembridge,' Rose said quietly. 'It's very good of you to invite us to tea.'

The voice was what she expected, Arabella thought, and denoted the girl's beginnings, and yet even that wasn't quite true. Whilst most of their social circle took care that their children were educated in a way that made sure they had no trace of an accent, there were still one or two who spoke with the Northern burr. 'It's a pleasure,' she said softly. 'Any friend of Alexander's is welcome in our home.' She smiled down at the child, who was looking up at her while clutching a handful of her mother's skirt. 'Alexander tells me you like cats, is that right, Betsy?' And as the child nodded, she said, 'Dogs too? Good. I have a little spaniel who has just had puppies. Would you like to see them after tea?'

Betsy stared at the grand lady who was dressed so beautifully. Her childish intuition told her that although the lady was being nice and happy she was sad inside, and this took away some of her shyness and enabled her to say, 'Yes, please. What is your little doggie's name?'

'Her name is Flossie.'

The child is quite enchanting, Arabella thought, and it softened her voice still more when she said, 'She's five years old today, as it happens.'

'Really? It's her birthday?' Betsy let go of Rose's skirt. 'Have you bought her a present?'

Arabella shook her head. 'No, but that is a very good idea, Betsy. Shall we save her some cake this afternoon and then perhaps you would like to give it to her when you see her puppies?'

Betsy nodded and then said solemnly, 'But are you sure you wouldn't like to give her the cake because you're her mammy?'

Arabella was surprised by the rush of affection she felt for this quaint little girl who seemed older than her years, but then growing up without a father must have had an effect on her. 'Quite sure,' she said smilingly, just as the door opened and the butler entered, carrying an enormous silver tray on which reposed a fine bone china tea service. The footman who had opened the door to them followed pushing a tea trolley. It had three shelves and these were laden with plates holding small, daintily cut sandwiches, pastries and a variety of sweetmeats.

'We'll serve ourselves, thank you, Henderson,' Arabella said to the butler who bowed before arranging the tray on a gilt table at his mistress's side, and then he and the footman brought other small tables alongside the two couches where Alexander, Rose and Betsy were sitting before leaving the room.

There was an awkward pause for a moment and then Alexander said, his voice over-hearty, 'Well, I'm famished, it seems a lifetime since lunch. Come along, Betsy, let's have a look and see what we've got.' He took Betsy's hand and led her over to the tea trolley which the footman had placed in the centre of them. 'Sandwiches first. This lot is cucumber and these are salmon and those are chicken in some sauce or other. And look, ham I think? And cheese and pâté. My, my, Cook's done us proud.'

Betsy smiled at him. 'They look as good as my mammy makes.'

'They do, don't they. Come along, fill your plate, and would you like tea to drink or perhaps milk?'

'May I have milky tea, please?'

'Indeed you may.'

Rose was feeling inordinately proud of Betsy. Although initially overawed, the little girl had bounced back and was conducting herself perfectly, remembering her manners and not being too forward as children can be when they are excited. She, on the other hand, had never felt so uncomfortable and awkward in the whole of her life. Alexander's mother had been gracious but she had detected the disappointment and disapproval the woman was attempting to hide, and in truth she could see her point of view. Out of the blue her son had told her that he was in love with a woman from a different class. Not only that, but this woman was a widow with a young child and worked for her living. She had mentally prepared herself for the fact that at some point in the proceedings her unsuitability would be remarked on, but discreetly and politely of course.

Arabella poured them all tea and they had helped themselves to sandwiches and were sitting listening to

Alexander's opinion of the Sidney Street siege in the East End of London, where three anarchists had had a gun battle with over a thousand troops and armed police, when William opened the door to his wife's drawing room and strode in.

'There you are, dear.' Arabella smiled at her husband but there was a warning in it he could not miss. They had spent a good deal of the night talking about Alexander and Rose, William stomping about their quarters and ranting and raving. In the end, at nearly four in the morning, Arabella had had enough. She had told him in no uncertain terms that as far as she was concerned, unhappy as she was at the situation, they had to make the best of it if they wanted to see Alexander in the coming months and years. 'And I do, William,' she'd said, a steely glint in her eyes. 'So if that means accepting this woman and her child into the family, then so be it. I won't lose him and I expect you to be with me on this.'

'And have you considered the fact that any children of their union will grow up having one foot in one class and one foot in another? And they won't belong in either. Is that really what you want?' William had said testily.

'It is not what I would have chosen, no, but as it is a fait accompli and there is nothing we can do, I shall make this woman and her child welcome.'

William remembered this conversation now as he took in the quietly dressed, quite stunningly lovely woman sitting beside Alexander, and as his son rose to his feet and she followed, he said, 'Good afternoon, Mrs O'Leary.

I'm William Bembridge, Alexander's father,' as he walked across the room and held out his hand.

Last night he had told himself that his wife was wrong and there was plenty that could be done about the situation. Now, having seen the woman in question, he wasn't quite so sure. Like Arabella had been, he was taken aback.

The next little while was tense and uncomfortable, and it was a relief to everyone when the tea was finished and Arabella said, 'I have promised to take Betsy to see Flossie and her puppies, William. Would you like to accompany us?'

Part of him wanted to refuse because he knew full well his wife didn't trust him to be left alone with Alexander and Rose, but the other part, the part that felt he had been knocked on to the back foot through no fault of his own now he had seen the girl, was keen to escape. Arabella had risen to her feet and was holding out her hand to the child, who he had to admit was a pretty little thing, and now he forced a smile as he too stood up. 'Just for a few moments, I have things to attend to.' His voice stiff, he added, 'Goodbye, Mrs O'Leary' – she had asked him to call her Rose but he wasn't about to do that – 'I hope you enjoy your stay in Scotland.'

'Thank you, Mr Bembridge. I'm sure I will.'

There it was again, the cool dignity and composure that seemed all wrong from someone of her class, and it was even more irritating because he could see it was genuine. In view of the enormous gulf between their social standing he had expected this widow – if the girl ever had been married, of course – to be subservient and eager to please, or at the very least deferential, but although she had been polite and civil enough there was no humbleness in her manner.

As Arabella led the child from the room he followed, but once outside in the corridor, he said tightly, 'I'll see you later at dinner.'

'William, please.' Arabella's voice was low and urgent with a plea in it he ignored. He was furiously angry; with Arabella, with the couple still sitting in the drawing room and even with this child who was looking up at him with a slight frown as though he had committed a faux pas of some kind.

He strode off, and as he went Betsy said in a very small voice, 'He doesn't like my mammy and me, does he.'

'Of course he does, my dear,' said Arabella, completely at a loss. 'He's just – just not himself today, that is all. A – a touch of indigestion, I fear.'

A pair of big brown eyes surveyed her unblinkingly, and it was Arabella's gaze that fell away as she said brightly, 'Let us go and see Flossie and her babies, shall we?' The feel of the little hand in hers had brought a lump to her throat and she was as angry with William as she felt he was with her. He was being positively churlish, she told herself indignantly, and his curtness with this dear little child was unforgivable. She would have words with him later but for the moment she would forget about him and try to make the afternoon pleasant for Betsy.

In the drawing room, Rose was voicing the same sentiments as her daughter. 'Your father doesn't like me.'

'Nonsense. He doesn't know you.'

'Nevertheless.'

'Rose, even if that were the case, which I am sure it is not, it doesn't matter, not really.' There was a long pause in which she just stared at him, and then, his words seeming to come from deep in his throat, he said, 'Nothing matters except you and me, and Betsy of course.'

'That's not true—'

'It is true.'

'Your mother was being kind but underneath she feels the same way your father does, and I don't blame them, Alexander. If you were, well, moderately wealthy, that would be one thing. Even then our relationship would be difficult but not insurmountable. As it is' – she waved her hands expansively – 'all this . . .'

'Is my parents', not mine, remember.'

'You are your parents' only child.'

'That doesn't mean I have to inherit. If I make it plain I am walking away from this, then there are cousins and other family members who would be only too happy to step up.'

She stared at him, horrified. 'And you think I would let you do that for me?'

'I would be doing it for myself, first and foremost. I have had two years to think about it all and you are the most important thing in my life. You always will be. And don't look at me like that. I can't help how I feel any more than the sun can help rising every morning and setting each night. I have an inheritance from my grandparents which would suffice to keep us in comfort and we could go abroad to live, somewhere warm where Betsy can grow up in freedom far away from narrow minds. I was going to talk to you when we were in Scotland, but Rose' – he took her hands in his – 'think about what I have said, please. And we can talk about it some more.' He brushed a stray curl from her forehead as he spoke, his gaze lingering on her mouth, and then suddenly he pulled her in to him.

For one infinitesimal moment they were staring deep into each other's eyes, and whatever he read in hers caused him to start kissing her face, not just her mouth, but her eyes, the tip of her nose and then her lips. And she responded, straining in to him as though she would merge her body with his, knowing she had never been kissed like this before, in such a way that time stopped and the world disappeared. When at last his lips moved away from hers she was gasping for breath and trembling with the passion that had consumed them both.

Even before he said softly and deeply, 'You see? You see how it is, my darling? You are the other part of me and me of you,' she knew she was lost. She was his, she couldn't fight this love that had come into her life like a whirlwind the first time she had set eyes on him in the market. Even then, in some deep recess of her mind, she had known she didn't want to live a life that did not hold him in it. But the cost, especially for him, would be huge. Could she subject him to that, loving him as she did?

He was reluctant to let her go but she moved out of the circle of his arms, recovering her composure as she tidied her hair and smoothed her clothes. When she knew she was sufficiently in charge of herself again, she said quietly, 'Alexander, you must see—'

'No.' He stopped her continuing by putting a finger on her lips. 'No more words, not today. We have time enough in Scotland for you to list all the obstacles in our path and for me to dismiss them.' He smiled gently. 'For now I just want to hold you until Betsy and my mother return and the world intrudes once more. But one thing I promise you, my love. It won't always be this way. We will make our own world, you and I.'

He nestled her against him, the top of her head beneath his chin, and with her emotions in turmoil she said no more. But she was going to have to tell him about her past, all of it, if they had any hope of a future together and right now she didn't know where the strength would come from. If the light in his eyes faded, if he looked at her differently, she would die. She might go on living and breathing and functioning, but inside she would be dead. But he had said he would speak the truth to her at all times and she could do nothing less, and the truth was that she was not the woman he thought her to be.

The fire crackled and spat in the grate, and outside the snow was falling. The room was peaceful and quiet and Alexander made a sound of contentment in his throat, all at odds to what she was feeling. She had reached another crossroads and the path that beckoned could turn into the most painful one yet if she lost him.

Chapter Twenty-Five

The journey to Lawrence's small estate on the borders of Scotland and England was an uneventful one. Alexander had sent a telegram to say they were coming and when they stepped down from the train at a small country station near Hawick, Lawrence's carriage was waiting for them. Betsy had been fascinated by the train and was excited at the thought of seeing Rosaleen again, but was wilting by the time the coachman drove through the open iron gates set in a high drystone wall and into the grounds of Lawrence's property.

Alexander had explained to Rose that his friend's estate was comprised largely of a very productive farm with many acres of arable land, but she saw immediately that it wasn't on the scale of the Bembridge landholding. The house came into sight immediately and although it was impressive it looked to be a third of the size of Highfield Hall, with a long lawn and trees in front of it but none of the sculptured grounds of the Bembridge estate. According to Alexander the farm was situated in a valley to the north of the house and screened from view by woodland. Lawrence's father was apparently a financier and the family home was in London, but a childless great-uncle had left Oakwood, as the little estate was called, to Lawrence in his will, which – in view of the accident – had given Lawrence an independence he might not otherwise have had. The farm was profitable and gave them an adequate income, but Alexander said they'd had to cut down on indoor staff in the house so he wasn't sure if he was getting the full story from his friend.

The weather had worsened through the last part of the journey and it was now snowing quite thickly, big fat flakes falling from a low white sky. The carriage pulled up outside the house at the bottom of a set of half-circle stone steps which Rose would have considered grand if she hadn't seen Highfield Hall, and it was a maid who answered the door to them, not a footman. They were ushered into a pleasant drawing room where Lawrence and Estelle were waiting for them and Rosaleen was sitting on a thick rug in front of a roaring fire playing with a number of dolls.

Rose liked Alexander's friends immediately. Lawrence was a thin-faced man with a crop of black hair and deep-set brown eyes, but although Alexander had told her they were the same age Lawrence looked ten, twenty years older, probably – Rose thought – because of what he had gone through. His wife was a tiny, pretty woman who spoke with a slight French accent and was beautifully dressed, but there was a depth of sadness in her blue eyes that again revealed that the last years hadn't been easy.

The introductions over, Rose found herself seated beside Estelle on a damask couch which had been pulled close to the fire, while the men sat back from the warmth a little, Lawrence in a wheelchair and Alexander in an armchair beside him. Betsy and Rosaleen had immediately started chattering as though they had seen each other the day before rather than two years ago and were soon engrossed in a game of their own making with Rosaleen's numerous dolls.

Estelle had told the maid who had shown them in to bring coffee and cakes and hot cocoa for the children, and once they were settled, she turned to Rose, speaking in a soft, gentle tone as she said, 'It is lovely to meet you at last, we have heard so much about you.'

Rose blushed, she couldn't help it. There hadn't been a trace of disapproval or condescension in either Lawrence or Estelle's manner, but the situation was what it was and she suspected they wouldn't have chosen someone like her for their friend, not with all the difficulties such a match presented.

'I've heard a lot about you too,' Rose said quietly. 'Alexander is very fond of you both, and the children of course.'

'Ah, yes, he is a very – how do you say it – "hands-on" godfather. When Nicholas was born he was nearly as excited as Lawrence.' Estelle's smile faded. 'That seems a long time ago now.'

The men were having their own conversation and it

emboldened Rose to murmur, 'I'm so sorry about Lawrence's accident. Things must have been very difficult for you both.'

'Yes, this is true. Lawrence has fought his disabilities every inch of the way but has finally accepted what the doctors said all along – that he will not walk again.' Estelle was speaking in such a low voice now that Rose, even seated next to her as she was, could barely hear her. 'My mama thinks this is a good thing but I am not so sure. While he was fighting, hard though it was, it gave him purpose, something to strive for, yes? But now this is not so. The army was his life and he needs something to replace it, and I fear family life is not enough.'

'What about the farm? Alexander said it is a good productive business.'

'Yes, this is so, but my husband is no farmer, besides which we have a very able farm manager who takes care of it all, so there is little for Lawrence to do. He – he suffers more in his mind than his body.'

Again Rose murmured, 'I'm so sorry.'

'But you also have known heartache, losing your husband and being left with a young child. She is delightful, your Betsy. Rosaleen has been so excited to know that you were coming to stay. With Nicholas away at school I fear life is dull for her most of the time. She has her lessons with her governess, of course, but poor Miss Lyndon is herself rather staid and unimaginative, timid, you know? An excellent governess in many respects, of course, but both the children take after their father and are, shall we say, adventurous?' She glanced across at her husband then, whose venturesome days were over. 'But here am I, talking about adventure when you have begun your own business. You know all about adventure, yes?'

Rose smiled. 'It's more hard work than adventure.'

'That was so brave of you.'

'Not really. It was simply something I could do to provide a living for myself and Betsy, that's all.' Now the subject had been brought up she wanted to make it clear that Alexander had not been involved and so she added, 'I had some money of my own and it seemed the right time to invest it for our future, rather than it possibly dwindle away. I am responsible for Betsy, and Davey, my husband, would have expected me to provide for her.'

'How did he die, if it is not too painful to talk about?'

'No, it isn't painful, not now.'

Over the next few minutes she spoke frankly about her life in Sunderland, her beginnings in the workhouse, her marriage, Davey's accident and her coming to Consett, but she did not mention Nathaniel or the miller. She knew she had to tell Alexander about both those things before long – she owed it to him to explain before things went any further between them – but she was dreading it. The moment would come, however – she knew it would – and she would recognize it when it happened.

It was two days later before Rose and Alexander were alone again for any length of time. Alexander had spent a lot of time with Lawrence, and the result on Lawrence of having his old friend staying had been evident in his lighter demeanour and frequent laugh. As Estelle had said privately to Rose, Lawrence was a different man when he was in Alexander's company. 'It lifts this – oh, what is the English word – ah, yes, this melancholy that afflicts him at times like a dark fog. He adores us, the children and I, but it is not the same as having male company.' There had been a pensive note in Estelle's voice when she had spoken and Rose knew she was thinking about the future. Rose herself had heard Lawrence refer to his home as a gilded cage, and although she wouldn't have said so to Estelle, she feared for his state of mind and their marriage.

'One of the women who was in charge of the children in the workhouse used to get depressed at times,' she'd said to Estelle. 'She was an unmarried mother and so she knew she had years ahead of her before she could leave when her child reached the age of fourteen. She used to call it "the black dog sitting on her shoulder".'

'Yes, yes, that is it. It is like the black dog.' Estelle had looked at her enquiringly. 'What happened to this woman?'

'I don't know. Her daughter was younger than me so she was still there when I left.'

'And the workhouse? It was bad?'

'Very bad.' Rose thought back to those days of humiliation and needless cruelty and the feeling of dread that had been with her day and night. 'Yes, very bad.'

'I am sorry that your childhood was so hard, Rose.'

Rose shook herself mentally, throwing off the memories. 'But Betsy's won't be and that is all that matters. The past is the past and can't be changed but the present and the future are ours to make of what we will.'

Estelle had touched her arm. 'I can see why Alexander is so in love with you,' she said softly. 'And you are good for him as he is for you. Don't let anything come between you. What you have is precious.'

That conversation had been the day before and now, with Lawrence taking an afternoon nap and Estelle keeping an eye on the children who were painting pictures in the nursery, Alexander and Rose had slipped out for a walk in the grounds which had become a winter wonderland over the last days.

'At last,' Alexander murmured as they left the house, pulling her arm through his and tucking her against his side. 'I am very fond of Lawrence and Estelle but I have been aching to have you all to myself.' He kissed the tip of her nose. 'They adore you, you know. You have completely won them over simply by being yourself.'

Rose smiled but said nothing. The moment had come. She couldn't let this go on for another day without telling him everything, and if he didn't want her after he knew then she would go back to her life as owner of the bakery and Betsy's mother and thank God for what she had.

A pale winter sun, a weak image of its summer glory, was illuminating the snow covering the grounds as they walked arm in arm in the direction of the woodland behind which sat the farm. The sky was high and blue and although it was bitterly cold the frail promise of spring was in the air. It was a beautiful day and all at odds with the ugliness of what she had to say.

And then he suddenly took her by surprise, lifting her up and twirling her around until she was squealing in protest whereupon he set her on her feet, grinning at her as he said, 'I am the happiest man in the world right at this moment. Do you know that? I want everyone to know just how much I love you. *I love Rose O'Leary*,' he shouted to the heavens, causing several large crows sitting in a nearby tree to squawk in protest and fly off. 'The only thing that would make me happier is for you—'

'Alexander.' It was just one word but it stopped him in his tracks, the smile sliding from his face. 'I need to tell you something, to explain what – what happened to me before I came to Consett.'

'I know what happened to you. Your husband died and—'

'That is only part of it. There is more, much more. And – and it is not pleasant. But I have to tell you it all before we get any closer and if you want to walk away afterwards I will understand.'

'Walk away? Nothing that you could tell me would make me want to walk away, Rose. You must know that?'

'No, don't say that now. Make no promises.'

'Rose, what is it?' His face was grim now. 'Tell me.'

'You know I was born and brought up in the work-house and that I never knew my mother. That I met Davey when I was sixteen. He was a good man and I was happy as his wife. When Betsy came along it seemed like everything was set for the future. More bairns in time, brothers and sisters for Betsy, but then—'

'He was killed,' Alexander said softly.

'Yes, he was killed. Can we begin walking again while we talk?' She couldn't tell him what she had to say with him looking at her with such love in his face.

'Of course.' He took her arm again and they made their way along the snow-covered path that led them away from the house.

After a moment or two, she said, 'When Davey was killed it was his best friend, Nathaniel Alridge, who worked with him who came to the house to tell me about the accident. That was the beginning of it.'

As she continued to talk, Alexander listened without interrupting. His temper was aroused when he learned of how she had fled her home, and everything she had known because of this friend of her husband's hounding her, and he had to grit his teeth not to speak out; but when she came to the part the miller had played in her past he missed a step and almost stumbled before pulling her more closely in to him as they walked. He still made no comment, however, even though he was burning with fury and silent frustration that he couldn't get his hands on the man and throttle him. He felt physically sick at the thought of what she had gone through but was full of awe at how she had carried on in the face of such abuse, creating a home for Betsy and a new life for them both. But that man, that foul man taking her— He checked his thoughts. He couldn't think of it now, time enough when he was alone and could punch some inanimate object until he felt relief. For now he had to comfort her, to be everything she needed him to be.

When she ceased talking she still hadn't looked at him, and now, as they reached a point in the path just before the woodland, he stopped and turned her towards him. His rugged face was more handsome than she had ever seen it as she stared up at him, wondering how she could bear it if he told her that things had changed. She held herself stiffly, fighting the feelings of shame and humiliation and degradation that time hadn't been able to erase, her eyes unwittingly begging him to understand that none of it had been her fault.

He touched her face in the lightest of caresses, his voice deep and husky when he said, 'A few minutes ago I would have sworn on oath that it was impossible to love you any more than I already did, but you have proved me wrong. I shall for ever suffer because you have suffered so cruelly, my beloved, but for the rest of my life I want to love and cherish and protect you. Will you marry me, Rose? Will you become my wife?'

She made no reply, her eyes glittering with unshed tears.

He took her in his arms gently, almost reverently. 'I damn that fellow to hell, my darling, and this other man too, the friend of your husband's who caused you to flee and be at the mercy of beasts like the miller, but can you find it within yourself to look on this as a new beginning? Can – can you trust me to make you happy?'

'Alexander?' Her voice was no more than a choked whisper and as he moved her slightly to look down into her face, he saw the light that seemed to be emanating from it. It told him all he needed to know, even before she murmured, 'Yes, yes, I'll marry you and I love you with all my heart.'

Then there was no need for words. His mouth took hers and he was kissing her like he'd done once before, until heaven and earth merged and the only thing in the universe was him.

PART FIVE

Orange Blossom and Black Roses

1912

Chapter Twenty-Six

Eighteen months had passed since the trip to Scotland and the wedding date was fast approaching. It was a beautiful soft Sunday morning in late August, and Rose was standing looking out of the flat's sitting-room window into the street below. When Alexander was home on leave there was never a day that passed that they didn't see each other, and he often took her to Highfield Hall if only for a short visit. She understood that he was anxious to keep relations between them and his parents as amenable as possible, but had also faced the fact that his father in particular would always be unhappy about their match. His mother never said a wrong word to her, but she sensed Arabella's pleasant stance covered deep disappointment and concern.

Alexander's parents were the main reason she had insisted on waiting for a while before fixing a wedding date. He would have rushed her down the aisle the day after their engagement if he could have, but she knew his parents needed time to come to terms with it all. And to be truthful, so did she. Alexander had spoken about resigning his commission and leaving the army once they were wed, but she'd impressed upon him that they didn't need to make a decision about that initially. She knew a large part of Alexander's intention to leave the job he loved was so that they could move abroad, but that didn't sit easy with her. In fact, little sat easy with her except that she knew she wanted to be his wife.

She turned restlessly from the window and glanced across at Betsy who was lying on the rug engrossed in one of the storybooks Alexander had given her. Once he'd discovered Betsy's passion for reading he had made sure he never came to see them empty-handed. Rose smiled to herself. Her daughter adored 'Uncle Alexander' and he her, and that at least boded well for the future. And Betsy was thrilled she was going to be a bridesmaid.

The thought of the wedding tightened Rose's mouth again. Alexander's mother had wanted it to be a grand affair, almost in a form of defiance, Rose suspected, against those of her social circle who'd looked askance at the Bembridge son and heir marrying a widow from the working class. But neither she nor Alexander had wanted the travesty of a high-society wedding. Instead they were getting married at the local parish church with just family and close friends invited back to Highfield Hall for the reception. She was wearing a long cream dress and hat and Betsy was going to look as pretty as a picture as the only bridesmaid in pink and white. The day would be nothing like her marriage to Davey, when they hadn't had two pennies to rub together and their reception had been a meal at a local hotel which Nathaniel had treated them to. The three of them had had a roast dinner and a glass of champagne, and afterwards she and Davey had made their way home arm in arm as Mr and Mrs O'Leary.

She had been thinking about Davey more since her engagement and always with a feeling of guilt that she hadn't loved him as much as he'd loved her. She had cared for him, of course, but the feeling she had for Alexander so far transcended what she'd felt for Davey that the two weren't comparable. But she had made Davey happy. She turned back to the window again, hugging herself round her waist. And that was a comfort. And if the accident hadn't occurred, she would have gone on being a good wife and mother and making him happy. Of course there would always have been Nathaniel in the background, but if Davey hadn't died she would never have discovered how his best friend really felt about her. Or would Nathaniel have caused trouble for them further down the line?

She sighed irritably. She was thinking too much. Ifs and buts and maybes were pointless, and when Alexander was home she didn't feel like this. He filled her with boundless optimism and confidence for the future, and in truth she knew they were blessed to have found each other. The terrible tragedy of the *Titanic* sinking in April had forcibly brought home the fact that every moment was precious.

Nearly four thousand men, women and children, even

babies, had perished in the icy waters of the North Atlantic when the great ship had hit an iceberg on its maiden voyage to New York. There had been so much excitement about the launch of the liner; Alexander had even asked her if she would like to travel on it one day, but now it was lying broken and mangled on the seabed. Who would have thought it? Life was so uncertain.

She walked over and kneeled down beside Betsy, stroking her daughter's rich curls from her forehead as she said softly, 'I love you, hinny, so much.'

Betsy grinned at her. 'I love you, Mam.' She sat up, crossing her legs. 'Mam . . .' she began, in the voice that told Rose Betsy had been thinking about something for a while.

'Yes, what is it?'

'When you marry Uncle Alexander, can I call him Da instead of Uncle?'

Trying to hide her surprise, Rose said quietly, 'Do you want to?'

Betsy nodded, her big brown eyes solemn. 'But not if you think it would upset me real da in heaven.'

Resisting the impulse to gather the child into her arms and smother her in kisses, Rose said, 'I don't think your da would mind at all. He would want you to be happy and if that would make you happy he'd be happy too.' She could just imagine the look on William and Arabella's faces if Betsy called Alexander by the working-class idiom for father in front of them, but that was by the by.

'I think Uncle Alexander would like it,' Betsy said reflectively. 'Don't you?'

'Most certainly.'

'And he *would* be my da, wouldn't he. Once you were married.'

'Yes, hinny.'

'We'd be a proper family then,' Betsy said with some satisfaction.

'Well, we've been a proper family, the two of us. Just a very small one.'

Betsy nodded but without any enthusiasm, and looking at her child Rose realized the longing for a father she could call her own must have been with her daughter for a long time. Unspoken, but real. She had done everything in her power to be mother and father to her daughter but of course it wasn't the same. Daisy's three older girls talked about their father all the time; at least they had memories of him, but Betsy had nothing except what Rose had told her about Davey.

'Will Uncle Alexander's mam an' da want me to call them Grandma and Granda?' Betsy asked after a moment of contemplation.

Rose stared at her. How on earth did she answer that?

''Cause his mam's nice, I like her an' she's bought me some nice things, hasn't she, but I don't like his da.'

'You don't?'

'No, and I don't think he likes me either.'

'I don't think that's true, Betsy. He likes you but' – she was going to have to be careful how she put this – 'he wanted Uncle Alexander to marry someone else, not me.'

'Who?'

'I don't know.'

'Someone more like them? Rich and everything?'

'Yes, I suppose so.'

Betsy considered this for a moment before picking up her book again as she said, 'Well, it's nothing to do with him who Uncle Alexander marries, is it. Just 'cause he's his father doesn't mean he can tell Uncle Alexander what to do now he's grown up. Anyway, Uncle Alexander loves *you* and that's all that matters.'

Out of the mouths of babes. Rose ruffled Betsy's curls and stood up. Yes, it was all that mattered. Everything else – where they would live, whether Alexander stayed in the army, her continuing to run the bakery, even Betsy's schooling – was secondary to the fact that they loved each other and they would make a success of their marriage.

She and Alexander had had endless discussions – some face to face and some in the letters that they wrote to each other when he was away – about those things. He wanted her and Betsy to live at Highfield Hall until he left the army and could be with her all the time and for Betsy to have a governess rather than attend the local school, both of which she had refused to do. She had conceded that they would come and stay at the Hall when he was home on leave, but the rest of the time she intended to live in the little home she had created above the bakery.

And she would keep on working, she'd made that plain too, and Betsy would carry on at the Consett school where all her friends were.

It made sense, she told herself as she walked into the kitchen and put the kettle on the hob to make a pot of tea. She knew Alexander was worried about the prospect of war looming in Europe with the arms race threatening to run out of control; it was the main reason he had agreed to continue in the army for the time being. The average person knew little of such things but Alexander's privileged position made him only too aware that certain countries were boosting their peacetime armies. Whether war came or not, until she could be with Alexander all the time and they decided where their future lay, she didn't intend to give up her hard-won independence and be isolated at Highfield Hall with William and Arabella. And Alexander had seen her point of view, up to a point. It would be an unusual state of affairs and no doubt eyebrows would be raised, but then they were an unusual couple in every respect and the gossip about them was rife anyway. With the reading of the banns at the local church, Daisy had told her with some glee that certain members of the community had been beside themselves.

'I dunno what some of the old biddies will do for their dose of tittle-tattle if you and Alexander ever leave here,' Daisy said, grinning. 'It'd spoil all their fun.'

'I'll be sure to bear that in mind when Alexander and I make any decisions,' said Rose drily.

The tea brewed, she poured herself a cup and a milky

one for Betsy and sat down, lost in thought. She'd soon be a married woman. She shut her eyes for a moment. *It would be all right. The wedding night, it would be all right.* Since their engagement she had been plagued by nightmares where she was in a dark room and being held down by iron-hard hands while Betsy screamed somewhere. However much she struggled she couldn't get free, and she knew what was going to happen but was powerless to prevent it and then, when Betsy's cries had merged with her own and she couldn't breathe, she woke up, bathed in perspiration and trembling violently.

She took a sip of tea, the cup rattling slightly as she put it back on the saucer. It would be fine, she told herself again for the hundredth time. It was Alexander who would be making love to her, not a spectre from the past, and even in their most passionate embraces he was gentle and in control. It was him, after all, who wanted to wait until their wedding night before their union was consummated.

'You know I've had women in the past,' he'd said to her shortly after they had returned from seeing Lawrence and Estelle in Scotland, 'but this, you – us – is different. You will be the mother of my children and I want us to start right before God and man, Rose. I want you, hell how I want you, but within the sanctity of marriage so that you have my name protecting you. Do you understand, my darling?'

She had said she did at the time, and there had even been a certain amount of relief knowing that she had months to come to terms with the prospect of full intimacy. She loved him and she wanted to be his in every sense of the word, and yet she was afraid.

She took another sip of tea, her thoughts racing.

She was afraid she would freeze when they were finally in bed together; that it would be Arthur Vickers and his brutality that she would remember; that she would disappoint Alexander and ruin their wedding night and the nights to come. In the day she could put the rape out of her mind, but at night her subconscious forced her to relive it over and over again in her dreams. What if she failed Alexander? What would it do to their love?

More than once when their lovemaking had become passionate she had wished he would forget his principles and just take her then and there so she didn't have to think about it, rather than their wedding night building in her mind like a huge obstacle, but his control had always been absolute. So far and no further.

She finished the tea and went into her bedroom, tidying her hair and taking off the apron she tended to wear in the house before she returned to the sitting room. 'Would you like to go and see Auntie Amy and take her some of the coconut ice we made yesterday?' she asked Betsy, who immediately closed her book and jumped up. Coconut ice was Amy's favourite sweet and because she was eight months pregnant – the longest she had ever carried a baby – she was being careful and following the doctor's orders to stay in bed until the child was born. For the bubbly, lively Amy the enforced confinement had been onerous in the extreme, especially with the ever-present fear that this pregnancy would go the way of all the others forever at the back of her mind, but as she said to Rose each time she visited, she would do anything – *anything* – to have a healthy baby. Amy's mother came in every day to prepare and cook the evening meal and do any washing and ironing, and Daisy went first thing in the morning on her way to the bakery to get breakfast for Amy and Frank and see to Frank's bait that he took with him to the works. When Rose had asked why Frank couldn't help out in the house due to the circumstances, Amy had looked at her as though she'd grown two heads. 'He's a man,' she'd answered as though that explained everything.

Which, Rose thought now as she put on her straw bonnet and summer coat, she supposed it did, for Amy and Daisy and probably most folk hereabouts. Men didn't lift a finger in the house – it was beneath them to do 'women's work' – and it was up to other women to rally round if the lady of the house was incapacitated, but she didn't see it that way, not in recent years anyway. The more she'd had to fend for herself and Betsy, the more she had questioned the rigid dos and don'ts of working-class society. Why shouldn't a single woman without a man run a bakery and provide for herself? Why should it have prompted the virtual scandal that had followed when she'd done just that? And someone like Frank, who loved his wife dearly, feeling it was unmanly to make even a cup of tea in his own house was wrong.

She had said as much to Alexander the last time he was home on a short twenty-four-hour leave two months ago to finalize the wedding arrangements, and he had shaken his head, looking sheepish. 'I agree with you, Rose, in principle,' he'd admitted, 'but I feel I'm being somewhat hypocritical. At home everything is done by the servants and even in the army my batman attends to my needs. I confess I have never made a cup of tea in my life either.'

'Not ever?' She'd stared at him incredulously.

'Not once.'

'But you wouldn't be averse to doing so on the grounds that it's women's work?'

'Not at all.'

'Good.' He had just brought her back to the flat from Highfield Hall, where they had been discussing the reception with Arabella. It hadn't been an easy conversation. Alexander's mother was determined to turn the ballroom, where they would sit down to eat, into a vision of loveliness and the flowers she had spoken of alone would feed a family for months. Rose was in great need of a cup of tea and she'd said, 'Then you can make us both one now while I put Betsy to bed.'

His face had been a picture.

'You will find everything you need in the kitchen,' she'd said briskly, resisting the laughter bubbling up inside, 'and it's three teaspoonfuls of tea in the brown teapot. And make sure the water is boiling, all right?'

After settling Betsy and reading her a story, something

Betsy still loved even though she could read herself, she had returned to the sitting room to find Alexander looking inordinately pleased with himself. A tea tray complete with a plate of biscuits was waiting for her. He had looked so sweet, she had surprised him and herself by flinging herself into his arms and covering his face in kisses. By the time they'd eventually got round to drinking the tea it was lukewarm, but neither of them had minded.

She was still smiling to herself at the memory when she and Betsy left the house and emerged on to the pavement, Betsy clutching the bag of coconut ice for Amy. After locking the door she took Betsy's hand, and it was then that a figure emerged from the shop doorway to their left.

'Hello, Rose,' said Nathaniel softly. 'It's been a long time.'

Chapter Twenty-Seven

Nathaniel watched the shock on Rose's face turn to fear, but his voice expressed none of the satisfaction he felt when he drawled, 'You left without saying goodbye all those years ago, didn't you. Now I ask you, was that any way to treat me? What made you do a thing like that?'

Rose stared at him. On the perimeter of her mind she was aware of the sunny street and warm air, of Betsy's hand in hers, but it was Nathaniel's blue eyes that filled her vision and they were as cold as ice. It was nearly a decade since they'd last met and then he had been a strikingly handsome young man. He was still handsome, but the cruelness she had always sensed beneath the surface was now evident in his face. He was bigger, broader, not fatter though, and the lines at the corner of his eyes only served to enhance his good looks. He was the same age as Davey and not yet thirty, but seeing him now he could easily pass for forty. She had to swallow deeply before she could say, 'What are you doing here?'

He smiled. 'Well now, I suppose I could be clever here

and say I just happened to be passing but we'd both know that was a lie. The truth is, I was looking for you. I've been looking for you for a long, long time, Rose.' His gaze moved to Betsy, who was staring up at him. 'And this must be Betsy. Hello, hinny,' he said softly. 'By, you're a big girl now. The last time I saw you, you were a little baby in your mam's arms. I'm your Uncle Nat, Betsy, and your da and I were best pals.'

He put out a hand to stroke the chestnut curls and Rose said sharply, 'Don't touch her,' as she pulled Betsy closer in to her.

His face darkened, the blue eyes narrowing. 'Don't be like that, lass, not you. I suggest you're nice to me and show a little respect. You've got a lot to lose if you upset me.'

'I don't know what you're talking about.'

'No? Then let me refresh your memory. Rowlands Gill mill? Ring any bells? Seems the miller there had a nasty accident, but then you know that, don't you.'

Her eyes flickered and he knew then for sure that he was on the right track. Ten damn years give a few months he'd been trying to find her and what had he discovered? By all accounts she was engaged to some top-drawer major or other who'd been born with a silver spoon in his mouth. When he'd made his usual enquiries a few weeks back in a pub at Shotley Bridge it had been more out of habit than with any hope of tracing her. He had told himself that this summer would be the last of attempting to hunt her down. He'd told himself this before for the last two or three years but this time he had meant it. Since walking out on Maria he'd regretted it more than once, especially in the winters when work was harder to come by and the nights could freeze your innards. He'd been sitting pretty there, and he could have had an easy life, but for the thorn in his flesh that was Rose. But Maria was gone, she'd topped herself like she'd threatened she would if he ever left her, and when her brothers-in-law had come after him, he'd left one crippled and the other threatening he'd get even with him if it was the last thing he ever did. Aye, Chester-le-Street wasn't an option. There were other towns and other Marias, however, and it made sense to get himself settled before he was too much older. But then an ancient little man had sidled up to him. He'd used to be a carrier and he'd taken a lass to Consett once, and she sounded like the girl he was looking for. A beauty she'd been and with a bairn an' all like he said. The old man's hand had been tapping his empty beer glass as he'd spoken and Nathaniel had taken the hint and refilled it. He refilled it several more times over the next couple of hours and got the old man's life history in the process. It seemed his wife had died and he'd come to Shotley Bridge from Consett to live with his daughter, but after rambling on for a while he came back again to the lass he'd given a lift to.

'Got herself set up in a nice little bakery by all accounts, the last I heard, but then with her looks you'd expect something of the kind, wouldn't you.'

'The kind?' Nathaniel's stomach muscles had tightened.

'You know what I mean, lad. It caused a bit of a hoo-ha, of course.'

'You're saying someone, a man, got the bakery?'

'Aye. Now she might be your sister' – Nathaniel's latest variation on a theme was that he was searching for his sister with whom he'd lost contact after a family quarrel years before – 'but I have to say she's no better than she should be, if you don't mind me talking straight. Mind, she's got her head screwed on and knows how to look after number one, I'll say that for the lass. She'll be in clover if he goes through with it an' marries her. The whole town was talking about it, I don't mind saying.'

Keeping a hold on his patience, Nathaniel had said, 'If who marries her?'

'The Bembridge son and heir, of course. Got betrothed, they did, a while back. He's an officer, a major, in the army.'

'And he bought her the bakery?'

'Sure as eggs are eggs. He probably thought he could get away with just that – you know what these lord-of-the-manor types are like – but somehow she's hooked him in. That's if the marriage happens, of course. Me wife was full of it when she was alive – you know what women are like. Even used to go an' buy the odd loaf or two from there, she did, an' her a woman who always baked her own.' The old man's eyes had narrowed and his voice had taken on a sceptical tone. 'An' you say she's your sister, lad?'

'Yes.' Nathaniel had bitten the word out.

'Well, you needn't worry about her any more, to my mind. She's done all right for herself and the bairn. She told me she was a widow when I picked her up that day. Was that right or was that what the family trouble was about, her having a bairn out of wedlock?'

Nathaniel had had more than enough by now and would have liked to take out his fury at what Rose had done by battering the old man to a pulp. Instead he said shortly, 'She was a widow,' and stood up, leaving the pub and walking back to the lodging house where he had taken a room. He'd sat up all night, simmering with rage and drinking a whole bottle of whisky that he had bought the day before.

She was a whore, he'd told himself, nothing but a whore. First the miller and now this rich bloke, and they were just two he knew about. She'd made a monkey of him, that's what she'd done. He'd searched the whole of Durham for her and all the time she'd been prostituting herself. He'd kill her, he would, he'd kill her. He'd done murder for her, turned his life upside down and moved from place to place for nigh on ten years and all the time she'd been laughing at him.

When eventually he'd fallen into a drunken stupor he had slept the whole of the following day before waking with a thick head and a curdled stomach in the middle of the night. The next morning he had washed and shaved and made himself presentable, and then walked the three or four miles to Consett. After asking around he'd quickly discovered where the bakery was, and had stood a few doors down on the opposite side of the road watching the comings and goings in the shop for a while, before having a meal and a pint at a nearby public house. He had used his charm on the barmaid, and after a series of seemingly innocuous questions had received confirmation of all the old carrier had said. When he'd asked about lodgings in the area Myra had told him one of the rooms at the inn was vacant, and after speaking to the landlord and inspecting it, he'd paid for a month up front. The room was a small single and basic in the extreme but it was cheap, and it was the locality that appealed, being on the corner of the street in which the bakery was located. From the window he had a perfect view up the street.

He had walked back to Shotley Bridge and collected his few belongings before returning to the public house, and once in the room had taken up a stance at the window. That was when he had seen Rose for the first time. The sight of her had hit him like a punch to the solar plexus. She was even more beautiful than he remembered; the girl had gone and in her place was a stunningly lovely woman who had walked with her head held high and all the confidence in the world. She'd had a child with her whom he had assumed was Betsy because of the colour of her hair, and some other little girls, and they had all disappeared into the shop.

He had sat glued to the window for the next two or three hours until the bakery closed, and shortly after this a woman had left the premises with the other bairns he had seen with Rose and walked away. After that there had been no activity, and a while later he had gone downstairs and had another meal and a few pints before going to bed, but not to sleep. He had lain awake for hours, tossing and turning and planning his next move. If she had this major toff in her pocket then he had to tread a mite carefully. He knew full well that money was power, and by all accounts the Bembridge family was rolling in it. It was one thing tackling someone of his own kind but the gentry were another matter. But he'd work something out. One thing was for sure, she'd get what was coming to her. She'd ruined his life and she didn't give a damn. But she would. Oh aye, she would.

Over the next days he had watched and waited. He'd seen no sign of her bloke but from the number of customers in and out of the shop it seemed like it was a nice little business she'd got herself. And Consett wasn't a bad town. He could see himself settling here.

Myra had made it plain she was up for a bit of slap and tickle and he had invited her to his room, but for once the easing of his body hadn't brought its normal relief. Not with Rose just a few hundred yards away. He'd had a hard job to be civil to Myra afterwards and had all but kicked her out. He wanted to really hurt someone, that was the thing. No, not someone. Rose. But although the feeling he had for her now was a long way from the love he'd once felt, it was still born of the need to possess her, mind and body. He wanted her to acknowledge that it was him who owned her. Not Davey, not any of the blokes who'd had her since then and definitely not this damn major type she'd got twisted round her little finger. But then he didn't know her, did he, the major. He was just another poor sap she'd made a fool of.

'So,' he said now, looking into the sea-green eyes that had haunted him for years, 'you going to do this the easy way or do you want me to play rough? I dunno if the law's still looking for the woman who left Rowlands Gill mill in such a hurry and a dead man behind her, but I'm sure they'd be interested in a tip-off. What do you reckon, me fine lady? And if you go down the line, what'll become of the bairn? Consider that. Your fancy man wouldn't want anything to do with either of you then, you can bet on that. Wouldn't see him for dust. An' as you know only too well, the workhouse is no place for a little lassie, certainly not one as bonny as her. I dare say that's where you learned your tricks, thinking about it. Am I right?'

Rose was glaring at him now, the fear that had first gripped her when he had suddenly appeared from nowhere burned up by the hate and loathing she felt. Her voice like the crack of a whip, she said, 'Do your worst, I don't care. I've got nothing to hide. If the miller is dead as you say it's nothing to do with me.'

'I doubt that, lass. I doubt that very much.' His voice was still soft and low, eerily so. 'But let's just suppose for a minute that's true, mud will stick if I open me mouth. You know that as well as I do. Folk'll make the most of it and how will that affect her?' He jerked his head at Betsy. 'Or your fancy major and his fine family?

Whereas you can quietly give him the elbow, say you've met someone else—'

'You're mad.' Those green eyes were flashing now.

'About you? Aye, I was once. Thought you were the be all and end all, fool that I was. But me eyes are wide open now. I'll take you on but it'll be me that calls the tune. I'd have married you years back, do you know that? An' brought the bairn up as my own. But I wasn't good enough for you, was I? Always had an eye for the main chance, haven't you? Aye, I see it now. How long would you have stayed with Davey before you upped an' broke his heart, eh? I reckon I did him a favour—' He stopped abruptly, aware that he'd let his tongue run away with him.

For a moment Rose didn't connect his last words with Davey's accident. She might never have done so, but for Nathaniel's expression as he broke off talking. She stared at him, and as the screaming silence lengthened, a kind of sick horror gripped her. Swallowing hard, she said, 'What do you mean, you did Davey a favour?'

He shrugged. 'Nowt. I meant nowt.'

His reply along with everything about him and not least the way his whole manner had changed from aggressive to defensive told her the unthinkable, the impossible was true. Betsy's hand was tugging at hers and praying that most of their conversation had gone over the child's head, Rose said, 'Wait a minute, hinny, there's a good girl,' without glancing down at her daughter, her eyes fixed on Nathaniel. 'You were working with him when he fell,' she said in a voice that didn't sound like hers even to herself. 'It was just the two of you.'

The piercing blue eyes had narrowed and as he took off his cap and raked back his thick blonde hair before replacing the cap on his head, he said, 'So? What of it?'

'So what really happened that day?' Already she could see his old bravado was returning and with it his composure, and while part of her was saying she must be mistaken, that what she suspected was inconceivable, she knew she wasn't wrong. He had killed Davey, her Davey, his best friend. Fighting the nausea that came with the thought, she said again, 'What happened? Tell me.'

He straightened, the movement impatient. 'You know what happened.'

'I thought I did.'

'Well, go on thinking it then and while you do, consider what I've said. You're nicely set up here and it'd be a shame to lose everything you've no doubt worked so hard for, one way and another.'

The double meaning wasn't lost on her. Before she could reply, he went on, 'You're mine, Rose. Get used to the idea. You don't want this major of yours to meet with a nasty accident, do you? Or the bairn maybe? It's a bad, bad world, you know.'

'You're threatening me?' Talking about Alexander and Betsy that way only confirmed she was right about Davey.

He smiled coldly. 'I'm just saying accidents happen, as we both know only too well.'

She glared at him with such ferocity that Nathaniel

was taken aback in spite of himself. 'If you were the last man on earth I wouldn't have you, and if you come near Betsy and me or Alexander I'll go to the police myself and tell them everything you've said today. Like I said, I've got nothing to hide and you can do your worst regarding the miller, but just remember I've got Alexander and his family to back me up. Who have you got? You're a bully at heart, you always have been and I never understood why Davey was so fond of you. He was such a good man and you, you're scum.'

'Don't talk to me like that.'

'Or what?'

'I mean it, Rose. Don't try my patience.'

'Try your patience?' Part of her couldn't believe they were having this conversation. He was acting as though he was the wronged one. 'Just leave me alone, I mean it. And for the record, Alexander knows everything there is to know about me and I wouldn't be responsible for his actions if he met you.'

'I don't believe you.'

'I don't care what you believe, Nathaniel. Can't you understand that? I don't have to answer to you. You were Davey's friend and for that reason I tolerated you because he thought a lot about you, but even then, before the accident, I didn't think you were worthy to lick his boots. You always looked down on Davey in your heart of hearts, didn't you. You were the big I am, able to get any lass you wanted at a click of the fingers because of your looks and the way you acted, but inside you're ugly, dirty.'

He was staring at her with a look on his face she could only describe to herself as demonic, and she turned from him, holding Betsy's hand tightly as she began to walk away. She half-expected that he would call to her or even try to grab her but nothing happened. Betsy was saying, 'That man, Mam? Who's that man? Did he really know me da? Was he being nasty to you?' but she didn't answer her, not until they had reached the corner of the street and were out of sight.

She stopped, breathing hard and still holding Betsy's hand so tightly that her daughter wriggled and said, 'Mam, you're hurting me.'

'Oh, I'm sorry, hinny.' She forced a smile. 'Don't know my own strength, do I. As for that man, he was never really a friend of your da's. Not a good friend, anyway. He's – he's not very nice and if you ever see him again I don't want you talking to him, all right?'

Betsy nodded. 'Are we going to Auntie Amy's now?'

'We are, and if you ask her nicely she'll show you all the baby clothes again, I dare say, and the little crib with the lace round it.'

Betsy forgot about Nathaniel in a moment and for the rest of the walk she bounced along at her mother's side, talking non-stop about Amy's baby and content with only monosyllabic replies. Rose glanced behind her a few times before she reached Amy and Frank's little house but she could see no sign of a tall figure following them, although she felt his presence and it made her skin crawl.

Deep down she'd always known he would find her,

but that paled into insignificance now with what she suspected about Davey. She'd never know exactly what happened that day but Nathaniel had killed him. She couldn't prove it but she knew it all the same. He had killed Davey because he had wanted her. Her mind had always been at war within her since Davey had died and Nathaniel had tried to take his place. Part of her had tried to believe that once she'd left Sunderland Nathaniel would forget about her and get on with his life, but the other part had been waiting for this day. And it had happened. He had found her. She wished Alexander was here. He was due home on leave for the wedding any day now, but she wished he was here this minute.

Betsy had reached up and banged the little brass goblin door knocker and within a moment or two Frank opened it but Rose saw immediately that he was harassed and worried. 'What's the matter?' she said urgently as they stepped inside the hall.

'It's Amy, she reckons the babby's coming.' He glanced up and down the street before shutting the door. 'Next door's gone for the midwife, I thought you were her.'

'Have you told Amy's mam an' da?' She knew Tessa had promised to come and be with her daughter during the birth.

'I can't. They've gone to Muggleswick to see Wilbur's mam. They got a message first thing to say she's not expected to last the day. Daisy's gone an' all. They called in afore breakfast to say they were going.'

'Why didn't Amy say about the baby?'

'She wasn't having any pains then. They come on shortly after they'd left but as there's another month to go we thought if she lay still it might all die down.'

'But it hasn't.'

'No.' He cast her a hunted look as a faint groan from upstairs filtered down. 'What am I going to do, Rose?'

'Right.' Rose went into practical mode. If the baby was coming it was coming and they had to make the best of it. 'Put plenty of hot water on to boil and sort out some towels. Betsy will help you. I want you to stay down here and look after your Uncle Frank, hinny, all right? When did next door go for the midwife?'

'A while back now.'

'Well, when she comes send her straight up.' She was taking off her hat and coat as she spoke. 'I'll stay with Amy now, you look after things down here.'

The look of relief on Frank's face would have been funny in any other circumstances.

When she entered the bedroom it was to see Amy lying amid rumpled covers, her knees up as she groaned horribly. It was a few moments before she could say, 'Rose, oh, thank God. Thank God. I asked Him to help me and He's sent you.' As the contraction died down a little, she added, 'The baby's coming whether it's time or not.'

Rose could see that for herself. When she felt the sheet under Amy it was soaked through; her waters had broken. 'You're going to be fine,' she said firmly, 'the baby too. Eight months isn't that early, Amy. It might be a bit small but it's going to be bonny and healthy, I promise you.

Now just you concentrate on doing your bit and soon you'll be holding your son or your daughter in your arms, all right?'

'Where – where's the midwife?'

'She's coming, she'll be here any minute,' said Rose, praying desperately that that was true. Amy had had so many miscarriages, so many fruitless births, this had to be different.

The next half-hour was traumatic. Frank appeared at some point with towels and hot water, took one horrified look at his wife and disappeared again.

Rose held Amy's hand throughout, encouraging her friend, urging her on, telling her how wonderful she was and what a great mam she was going to be, and all the time secretly cursing the hapless midwife. By the time the birth was imminent and the baby's head was showing Rose had resigned herself to the fact she would be delivering the child.

'I can see its hair, lass,' she said, as Amy sobbed that she couldn't do this any more. 'Just one more push and it'll be out. Come on, there's a good girl, just one more.'

When, in the next instant, Amy gave a long high scream and strained with all her might, the baby shot out from between her legs straight into Rose's hands. For a moment Rose was too surprised to do anything and the baby seemed equally astonished, blinking in bewilderment before it started bawling. 'It's a boy, Amy, and he's beautiful,' she said. 'Hark at him cry, lass. He's all right, everything's all right.'

She wrapped him in a towel and passed him to Amy, still with the umbilical cord attached, and it was in that moment that the midwife appeared, red-faced and breathless. 'I'm sorry,' she panted. 'I've been at another birth but I came as soon as I could.'

'It doesn't matter,' said Amy, a blissful smile on her face as the tears ran down her cheeks. 'I had my best friend with me and we did it together, didn't we, lass?'

Rose nodded. In that moment she couldn't speak.

Chapter Twenty-Eight

'That settles it then.' Alexander's voice was grim. 'Because believe me, my love, there'll be murder done if he touches a hair of your head. You and Betsy are coming to live at Highfield Hall where I know you will be safe when I am away. Betsy can still go to her school if you insist, and you could continue at the bakery in the day when Daisy is around, but I'm not having you live there by yourselves. I mean it, Rose. I wouldn't know a moment's peace.'

It was the same day Amy's baby had been born and she had seen Nathaniel. Alexander had surprised her by turning up at the bakery late at night when he had got home on leave for the wedding, and when she had heard someone knock she had been terrified it was Nathaniel. She had gone downstairs carrying a kitchen knife and had felt quite faint with relief when she had seen Alexander outside. Once she had told him what had happened he had been both incandescent with rage and beside himself with worry.

She stared at him, shaking her head. 'He's probably

left the area and won't come back, not after what I said to him.'

'You don't believe that any more than I do. And bear in mind we are not just talking about you and me here. There's Betsy too. What would you do if he took her or hurt her? From what you've told me he is more than capable of it, if it would mean he could get to you. He is deranged, Rose.'

Yes, Nathaniel was deranged. She and Alexander were standing facing each other in the sitting room and she suddenly flung herself into his arms, bursting into tears.

He held her close, soothing her with terms of endearment, before pressing his case. 'You've already said you'd like to get Daisy used to everything that is involved with running the bakery so that she can take over when we make our lives together somewhere else, so why not bring certain elements of that forward now? Daisy and the girls could move into the flat, for instance, and that would save her paying rent where she is now, and she could be more of a manager for you. You were talking about hiring another assistant soon with the business going so well, and if you do it would mean you're not so tied every day. But the main thing is you must be safe, you and Betsy. You can't take risks with a man like this Nathaniel, my love.'

She knew he was right. She had to keep Betsy safe. But the thought of living at Highfield Hall with Alexander's father filled her with dread. She had warmed to his mother over the last months but his father was a different kettle of fish. She drew away a little to wipe her eyes with her handkerchief. 'What will your parents say if we tell them Betsy and I are coming to live at the Hall permanently?'

'They would no more want you to be in danger than I would,' said Alexander firmly. 'And on that subject I am staying here tonight. I'll sleep in the chair, and tomorrow we will move your things to the house.'

'But with the wedding so close —'

'It makes it all the better,' he finished determinedly. 'You will be on hand to discuss any details. We'll talk to Daisy tomorrow and she can give notice where she lives whenever she's happy to do so, but I'm going to have a sign made for the shop window to say the bakery is under new management so Nathaniel knows you are not living here any longer. I want you on the estate with all the protection that affords. And don't forget, you will be my wife soon, not a young woman with a child living alone and unprotected.'

'I hate the fact that he'll think he has managed to drive me out of my own home.'

'He won't know that, Rose. After all, most people would expect that you would live at Highfield once we are married.'

Yes, that was true. She nodded again.

'And frankly, I was always concerned that you wanted to carry on here when I was away. I wouldn't have wished for this to happen, of course, but it will be a great relief to me to know you and Betsy are safe and secure until I leave the army and we have our own home.' Although when that would be he had no idea. The possibility of war was gathering steam by the day. Only a month ago Britain had withdrawn her battleships from the Mediterranean and had placed them on patrol in the North Sea in response to the continuing German naval build-up. It had followed the breakdown of Anglo-German talks aimed at slowing down the rate of expansion of the two countries' navies, which was a growing concern on both sides of the North Sea. There was now a definite threat from Germany, and the naval budget was being expanded as well as a recruiting drive in all the forces. He had been chatting to his commanding officer just before he left for home today, and he'd said he wouldn't trust the Kaiser any further than he could throw him.

'War's coming, Alex,' the colonel had said, puffing his pipe, his face dour. 'In my opinion it's no longer a matter of if but when. And it'll be the same as all wars – tens of thousands will die without having any real idea of what it's all about but they'll do as they're told by men like us, and we'll do as we're told by the generals.' He'd shaken his grizzled head. 'Greed and power, the two great vices.'

'You really think the Kaiser will force the issue, sir?'

'He already is. The writing's on the wall for anyone with the sense to read it. He's not a man of peace, Alex. He never was. And I tell you one thing, we'll need men like you out in the field. Experienced soldiers who know what's what. But enough of this, m'boy. You get off home to your bride-to-be and enjoy your leave.'

'I will, sir, and thank you.' Alexander knew the colonel

had pulled strings to get him an extended leave of four weeks and he was grateful. It meant he could take Rose on honeymoon and show her a little of Europe before they were separated again.

Now he looked at the woman he adored with every fibre of his being and said softly, 'A few more days and we'll be Mr and Mrs Bembridge. You'll love France and Italy, especially Italy. If I was going to live anywhere but England that is where I would like to settle.' He sat down, pulling her onto his lap and kissing her. 'The Italians love children, they're very family orientated. Betsy will be a great hit.'

He had been all for taking Betsy with them on honeymoon, something Rose hadn't expected but had been very grateful for. Much as Betsy liked Alexander, her daughter was going to find her life changing – it was inevitable, and especially now they were going to live at Highfield Hall. A time of just the three of them being together and Betsy getting to know Alexander properly would be wonderful.

'Thank you for letting her come with us,' Rose said, stroking his cheek. It was stubbly under her fingers – he needed a shave – but he'd told her he had dropped everything at the house and come straight here, such had been his desire to see her.

'Of course she must. We're a family.'

'Some folk will think it strange.'

'I think we are well past worrying about what people think,' he said drily.

'I love you so much.'

'And I you.' He nestled her against him. 'My beautiful winter rose.'

Since the New Year's Eve when he had first called her that, it had become a term of endearment, and now she reached up and kissed him, feeling safe again in his arms.

The move to Highfield Hall was accomplished with little trouble the next day, and by that evening Rose and Betsy were installed in one of the sumptuous guest suites boasted by the huge house. Arabella and William had welcomed them graciously but there had been real warmth in Arabella's voice when she had taken Betsy off to show her the walled garden at the back of the house that had a big swing seat hanging from one of the trees. 'This is where Alexander loved to play when he was a little boy,' Arabella said. 'He preferred it to the more formal gardens and so he had his own vegetable plot where he loved to grow flowers and strawberries and things like that, and the gardener made him a tree house that Alexander pretended was a fort.'

'It's lovely.' Betsy gazed round. She hadn't been in here before, although on previous visits she had explored the rest of the grounds which housed a special rose garden, various greenhouses and outhouses tucked well out of sight, and several ornamental areas with fountains and bowers and little grottos. A large lake with its own small landing stage and a selection of rowing boats shimmered in the distance, bordered on the far side by massive oak trees.

'You could have this as your special garden if you like,' Arabella said gently, touching the red curls as she spoke. 'It could be just yours. Would you like that?' She had fallen in love with this sweet little girl over the past months, and it was a cause of pain to her that William refused to open his heart to the child. She knew better than to make it an issue with her husband, though. William would merely dig his heels in. 'You could bring Queenie here to play and once the door is shut she would be quite safe. It would give her a chance to get used to her new surroundings with you. What do you think?'

Betsy nodded. The high stone walls of the garden were covered in a mass of climbing roses and clematis, and the scent of the flowers was rich in the still air. 'I think Queenie would like it here,' she said seriously. The little cat was shut in their new quarters for the present and had objected to her lack of liberty. 'But would Uncle Alexander mind if this was his own garden once?'

'We can ask him but I know what he will say. He will be delighted.'

Betsy smiled up at the lady she always thought was sad inside. She didn't know why she thought this but it made her like Alexander's mother even more. 'Will you come here with me and Queenie?'

'Do you want me to?'

Betsy nodded firmly. 'Yes, please. We could play with Queenie together and perhaps paint Uncle Alexander's tree house a different colour?' The den looked the worse for wear, its green paint flaking.

'Well, you could choose what colour you want and we'll ask one of the gardeners to paint it, as it is a little high for us. He can check the ladder is still safe and maybe make a small table and chairs for inside? We could have tea parties there and you could invite your friends to come and play. You could pretend it's a magic castle and you're a princess.'

Betsy beamed. She slipped her hand into Arabella's as they walked on, exploring the garden together. There were some of Alexander's little lead soldiers still dotted about here and there, and in one corner, near a small shed overgrown with ivy, a large grassy mound with a deep groove running round the bottom of it. 'That was Alexander's hill he made for his soldiers and he used to fill the moat with water,' Arabella said fondly. 'I've forbidden the gardeners to come in here and change anything. I wanted his children to see it as it was and now you have, my dear.'

Betsy looked up at Alexander's mother. 'When Uncle Alexander and Mam are married I'm going to call him Da.'

'And so you should because he will become your father.'

'Can—' Betsy stopped. When she'd talked to her mother about this she had sensed it was a thorny subject.

'Yes, my dear?'

'I was just wondering what I should call you,' Betsy said after a moment or two.

They had come to a small stone bench set between two lattices heavy with sweet-smelling roses, and now Arabella sat down, careless of her fine gown, and Betsy sat with her. 'What would you like to call me?'

'Well . . .' Betsy chose her words carefully, with a natural wisdom beyond her years born of innate kindness. 'I would like to call you Grandma because I've never had a grandma. My da's mam an' da live a long way away but I've never seen them. I don't think' – she paused, and then went on – 'I don't think they liked my mam. She's never said that but that's what I think.'

The child's request had brought a lump to Arabella's throat and a prickle of tears at the backs of her eyes, but she kept her voice matter-of-fact when she said gently, 'I would very much like you to call me Grandma, Betsy.'

'Good.' Again Betsy hesitated. 'And – and Mr Bembridge?'

'Well, I think you should call him Grandfather, don't you?'

'I – I don't know if he would like that.'

Concealing the anger that the child's words had caused towards her husband, for his treatment of this beautiful little girl, Arabella said calmly, 'Would you like me to ask him about that privately for you?'

Betsy nodded solemnly. 'I think that would be best, don't you?'

'Then that is what I will do, my dear.'

A robin came to say hello, its bright red chest puffed out, and Betsy's delight in the little bird coming so close brought the conversation to a natural end, but not before Arabella resolved to have the matter of her son marrying Rose out with her husband once and for all. It had driven a wedge between them for one thing, and for another she wasn't going to have Betsy feeling uncomfortable in what was now her home. The wedding was in four days' time; it was ridiculous William hadn't come to terms with it before now.

Betsy was oblivious to the consternation she had unwittingly caused. She sat beside Arabella in the tranquil surroundings, happy with her lot. She was going to like living here, she decided. She hadn't been very sure at first and it had all seemed to happen so quickly, but they had never had a garden before and now she had one of her very own. And she liked Alexander's mam, even, she thought shyly, loved her. Alexander's da was a different matter but she didn't have to see much of him anyway. No, overall she was glad they were here and there was the wedding to look forward to when she would wear her beautiful dress, and then a holiday with her mam and her new da when they'd go on trains and ships and see the seaside.

The robin flew off but they sat on in the scented air, and it seemed natural when Betsy leaned into Arabella's side and Arabella put her arm round her. It was what a grandma would do.

Later on when Betsy was lying in bed with her rag doll tucked under one arm and Bruno under the other, she watched her mother getting ready to go downstairs for dinner. She had never imagined a bed could be so soft as this one, and the linen sheets were embroidered with little flowers at the top and smelled of lavender. Her mother's bed, which was divided from hers by a small table with a lamp on it, was exactly the same and they both had a top cover that matched the pale lemon curtains at the big bay window.

She was comfortably full after having her tea as usual at six o'clock but apparently here the adults all ate later in the beautiful dining room with its grand upholstered chairs and chandeliers. Her mam had put her best Sunday dress on with the lace collar and cuffs and she looked so bonny, Betsy thought, with her hair piled high on her head and the glittery necklace and earrings that Uncle Alexander had given her for Christmas sparkling like stars.

She voiced the thought, and Rose smiled at the small figure in the big bed. In the past there had been occasions when she had come to the Hall for dinner when Alexander was home on leave, and she had always been conscious of the dowdiness of her clothes and scant knowledge of the custom of fine dining. There seemed to be so many items of cutlery, umpteen courses one after the other and even different wines to accompany certain dishes, and the food was of such variety that she was rarely able to finish what was put on her plate. She had got a little more used to the niceties of upper-class etiquette which Alexander called a load of tosh, but still felt awkward, especially with William's eagle eyes taking in her every move. But now this was her home, at least for the foreseeable future. She would have to do something about getting some new clothes, she thought, as she smoothed down the bodice of her dress, especially as they would be travelling round Europe on honeymoon, but she doubted whether Consett had the sort of garments she would be expected to wear as Alexander's wife and she had no idea where else to shop.

A polite knock at the door interrupted her thoughts, and thinking it was one of the maids, she called, 'Come in,' and then stared in surprise when her future mother-in-law came into the room with several dresses in her arms.

Arabella appeared flustered, and her first words were in the form of an apology. 'Rose, these were meant to be a wedding gift to you from me, one woman to another, but as you are here I thought it might be easier to give them to you now. I have taken the liberty of buying you a few things as I didn't think you would have the time before the wedding with all there is to do and—'

Rose gently interrupted the embarrassed flow of words. 'Arabella, that is so kind of you.' Deciding to be honest, she added, 'I'm aware I don't look the part but I have never been in a position to buy myself many clothes before.'

'You always look beautiful.' The words were genuine and not patronizing. 'I – I never had a daughter as you know, but it would have been wonderful to indulge her if I had, especially with her trousseau. I confess I got a little carried away when I was choosing items – there are more for you in my rooms if you would like to come and see them tomorrow. I – I thought with you going to Italy and it being so hot—'

Rose came forward and took the garments, laying them carefully on her bed before she said softly, 'They're exquisite, Arabella. I wouldn't have known what to choose or where to go.'

Arabella was visibly relaxing. 'I didn't want to do anything to offend you.'

'You haven't, I promise.'

'I got some things for Betsy too.' Arabella smiled at the wide-eyed figure in the bed who had been watching the proceedings with great interest. 'I've never had a granddaughter before and it was such fun to shop for you both.'

There was a lump in Rose's throat. Arabella's kindness coming on a day when she had been feeling wretched was almost too much. Not so Betsy. She jumped out of bed and ran to Arabella, throwing her arms round Arabella's waist as she said, 'Thank you, thank you. Can I see my things tomorrow too?'

'Of course.' The two women smiled at each other over Betsy's head. 'But for now why don't you help choose a dress for your mama to wear tonight to welcome Uncle Alexander home?'

There followed a lovely few minutes for the three of them, and when Rose was dressed in a pale blue silk gown that showed off her figure perfectly, it wasn't just

Betsy who stared in wonderment. 'You look utterly delightful, my dear,' Arabella murmured. 'Alexander won't be able to take his eyes off you.'

She was right. He couldn't.

Chapter Twenty-Nine

The next days proved hectic, not so much concerning the wedding arrangements because Arabella was taking care of that, but because Rose was busy at the bakery every day going through everything with Daisy to make sure the business would tick along smoothly when she was away. She popped along to visit Amy and the baby for an hour every evening before Alexander collected her and Betsy to bring them back to Highfield, and she'd told Amy and Daisy that she'd decided to live at the Hall because Alexander felt it was the right thing to do once they were wed. Which was true, just not the whole story.

Daisy had been enthusiastic about the prospect of moving into the flat. With her promotion to manageress and the accompanying rise in wages, and without having to pay rent on the house where she had been living, she was much better off financially. The children were still off school for the summer holidays and her girls had great fun organizing their bedrooms, the three eldest sleeping in the largest and Sarah and Katy in the room which had been Betsy's. Daisy was sleeping on a sofa bed in the sitting room.

It had been strange for Rose to see the little home where she and Betsy had been so happy changing, but she knew she was doing the sensible thing. Alexander had put a notice advertising a change of management in the shop window, and one outside for good measure, and so the die was cast.

Amy had been delighted for Daisy and thanked Rose each time she called in. 'It's made all the difference, you taking her on at the bakery and now this,' she said as she sat feeding the baby, John Wilbur, who was named after his two grandfathers. 'Our family can never thank you enough, lass. You know that, don't you?'

'Don't be silly. Think how you all helped me when I arrived here not knowing a soul, Amy. And Betsy loves Daisy's girls. They're the sisters she's never had and I'm so grateful for that. She could have been lonely, being an only child.'

It was the evening before the wedding and Betsy had stayed at the Hall helping Arabella with the last-minute details. Both the parish church and the ballroom at the Hall where the wedding breakfast was being held were a mass of flowers; Arabella had had the staff working from sunrise to sundown but both she and Betsy were delighted with the result. Even William had unbent a little and got involved, and the day before he had taken Betsy for a walk in the rose garden, naming all the different roses growing there. She had sensed a softening in

Alexander's father – certainly towards Betsy – over the last days and although she didn't understand why, she was thankful for it.

Amy had finished feeding little John and she had just passed him to Rose when Betsy arrived with Alexander, full of the day's happenings. All of that paled into insignificance, though, once Betsy was settled in a chair holding the baby on her lap. She adored him and her greatest delight was being allowed to cuddle him before they had to leave.

Once they had said their goodbyes and were on their way home, out of the blue Betsy piped up, 'Are you and Uncle Alexander going to have a baby, Mam? Alice said that's what happens when people get married.'

Alexander swerved slightly but kept his eyes firmly ahead.

After a moment, Rose said, 'Perhaps, hinny, I don't know. We'll have to see.'

'I always thought I wanted a sister,' Betsy said thoughtfully, 'like Alice an' Rachel an' Violet, but now Auntie Amy's had John Wilbur, I think I'd like a brother.'

'What about one of each?' Alexander suggested, deadpan.

'Oh, yes, one of each,' Betsy agreed delightedly. 'Can we, Mam?'

'Like I said, we'll have to see.' Rose glanced at Alexander for help; he pretended to be oblivious although a quirk to his mouth indicated that he was enjoying the conversation. 'Sometimes people have to wait for a long time for a baby, Betsy. Like Auntie Amy.'

Betsy considered this for a moment or two. 'Did you have to wait a long time for me?' she asked interestedly.

'Not really.'

'And Auntie Daisy didn't for Alice and the others?'

'No, I suppose not.'

'So I think it will be all right,' Betsy said contentedly. 'We could have twins, couldn't we, a boy and a girl, like Patience and Donald McArthur at school, although they don't really look much alike. It might be nice to have twins like Sarah and Katy that look the same. What do you think, Mam?'

'I think we'll have to wait and see what God sends us,' Alexander put in, taking pity on Rose.

Betsy nodded. 'Well, I'll ask Him for twins and let Him decide if it's two boys or two girls, or one of each,' she decided.

Alexander was smiling now but not so Rose. She felt her daughter's words revealed her longing for brothers or sisters of her own and it made her sad. She had done her best for Betsy but there were some things she hadn't been able to provide. Of course, Betsy had benefited in other ways, receiving her full attention and having her all to herself. Now that was changing and Betsy seemed more able to adapt than she did, Rose thought ruefully.

Once they were home they found Arabella waiting for them in the hall. 'Come and see if you like your bouquet,' she said to Rose. 'The head gardener only brought it to the house with Betsy's little posy a few minutes ago. Oh, and something was delivered for you this afternoon, my dear.' Turning to Alexander, she added, 'Your father is waiting in the drawing room. He said to tell you it is the only place where there is a little peace in what has become a madhouse, and he wondered if you would like a quiet drink with him?'

Alexander grinned. His father liked his routine at home and such disorder as there was at present would be hard for him to accept. He rather thought the invitation was in the form of an olive branch too. William had been shocked and alarmed when he'd told his parents about Nathaniel and the threat to Rose and Betsy, but they had ended up having a few words after his father had intimated that maybe the fellow had some claim on Rose she hadn't told him about. William had apologized later, but relations between them had been a mite frosty since. 'I'll go now,' he said to his mother, earning a smile of thanks in return.

Rose and Betsy followed Arabella through to the ballroom which had its huge set of three floor-to-ceiling glass doors open to the gentle evening breeze in an effort to keep the flower arrangements from wilting. The perfume of roses and other sweet-smelling flowers was heady, and a number of tables were set in the shape of an open-ended square glittering with silver and crystal and fine linen.

Rose had let Betsy choose the flowers for their bouquets, and the little girl had settled on orange blossom, pink rosebuds and clouds of baby's breath tied with trailing white ribbons. The result was breathtaking. Rose's bouquet would almost reach the floor when she held it,

419

and Betsy's little posy was delightful. After she had paid sufficient homage to the head gardener's exquisite work and gone outside to the veranda off the ballroom where he was tending more flower displays to thank him personally, Arabella handed her a long thin box tied with ribbons which was addressed to Rose O'Leary, care of Highfield Hall.

'It came earlier,' said Arabella, trying not to appear too inquisitive. 'Apparently a young boy had been paid to deliver it but he didn't appear to know who the sender is.' And then, as there was a loud crash from the veranda followed by some choice words from the head gardener, Arabella hurried outside, leaving Rose and Betsy together.

'Would you like to open it, hinny?' It was bound to be something from Amy or Daisy, Rose thought fondly, or maybe their parents. She had told all of them that she and Alexander didn't want wedding presents – their attendance at the church and then the wedding breakfast would be gift enough – but Amy in particular had been unhappy about that.

'No, Mam, it's for you,' said Betsy seriously.

Rose smiled at her daughter. She untied the ribbons and then carefully raised the lid of the box. Inside, nestled in a bed of tissue paper, there lay a single decaying rose, its petals black and shrivelled.

'I'll kill him. If I get my hands on him I swear I'll kill him.'

It was later that evening. Lawrence and Estelle and the

children had arrived for the eve-of-wedding dinner – Lawrence was Alexander's best man – but they had all retired to their rooms, Lawrence being tired after the journey. Now it was just Rose and Alexander, and Arabella and William, having a last cup of coffee along with glasses of brandy for the men in the drawing room. The atmosphere had been convivial and for once William had appeared relaxed and even jolly, and Rose had almost asked Alexander to say nothing about the rose, but it was right that they knew.

Alexander had been enraged earlier when Rose had taken him aside, but she had asked him to say nothing for the time being until they could talk privately to his parents. She had played the matter down in front of Betsy, merely telling her daughter that someone had kindly sent her the flower but that unfortunately, no doubt because of the hot weather, it must have died en route. Betsy had accepted this quite happily and Rose had disposed of the box and its contents before Arabella's return, harassed about the mess on the veranda and her mind now occupied elsewhere.

That the dead rose was a threat, Rose was in no doubt. Nathaniel was telling her she was still in his sights. She hadn't expected anything else if she was being truthful, not after seeing him that day and looking at his face in the moments before she had turned and left him, but the calculated reminder of his presence on the eve of her wedding was still upsetting. Alexander had called him insane but she didn't think Nathaniel was mad, at least not in the way the poor unfortunates locked away in the lunatic asylums were. He was more dangerous than that. Outwardly handsome and charming when he wanted to be, but inside dark and foul and capable of anything. She was frightened of him, terrified. She didn't like her fear and though she could do nothing about it, maybe in a way it was a good thing? she told herself. It meant she wouldn't take any chances and would always be on her guard.

Alexander had just explained about the rose and William stared at them both. It was clear to him that this Nathaniel fellow was a blackguard, but he still had his doubts as to the part Rose had played in it all. She was a beautiful woman, and when all was said and done, women liked to flirt and even lead a man on now and again.

Rose sensed what her future father-in-law was thinking. She had only told Alexander about her suspicions regarding the part Nathaniel had had in Davey's death, and they'd agreed to keep silent about it in case it worried his mother. But the time for that was past. They needed to know what they might be dealing with now she was living with them. Taking a deep breath, she said, 'I think it is only right that I tell you something. We didn't want to worry you but we believe now that was a mistake. I think Nathaniel murdered my first husband.'

There was a sharp intake of breath from Arabella, and William sat up straighter.

'The accident at the works when Davey fell – it was just him and Nathaniel present. In the days following,

Nathaniel made it clear he wanted to take Davey's place and that was the reason I left Sunderland. I didn't suspect this at the time or else I'd have gone to the shipyard or the police while everything was still fresh, but something Nathaniel said when he came to the bakery makes me sure he was behind Davey's supposed accident. Of course, it is too late to prove anything even if it had been possible back then.'

Arabella had gone white. 'Might he attack Alexander?'

'If he attempted to do so he would get the worst of it.' Alexander's voice was grim. 'But I think it is Rose he is after. That is why I insisted she come here.'

'I see.' William stared at Rose. 'I have to ask this. Did you lead this fellow to believe, even by default, that he had a chance with you?'

Rose pressed Alexander's hand when he would have leaped to her defence. Her voice firm, she said, 'No, I did not.'

'Then what led him to believe . . .'

'I don't know. He was Davey's best friend, they'd been inseparable from childhood and Davey loved him like a brother. Nathaniel was best man at our wedding and a frequent visitor to the house but I never liked him. There was always something about him I couldn't put my finger on.'

'Probably the fact that the man's unhinged,' Alexander growled.

'And he never made overtures to you when your husband was alive?'

'No, not really. As I say there was always something that unsettled me, the occasional look and things like that, but no, he didn't try anything and of course Davey was oblivious to how Nathaniel felt. I am sure of that.'

Alexander was glaring at his father and his voice was acidic when he said, 'Satisfied? Or would you like me to see if there's a pair of thumbscrews in the house so you can continue your interrogation?'

'Alexander, stop,' Rose said softly. 'It's perfectly reasonable that your parents need to know the background. Betsy and I are living here now and that entitles your father to know the facts.'

'Let me say one thing more and then we will not speak of this again.' William glanced at his wife before continuing. 'Tomorrow you will become man and wife, and we will gain a daughter and a granddaughter. Arabella and I want to give you our blessing and support, and that includes anything that may transpire as a result of this fellow Nathaniel. Rest assured, in Alexander's absence, I shall deal with him as my son would and you have my protection, Rose. You and Betsy.'

Arabella had clearly been trying to compose herself and now she said, 'Everything will be all right, my dear. I am sure once you are married he will see that there is nothing to gain from continuing this preoccupation with you.'

William didn't contradict this – he didn't want to worry his wife further – but the facts spoke for themselves. If this fellow had been after her for practically a decade he wasn't going to let a mere marriage stand in his way. Added to his previous reservations about this union there was now this nasty element which posed real danger, not only to Rose but to Alexander as well. If Rose was right and this fellow had killed once, and his friend at that, then he wouldn't baulk at doing Alexander harm. But nothing would be gained by objecting further to this marriage. As Arabella had pointed out when she had spoken to him concerning the child a few days ago, he was in real danger of losing Alexander if he didn't accept the situation. But it was a damn mess whatever way you looked at it. A damn mess.

Rose and Alexander sat together after William and Arabella had gone to bed, his arm round her as she nestled into his side. Alexander had so many emotions churning inside him he couldn't have named them, but his overriding one was of intense love for the beautiful woman beside him who tomorrow would become his wife. That Nathaniel had tried to mar the day filled him with impotent rage but also deep concern, and but for the impending threat of war with Germany he would have resigned his commission and left the army forthwith. Never had he felt so torn about his duty as an officer in His Majesty's army and his love for Rose. He kissed the top of her head and as she lifted her face to his, he murmured, 'Don't let him spoil the day tomorrow, my darling.'

'I won't.' And it was true, she didn't intend to. She had lived so long with the threat of Nathaniel in the background that once the shock of seeing him again had receded, she had determined she wouldn't give him the satisfaction of ruining their day – and in a strange way the dead rose had only strengthened her resolve. Besides which, the spectre of Nathaniel was nothing compared to her fears that she wouldn't be all Alexander deserved her to be on their wedding night. Even his father's obvious reserve about her didn't worry her any more; she had Arabella's support and that was more important. She reached and kissed Alexander hard on the lips, and as he responded, she thought, it will be all right. Everything will be all right. This is Alexander and I love him.

And it had been all right, more than all right. Rose lay entwined in Alexander's arms, listening to his breathing as he slept, her heart full of thankfulness.

The service at the church and the wedding breakfast at the Hall had passed without a hitch, and she would never forget the look of wonder on Alexander's face when he had turned and seen her walking down the aisle on Frank's arm. It had brought all the women's handkerchiefs fluttering. It had been a happy day, surrounded by family and friends, real friends, and although Amy and the others had been overwhelmed by the splendour of Highfield Hall, they had enjoyed themselves. Betsy and the other children had had a wonderful time and Betsy had stolen the show in her bridesmaid's dress and sparkly shoes.

William and Arabella had made everyone welcome, pressing all their guests to stay for an evening buffet

which had been held in the grounds of the house, much
to the delight of the children who had run wild after
being on their best behaviour.

And later, when all the guests but Lawrence and Estelle
and family had departed, Rose and Alexander had put
Betsy to bed in the child's new rooms which Arabella had
organized. They held everything a little girl could possibly
want, right down to a magnificent life-size rocking horse
which Betsy immediately christened King, saying she now
had a king and queen as pets. Alexander had read her
the bedtime story, and once she was settled with Queenie
purring in her basket on the floor beside the bed, they
had gone to Alexander's suite, which was now Rose's
too.

She had been tense in spite of herself when he had
taken her into his arms, but he had merely drawn her
over to a couch in front of the big bay window that
overlooked the gardens, pulling her onto his lap. 'We
have all the time in the world,' he'd murmured throatily,
sensing her tension and understanding the reason for it.
The window was open and the climbing roses on the
stone wall outside perfumed the room with their sweetness, and gradually, as the shadowed night and Alexander's
kisses and caresses soothed her, it was she who turned
more fully into his embrace.

He undressed her slowly and then himself, and she
matched him caress for caress, wanting to touch every
inch of him and glorying in his virile maleness. Their
lovemaking was so different to anything she had known

before, tender and passionate on his part as he brought all his experience to the fore in an effort to please her without rushing her, vitally aware that this night would cement their life together and wanting every moment to be perfect for her. She could hardly contain the pleasure he was bringing forth with his lips and tongue and hands, her body coming alive as though for the first time as he explored her curves and hollows; and when he found her most intimate place with his tongue she gasped his name, tangling her fingers in his hair. She hadn't known that men and women did things like this to each other; Davey had been a kind but unadventurous lover and there had been little foreplay before the act itself.

When Alexander eventually took her she was ready for him, her body moving to draw him further and further in as he made her his at last, their mutual climax transporting them to another dimension of splintered light and sensation.

He had spent a long time afterwards just kissing and caressing her and murmuring words of love, and when his breathing had finally told her he was asleep, she had fought her own drowsiness, wanting to relive the most wonderful night of her life over and over again. She was his, body, soul and spirit, she told herself, and in that there was no fear, no concern about the loss of her own identity, but rather the knowledge that for the first time in her life she was who she had been made to be, a whole woman, fulfilled and at peace with herself, adored and loved.

She nestled further in to him, luxuriating in the close-ness, her arm across the furry pelt of his chest as she breathed in the delicious, faintly lemony smell of the soap he favoured, and even in his sleep he murmured her name, loving her. And that was how, with her lips curved in a smile, she drifted off to sleep.

PART SIX

War and Peace

1914

Chapter Thirty

Rose was nearly seven months pregnant and Betsy had got her wish – it was twins. This, along with the fact that a month ago, at the beginning of August, war had been declared as Britons had returned from the Bank Holiday, had caused considerable changes for the occupants of Highfield Hall.

Britain's declaration of war against Germany had sent cheering crowds onto the streets of every big city in the country, singing the national anthem and working themselves into a fever of patriotism. Young men had sung on the way to the recruiting office, desperate to do their bit for King and country before the war was over, as everyone knew they'd beat the Germans before Christmas. Right was on their side after all, and the Kaiser should be strung up for what he was doing to the poor Belgians. This sentiment had been felt at Highfield and several of the servants, including Franklin and the other footman and four of the outside staff, had joined up in the first few days, followed a week later by the groom, the eldest stable lad and the remaining under-gardener.

Earlier in the year, when Rose had discovered she was pregnant with twins, she had made the decision to gift the bakery over to Daisy – lock, stock and barrel – feeling that whatever the future held, her time there was done. A few days after this she had received another of the envelopes filled with black rose petals – the third since her marriage to Alexander. She didn't know where Nathaniel was living or what he was doing but it was an indication that he was still around and wanted her to know so.

She hadn't mentioned the letters to anyone – she didn't want Alexander worrying when he was away, besides which envelopes with dead petals inside them was hardly a crime, but she watched over Betsy like a hawk and fretted every minute her daughter was at school. Betsy, who had had her twelfth birthday in the summer, had accepted her fussing good-naturedly at first but over the last months had begun to object when she couldn't go anywhere without an escort. Rose agonized over whether to tell her daughter about Nathaniel but always came to the conclusion that she didn't want to frighten her unnecessarily. Childhood was supposed to be a time of carefree days and enjoyment; this was something she herself had never experienced in the workhouse, and she didn't want Betsy to miss out too. Besides which, they were all worried about Alexander fighting in France and that was enough for the child to cope with.

Germany was determined to overwhelm France with a massive flanking movement through Belgium, and every day the news from the front seemed to get worse. Alexander's unit was part of the British troops in action alongside their French and Belgium comrades in a bitter struggle for the town of Mons, and despite the fighting skill of the British Expeditionary Force, the enemy was proving too much. British forces were suffering heavy casualties as they pulled back, and bloody battles were being fought along an ever-shifting line from Belgium to the north of Alsace and Lorraine in the south, but Alexander had written that the main danger was in the north. In under a month the Germans had swept over most of Belgium, crossing the Sambre and Meuse, forcing a retreat to the Somme, the last barrier before Paris. Names Rose had never heard of were now burned into her psyche and featured in her prayers, and the newspapers spoke of a bloodbath at Mons, conjuring up pictures in her mind that kept her awake at night.

One thing became clear by the end of August, which was that the view expressed by Field Marshal Sir John French, the commander of the British Expeditionary Force, that the war would be over by Christmas – a view which had been taken up with such gusto by many young men – was wrong. The Germans had been well prepared and were inflicting severe losses on the Allies.

Alexander had never believed the field marshal was right; rather he had thought Lord Kitchener, the newly appointed Secretary for War, had a better handle on the situation when he forecast that the struggle would be a long and arduous one. Rose had suspected Alexander was right but had prayed that he was wrong; she wanted him home and safe with her and Betsy as soon as possible and able to see his children when they were born. She had been prepared for the prospect of war by Alexander in the days leading up to the declaration, but right to the last moment had hoped it wouldn't happen, especially when she had discovered she was pregnant.

Arabella had been ecstatic at the news and even William had mellowed, and when twins had been confirmed by the Bembridge doctor, a renowned physician from London, Arabella's mollycoddling of Rose had risen to new heights. If her mother-in-law had had her way Rose would have been confined to bed for the whole of the pregnancy, and when she had insisted on going about her daily business the same as usual it had caused quite a few difficult moments, until Arabella accepted that Rose was going to do as she saw fit.

The babies were due to be born in the middle of November and the nursery had been redecorated already and new furniture bought in readiness. Arabella had indulged in stacks of baby clothes – as William had said, it would take several sets of twins to use them all. Another battle – albeit a gentle, civilized one – was fought with Arabella over the matter of a nanny. Her mother-in-law couldn't see how Rose could cope without one, especially with twins, and Rose was equally determined that she would look after the babies herself. Two cribs were already in place in her bedroom and Rose had stated she would keep the babies with her, at least for the first few months until they progressed to their own bedroom in the nursery suite. After much persuasion it was agreed that Rose would choose a nursery maid to help with the practicalities, although Arabella had scarcely been consoled by this compromise on Rose's part.

'My dear, I had the nanny and two nursery maids when Alexander was born,' Arabella had said earnestly.

'And I had no one when I had Betsy and coped perfectly well.'

'But one feels so exhausted after having a child.'

'Yes, that's true, but bear in mind that as well as caring for Betsy I was keeping house. I shall be waited on hand and foot here, no doubt.'

'You would still be able to see the babies whenever you like, my dear. I practically lived in the nursery for the first few years of Alexander's life.'

'Arabella, I'm sorry but I intend to bring my children up myself and Alexander agrees with me on this. We have discussed it at length.'

'But *twins*, Rose.'

Rose had had to smile at the agonized note in her mother-in-law's voice. 'You have Betsy to thank for that. Apparently she has been praying for that very thing since Alexander and I got married.'

This was no comfort to Arabella but eventually they agreed that the engaging of a nursery maid would take place a few weeks before the babies were due, and that Rose would have sole choice in the matter.

September proved to be a trying month. Rose felt as big as a house and the babies were at their most active at night when she was trying to sleep. This, combined with her worry about Alexander and the longing to see him, and the occasional altercation with Betsy who was growing up fast, made her exhausted most days. The war news was mixed; on the one hand the first decisive battle on the Western Front was fought in the middle of the month and the Allies had driven the Germans back to the Aisne and removed the threat to Paris; on the other German submarines sank three British cruisers off the Netherlands in the new war at sea, which was a major setback for the Royal Navy. The army was calling for five hundred thousand more men to sign up, with the aim of placing well over a million soldiers in the field as soon as possible, and although Alexander's letters were invariably cheerful and positive Rose knew he wasn't telling her the whole story.

In October, as Belgian cities fell to German troops and the first bombs dropped on London, an advertisement in several Northern papers for a nursery maid brought a number of replies. Rose had insisted she wanted a local lass, someone she could feel at home with, and as soon as the third applicant walked into the room Rose knew she was the one. The first two women had been older and had related a long history of dealing with children, but she hadn't liked either of them, not least because neither had bothered to hide their surprise and what amounted to almost disdain that she wasn't from the upper class as they had expected. Snobbery, Rose was finding, wasn't confined to the aristocracy.

The third woman was considerably younger than the others, only eighteen according to her letter of application, although on seeing her Rose thought she looked barely that. She had bright blue eyes and blonde fuzzy hair and her hat looked as though it would spring off the riot of curls at any moment. She was also clearly nervous, and after the maid had left sat perched on the edge of her seat in the morning room where Rose was lying on a couch, resting her swollen ankles.

'Good morning,' Rose said warmly. 'And your name is?'

'Davidson, ma'am. Jinny Davidson.'

'And you say you've had experience with children?'

'Oh, yes, ma'am. I helped bring our lot up, me brothers and sisters, I mean, 'cause I'm the eldest, and then when I was twelve the vicar's wife had twins and as I'd just left school they set me on, helping her like. She was weakly, poor Mrs Kirby, after the birth an' that, and she'd no sooner got round when six months later she was expecting again, and this one – Miss Grace – well, she cried night an' day, ma'am. Me brother, Joe, was the same when he was born so I gave Miss Grace the same as I'd given him, a pap bottle with me mam's beef broth in it but well watered down. Mrs Kirby's milk wasn't enough, see.'

Arabella would have a fit if she heard that. Rose was feeling weary that morning; she hadn't heard from Alexander in two weeks, but as she listened to the girl chatter – because Jinny was barely more than a girl – she felt less tired. 'And why are you leaving the vicar's employ?'

'They're moving, ma'am, down South.'

'I see.'

'They said I could go with them, ma'am, but I don't want to be so far away from me mam an' da, not with the war and everything.'

'I can quite understand that. Where do your parents live?'

'Not far from here, ma'am, in Leadgate. Me da's the blacksmith.'

'And you say you've had experience with twins before at the vicarage?' Rose touched her stomach. 'They tell me I am expecting two, although at times it feels like three or four in there.'

Jinny grinned. She was relaxing a little now. The grandeur of the house and grounds had taken her aback at first. She had nearly turned on her heel at the gates, convinced she didn't have a chance of securing a position here, but Mrs Bembridge was lovely. She had heard that the son of the family had married an ordinary working-class lass and properly set the cat among the pigeons, but to her mind there was nothing ordinary about Mrs Bembridge. 'When are the babies due, ma'am, if you don't mind me asking?'

'In just under a month. The middle of November.'

'Well, ma'am, me mam always says that the last weeks are the most trying and she's only ever had one at a time. She swears by a dose of peppermint cordial at night to help with the heartburn and such. I don't know if the doctor has recommended anything like that, ma'am?'

'No. No, he hasn't.' Mr Smethington-Blythe, the doctor from London, had been stiff and highfalutin as befitted his exalted position, and Rose hadn't liked him at all. He had apparently brought Alexander into the world, though, and Arabella had great faith in him, despite him being in his seventies, so she had agreed to see him but once having met him she had put her foot down. She wanted a local doctor or midwife. So Dr Price had visited Highfield with his nurse, had pronounced her fit and well and was due again in a few days unless he was called before then. Rose had found him brisk but approachable and he'd had none of the other man's condescending manner when he had attended her. She smiled at Jinny. 'But I'll send someone to collect a bottle today.'

By the time Jinny left the house she had been engaged as Rose's nursery maid and was due to take up residence at the end of the week. One of the maids had shown her the day nursery, the night nursery, and the nursery maid's bedroom and sitting room and bathroom. Jinny had been overwhelmed by the luxury of it all but reassured by the person of Rose herself. She felt she and her mistress would get along fine.

Rose felt this too, and she went to bed that night more

at peace than she had been for a while. She hadn't left the house and grounds for some time as the pregnancy had progressed and she had felt uncomfortable, but the inactivity coupled with her physical condition was frustrating. Even after her marriage to Alexander she had been used to going into town and helping out at the bakery most days before popping in to see Amy and little John. She and Alexander were the baby's godparents and she had used this as an excuse to shower him with gifts, buying his cot and pram and highchair as well as lots of clothes as he grew. It was a way of helping Amy and Frank financially by the back door, as Alexander had put it, because Frank was a proud man and wouldn't accept what he would have termed as charity. Amy had come to see her the week before and she had almost felt like crying when they had said goodbye which was ridiculous, she knew, but in a house full of people she felt lonely.

She shook her head at herself. She was being silly, she had so much to be thankful for but nevertheless, it would be lovely to have Jinny on hand. Jinny was one of her own kind, that was the thing. She'd realized very shortly after coming to live at Highfield that what she termed as being friendly and informal with the servants wasn't encouraged by the family or the staff themselves. They saw it as over-familiarity and it made the servants uncomfortable. She felt instinctively that Jinny wasn't like that, and that the girl would neither feel awkward if she talked frankly with her nor take advantage of it. She had found a friend.

She turned over in the big soft bed, trying to find a position that was more comfortable for her swollen stomach and wishing Alexander was with her. Keep him safe, God, she prayed silently. In all the madness, keep him safe. Let him live to see his children. Bring him home to me.

Chapter Thirty-One

Alexander stared at his commanding officer, his face expressing his relief and surprise at what the colonel had just told him. His leave had been granted on compassionate grounds.

'I see no reason why you can't disappear for a week or two, m'boy,' the colonel continued, puffing on his pipe. 'There isn't much happening here, let's face it. I wouldn't be surprised if we're dug in for the winter so you make arrangements to get yourself off home to that pretty little wife of yours.'

Over the last weeks a continuous line of trenches, full of weary soldiers, had been dug to stretch from the North Sea to Switzerland, but with little movement since the Germans had failed to reach Paris. It was now the middle of November and a stalemate existed amid the mud and barbed wire, with reports from the front talking of little else but 'alternate advances and retirements'. Nobody on either side had yet developed a tactic to break the deadlock.

The bloody battles of August and September had settled into relative quiet, and in some areas in the trenches men were playing football behind the lines. Elsewhere soldiers were daring each other to go and attack the enemy machine-gun posts and return with their weapons to ease the monotony, something the colonel and Alexander had expressly forbidden for their men. It was a strange state of affairs, and the cold and rain did little to lighten spirits. Elsewhere, European colonies were being sucked into conflict and in Constantinople Turkey had declared war on Russia, the United Kingdom, France and Serbia. In the steaming malarial country of West Africa, commonly known as the 'white man's grave', a combined British and French force had defeated the Germans, and on the Eastern Front Russian troops were reported to be advancing on Königsberg in east Prussia, which made it all the more frustrating for Alexander and his men to be stuck in what they all saw as no man's land.

War was one thing but sitting on their backsides picking their noses was another, as one of the soldiers under Alexander's command had put it only that morning. Alexander had smiled at the time but he shared the man's sentiments.

'So,' the colonel said briskly, 'what are you waiting for? I'll see you in two weeks, Alex.'

'Thank you, sir.' He wasn't about to argue. The thought of seeing Rose was like a lifeline to a drowning man. Not that he was drowning, not really, he told himself as he took his leave of the colonel and went to find his batman in the dugout to tell him the news. Although there had been moments, especially in the bitter struggle for Mons, when he'd felt like it. Blood and guts and bits of bodies had even been with him in his dreams – when he could sleep, that was. All the years he'd spent in the army had been unable to prepare him for the wholesale slaughter, and he'd felt sorry for the men, some of them mere fresh-faced boys, who had joined up in a furore of enthusiasm only to find themselves cast into a living hell.

Hopkins was waiting for him when he got back. 'Trouble, sir?'

'On the contrary.' Hopkins had been with him for years and Alexander thought a lot of the man. He was the sort of fellow you'd want with you in a tight spot. 'I'm off home for a bit.'

'Aw, that's good, sir. You might be in time to see the nippers arrive.'

'I hope so.' Rose had a few days to go yet and there had been no news thus far. Highfield seemed so far away, another world of soft calm voices, loving arms and peace and quiet. Rose had written to say that she had engaged a nursery maid and he was relieved about that. He'd been worried she would insist on trying to take care of the babies without any help at all.

An hour later and he was on his way, unutterably glad to leave the stink of the trenches behind him if only for a few days. He'd never thought of himself as a particularly fastidious individual, but the mud and foul water and lice would try anyone. He hoped the colonel was wrong and they weren't going to be stuck in limbo for months on end; trench warfare was not his idea of fighting the enemy.

But now, now he was going home to Rose and Highfield.

Rose awoke from a fitful sleep in the middle of the night and she realized the babies were coming. The unmistakable cramping pains that had heralded Betsy's birth were beginning and she knew they would get worse. But she was glad. The last two weeks her stomach had been as tight as a drum and so distended she'd wondered if her skin would split, and she knew from the gradual lack of movement inside that the babies had very little room to manoeuvre. As though to deny this she felt a series of kicks that made her wince even as she smiled to herself. 'Come on then,' she whispered. 'Come and meet your mam.'

She got out of bed, walking slowly into her bathroom, and once she had finished in there she didn't return to bed but took the armchair in front of the window and sat staring out into the dark night. It had snowed for the first time the day before, a light dusting that was pretty rather than an inconvenience, but inside the room it was warm and comfortable, the fire in the ornate grate having been piled high with coal before the maid attending it had retired. Now it cast a flickering glow over the two cribs swathed in white lace that were waiting for their occupants.

At the moment the pains were no more than if she had indulged in too much fruit and she didn't want to wake anyone yet, enjoying these last moments with the babies before they were born and the unique closeness between a mother and her unborn children was gone. For nine months only she had known when they were awake and moving about, or sleeping.

By six o'clock when the household was beginning to stir the pains were more frequent but still quite bearable. One of the maids brought her a cup of tea and biscuits at six-thirty as she'd requested for the last month with her sleep being so disturbed, and she asked the girl to fetch Jinny. Within a minute or two Jinny was with her and as soon as the nursery maid walked into the room, she said, 'It's starting, ma'am?'

Rose nodded.

'Shall I fetch the mistress?'

'No, not for a bit. I want to enjoy my cup of tea.' They smiled at each other. Arabella had been like a cat on a hot tin roof the last weeks, panicking at the slightest twinge Rose experienced and hovering close whenever she could. Rose appreciated her mother-in-law's concern but it was wearing. She had given birth to Betsy without any complications and didn't see why this confinement should be any different, although she understood that Arabella's excessive solicitude was a result of her own experience of childbirth, which had been traumatic.

By nine o'clock the doctor had been sent for and Rose was relieved when he walked in the door with his nurse.

The pains were coming at regular intervals and they were excruciating. Betsy had come in to see her before she was taken to school and Rose had managed to chat quite normally and reassure her daughter that all was well, but within an hour of the child leaving she would hardly have been able to speak at all with the spasms attacking her every two minutes.

Arabella and Jinny sat at one side of the bed and the doctor and the nurse at the other. Rose had wanted Jinny there but not her mother-in-law; she had known Arabella would be panic-stricken and that proved to be the case, so much so that after a while the doctor had taken it upon himself to usher Arabella from the room, kindly but firmly ordering her to wait downstairs. Arabella, who was now in a state of nervous collapse, did not protest.

The first of the twins was born at eleven o'clock in the morning and his bellow of a cry expressed his indignation at being expelled from the warm safe place where he had been so comfortable for nine months. His brother followed a few minutes later and he, too, was a lusty, healthy baby and a good weight like his twin. In fact, as the doctor remarked privately to his nurse on the way back to his surgery later, it was quite remarkable how Mrs Bembridge had managed to fit both of them into her normally slim frame.

Jinny had held Rose's hand throughout, and it was she who told her mistress that she was the mother of two fine lads. Once the nurse and Jinny had washed the infants and made Rose comfortable in a fresh nightdress and bedding, they placed the boys in her arms, and as though by magic their grizzling stopped and they went to sleep. It was then that Rose heard a pounding on the stairs outside and the next moment the door was flung open and Alexander stood in the aperture.

He stared at the tableau in the bed, unable to speak or move for the wonder of it, and it was Rose, her face alight, who murmured, 'Alexander, my darling, come and meet your sons.'

It was midnight of the same day and Rose was lying in Alexander's arms in their big bed. Her husband was fast asleep but in spite of her exhaustion, Rose found she couldn't drift off. She had napped on and off for most of the day but now, when the rest of the household was at rest, she was wide awake. She lay thinking about the events of the last twenty-four hours, picture after picture flashing through her mind.

Alexander's face when he had seen his sons and held them for the first time. Betsy, almost delirious with joy at having two baby brothers. Arabella, beside herself with relief that all was well and crying unashamedly as she held her grandsons. William, uncharacteristically mellow, saying that she had done Alexander proud, although, as Alexander had pointed out, he himself had had something to do with it. There had been more tears of joy from Amy when Alexander had sent his father's valet – the family chauffeur having long since signed up – to pick Rose's friend up for an hour or so, knowing Rose would love to see her. And Jinny, Jinny had been marvellous, Rose thought. She had let Betsy help her change the babies and give them a pap bottle each until Rose's milk was in, and the friendship between her daughter and the nursery maid that Rose had noticed over the last two weeks had been further strengthened, which was good for Betsy. She needed someone to talk to closer to her own age in this house.

Everything had gone so well, Rose thought contentedly, and the only thing that marred her happiness was the knowledge that in due course Alexander would have to return to France. She had been shocked at the change in him and she knew his mother had too. He had always been lean but now he was gaunt, and there was something in his eyes that hadn't been there before he had gone to war. Of course, the bloodbath at Mons had been heavily reported and Alexander had been there in the thick of it, which must have been horrendous. He hadn't really talked about it except to say that as the British forces, suffering heavy casualties, had pulled back, some men of II Corps had claimed to have been transfixed by the vision of a shining angel. Briefly, Alexander told her, the men said that while it remained, the oncoming German cavalry had been halted.

She had asked him if he believed the account – he hadn't seen it himself – and he had admitted he didn't know. The men in question were seasoned soldiers and not given to fancies, but he still found it hard to accept.

'I think someone's mother or wife or sweetheart was

praying for protection for their loved one at that moment,' Rose had said quietly. 'And before you say anything I know that not everyone can be spared, but perhaps there was a special reason for whoever it was.'

'I wasn't going to say a word to the contrary.' Alexander had pulled her close. 'And you could well be right, my darling.' He had glanced across at his sons, snuggled in their cribs. 'I am not a praying man, as you know, but I've asked God on numerous occasions to let me come back to you and our family if He exists. I want to do my job as a husband and father and look after you all.'

He hadn't mentioned Nathaniel and neither had she, but she knew the spectre of the man who had hunted her down was present nonetheless. She wanted to allay his fears but of course she couldn't; the withered rose petals in the envelopes spoke for themselves. But she was safe here on the estate, and more importantly so was Betsy and now the twins. She had to believe that or she would be a nervous wreck and she wasn't going to let Nathaniel spoil the present; he'd had his way too much in the past.

The next two weeks before Alexander returned to the front were full of peace and happiness, made all the more poignant by the knowledge that each day was precious and had to be made the most of. To her relief, once her milk came in Rose found she had more than enough to content the babies, who fed every two or three hours and seemed to have voracious appetites. They were very different to how Betsy had been as a newborn; both of them had chunky limbs and large hands and feet and seemed very aware of their surroundings. Alexander walked about like the cat who'd got the cream and a feeling of joy pervaded the house despite the happenings at home and abroad with the war. Alexander had thoroughly approved of her choice of nursery maid and often could be heard joking and laughing with Jinny, and once Betsy was home from school she couldn't be torn away from her baby brothers.

They had let Betsy name the twins, which had thrilled her. The first was duly called William Alexander, which had brought a tear to his grandfather's eye, and the second James David. Rose had wondered if Alexander would mind Betsy using the name of her own father, but he had assured her he didn't and she believed him. He knew that she was his in a way that she had never been Davey's. They had not discussed this, they didn't need to. A love such as theirs only came once in a lifetime.

On the day that Alexander left Highfield Hall, Rose insisted on accompanying him to the train station. It was the end of November and the weather was bitterly cold. There had been intermittent snow showers for days and Alexander had tried to persuade her all morning to stay in the warm before eventually admitting defeat. They left Hammond, the valet, sitting in the car outside the station and once Alexander had his ticket they passed through the barrier. Rose was clinging on to Alexander as though she would never let him go and he had his arm tightly round her. He led her to a seat at the far end of the platform, where they sat.

'You should never have come, you should still be resting.'

'Nonsense, I'm as strong as a horse.'

'My mother was in bed a month after me, she's horrified you were up and about within days.'

She didn't want to talk about Arabella. She turned her face to his and immediately his lips were on hers. They clung together, willing the moments to stretch into eternity, and when at last he lifted his head, his voice was husky when he murmured, 'I hate leaving you.'

'I hate you going.' She had promised herself she wouldn't cry. She didn't want his last memory of her to be in tears but it was taking all her strength not to break down.

The platform had been virtually empty but now it was filling up in readiness for the next train, and Rose saw a couple of women she knew saying goodbye to men in uniform. This war, this wretched war.

'When do you think you'll be able to get leave again?'

She'd asked the same question in various forms several times and he replied as he always did. 'I don't know, my love.' Things were rapidly getting worse. Belgium was now under the control of the German army and every day the news seemed dire. But it was no good saying this, and so he added, 'As soon as I possibly can, I promise you.' He knew that with the flood of young volunteers who hadn't known one end of a rifle from the other when they'd joined up, experienced officers were needed on all fronts. It wasn't going to be any easier when they brought conscription in, which they were going to have to do sooner or later. At least the volunteers, rose-coloured glasses or no, had wanted to fight the Germans even though few of them had had any idea what that entailed.

'I'll write to you every day,' Rose whispered.

'And I'll write to you but don't worry if you don't hear at any point. Sometimes there's a delay in getting the letters away and it might be that you get two at once.'

'I don't mind as long as you keep writing. I'm going to miss you so much.'

'And I you.' He kissed her again, oblivious to the glances from other folk. 'It's your letters that keep me going, my sweet. And try not to worry, my darling. I'll be all right. I promise.'

They both knew it was a promise he might not be able to keep and as they heard the train approaching, Rose pressed closer still, suddenly frantic. 'I love you, I love you, I love you.'

The train slowed down and stopped, doors opened, and Alexander stood up, holding his bag with one hand while he kept his arm round her with the other. 'Look after the boys and Betsy for me,' he said gently before kissing her again, but a swift goodbye kiss this time. 'I'm carrying you with me in my heart, you know that, don't you. I love you, my darling girl.'

She had broken her promise to herself, the tears streaming down her face, and could only hold on to him one more moment before she let him go, unable to speak.

He crossed the platform and got into a carriage; the door closed, the whistle blew and before he had even sat down the train was moving. She saw his face at the window and mouthed, 'I love you,' and then he was gone and she was standing on the platform, alone.

She stood for a few moments more, trying to pull herself together, and didn't notice the big blowsy woman further down the platform who was staring at her with such interest. After she had wiped her eyes and blown her nose, she made her way out of the station to the waiting car, Hammond opening the door for her as she slid into the leather-clad interior.

He had gone, and she didn't know if she would ever see him again. How could she bear it? But she'd have to, the same as countless women in this country and all over the world were doing, though somehow that didn't make it any easier. But she had the twins, a part of him, and already her breasts were telling her they were due for a feed.

She stared silently out of the window on the way back to the Hall, not seeing the snow that had started to fall, her whole being on the train with the man she loved.

'How do you know it was her?' Nathaniel stared at the woman in front of him. He had arrived back at the lodging house already the worse for drink after stopping at the Pied Piper on his way back from the works with a bunch of his cronies.

Polly Stamp stared back at him, hands on hips. 'I've seen him, the Bembridge son and heir before, haven't I, and it could only have been her with him the way they were carrying on.'

She took a perverse pleasure in throwing that in Nathaniel's face. She'd lost her husband twenty years ago after only a few months of marriage, but those months had been enough for her to discover that she liked the intimate side of marriage, she liked it very much, and furthermore she didn't intend to do without just because her husband had been foolish enough to walk in front of a tram when he was three sheets to the wind. Along with 'obliging' the four male lodgers who slept two to a room upstairs, she had what she called 'gentlemen callers' in her bedroom which was the front room of the two-up, two-down terrace in Pitt Lane. All this enabled her to pay the rent, live comfortably and indulge her addiction to hard liquor which she'd been introduced to as a child back in Ireland. And then Nathaniel had come knocking at the door seeking lodgings, and she'd fallen for him like a ton of bricks.

He'd only been sleeping with her for a week or so when he had got blind drunk one night and gone on about Rose O'Leary, the woman who had ruined his life, and who was now married to Alexander Bembridge. Polly had recognized obsession when she'd seen it and was bitterly jealous of this woman who had captivated him, especially because most of the time he treated her, Polly, like dirt, even though she never charged him a penny for her favours like she did the others and most of the time he didn't even pay her his rent.

She'd been at the station as moral support for her mother as her youngest brother, the apple of his mother's eye, had enlisted and was leaving that day for army camp. She'd recognized the Bembridge man straight away but it was the first time she'd seen Rose. The fact that she was so bonny had been a blow and made her want to hurt Nathaniel just as he hurt her. She was under no illusion that Rose was the reason he'd taken a job at the ironworks which he hated, and that it was his strange love/hate for her that caused him to drink himself into a stupor most nights. Rose was his motivation for life, it was as simple as that.

The thought brought the jealousy surging again. 'I'll tell you another thing an' all,' she said flatly, knowing each word would be like a knife in his chest. 'Gertie Bell was at the station, seeing her man off after he'd been home on leave, and after the train had gone and we were talking about the Bembridges, she said they've just had twins. Twin boys. Her sister's a maid up at the house and she told Gertie that the husband, Alexander, got special leave to come and be with her, him being an officer an' all. Devoted, Gertie says they are. She says her sister told her she'd never seen a couple so besotted with each other.'

'*Shut your mouth*.' Nathaniel had been sitting at the kitchen table drinking a glass of whisky she'd poured him when he had walked in, but now he stood up so suddenly the chair went skidding backwards to fall with a clatter on the stone flags.

'No, I won't shut up,' Polly said defiantly, knowing two of the lodgers were upstairs and they would come running if she screamed. 'This is my house, remember, and I'll say what I like in it.'

They glared at each other, Nathaniel's face red with fury and the alcohol he'd consumed, and then he swore viciously as he hurled his glass into the range where it shattered into a hundred pieces. He brushed past her, almost knocking her off balance as she'd had a few while she'd been waiting for him, and she heard him going up the stairs and then the bedroom door slamming which wouldn't go down well with the other occupants.

'That told him,' Polly said out loud, before sinking down onto a hard-backed chair and bursting into tears. After a minute or two she reached for her panacea to all ills, the whisky bottle. She poured herself a good measure, knocking it back in three gulps before filling the glass to the brim.

All the men she'd had in her time, she thought bitterly, and she had to go and fall for the biggest swine of 'em all. More than one of her lodgers would have married her if she had said the word, and though she'd discovered she liked her independence and didn't want to be tied to one man, all that had changed the day Nathaniel came knocking. He treated her as less than the muck under his boots most of the time and he didn't even pay his rent or buy her the odd thing, so why couldn't she tell him to sling his hook? She had worked herself up to do just that more than once, but then he'd be nice and sweet-talk her and before she knew it she was putty in his hands. More fool her.

She sat drinking and crying into her glass for more than an hour, and by the time she staggered into the front room she was so drunk that she fell on the bed fully clothed and was snoring within seconds. She didn't hear Nathaniel leave the house at just after midnight.

It had stopped snowing and the air was crisp and bitingly cold, but Nathaniel didn't feel the chill. His face was grim as he made his way to the Bembridge estate some miles away. The snow lit up the surrounding countryside but he would have known the way without it; it wasn't the first time he had trod the path. Many a night he had left the house when he was sure the other occupants were dead to the world and walked to Castleside, climbing over the wall into the Bembridge estate grounds and taking his time exploring the gardens. The vegetable garden didn't interest him and neither did the walled garden, which looked as though it had been set up for a child with the swing and tree house it contained. No, it was the rose garden situated a short distance from the house and entered by an ornate scrolled iron gate set in a high, ivy-covered wall that drew him again and again. In the summer the scent of the flowers was overwhelming and he would sit in the shadowed silence thinking of Rose and pleasuring himself until, having reached a climax, he would wander out and stand in the darkness, looking up at the house for sometimes over an hour or more. Maria and several of the other women he'd stayed with for a time had slept naked, and he liked to think that Rose did the same. He would take his time imagining her body spread out on the bed, her legs open to receive him and her hair cascading over the pillow, and when he was hard enough he would shut his eyes and pleasure himself again, groaning her name. Other times he visualized her pleading for mercy as he subjected her to various indignities before putting his hands round her throat and squeezing the life out of her. That picture in itself was arousing.

He knew exactly what he was going to do tonight, he thought as he strode along. It was high time she was reminded of his claim on her again. Did she know that the rose petals he sent her in the envelopes had come from the blooms on the estate? He doubted it. So it would be nice to let her know she wasn't as invincible as she thought in her comfortable ivory tower. Twins. She'd had twins with that fancy gentleman of hers. She'd let him penetrate her and distort her body and then she'd brought forth the results of their filth. He ground his teeth, his jaw working. But a husband, bairns, they were nothing; it was him who owned her and he would make her see that she belonged to him. He'd done murder for her and sold his soul to the Devil – no other man would have done that. No one was capable of loving her like he did. And now look at him, he was working at the stinking ironworks and living with the lowest of the low, and all because of Rose.

She had to be made to understand that the bond between them could never be broken until death. Aye, he told himself grimly, until death.

Since the outbreak of war, old Stubbs, the head gardener at Highfield Hall, had lost the three gardeners under him – two of whom were his sons – when they had joined up. He'd found a couple of young lads from the nearby hamlet who came in to help him at weekends when they weren't at school, but otherwise he'd been forced to cope on his own and at seventy years of age he was finding it increasingly difficult.

He had been employed at Highfield from a lad of twelve; he knew and loved every inch of the grounds, and revered the Bembridge family. The master, in his book, was only a step down from God Himself. He disapproved strongly of the increasing trend in the young not to know their place any more, which made it all the more surprising when he so far forgot himself as to burst through the front door of the house rather than using the servants' entrance. He further compounded this disgraceful act by pushing past the butler when he tried to stop him, and rushing in on the family when they were having breakfast.

William, Arabella, Rose and Betsy looked up in astonishment as the door flew open and Betsy even gave a little scream.

His rose garden, he cried. His beautiful rose garden that had produced the finest blooms in the North for decades. Gone, all gone.

William, fearing that the old man was having a break-down due to overwork and worry about his two sons, who were both at the front, stopped the butler and the valet when they would have forcibly removed the old man from the room, and instead sat him down on a chair, telling a maid to get a glass of brandy.

Visibly shaking and hardly able to form his words, the gardener described the scene that had awaited him that morning. Every single rose bush in his precious protected walled garden had been uprooted and savagely mutilated, and the paraffin for the heaters used in the hothouse had been poured onto the mangled remains before being set alight. The hothouse windows had all been smashed and the roses therein, cultivated for the flower displays in the house, had received similar treatment. Nothing remained. His own spade and shears were lying amidst the devas-tation, and even the stems of the climbing roses on the stone walls had been hacked away.

What madman would do such a thing? And why, why?

Chapter Thirty-Two

Once Betsy had been taken to school in the car by
Hammond, Rose had gone to see William in his study.
Her father-in-law had told the gardener to go home and
rest for the day and that he would deal with the clearing-
up involved, and to that end the rest of the remaining
staff, even the butler much to his indignation, had been
dispatched to the scene of the crime with orders to dispose
of the debris.

William was sitting at his desk but staring across the
room into the fire burning in the basket grate, and
although he smiled at her entrance it was forced. Before
she could speak, he said, 'I have been thinking, Rose.
Is it possible that this fellow you told us about could
be responsible for the wilful destruction of the rose
garden?'

'I'm sure of it.' She sat down, and then told him about
the dead rose petals she had received. 'I think it is his
way of telling me he's still somewhere close.'

'You should have told me before.'

'I didn't want to worry you, and after all what are a few petals – but this, this is different.'

'Does Alexander know about the envelopes you received?'

'No, and I don't want him to, or to learn about the rose garden either. He has enough to worry about.'

'I agree, and I would prefer your mother-in-law to be kept in ignorance about the envelopes too. She's very distressed about the rose garden as it is.'

'I'm sorry.' She had brought this upon them, she told herself wretchedly. She should never have married Alexander. She was putting them all in danger. 'This is all my fault. I should leave and go away somewhere.'

William stared at the young woman he had come to like and even admire over the last couple of years. If he was being absolutely truthful he still wished Alexander had married one of their kind, but nevertheless his son could have done a lot worse than Rose. 'That is ridiculous, Rose, and you should dismiss such a thought from your mind. There is only one person to blame for this and that is this fellow Nathaniel. I agree with old Stubbs, he's a madman but clearly a resourceful one. I shall have enquiries made as to his whereabouts. I should have done it when you first mentioned the wretch but I suppose I hoped he would disappear once you were married to Alexander. Obviously not.'

She stared at him helplessly.

'Now I don't want you worrying about this. He clearly wants to intimidate us and in that he will not succeed.

When I find out where he is residing I shall put the fear of God in him regarding this latest outrage. I have friends in high places in the police force and if the man's liberty is put in jeopardy no doubt he will think twice in the future.'

'But we can't prove anything.'

William smiled. 'Let's just say intimidation can work both ways, m'dear. The fellow is a scoundrel but not a fool and the police can be most persuasive when they want to be. In the meantime there are a couple of chaps I know from way back, gamekeepers who are retired now but still active enough. I shall get them to patrol the grounds at night from now on. I'm sure they could use the money and there will be men they can use if they are incapacitated. You and my grandchildren will be safe, you can count on that.'

Rose made no comment to this because of a sudden it seemed that all her strength was draining out of her. She did not feel the need to cry, but a great need to sleep. The shock of the gardener's revelation and Nathaniel's audacity coming on top of the birth of the twins and the heightened emotions of Alexander being at home and then leaving again had taken their toll, just how much she hadn't realized until this moment in time. She was tired, tired of being in a state of anxiety and worrying about Betsy if her daughter was out of her sight. Nathaniel had killed Davey, she was sure of it, and that meant he was capable of anything.

She sat back in the chair and let a long-drawn breath out before she said, 'He is dangerous.'

'He is a good-for-nothing and a coward to boot. To hound a woman as he has hounded you is unforgivable. Now you are looking pale, m'dear, and I insist you retire to your quarters and rest. I have everything in hand, please believe me.'

She wanted to, but he had never met Nathaniel. Nevertheless, as he came over to her and helped her up, she said softly, 'Thank you, I think I will take a nap.'

'Do, do.'

Once in her own rooms she found Jinny waiting for her, jogging a baby on each arm. 'I'm sorry, ma'am, they won't be pacified until they've been fed. I've tried everything.'

'I'm sure you have.'

The feed worked its usual miracle, and once the babies were sleeping in their cribs after Jinny had changed their nappies, Rose told the nursery maid to go down to the kitchens and have her breakfast. Her sons' need of her, their total helplessness, had banished the earlier feeling of weakness and replaced it with anger. How dare he come into the grounds of the house, right to where her bairns were, how dare he? And William was right, she wouldn't allow herself to be intimidated and neither would she let him drain the joy out of her days. Her thoughts and prayers needed to be centred on Alexander, keeping him safe, and she wouldn't let herself brood about Nathaniel.

She lay down on the bed, drawing the coverlet over her, and within a few minutes was sound asleep, and when Jinny returned from the kitchens and gently wheeled the babies through to the nursery she didn't wake.

Christmas came and went, and although the adults put in the effort to make it a happy time for Betsy with a magnificent tree in the drawing room and lots of presents on Christmas Day, each one of them was vitally aware of the missing place at the table.

Among all the dire news, there was one reported incident about a truce in the trenches on Christmas Day that shocked the generals and heartened many a mother and wife. In one corner of the Western Front, where the British Tommy in his trench was only a few yards from the enemy in his, the war came to a halt, briefly, on the day of Christ's birth.

A second lieutenant of the Royal Field Artillery raised his head above the parapet, and was astonished to see British and German soldiers standing in the open and making no attempt to shoot at each other. The lieutenant met another officer and together they walked along the line as Germans waved and called out. Speaking in simple French, the Germans, holding out cigars, asked for English jam, and for a while the rival troops put the war behind them.

'It just shows, doesn't it, ma'am, that them German soldiers are no different to our lads at heart,' Jinny said when she and Rose were discussing the incident, a baby each on their knees as they undressed the twins ready for their evening bathtime. 'Me da says it's them few at the top like the Kaiser and his cronies who make the wars and it's ordinary men and lads on both sides who have to fight each other.'

'I think your father is right, Jinny.'

'Me da reckons the Kaiser has a few surprises for us up his sleeve. What do you think, ma'am?'

'I hope he's mistaken.' Rose cuddled little James's naked warm body into her, kissing the top of his downy head. Once the Kaiser and all these men of war had been small infants, innocent and dependent on others. What happened in a man's mind to turn him into a creature intent on violence and domination? What had happened in Nathaniel's? In spite of herself she always was on tenterhooks once darkness fell and she wasn't sleeping well, even though William's men were outside. She had spoken to them once when they were sitting hunched over the brazier in a sheltered spot near the stables, and they had assured her that no one would get past them.

'We can hear a deer breathing at a hundred yards,' one of them had said cheerfully, his gnarled hands stretched out over the coals. 'Years of watching for poachers, see, ma'am? It sharpens all your senses, does gamekeeping. Whoever this bloke is, he won't get the better of us.' He'd adjusted the shotgun at his feet. 'You sleep easy, ma'am, you and the bairns.'

She had appreciated their sentiments but they thought they were just dealing with a vandal or thief, or someone with a grudge against William, because that was what her father-in-law had told them. Nathaniel was different, he wasn't normal. She knew William had employed someone, a private investigator, to find out where Nathaniel was living, but even if they found him and, as her father-in-law had put it, put the fear of God in him, she had no hope that that would be the end of the matter.

In the middle of January Jinny's father's prediction came true as a sinister new development of aerial warfare was experienced in Britain. German Zeppelins crossed the Norfolk coast during the night to bomb unsuspecting British towns, resulting in civilian deaths. Great Yarmouth and King's Lynn were the targets and both towns were fully lit as the enemy approached from the south. More bombs fell near Sandringham, the King's Norfolk home, and for the first time in the war civilians didn't feel safe in their beds. In December three German warships had loomed out of the mist off the east coast and shelled the towns of Scarborough, Whitby, Hartlepool and West Hartlepool, killing and injuring hundreds, but the Zeppelin attack was different, everyone agreed. And to target the King's residence caused a national outrage.

By the middle of the year even ordinary men and women knew they were in the war for the long haul and that the earlier claims of a swift defeat for the Germans were false. The enemy's terrible new weapon of choking chlorine gas had caused panic in the trenches on the Western Front in April.

Alexander had written that the gas, drifting across from the German lines, was a swirling greenish-yellow vapour and looked fairly innocuous, but its effect had been deadly, allowing the Germans in their gas-proof helmets to tear a four-mile gap in the Allied front. Rose didn't know if he had been stricken by it, he hadn't said, but since that letter she had ceased to worry about Nathaniel and all her thoughts concentrated on Alexander. There was a lot of talk about trench warfare in the papers now and less glorifying of the war. Alexander hadn't been home since the year before when the twins were born, and now they were both sitting up and were very different to the small newborns he had left. Once the infants were sleeping through the night they had gone into their cots in the night nursery, and although Rose found she slept a little better without their snuffles and squeaks keeping her awake, she missed them.

William had told her his man had found Nathaniel. Her father-in-law's friends in the police force had paid Nathaniel a visit, but William had told her nothing more and she hadn't asked. She didn't want to know where he was living or what he was doing or his response when the police had been to see him. She wanted to put him out of her mind and allow him no access to her thoughts.

Jinny was proving a great help with Betsy as well as the twins. The friendship which had sprung up between the two early on had strengthened as the months had gone by. After the garden incident Rose had decided to confide in the nursery maid about Nathaniel, confident that she would not gossip to the other servants. Betsy was spending more time with Jinny and the twins when she was at home than anyone else, and often took walks in the grounds with the nursery maid, Jinny pushing one pram and Betsy the other. Rose felt that if Nathaniel should materialize, unlikely though that was, she wanted Jinny to be fully aware of who he was and his intent. To that end she had given Jinny a detailed description of him and Jinny had promised she would keep her eyes skinned at all times.

'One of me sisters had trouble with a man like him,' Jinny had told Rose at the time. 'He was double her age and her only fifteen, but he wouldn't leave her alone. Worried me poor mam to death, it did, ma'am. Then me da and some of his mates paid him a visit in the middle of the night. When he come out of hospital he took off to pastures new, and good riddance, we all said.' She'd smiled at Rose and Rose had smiled back, but inside Rose had wished that Nathaniel could have been got rid of so easily.

But now it was June, and after a late spring the lanes and byways were in full leaf as the trees luxuriated in the sun and the scent of flowers was everywhere. Rose was hoping that Alexander's long-awaited leave would finally happen; twice he had been going to come home and twice it had been cancelled at the last moment. He had written in his last letter that it was common knowledge among the officers that there was dissension among the generals as to tactics, and that Lord Kitchener was at loggerheads with certain politicians, which all made for confusion and error at the front. General Joffre, the French commander-in-chief, had been told by Kitchener to instruct the British Army but as there were British commanders who didn't speak French and had to take their orders through an interpreter, this had added fuel to the fire among the generals and Kitchener's critics.

We don't know what the situation is from one day to the next, Alexander had written, his frustration clear on the page, *and it's a recipe for disaster. We advance a few hundred yards and then we pull back, and I have to pretend to my men that we know what we're doing.*

It was rare he let his feelings show – he was invariably cheerful and positive in his letters – so she knew how angry he must be feeling and ached to be able to see him, to hold him and comfort him, but there was a sea between them. All she could do was pray, and she did, constantly. Men were dying in their thousands and still the government called for more to enlist; the world had gone mad and might seemed to be winning over right, but she had to be strong. For her babies and Betsy, for Arabella who was making herself ill worrying about her only child in the thick of it, even for William who was walking around as though he had the weight of the world on his shoulders, but especially, *especially* for her love, her Alexander.

Chapter Thirty-Three

'Well, sir.' Hopkins's voice was bright and cheery. 'It looks like this is it. We've been waiting for it long enough.'

'You're right, we have.' Alexander smiled at his batman, who had been busy brushing him down.

Hopkins took a step backwards to inspect his handiwork and make sure there wasn't a speck of dust on Alexander's uniform. He prided himself that his officer was the best turned out in the regiment, and the major was a fine figure of a man to boot. 'Strange it should happen today, sir, it being my birthday. I think that's a good omen.'

'I'm sure it is.' And they would need all the luck they could get. The long-prepared British and French offensive on the Western Front, coordinated with Russian and Italian assaults, was about to begin, astride the River Somme in Picardy. They had come up to the front during the night in Alexander's staff car, passing endless lines of heavily laden soldiers marching at a smart pace, some of them singing music-hall tunes accompanied here and there by a mouth organ. Numerous other staff cars and motor-cycles of dispatch riders had been on the roads, all making for the points of flame stabbing the blackness where the British shells were falling.

Alexander knew it was the biggest British army yet sent into battle. His colonel had told him that twenty-six divisions, every man a volunteer, were stretching along a fifteen-mile front. The French were doing their part but of the original forty divisions they had promised, they'd only been able to muster eighteen, their strength drained by the savage five-month German attack on Verdun. This had worried the colonel and it worried Alexander. It had felt like they were going into battle with their forces already heavily depleted. But the old generals had insisted the assault go ahead and so go ahead it must. It was now almost two years, give a month, since the beginning of the war and over eighteen months since he had seen Rose and the children. He'd stopped hoping for a decent period of leave until something changed. This, as Hopkins had said, could be it.

Alexander glanced to where his friend, Captain Palmer, was marshalling their men. He lifted his hand, receiving the same in reply. He hadn't known Philip Palmer more than twelve months but they'd struck it off immediately. On the couple of times they had been granted a forty-eight-hour leave, they'd spent it in a nearby village getting drunk together and talking about home and family.

Although they were the same age, Philip had been married to his childhood sweetheart for over a decade and had three children, the eldest a boy of nine and the youngest a girl of three. Philip's two brothers had been killed in the first year of the conflict, but he'd told Alexander that his parents were army people and had accepted the loss of their sons stoically. Alexander hadn't known quite what that meant. Already he knew he wouldn't be able to stand it if anything happened to his boys, or Betsy for that matter.

Philip was a strange mixture, Alexander thought now. An army man through and through, but a poet too. He was exceptionally well read, having taken English Literature at university, and he had shown Alexander some of the poems he'd written. In Alexander's humble opinion, they were amazing. One in particular, entitled 'A Summer's Morn', had transported him back in time to when he was a boy at Highfield. He'd almost been able to smell the scent of climbing roses and newly mown grass, and hear larks calling in a blue sky. For a few precious moments it had taken him away from the grim reality of the trenches, of men dying, or being horribly crippled or burned alive.

'Nearly time, sir.'

Hopkins's voice brought him out of his reverie. At half-past seven that morning the artillery barrage would stop and they would go over the top. The orders were to push forward at a steady pace in successive lines, but as each soldier was expected to carry entrenching tools, two gas helmets, wire cutters, two hundred and twenty rounds of ammunition, two sandbags, two Mills bombs and other essentials totalling almost seventy pounds of equipment each, Alexander knew the most they could hope for was a slow walk into No Man's Land. The aim was to seize, according to Field Marshal Haig's calculation, some four thousand yards of enemy territory in the first day.

Alexander and Philip had privately agreed that this would take a miracle to achieve, but orders were orders and the officers had to present a united front to the men however they felt about leaders who seemed to have no real grasp on reality.

Alexander began to walk along the duckboards and he saw Philip doing the same, speaking to the men and encouraging them. Hopkins was right behind him as ever, and he heard his batman joking with a sergeant about having a beer or two when they reached their new quarters. He grinned to himself. He was sure every man present felt like him, sick to their stomach, but one would never have known. It wouldn't be guns and bombs and military power that won this war, he told himself, but the spirit represented right here.

At seven twenty-eight he joined up with Philip again and they stood together for a moment. 'Good luck.' They spoke at the same time and both smiled. Then they parted to take up their positions and await the countdown. Strangely, now the moment was here, Alexander found he didn't feel anything – not fear or relief or panic or resignation – nothing. It wasn't exactly a numbness and neither was it peace, it was . . . unexplainable.

All along the trenches sergeants were bellowing, 'Thirty

seconds, twenty, ten,' and then, as the artillery barrage stopped right on cue, 'Over, over, over.'

Alexander didn't know that in the first five minutes of the battle thousands were cut down by relentless enemy fire; he was just aware that he had walked into hell and his men were following him. The bombardment of previous days meant to destroy and weaken heavy barbed-wire obstacles hadn't done its job, and sweeping machine-gun fire mowed down men without mercy. All around him they were screaming and falling and being blown apart; it was slaughter at its most spectacular and it went on and on and on. A shell exploded near him and he was thrown to the ground, but he was up again in a moment, his ears ringing and dirt in his mouth. He turned to speak to Hopkins but all that remained of his batman was his upper torso and head; the shell had scored a direct hit.

The German defences were formidable and deep, so that the capture of the first and second lines brought little advantage and no respite from the carnage. On every side of him there were dead and wounded but there was no going back, just forward even though it was into the mouth of the beast. Shells were bursting overhead, timbers and clay from the trenches were being thrown into the air and the machine-gun fire was merciless. He thought he had seen it all at Mons in the first weeks of the war but even though this wholesale annihilation was worse, still he found himself shouting, 'Come on, forward, forward,' because that was what officers did, wasn't it? Damn it, that's what they did. Every one of them, officers and men, were just pawns in some sick game the Kaiser and the generals had thought up.

As he pushed on, men stumbling and falling behind him, the barbed wire they'd been told would be destroyed tore at his uniform and hands, trying to catch him and pin him so that the enemy had a sitting target. The noise was indescribable, guns and shells and shouts and screams – some from dying and wounded men and some from officers trying to give orders. It was Mons all over again.

He didn't feel any pain when the explosion lifted the ground from beneath him, just a force like a mule kicking him in the chest, so when he got to his knees and tried to lift his rifle he experienced a feeling of surprise when his right arm wouldn't obey him. It was then he realized it was all but gone, blood pouring from a wound above his elbow and the flesh beneath and his hand looking like something on a butcher's block. Somehow he got to his feet and staggered a few more yards only to go headlong into a German trench which fortunately had already been taken by their lads. There were bodies of Germans and some British soldiers strewn here and there along the dugout, and he fell onto one, before rolling over and trying to sit up with his back to the wall of the trench. His blood was soaking his uniform and everything was going hazy, and it was then a voice said, 'Major Bembridge, is that you?' and one of his own men was kneeling in front of him. 'Let me look, sir, I've done first aid.'

He didn't protest, he couldn't have; he was losing consciousness fast and it was a blessed relief to go into the darkness, his only thought being, 'Sorry, my love. Sorry, Rose, I promised I'd come back to you,' before he sank into oblivion.

The telegram arrived a week later and by that time Rose and the others knew from the news reports that nineteen thousand men had died on the first day of the Somme campaign, and a further fifty thousand been injured.

At Highfield they'd all been frantic with worry, and but for the twins Rose feared Arabella would have made herself ill. As it was, her mother-in-law practically lived in the nursery, taking comfort from the fact that as Alexander's sons grew they looked more like their father every day. The babies were identical in appearance but were developing distinct personalities of their own. William was a demanding, determined and impatient little person, whereas James was a far more placid individual, always smiling and ready for a cuddle.

Rose stared at the telegram which the maid had just put in front of her plate in the breakfast room. Arabella's fingers were clutching her throat and William was perfectly still; even Betsy had frozen, her hand halfway to her mouth.

When she opened it the words danced in front of her eyes for a moment and then she raised her gaze, looking at the three faces watching her. 'He's injured,' she said shakily, 'but he's coming home. He's coming home.'

In the event it was some time before Alexander was to return home. The shell that had taken his right arm had also kindly left its handiwork in his chest with pieces of shrapnel. When he was shipped back to England it was to a hospital in the South where a surgeon who specialized in the intricate form of operation he needed was based.

He didn't remember being brought over from France, but apparently, according to the other men in the ward, he'd been in a bad way.

'Touch an' go, it was, Major,' Montgomery, a lieutenant in the next bed, told him when Alexander had returned to the land of the living. Montgomery, an Eton man, also took pleasure in informing him that they'd taken bets as to whether he would pull through or not, which Alexander thought was a strange introduction to his fellow patients, all of whom were – or had been – seriously ill. Most of them were minus at least one limb like him and a couple had lost both legs. Several had extensive burns, like Montgomery, and all had pieces of shrapnel lodged somewhere or other in their battered bodies.

'It's a common problem with you chaps, I'm afraid,' his doctor, a middle-aged man with a stern face but a warm smile, had informed him. 'But don't worry about it. We'll get the little beggars out of there sooner or later.'

'Could you make it sooner?' Alexander had asked with a smile. The sister had already told him that until Dr Jefferson was satisfied that he had done all that he could, he'd be remaining where he was. Which was all very well – the hospital was an excellent one and the staff were a nice bunch although Sister Shawe was a bit of a dragon – but it was a good two hundred and fifty miles from where he wanted to be. Visitors were discouraged on the ward owing to the fact that the men had just had, or were about to have, major operations, but Rose had made the long journey by train once already despite the frosty disapproval of Sister Shawe, who had only allowed her to stay for ten minutes. Ten minutes for a day's journey. He had made her promise she wouldn't come again; he'd be transferred to a hospital in the North soon, he'd assured her, but the ten minutes had done him more good than any of his medication. They had kissed and she'd sat and held his hand and told him about the twins and they'd both cried a little, but seeing her had meant the world even though it had exhausted him and he had more or less slept for the next twenty-four hours.

It was shortly after Rose's visit that a strange incident occurred. He had been dozing when one of the nurses had dropped a tray of instruments on the tiled floor, the sound deafening in the confined space. And suddenly the ward had vanished and he was back in the trench in France, shells exploding overhead and screams and cries all around. He tried to grip one of the soldiers in the trench but he was a lifeless corpse, horribly burned, but then at his touch the corpse came to life and began to shout, 'You told us to go over and so we did, we did,' and then the bottom of the trench opened up and he could see fire below them and he was falling, falling into the flames and sulphur.

'It's all right, Major, it's all right.' He clawed his way up out of the pit to find he was in the ward again, the curtains closed round his bed, and Sister Shawe stuck a needle into his arm as he tried to tell her about the flames. 'This happens, Major, it happens and it's nothing to worry about. Go to sleep and when you wake up you'll be yourself again.'

And he had been, until the next time. Dr Jefferson had told him that these 'incidents' were akin to nightmares but when you were awake, and that they would gradually get better. 'Your mind is exhausted as well as your body, Major,' he had said in his deep voice. 'We don't quite understand "shell shock" as they're calling it, but it improves with time, take my word on that.'

'I'm going mad?'

'Far from it, Major. You're as sane as me, if that's any comfort.' He'd smiled his warm smile and Alexander had tried to smile back. 'Loud noises can set this off, or exhaustion or extreme agitation, things like that. It's nothing to be ashamed of, no more than any other injury or illness as a result of this damn war. Just go easy on yourself, that's all I'm saying. You're doing very well after your operation and it was highly successful. If you continue to improve as you are doing we'll soon have you out of bed and taking gentle walks.'

'Can I take a gentle walk up North?'

'All in good time, Major, all in good time. You understand that the loss of your arm, although difficult for you, is not my main concern? The shrapnel is vicious and it's damaged your insides, it's as simple as that. We'll do all we can but it is time that's the great healer, and that calls for patience from you. Even once you are home you will have to take it easy for a long time unless you want to be permanently affected. If you *are* sensible I see no reason why, in a year or so, you shouldn't be back to full health.'

'A *year*?'

'Don't look so horrified, Major. You made it back to England, that's the main thing.'

Unlike poor Hopkins. He had thought about his batman a lot. He intended to write to the man's elderly mother when he could and tell the old lady that Hopkins had been an excellent soldier and a fine person and that he had been proud to know him. It might help her in her grief. Hopkins had never married and Alexander knew his batman had thought a lot of his mother. He had been an only child and his father had died when he was a boy, so now the old lady had no one. Such sadness and grief in the world, such loneliness. How did people like Mrs Hopkins get through each day?

But he had Rose and the twins and Betsy. Dr Jefferson was right, he'd made it back and that was everything. The loss of his arm he could come to terms with, and if it took twelve months to gain his strength, so be it. He was alive and he had Rose waiting for him. What more could a man ask?

Chapter Thirty-Four

Alexander was home in time for Christmas. Although a shadow of his former self, he appreciated every moment. He'd broken down when he had first seen his boys. Both the twins were crawling now and into everything, William in particular keeping Jinny on her toes. Perhaps it was indicative of his nature that his first word was 'No'. James's, on the other hand, was 'Mamma'.

It made it all the more poignant for Alexander that the stalemate in the trenches on the Western Front made this, the third Christmas of the war, the bleakest for those still in France. Two years ago the men of Europe had gone to war cheerily confident of 'being home for Christmas'. There was no such optimism now. Neither side had achieved the breakthrough they had sought and the cost in lives was immense. The great British offensive at the Somme had proved bloody and fruitless; six hundred and fifty thousand Allied soldiers had perished, most of them British, along with five hundred thousand Germans. In places the front lines were changed by a mile or two but rarely for long, and never to achieve the significant strategic gain the generals had predicted.

Rose was unutterably thankful to have her husband home, but at the same time she was frighteningly aware of just how fragile he was, not only in body but also in mind. Arabella's expression of concern about her son took the form of relentless fussing which tended to drive Alexander to distraction, so in between trying to keep him peaceful and rested and tactfully advising Arabella to give her son time to himself, Rose had her work cut out.

They celebrated the New Year quietly. Thick snow covered the North of England and the weather was bitterly cold. This, added to the harsh fact that a number of households had lost their breadwinner, meant whole families were struggling to keep warm and have enough to eat.

Rose met with Daisy in the second week of January, and put an idea to the other woman that she'd been mulling over for a little while. Betsy had left school now, and although she had decided she wanted to train to be a nurse in the future, for the time being she divided her time between helping Jinny with the twins and working at the bakery with Daisy. Daisy's assistant had skedaddled to a munitions factory in Newcastle and as Betsy refused any payment for her services, she was doubly welcome as far as Daisy was concerned. Rose's idea was that they open a soup kitchen at the bakery for those in need in the community, and Daisy embraced the idea wholeheartedly. So it was that every day thereon, from four in the afternoon until six o'clock, the bakery provided soup and rolls for everyone who came, all paid for by Highfield Hall.

At first folk seemed somewhat suspicious of this act of altruism, but once word spread that there were no strings attached the queues began to form as early as half-past three. Rose and Betsy put their pinnies on and dished out the soup and rolls while Daisy manned the kitchen. The customers were mostly weary-looking mothers and hungry children, and Rose made it a point to get alongside the women and find out who was most in need so she could discreetly do something about it, mindful of the fierce pride of Northerners. Even Mrs Finnigan came and was welcomed.

Over the following weeks, the number of customers increased so much that she asked the local vicar if they could move the soup kitchen into the church hall in order to accommodate more people eating in the warm, to which he readily agreed. Amy joined the others to do her bit, as she put it, and after a few men – mostly the old and destitute, along with a few disabled soldiers – started to come regularly, Alexander came with Rose each day. He sat in a quiet corner, chatting to the men and making them feel comfortable, and as an injured soldier they responded to him as they would never have done when he was just the Bembridge son and heir. Rose had worried about him accompanying her at first, fearing it would be too much for him, but she soon realized that it was enabling him to feel useful – and also it did him good to be away from the house and his mother's incessant worrying. He didn't want to feel like an invalid, even though that was unfortunately the case for the present at least.

Battles continued to be won and lost on both sides during the first part of the new year, and at Easter the spring offensive against the Germans manning the famous Hindenburg line began with prayer. British, Canadian and Australian troops accomplished the main objectives in the first hours of the assault, and now that the United States of America had entered the war on the side of the Allies at the beginning of April, some folk were saying the end was in sight.

Privately, Alexander wasn't so sure. He was glad America had finally made the decision, but it remained to be seen just how useful the Yanks would be initially. Although their resources in terms of manpower and industrial production were potentially greater than those of any of the belligerents, with the possible exception of Germany, he wondered how quickly the country's capacity could be translated into effective fighting power. The States manufactured no fighter aircraft whatsoever, and the total strength of the regular army was only five thousand officers and one hundred and twenty thousand or so men.

He recalled a conversation he'd had with Philip the year before when they had discussed the possibility of America entering the war. Philip's summing-up had been spot on. 'We could do with their help – any help from anywhere if it comes to that – but they're going to have to pull their finger out if they're going to make a difference in the short term. They're unprepared, and all the in-fighting that's gone on within Congress has meant they've procrastinated too long already. Wilson needs to silence the opposition and take control, but he's a great one for the middle course, which in the end pleases no one.'

Philip . . . Alexander shook his head sadly. His friend's wife had written to him shortly after he had come home to Highfield before Christmas. She'd told him that Philip had died of blood poisoning in France following injuries received on the battlefield. It seemed fitting to him though, that if Philip had to die, his death mirrored that of his great literary hero, Rupert Brooke. He remembered one night in the trenches when Philip had recited Brooke's poem entitled 'The Soldier' by memory. It had brought a lump to his throat then and it still did when he read it afresh. For the first time in his life he had really under-stood the power of poetry, and it was all thanks to his friend. And now there was another corner of a foreign field somewhere that was for ever England.

Alexander raised his head and glanced across the church hall. He was sitting at his table in a corner of the room and Rose and the others were standing waiting for the curate to open the door and let the first customers in. It was the middle of May, and at the beginning of the month the King had urged the nation to tighten its belt. At the same time it had been revealed that the royal household had been on strict rations since February.

Alexander grunted to himself. Worthy though the royal proclamation was, and well meant too he was sure, he felt it highlighted the difference between the prosperous South of the country and the poorer North. The food shortages which had begun to bite Britain were nothing new to the people of the North East in a way, because here ordinary families had always known what it was to be in need. Men had been struggling to feed their wives and children and keep a roof over their heads long before the war, and Rose had told him how the workhouses were seen as a terrible last resort where all hope vanished. Of course men like Lord Rockingham and Wynford wouldn't see it that way, he thought, remembering conversations from the past. They always had an answer for everything. The King had called for a national holding-back on bread consumption which was often the mainstay for poorer families, but no doubt Wynford would tell his employees to eat cake instead if they complained. The total unawareness of the French monarchy at a time of crisis had been its downfall; he would hate to see that happen in this country that he loved.

He had never really considered the big divide between rich and poor until he had met Rose; he supposed he'd had no need to if he was being honest, but men like Lord Rockingham and Wynford had always grated on him. That, at least, was to his credit.

The church hall door was flung open and an orderly queue progressed into the premises. Suddenly from outside a vehicle, probably a lorry or van delivering supplies to one of the shops, backfired with the force of a pistol shot. He saw Rose swing round towards him but he was already going down into the trench, down into the mud and bodies, and then the pit was opening and flames were licking up towards him. This time, though, he felt her arms holding him when she reached him and he could hear her voice talking, encouraging him to surface. He blinked up at her, ashen-faced, and the feeling of shame that the attacks always produced was strong, but she was murmuring in his ear, 'No one noticed. It's all right, my darling, no one noticed and that was better this time. It was just a few seconds, Alexander. That's much better.'

He clung on to her waist for a moment, his head against her breast and her chin resting on the top of his head, and then drew back a little. His voice shaky, he said, 'Go and help the others, they need you.'

'You need me.'

'Always, but I'm all right now, I promise.'

She kissed the top of his head and then went back to the trestle table holding the steaming pans of soup. He shut his eyes for a moment, the feeling of nausea the incidents always induced causing him to swallow hard. Dammit, when was he going to feel like a man again? He felt very tired now, exhausted suddenly, but Rose was right. This time had been much shorter. He *was* getting better, he had to believe that or else he really would go mad. And he wasn't the only soldier who had come home suffering in this way. Perhaps he was fortunate in that his physical injuries were so obvious, because he had heard stories of soldiers who were physically unimpaired being hounded by the army and civilians alike when they broke down. It made him incensed, and one of the old timers who came to the soup kitchen now and again had related how a young lad in the town, only eighteen years old, had been given a white feather by a bunch of women after he'd been unable to return to the front, and he had gone home and killed himself.

The hall was busy now but as Alexander sat there an idea he'd been mulling over since his return from the war came to the forefront of his mind again. He had broached it with Rose and she'd thought it was splendid, but how his parents would react he wasn't sure.

He'd like to see Highfield Hall used as a convalescent home for wounded soldiers, those sick in their minds as well as those physically ill. The extensive grounds were perfect for men to recuperate at their own pace, and there was the farm too for those who wanted to work and get their hands dirty. Being outside in the fresh air could be a tonic in itself, and the farm manager had only been complaining to his father the other day that he was finding it harder to keep things ticking along due to the number of men who'd left to join up.

Old Stubbs could use some assistance too, but he didn't quite understand why the elderly gardener had dug up all the rose bushes in the rose garden and replanted new ones when he was short of men. His father had told him it was something to do with a disease which had attacked the roses, but it seemed a rather extreme thing to have done. Nevertheless, the pleasure gardens and the grounds were tranquil and peaceful and men could find solace there.

He'd wait for the right moment and mention it to his parents over the next week or so, he told himself. It would take a great deal of organizing and financing to set up, but the need would only increase with hundreds of injured men being shipped home each month. It felt wrong to be living in such a beautiful environment when men who had fought for their country, the same as him, were suffering. He thought the family could live in one wing of the house and the rest of it could be modified accordingly. It was perfectly doable. After all, they had already shut up part of the house and closed down the labour-intensive and fuel-hungry garden greenhouses. That had been hard on old Stubbs, who still grieved for his precious hothouses and found it difficult to come to terms with the new order of things. He knew the old fellow used to spend many happy hours pottering about in them, especially in the cold winter months, while his under-gardeners saw to the outside work.

The changes had had to happen though, Alexander thought. They were part and parcel of the war effort, along with releasing more servants nationwide for 'useful purposes', as the government put it. All the younger staff apart from Jinny were gone now, just their elderly butler and valet and equally long-in-the-tooth housekeeper and cook remaining. With no kitchen maids on hand, their meals were simpler, and Rose assisted the cook in the kitchens most mornings, while Jinny helped the house-keeper when she wasn't tied up with the twins. The butler and valet had adapted, albeit grudgingly, to doing a range of jobs that they'd have considered beneath them before the war, and his father's beautiful motor car was rarely used unless William had to travel into Gateshead or Newcastle on business. They had the horse and trap and the larger carriage, which were perfectly adequate.

You had to adapt in life, that was the thing. Alexander nodded mentally to the thought. His arm was gone and his army life was finished, but he could still see and hear and move unaided, unlike some of the poor beggars who'd been shipped home alongside him. And he had Rose, his love, which was everything.

By the time the church hall doors were finally closed at just after six o'clock Alexander was exhausted and he looked it. Amy and Daisy insisted that they would do the clearing-up and Rose must take him home, and as Hammond was sitting outside in the horse and carriage, she didn't argue.

It was a truly beautiful evening that greeted the three of them as they walked out of the hall. A soft warm May twilight was just beginning to steal across the sky and the smell of summer was in the air.

Once in the carriage Alexander put his head back against the upholstered seat and shut his eyes, and as the two horses clip-clopped their way out of town, Rose and Betsy talked quietly together. Rose so appreciated what she saw as diminishing time with her daughter. One day Betsy would go away to train as a nurse, she was determined about that, but for the moment she was still at home and Rose tried to make the most of every minute with her. Betsy had grown into a beautiful girl and now she was on the cusp of womanhood, Rose thought fondly; Davey would have been so proud of her. She could see Davey in their daughter's big brown eyes and she had his caring, gentle nature. She would make a fine nurse.

They had left Consett and were only a few hundred yards from the entrance of the estate when Rose became aware of the carriage drawing to a halt and Hammond clambering down from his seat. She put her head out of the window. 'What is it?'

'There looks to be a soldier lying at the side of the road, ma'am. I'd better see what's what.'

Alexander was dozing, his head lolling, and signalling for Betsy not to wake him, Rose opened the door and stepped down onto the dusty country road, Betsy right behind her. The valet had just reached the prone figure when something, some deep dark instinct born of self-preservation that came from the subconscious rather than the conscious mind, made Rose call out, 'Hammond, stop,' but it was too late.

The figure on the ground moved, there was a shot and then Hammond crumpled as Nathaniel sprang to his feet. He was holding a rifle that had been concealed under his body and now it was pointing at Rose and Betsy. Rose froze for a split second before pulling Betsy behind her.

As Alexander called out, 'What's going on?' she shouted, 'Alexander, stay inside,' but he was already climbing down from the carriage.

Nathaniel moved towards them, stopping a few yards away. His lip curling, he said, 'Oh, he wouldn't do that, would you, Major? He's the great war hero, losing an arm an' all.'

Alexander was at Rose's side now and Nathaniel's eyes had narrowed into blue slits. 'I suggest you don't take another step, Major, unless you want your head blown off.'

'What do you want?' Alexander's voice was cool. 'Money? I've a few pounds on me.'

'Is that your answer to everything, money? But then it bought you her, didn't it. Perhaps you'd like to introduce me to your husband?' he added, looking at Rose. 'It's about time.'

'It's Nathaniel.' Rose didn't look at Alexander as she spoke, keeping her eyes on the man in front of her. When she had last seen him outside the bakery shop he'd still looked like the man she remembered. Older, harder, but he had still been handsome. Now he looked unkempt, and his nose had taken on the red veins associated with heavy drinking.

'Aye, it's Nathaniel. Alive and breathing, which will be more than can be said for the three of you in a few minutes.' His voice was mocking. 'Although, having seen Betsy again, I think I'll have a bit of fun with her before I let her join the two of you. She's bonny, your daughter,

Rose. Young, fresh, not like you. How many men have you had in your time, eh? Too many to count or remember?'

Alexander made a sudden movement and Nathaniel jerked the rifle higher. 'I wouldn't, Major. Make the most of the few seconds you've got left, don't throw them away. I won't be leaving any witnesses, I can promise you that.'

Rose could sense Betsy trembling, and along with her own fear and loathing, anger was rising. How dare he frighten her daughter? How dare he? 'You'll never get away with this. You know that, don't you?'

Nathaniel smiled. 'Now I'd take a bet on that but as you won't be around to pay, it'd be pointless, wouldn't it. I'm in the army now, see. The great faceless horde. Not using my real name, oh no, I was too canny for that, because I'd planned to settle with you for a long while and knew I'd have to disappear after. Robert Fletcher's the name, doing his bit for King and country.' He clicked his heels together but the rifle aimed at Alexander's chest didn't move. 'Poor old Nathaniel Alridge killed himself last year because he couldn't face being called up. At least that was the conclusion everybody came to when they read the letter I left and found the body in the woods some time later. Been messed about by wild animals it had, the face all gone, but it had the remains of the clothes I'd been wearing and was the right height, so . . .'

'You *killed* someone?' Rose murmured.

'Oh, it's not the first time I've killed for you, but then you know that, Rose. After the first time' – he shrugged –'it's easy. He was just a tramp, a nobody. No one will miss him. The hard part was making sure I stayed alive long enough for this day, but all good things come to him who waits, isn't that what they say? And so I dodged the bullets and the shells – not an easy task, as the good major found out – and waited for my first leave as Private Robert Fletcher, and what did I find? You an' him doing your lord and lady of the manor act for the poor peasants. Very touching.'

Alexander put his arm round Rose and in so doing shielded Betsy even more. 'You don't have to do this.' He had seen the slightest of movements from the valet who was lying at the side of the road. If Hammond was still alive and if he could get to his feet without Nathaniel turning round, there was the faint possibility that between them they could take the man. It was Rose and Betsy's only chance. He needed to keep him talking.

'On the contrary, Major. It's something I should have done a long time ago.'

'What has Rose ever done to you, or Betsy for that matter? Kill me but let them live.'

'That's very kind of you and exactly what I shall be doing in a few moments. You'll go first and they'll live a little longer. Rose's first wound won't kill her. I want her to see what happens to her daughter first, but once I've finished with Betsy, Rose will join you both. As for what she's done to me' – his voice had risen higher and for the first time Alexander saw madness in his eyes – 'you have no idea.'

Alexander saw that Hammond was on his knees now. 'No? Then tell me. I'm all ears.'

Betsy was sobbing, quiet, choked sobs, and Rose turned slightly to say, 'It's all right, hinny. It will be all right,' which seemed to enrage Nathaniel.

'Don't tell her that, tell her the truth,' he ground out.

Rose swung back to face him, 'You're an animal,' she said, coldly and very clearly. 'A filthy, dirty animal, scum of the earth. Davey trusted you – you were his best friend and he would have done anything for you – and however clever you think you've been, now you will pay for this at the end of a rope.'

'That's enough.'

She had taken a step towards him and as Nathaniel involuntarily retreated, he said again, 'That's enough, stay where you are or so help me I'll blast you to hell.'

Rose, too, had seen Hammond. The man was clearly in bad shape but if she could just distract Nathaniel, get him to step back a little more, then the valet would have the best chance of taking him off guard.

She ignored Alexander's, 'Rose, stay still,' as she said, 'For years I was frightened of you. Do you know that? Terrified of every dark shadow, and now I can't think why because you're nothing. You've always been nothing, just wind and water, a great bag of air. You'll go out of this world with no one remembering you or grieving for you. You're such a brave man with a rifle in your hands, aren't you, but without it you'd be crawling to lick Alexander's boots—'

Nathaniel's roar of rage coincided with Hammond lunging at his legs, knocking him off balance and towards

Rose. The rifle went skidding across the road but then Nathaniel was on top of her where she'd fallen and his hands were round her throat, squeezing as hard as he could, his face demonic. She couldn't breathe, there were lights in front of her eyes and a pressure in her head and she could hear voices, shouting, but the iron fingers were merciless and she knew she was dying, right here, now. But that didn't matter if Betsy was all right.

She was unconscious when Alexander used the butt of the rifle to smash into Nathaniel's head, knocking him off her. But the next moment Nathaniel had reared up again and Alexander, hampered by the loss of his arm, fell backwards as the other man's fist hit him full in the face. But Hammond had two hands and, bleeding though he was from the wound to his stomach, he reached for the rifle which had clattered to a stop beside him. Lifting it, he shot his target in the back and then, as Nathaniel turned to face him, he shot him again, and this time Nathaniel went down and didn't move.

Betsy's screams had alerted the occupants of a small hamlet some distance away, and as folk came running she shouted for them to get help. Rose was conscious now, choking and gasping as she drew breath, and Alexander, his face bloody, had crawled to her side and was holding her close; so Betsy, with great presence of mind, concentrated on Hammond, tearing her petticoat and making it into a ball which she held to the wound in the valet's stomach.

* * *

The attack on that nice Mr and Mrs Bembridge by a man who had been declared dead the year before was the talk of the county. It provided a welcome relief from war news for one thing, and for another hadn't Mr and Mrs Bembridge and their daughter been saved by the valet who was seventy if he was a day, but that hadn't stopped him putting an end to the scoundrel. He was a hero, that's what he was. And all was well that ended well, except for the attacker of course but he'd got his just deserts, everyone agreed on that. And the daughter, that little slip of a thing, she was a heroine too for hadn't the doctors said that but for her quick thinking the valet would have bled to death then and there on the road? As it was he was making a good recovery, bless him. Aw, it was nice when there was a happy ending, you didn't get a lot of them these days, but you had to live in hope, didn't you, and sunny days would come again. They always did.

Epilogue

They were calling it the 'Great War'. It had been over for six weeks and certainly there had never been anything like it in history before. More countries had been involved, and more people had perished, than in any previous single conflict. No class of society was immune from the war's impact. Casualties amongst junior officers were about three times higher than among ordinary soldiers, and they included the eldest son of Herbert Asquith, the former prime minister. The human cost of the war was over ten million dead and many more millions maimed for life, but one thing was certain, folk said. It had been a harsh lesson for the future, and such a thing would never happen again. That, at least, was something positive to come out of all the bloodshed and heartache and loss.

But for this first Christmas Eve in peacetime for four years, all Rose and Alexander could think about was each other. They were strolling arm in arm in the snowy grounds of Highfield. Betsy and the twins were running ahead of them, Jinny having gone home for Christmas stocked up with all sorts of goodies for her family from Rose. Betsy was leaving them in the New Year to begin her nurse's training and Rose was going to miss her, but now that Highfield was a convalescence home she knew she would be too busy to brood over her first chick leaving the nest. William and Arabella had decided to make the estate over to Alexander, after which they had retired to their London residence, although they visited frequently.

Rose and Alexander had invited Lawrence and Estelle to be part of their new venture, and Lawrence had subsequently sold his estate in Scotland and the family lived in a purpose-built house in the grounds of Highfield. The couple helped them manage the home, which boasted a resident doctor, physiotherapist, psychiatrist and several nurses, male and female, as well as the kitchen staff and housemaids and so on, all of whom were housed in new recently built quarters adjoining the back of the main house. The original floor plan of Highfield had more than doubled and the expense had been considerable, but the result was a beautiful residence that had lost none of its old charm but now served its new purpose well.

Lawrence had been a different man since he and Estelle had made the move; as he had said to Alexander on many an occasion, he felt he had a reason for getting up in the morning again. He had also joked that together he and Alexander made one good body between them, but Alexander knew that underneath the banter his own disability had helped Lawrence come to terms with his.

He looked down at Rose at his side and her gaze met

his, and as he bent his head and took her lips they swayed together for a moment in the clear cold air. Old Stubbs had a bonfire somewhere in the grounds and there was the faint tang of woodsmoke drifting on the icy breeze, but apart from the twins' squealing as they tumbled like puppies in the snow, all was quiet.

'I love you,' he whispered, drawing her even closer, thankful beyond words that she was his.

'I love you too.' She dimpled up at him. So much had happened since she had met him, good and bad, but they had come through it all and they were together. And although she had never voiced it, something had been lifted off her the day that Nathaniel had died. It wouldn't be an exaggeration to say that she had been set free, free of the past and all its heartache. And the future was theirs, a future rich with promise and fulfilment. Reaching up she took his face between her hands, her eyes tender, and now it was she who kissed him. They held each other tight, standing still and watching Betsy busily brushing the boys down before the three of them began to build a snowman.

The sun was beginning to set in a pearly sky, a bright red ball that sent rivers of scarlet and gold flowing into the silver expanse and tinged the snow pink.

Now was the moment, Rose thought. Turning Alexander's face to hers again with the tip of her finger, she murmured, 'I hope you have a wonderful Christmas, my darling, and you have already given me the best gift I could have asked for.'

'I have?' His brow wrinkled.

'Tucked away in here.' She patted her coat over the top of her stomach.

For a moment he stared at her blankly, and then, as comprehension dawned, his face lit up. 'You're having a baby?'

'Our baby.' A child conceived in the last days of the war but who would be born into peace. A child of hope and love. She smiled, and then they were both laughing and hugging, and Betsy and the twins stopped what they were doing and stared at their parents, laughing too but without knowing why, all joined together in one perfect moment.

Dancing in the Moonlight

By Rita Bradshaw

As her mother lies dying, twelve-year-old Lucy Fallow promises to look after her younger siblings and keep house for her father and two older brothers.

Over the following years the Depression tightens its grip. Times are hard and Lucy's situation is made more difficult by the ominous presence of Tom Crawford, the eldest son of her mother's lifelong friend, who lives next door.

Lucy's growing friendship with Tom's younger brother, Jacob, only fuels Tom's obsession with her. He persuades Lucy's father and brothers to work for him on the wrong side of the law as part of his plan to force Lucy to marry him.

Tom sees Lucy and Jacob dancing together one night and a chain of heartbreaking events is set in motion. Torn apart from the boy she loves, Lucy wonders if she and Jacob will ever dance in the moonlight again . . .

Beyond the Veil of Tears

By Rita Bradshaw

Fifteen-year-old Angeline Stewart is heartbroken when her beloved parents are killed in a coaching accident, leaving her an only child in the care of her uncle.

Naive and innocent, Angeline is easy prey for the handsome and ruthless Oswald Golding. He is looking for a rich heiress to solve the money troubles his gambling and womanizing have caused.

On her wedding night, Angeline enters a nightmare from which there is no awakening. Oswald proves to be more sadistic and violent than she could ever have imagined. When she finds out she is expecting a child, Angeline makes plans to run away and decides to take her chances fending for herself and her baby. But then tragedy strikes again . . .

The Colours of Love

By Rita Bradshaw

England is at war, but nothing can dim land girl Esther Wynford's happiness at marrying the love of her life – fighter pilot Monty Grant. But months later, on the birth of her daughter Joy, Esther's world falls apart.

Esther's dying mother confesses to a dark secret that she has kept to herself for twenty years: Esther is not her natural daughter. Esther's real mother was forced to give up her baby to an orphanage – and now Joy's birth makes the reason for this clear, as Esther's true parentage is revealed.

Harshly rejected by Monty, and with the man Esther believed was her father breathing fire and damnation, she takes her precious baby and leaves everything and everyone she's ever known, determined to fend for herself and her child. But her fight is just beginning . . .

Snowflakes in the Wind

By Rita Bradshaw

It's Christmas Eve 1920 when nine-year-old Abby Kirby's family is ripped apart by a terrible tragedy. Leaving everything she's ever known, Abby takes her younger brother and runs away to the tough existence of the Border farming community.

Years pass. Abby becomes a beautiful young woman and falls in love, but her past haunts her, casting dark shadows. Furthermore, in the very place she's taken refuge is someone who wishes her harm.

With her heart broken, Abby decides to make a new life as a nurse. When the Second World War breaks out, she volunteers as a QA nurse and is sent overseas. However, life takes another unexpected and dangerous turn when she becomes a prisoner of the Japanese. It is then that Abby realizes that whatever has gone before is nothing compared to what lies ahead . . .

A Winter Love Song

By Rita Bradshaw

Bonnie Lindsay is born into a travelling fair community in the north-east of England in 1918, and when her mother dies just months later Bonnie's beloved father becomes everything to her. Then, at the tender age of ten years old, disaster strikes. Heartbroken, Bonnie's left at the mercy of her embittered grandmother and her lecherous step-grandfather.

Five years later, the events of one terrible night cause Bonnie to flee to London, where she starts to earn her living as a singer. She changes her name and cuts all links with the past.

Time passes. Bonnie falls in love, but just when she dares to hope for a rosy future, the Second World War is declared. She does her bit for the war effort, singing for the troops and travelling to Burma to boost morale, but heartache and pain are just around the corner, and she begins to ask herself if she will ever find happiness again.

Beneath a Frosty Moon

By Rita Bradshaw

It's 1940 and Britain is at war with Germany. For Cora Stubbs and her younger siblings this means being evacuated to the safety of the English countryside. But little does Cora know that Hitler's bombs are nothing compared to the danger she will face in her new home, and she is forced to grow up fast.

However, Cora is a fighter and she strives to carve out a new life for herself and her siblings. Time passes, and in the midst of grief and loss she falls in love, but what other tragedies lie around the corner?

As womanhood beckons, can Cora ever escape her troubled past and the lost love who continues to haunt her dreams and cast shadows over her days?

One Snowy Night

By Rita Bradshaw

It's 1922 and the Depression is just beginning to rear its head in Britain, but Ruby Morgan is about to marry her childhood sweetheart and nothing can mar her happiness. Or so she thinks. An unimaginable betrayal by those she loves causes her to flee her home and family one snowy night.

Crushed and heartbroken, Ruby vows that, despite the odds stacked against her, she will not only survive but one day will show the ones she left behind that she's succeeded in making something of herself. Brave words, but the reality is far from easy.

Dangers Ruby could never have foreseen and more tragedy threaten her new life, and love always seems just out of reach. Can a happy ending ever be hers?

'Catherine Cookson would have been proud to put her name to this heartfelt and moving saga'
Peterborough Evening Telegraph

The Storm Child

By Rita Bradshaw

It's mid-winter, and in the throes of a fierce blizzard Elsie Redfern and her husband discover an unknown girl in their hay barn about to give birth. After the young mother dies, Elsie takes the infant in and raises her as her own daughter, her precious storm child.

Gina grows into a beautiful little girl, but her safe haven turns out to be anything but. Torn away from her home and family, the child finds herself in a nightmare from which there's no waking. But despite her misery and bewilderment, Gina's determined to survive.

Years pass. With womanhood comes the Second World War, along with more heartbreak, grief and betrayal. Then, a new but dangerous love beckons; can Gina ever escape the dark legacy of the storm child?

'Expect the unexpected in this enthralling story with a wealth of colourful characters'

Coventry Evening Telegraph